12/97

BREAD

for the

DEPARTED

BOGDAN WOJDOWSKI

Translated from the Polish by Madeline G. Levine
Foreword by Henryk Grynberg

NORTHWESTERN UNIVERSITY PRESS
Evanston, Illinois

Northwestern University Press
Evanston, Illinois 60208-4210

Originally published in Polish under the title *Chleb rzucony umarłym* in
1971 by PIW, Warsaw. Copyright © 1971 by Bogdan Wojdowski. English
translation copyright © 1997 by Northwestern University Press. Foreword
copyright © 1997 by Northwestern University Press. Published 1997 by
arrangement with Maria Iwaszkiewicz-Wojdowska and Irena Grabska. All
rights reserved.

Printed in the United States of America

ISBN 0-8101-1455-0 (cloth)
ISBN 0-8101-1456-9 (paper)

Library of Congress Cataloging-in-Publication Data

Wojdowski, Bogdan.
 [Chleb rzucony umarłym. English]
 Bread for the departed / Bogdan Wojdowski ; translated by
Madeline G. Levine ; with a foreword by Henryk Grynberg.
 p. cm. — (Jewish lives)
 ISBN 0-8101-1455-0 (cloth : alk. paper). — ISBN 0-8101-1456-9
(paper : alk. paper)
 1. Holocaust, Jewish (1939–1945) — Poland — Warsaw — Fiction.
I. Levine, Madeline G. II. Title. III. Series.
PG7182.O45C513 1997
891.8'5373 — dc21   97-27125
                                                            CIP

✤

Contents

❖

Foreword

Bogdan Wojdowski, My Brother

He was older than me by six years, which is to say he was much more experienced, grievously experienced, because those years have to be counted differently. Also, our common fate as children of the Holocaust was kinder to me, because I was not in the Warsaw Ghetto and therefore saw and knew less than he did. We both survived, but not completely, and not to the same degree, and afterward we paid a price for our survival—a very high price. So high that sooner or later our resources were exhausted. That's how it was with Piotr Rawicz, Primo Levi, Jerzy Kosiński; that's how it was with Wojdowski.

For a while we received food and clothing from America and from other countries whose consciences were not quite clear, but no one thought about offering help for our psychological needs. We coped as best we could, seeking deliverance in self-defense (Israel) or in flight. We escaped to distant lands and from Jewish identity. Communism was an escape, too—its presumed equality, acceptance, internationalism. Sooner or later all these escapes proved illusory. Once again it turned out to be impossible to escape from one's past, that is, from oneself. Our war did not end in 1945 and we continue to fall in the unequal battle. We put up resistance, we do not surrender, but new, dark powers are constantly joining the demons of our past. Time does not heal our wounds; on the contrary, they ache even more as old age approaches and we grow more alone and more in need of the help that does not exist for us. Our lives, saved with such difficulty, torment us and exhaust our diminished strength, while at the same time the sense of menace, which never left us, does not shrink but, to the contrary, swells within us.

I have often wondered how he managed to endure the years 1968–69 in Warsaw, which was the time of the worst antisemitic racial persecutions since the fall of Hitler's Reich, which none of us had anticipated. Once again, I was luckier than he was, because I escaped in the nick of time, and once again I wasn't there in the worst place at the worst time. I would not have been able to endure those additional two years of Hitlerism in its new Communist edition, and I know now that they depleted his endurance, too.

For a long time he fled from his most important subject, but there came a time when he had to return to it, and in the early 1960s he began his true narrative. When I read "Madagaskar," a fragment from a novel that he published in the Warsaw *Kultura* around that time, I knew I had a brother. The rest of the novel—*Bread for the Departed*, that is—appeared only in 1971 after the bloody events in Gdańsk (December 1970), when the next compromised clique (Gomułka and Moczar) stepped down and the antisemitic repression abated. *Bread for the Departed* is without a doubt the best novel about the Warsaw Ghetto and one of the best literary depictions of the Holocaust. The reduced "Second-Degree Prize" awarded it by the Minister of Culture and Art reflects poorly on both the minister and the culture. Jurors for literary prizes are not always aware that they are giving testimony about themselves.

Bread is the theme of this novel, since bread was the main subject of daily life in the Warsaw Ghetto. Wojdowski describes that life from the creation of the Ghetto until January 1943, or the "little action" of liquidation, which was to be the epilogue to the "great action" that had been carried out in the summer of 1942. By then the Jews began to mount an armed resistance and the epilogue turned into the April Uprising.

Wojdowski depicts the progressive and deliberate process of the diminution of human life in both the abstract and the concrete sense. An illustration of this phenomenon is the activity of Dr. Obuchowski, a physician who examines the Ghetto's inhabitants every day and understands better than anyone that "the belly rules the world of the hungry." His rhetorical question "When does a man cease to be a man?" refers equally to the moral and physical states. Bread became more important than life for both the children smuggling it across the ghetto walls and for their parents. It also carried a high price for those who tried to help the hungry by distributing it, like the Polish trolley car driver who "always had a loaf of bread in plain view behind the windshield . . . and when he drove through the Ghetto he would slow down, ring his bell for the beggars, and throw the bread into the street for them." In the end, one day "they pulled him out of the trolley and shot him" along with thirty beggars.

Wojdowski, who was in the Ghetto from age ten to age twelve, focuses on the adaptation of children to that particular human condition that became their natural reality. Fulfilling the animal function of obtaining food every day, the children developed appropriate instincts and applied the animal tactic of safety in numbers. For example, rushing across the wall: "The unruly kids . . . ran straight ahead in a mob, and the guard could fire off a couple of shots in haste, kill one or two on the spot, but the rest would clamber across the wall safe and sound, with a howl of triumph."

Wojdowski's novel contains some four hundred pages, but it has no plot. It is composed of epic descriptions and chaotic dialogues, voices recorded in their authentic, ungrammatical Polish, a sort of literal translation from the Yiddish. The author piously carries out this posthumous recording of voices. He does not develop scenes; he does not close them with resounding chords or clever points; and he rarely "introduces" them in the traditional literary fashion. They appear abruptly, spontaneously, and disappear together with their voices and dialogues, and others take over and fill their place—just as it must have been in the chaotic life of the overcrowded Ghetto. Wojdowski is faithful to remembered reality. With Old Testament scrupulousness he includes even the most repellent scenes of theft, plunder, prostitution, and sacrilege toward the dead, from whom the children known as "rats" extract gold teeth in order to buy bread for the living. The author seems confident that the truth, even the worst truth, cannot be an indictment of the inhabitants of the Ghetto, where thieves, prostitutes, and defilers were also victims, because in the inhuman conditions in which they were ordered to live and die, they could not possibly be responsible for conduct that ran counter to human norms.

Wojdowski does not comment and does not justify. The Ghetto inhabitants were justified by the unprecedented situation in which they were imprisoned. He condemns no one, nor does he offer praise. He treats te altruistic deeds of Dr. Obuchowski and the trolley driver as natural reflexes, just like the ugly deeds of others. Perhaps both the one and the other were dictated by a peculiar instinct of self-preservation: in one instance it was a matter of biological survival (the preservation of the species), in the other, the preservation of humanity. So, too, at the end, when we see the preparations for armed resistance, Wojdowski avoids all allusions to heroism, which in the banal traditional sense was inadequate to the reality of the Warsaw Ghetto. (I believe that Marek Edelman, one of the leaders of that uprising, expressed the same idea in his conversation with Hanna Krall, published in book form as *Shielding the Flame*.) Wojdowski even avoids symbolism, as if fearing to insult the victims of that reality which, as has been proved many times, does not fit into traditional literary dimensions. Instead of symbolic abbreviations, we have innumerable details, especially in the epic description of the mass deportation in midsummer 1942—the largest death march in human history. Yet every detail here has the weight of a symbol.

Our personal contact began only in 1990. I had received fervent letters signed with the three Hebrew letters that spell the name David. He wrote about his Polish-Jewish quarterly *Masada*, of which he was the initiator and co-founder. I did not like that title, because Masada, after all, was a fortress of suicides. He also sent me a typescript of a feverishly written "Open Letter to Writers of the Shoah Generation," whom he wanted to summon to a conference in Warsaw. I visited him in the Warsaw psychiatric hospital in February 1992, during my first trip to Poland since my escape in 1967. I arrived without prior notification, but he wasn't in the least surprised. He was haggard and unshaved, but in very good mental shape: intelligent, witty, sober-minded—a true writer. He spoke about his institutionalization like an observer, a reporter, not a patient. We talked for a long time, not at all feverishly. I understood his escape into alcohol, and he understood my escape across the ocean. We children of the Holocaust understand each other very well. I carried away a very pleasant impression from this our only meeting.

I understand his final escape, too. It was on April 18, 1994, on the eve of the anniversary of the Warsaw Ghetto Uprising. Only we children of the Holocaust understand each other this well. We are brothers and sisters, and not just in the metaphorical sense.

Henryk Grynberg

❁

Translator's Note

The reader of *Bread for the Departed* is asked to bear in mind that one of the most striking stylistic features of this novel—its multilayered linguistic complexity—is necessarily obscured in translation. *Bread for the Departed* is in large measure an auditory novel, a novel of voices recorded in dialogues and snatches of overheard speech. In the scenes involving the children's gangs, the smugglers, the provincial Jews whose first language is Yiddish, Wojdowski employs a complex and ingenious blend of standard Polish, Warsaw dialect, thieves' argot, Yiddish and Hebrew words or phonemes. There being no equivalents in English that would not introduce inappropriate cultural associations, I have chosen to render these passages in an only marginally defective English. Passages in German have been left untranslated in order to preserve their alien sound.

Madeline G. Levine

Bread for the Departed

❖

I

Cainan begat Mahalaleel. Mahalaleel begat Jared. Jared begat Enoch. Enoch begat Methusaleh. Methusaleh begat Lamech, and Lamech . . . Over and over again he repeated this until he himself, Grandfather, Father's father, with his long, red, rain-soaked beard, appeared at the end and announced, "I do set my bow in the cloud." The rain stopped and he saw a rainbow stretched across the clear sky outside the window, and water dripping from the trees and from Grandfather's beard. He knew by now who had sat him on his knees all these years and jounced him rhythmically up and down, calling out in a singsong voice the names of all the generations from Adam to Japheth. Father used to rock back and forth, praying out loud, with a shawl thrown over his head. It was a wide shawl, made of cashmere yarn, white with black stripes. That was Father's *tallis*, and his forehead and left arm were bound with a long strap, and that was called *tefillin*. When Father stood near the window at sunrise with his shawl falling over his face and with the straps wrapped around his arm, he was terrified and hid behind Mother, peeking out to watch the praying. It was better that way. Mother ran through the orchard with her arms outstretched, and her fingers brushed the branches, brushed the tree trunks, and showers of fruit fell to the ground and rolled onto the grass. Mother's footsteps were loud. *David! David!* It was she who first pronounced his name. A wind blew up, swayed the trees, swayed the clouds, the sun clung to Mother's face, the wind clung to her hair, flapping a small strand near her temple, it flapped the branches and it flapped a swarm of bees, which had abandoned their hive and were now hanging in a huge, brown, shaggy sphere at the top of the tall pear tree.

A long, long time ago, when he was very little, Mother told him in a whisper, "Once there was a black, black forest, and in the black,

black forest there was a black, black house, and in this black, black house there was a black, black room, and in this black, black room stood a black, black coffin, and in that black, black coffin lay a black, black corpse!" Convulsed with shudders, he had listened to that story as darkness fell. There was a block of ice under his skull and he could feel every single hair on his head.

He is awake now and he sees how his father stealthily kisses the hem of his holy shawl and hurriedly, quietly, almost in a whisper, pronounces the final words. Mother is on her knees, her forehead smudged with soot, her cheek baked by the rosy light from the flames; she takes long, controlled breaths, inhaled deep into her chest, and blows on the fire in the cook stove. The golden gleam of the flames lightly strokes her hair. Father folds his shawl in silence, frees his arms and neck from the leather straps, turns around, and erupts in raucous laughter. She stands in front of him, timid, with smudges of ash on her face. Her rapid breathing lifts her breasts, her hands hastily pin and smoothe her hair, her elbows move above her like the wings of an angel in flight, and behind her the sun is rising. What do you want, he asks, what do you want from her? Father laughs cheerfully. That's what mornings were like. If there wasn't enough time, she would slip a herring wrapped in newspaper into the ash pan. The herring crackled in the fire, the herring hissed in the fire, the herring sang in the fire, and when it was thoroughly baked, breakfast was ready. Oh, David loved such days.

Grandfather opened the *Kisvey Hakoydesh*, the Holy Scriptures, and, rocking back and forth, he began to wail in a strange voice that didn't belong to him. "'At any hour it can begin, and it can end in any place.' David, listen," he crowed in a high soprano voice, "*Bereyshis* . . . In the beginning . . . "

And thus began that innocent nightmare, life. *Bereyshis boro Elohim es hashomayim v'es ha'orets.* Which he was supposed to translate as: "In the beginning God created the heaven and the earth." Heaven and earth? He couldn't imagine that. How, what did He make it out of? Why? In the meantime Grandfather droned on in a mournful voice and dragged the boy after him, straight into chaos, into darkness, into the void. From which the first light was supposed to burst forth. There was a vague threat in these words. *Nu, nu,* now. And God said, Let there be light: and there was light. Not like that, no, *Yehi! Yehi!* Stop it. One more time. *Vayoymer Elohim yehi or vayehi or.* Grandfather showed him a faint mark that was lost under the verse like a blurry trace left on a road by nomads. And then, lowering his voice, he explained patiently and at length the secrets of the voiced and unvoiced schwa. He raised his shaggy brows and then slowly lowered his eyelids. Onward, onward. And God called the light day, and the darkness he called night. And the evening and the morning were the first day. Grandfather's eyebrows lived their own life, as restless and agile as two little animals. When Grandfather lowered his eyelids, David had to repeat, imitating Grandfather in his own thin little voice.

And the evening and the morning were the sixth day. In his mournful voice Grandfather drew out verse after verse and dragged the boy after him, deeper and deeper into the world. The clouds were already spreading over the sea, the earth was already covered with grass and trees. Birds were fluttering under the sky; fish were swimming in the watery depths. In the forests lived men and beasts. Grandfather closed the Bible and tenderly caressed the spine of the black tome, the mournful chronicle of life. Yes, yes. When David grows up he'll learn everything. The most important book? The *Seyfer Toyreh*. Also the *Mesholim*, the Parables. He'll become acquainted with the shining, wise prophecies for kings and people. From the Book of Esther he'll find out about the miraculous salvation of the Jews. And the most beautiful of all beautiful things will be revealed to him in the Song of Songs, *Shir Hashirim*. But meanwhile, the alphabet slowly and painstakingly, *alef, beys, giml, daled, hey, vov, zayin.*

He mewed like a cat, crowed like a rooster, and sang the entire alphabet, striking his hand rhythmically on the table, and when he tired of that he asked David questions. They were very difficult, David remained silent, and Grandfather encouraged him and lamented over him, *tss, tss, tss, tss.* And it was like the hissing of geese, like the voices of village girls when they stand at the edge of a pond and call the birds. *Tss, tss, tss.*

The geese floated with the current, and on the river banks the stately Jews promenaded, dressed in their black clothing, and every one of them held a black prayer book in his hand, and every one of them nodded and swayed over it, and every one of them had a small black yarmulke on his head, *peyes* on his temples, and the fringes of his *tzitzith* at his waist sticking out like the white straps of long underwear. A day like this occurs once each year and it is called Rosh Hashanah. That's when the boys run down to the river with sticks, yelling and splashing water on the praying men.

"Hitler's on the way, Jew! Hitler's on the way, Jew!"

But that, it seems, is not part of the holy days, nor is the crashing noise of shattered windows.

"Close your eyes and don't look," Mother said. "If you look out the window when you wake up, all your dreams will escape."

At night he lay in wait for sleep like a cat hovering over a hole in the hope of catching a mouse. Nothing came of it. He would wake up and it was already tomorrow. He would wake up and look out the window, at the sliced-off piece of sky behind the smashed pane, at the cloud dangling above the tin roof. He looked out the window and forgot his dreams, and when he searched for them in his memory they quickly disappeared, floating away like kites on an autumn wind. He could feel the slight puff of air, the pressure of the line on his palm, and he could tell by these signs that the paper bird had not yet torn away from its string, had not taken flight, and that up there, way up high, it still belonged to him. But he couldn't reach it, just as he couldn't reach his dream through memory. But Jacob remembered *his* dream, the Bible says so, and other people must have remembered it afterwards, because that dream made its way into the Bible. And then it was repeated for such a long time that those ancient times passed, and then other times and still other times passed, and now the present time has come, and every child knows. About Jacob's ladder. This is how it started:

Jacob was running away from Esau and when night came he lay down and fell asleep. Jacob slept with his head on a stone. The first rung, the second rung, the third, fourth, fifth. Enough. The worst thing is when you have to tell it in your own words. "Jacob!" That's the voice of God. But the angels were blowing their trumpets, there was an awful uproar, could Jacob possibly have heard what God wanted of him? How many? He didn't tell anyone how many rungs there were and aside from him no one else knows. It's just that climbing up a ladder isn't at all hard, but climbing down—that's something else. End of the story about Jacob's ladder.

But Grandfather told it like this: "And from that time God made a covenant with Jacob and relations between them became tolerable."

If you could tell it like Grandfather did it would be great fun in class, but it has to be done in an entirely different way, and David doesn't remember how. He has to look at the book before class. *The Pentateuch: An Introduction for Children*. It has drawings and captions underneath the drawings.

He rubbed his nose across the greasy pages, which were damp and yellow and smelled of mildew. Cain murders Abel. Aha . . . Noah sails on the waters of the flood for forty days and forty nights. Abraham sacrifices his son, Isaac. Aha . . . Jacob's tents and flocks. Oh . . . The Jews flee the house of bondage in Egypt. The crossing of the Red Sea. Oh . . . The Jews eat manna in the desert. A miracle, a miracle. The Jews dance around the Golden Calf. Joshua lays siege to Jericho! The trumpets shatter the walls.

He filled in the outlines with colored chalk, blue for the sky, green for the palm trees, yellow for the desert, white for the sheep, brown for the faces of the patriarchs. A patriarch supported his arm on a long, heavy stick that was taller than his head. It was a shepherd's crook. He was standing in front of a tall, soaring tent, with palm trees waving above it. The palm trees cast a shadow on the well where the flock was being watered. The past had the color of brown steppes, of the unblemished azure of the sky above the altar, the cold waters of the Jordan, the woolly flocks on the hills of Gilead, the white of the fluttering cloaks on the backs of the patriarchs of Ur, the green of the slender trees in the land of Canaan. The blood shed by Cain sliced through the past with a thin thread of crimson and seeped into the desert sand. It pulsed in the slit throats of sheep and flowed onto the sacrificial stone. It was woven into people's cloaks from generation to generation, woven into their light tents. A drop of that blood dripped into the spring.

He halted the nomads, those free sons of the desert, in the midst of their distant journey. The patriarchs had bare torsos that exuded manliness. They spread their arms wide to welcome the angels and the newcomers from a foreign land, and that gesture signified for him an open friendliness and nobility. They had high foreheads and held their necks stiffly, and for him that signified dignity and pride.

They put their arms up against their temples and spied out their enemies; their eyes looked into the distance from under their sternly raised brows. They were strong, just, and free.

He colored their sunburned faces with blood, breathed life into them, and they were alive once again. With the tip of his tongue protruding earnestly between his teeth, he drew and filled in the colors of that world that did not exist, a world of nomadic shepherds that came to life before his eyes. How solitary and strong they were, herding their flocks along distant roads. How they raised their hands in fervent prayer. How they went in search of women who would give them sons. How they begat generations worthy of their Lord on the plush skins of lions and does from the mountains of Bethel.

In their language, in their ancient tongue, Father said his prayers and Aunt Chava conducted obscure conversations with Grandfather. It frightened David to think about how Aunt Chava drew the curtains, lit the candles in the silver candlesticks, and read the Bible, slowly moving her crooked yellow finger under the lines of the Book which has neither beginning nor end. And how she and Grandfather talked at length by the light of the candles about Haman, the cruel and majestic deputy of King Ahasuerus. In the blackness of her clothing, in the anxious blackness of her eyes, crumbling in her hand a flat, drily rustling pancake, she shouted words that made the flames of the candles flicker. And when those words issued from the lips of the king, Haman's face was instantly covered up. She had colorless, sparse, damp hair, which she concealed with a wig, and an obvious strip of hair—a moustache?—above her upper lip. Her speech was full of wild, snorting sounds that enveloped him in vague terror.

On Father's lips the ancient language sounded so melodious! And when he drew the words out there was something both kindhearted and authoritative in his voice. Grandfather's voice rose and fell in a soprano, and David could hear the voices of all the animals in it: the goat, the rooster, the horse, the sheep, and the lion. Haste and irritation summoned the impatient cry of the rooster. Laughter embellished his words with the melody of a sheep's bleating. But not even Father, with his bald spot covered with drops of sweat, nor Aunt Chava with her smudge of a moustache, traces of egg yolk, and tiny pancake crumbs above her upper lip, nor Grandfather with his beautiful beard, whose strands were combed into two wings as glistening and soft as the downy feathers of ducklings, merged in David's imagination with the image of those patriarchs whose faces he colored bronze, overpowered by the seductive force and truth of the legend. They were different, they were long ago and far away. They had generously condescended to lend their ancient language to Grandfather, Father, and Aunt Chava, so their brows might be illuminated with the light of distant suns.

David repeated after Grandfather the words of the *Bereyshis.* And Jared lived one hundred sixty and two years, and he begat Enoch: and Jared lived after he begat Enoch eight hundred years, and begat sons and daughters. And all the days of Jared were nine hundred sixty and two years: and he died. He repeated the verses in a state of stupefaction, and the ages of the patriarchs stretched ever onward, back into the endless past, where their restless fates had vanished in a cloud of dust, along with their flowing tents and their swift-legged flocks. What remained was the sounds of their ancient language. The carefree, unconstrained cries of birds, their primal note, remained. The sweet fluttering of the Song of Songs remained.

It was the music of the Hebrew language, full of deep, moist aspirations. The verses followed along evenly, unhurriedly, in the rhythm of the hooves of a herd moving along desert roads, with the creaking of harnesses, the rustling of the disturbed sand, the thundering of taut skins filled with water, across the distant space surrounding the hidden sources of rivers, far from the stone walls of the cities where the temple's tower shone golden, guarding the visage of the pagan idol. Their land, their fatherland, was the road—a broad track along which they had wandered for millennia. A space which was always mercifully open for the nomads, where they rested their flocks and set up their tents without fear. He could think about them over and over and over again. But a voice was summoning him from the Promised Land.

No longer were there long roads in the sunshine and dust, nor the unblemished azure of the sky. No longer were there the gentle nostrils of kids cautiously bathing in the waters of a spring. In front of him sat Grandfather in his long black coat that was shiny with age, with his parted beard. He was waving his arms in the air, impotent and furious, like a large old bird trying, too late, to take flight. David tried to place a shepherd's crook in those hands but it slipped out; in his mind's eye, he tried clothing the old body in the dignified robes of the desert patriarchs, but they slid to the ground without so much as a rustle. And all that remained was the voice that said it could begin at any hour and end at any place, a voice that was growing faint, the grating Hebrew words, and their distant, crippled echo.

Eli doesn't study religion, he just swears. He doesn't have a grandfather, but he does have an album full of postage stamps and a mark on his neck and cheek. The mark is the color of borscht, only it's a birthmark, not a borscht stain. He went with Eli across the railroad tracks to the area behind the freight yards. There were an awful lot of boys in *Gymnasium* caps whom they didn't know. They had sticks, knives, and pockets full of old coins. They called them *dytki*. They watched them fly through the air and then measured the distance between the coins with their hand, two fingers, or a thumb. They did long-distance spitting. They sang, "O Lord, the day it poured, Julek and Manka went out of town, and kissed so hard that the trees fell down." Back home, he got a whipping and he felt awfully embarrassed, just as when he heard that song. Eli told him not to say where he had been. Mother said he had to tell, and he didn't get supper that day. But Father only laughed; he called him an old horse and boxed his ears so they hurt. An old horse, an old horse. Saba, the mare who pulls Mordechai Sukiennik's wagon— now that's an old horse. But Eli gave him a triangular Tanganyika with an antelope on it for keeping quiet. O Lord.

So now he knew that the train tracks were close by. All you had to do was cross the street and they were right there. And when he was falling asleep he could hear the voices of the trains in the evening silence. The steam locomotives, switched from track to track, came closer and then moved away in the darkness. The long, slow freight trains clanged loudly as they crossed the street, then slowly subsided into the quiet, measured rhythm of their wheels, the whispering of the tracks, the strip of smoke that stretched out over the rooftops, the breeze caused by the stirring up of the air. Where were they going? Where to? Where to? Where did the trains go? All night long the locomotives howled painfully, heavily, through the outskirts of the city. That was terror. He wanted to run away, his legs were rooted in the ground, he was thinking: Any moment now and I'll fly. That was a dream.

A roar, a roaring noise. There was a furious roaring that kept growing louder, but still he couldn't see the train. He saw a man in black running across the roof with the lead ball and rope of a chimney sweep. A button, where's a button? He looked for a button and couldn't find it. He didn't have a stitch of clothing on, not even a button. He was naked. The passenger cars flew by, windows, heads went past him, and outstretched, threatening hands rode past. *Jew!* But he couldn't run away, he couldn't scream. Then Eli fluttered down from the roof amidst a flurry of scattered postage stamps. He had six wings like a seraph: two he used to cover his face, two to cover his legs, and two to fly. In his hand he held a glowing coal and he held it out toward David's mouth. I don't want it, no, no. He knew that Father would come to his rescue . . .

. . . And Father did float gently to earth by the same means. A black and white scarf fluttered above him. He was trying in vain to hold out his arms, which were restrained by thongs. He said what he always said. We don't know when we know too much. He could hear neighing in empty, dark Towarowa Street. It was Saba the mare, galloping along the tracks into the sky. She tossed her mane and acorns fell out of it, and chestnuts. Mordechai Sukiennik stood there on his sturdily planted legs and gathered them up in a sack. When he slashed his whip, the dust whirled up into the air. Mother appeared. David, what are you doing here? She was coming from far away, from the marketplace at Żelazna Brama, and she was carrying a grayish herring in one hand and a lemon in the other. That was for Friday dinner. Grandfather is supposed to come on Friday with a prayer on his lips. *Sh'ma Yisroel adoynoy eloheynu adoynoy ekhod.* No, that wasn't smoke, not smoke, it was Grandfather's beard fluttering in the clouds. Straight from the chimney where he had gotten stuck. It can end at any place. And it was from there that David heard his strange, changed voice, when he was calling above the city.

Ki adoynoy eloheynu eysh okhlo hu eyl kano.

And he opened his eyes to hear the painful, loud beating of his heart. On the other side of the transparent curtain a flash of lightning flickered, more fleeting than a sigh. Rain, the swaying lights of the street lamps. He strained to listen: everyone was fast asleep; he was alone.

That night he wanted very much to pray, but he didn't know which God to pray to. The one God belonged to the Jews and was called Jehovah; the other one God belonged to the Christians and was called Jesus Christ; but most gods belonged to pagans. There wasn't anyone left for David. When you squeeze your eyelids very tight in the darkness, stars float down and you can't count them. But Professor Baum says that the earth revolves around the sun at a speed of 30 kilometers a second. And is he revolving, too? Along with that skinny tree opposite his window? And the trolley car that clangs its bell at the intersection of Srebrna and Miedziana Streets? He is circling around the sun at a speed of 30 kilometers a second? When you're lying there with your eyes closed, and seeing the flight of the stars in the darkness, you can believe that. But Grandfather says God moves the moon and all the planets with his little finger and when he wants it to be day, it's day, and when he doesn't want it to be day, it's night.

Where did that inkblot come from? He spat on his finger, rubbed the paper, turned it over, and saw an ugly hole. He ripped the page out and the notebook fell apart; but there was still a stain on the paper. There was no way to hide it. Then Teacher said that it is not at all nice to tear up one's notebook. Shame on you. But what if a hair or a speck of dirt gets on your pen point? It troubled him that his handwriting was so ugly, and he was afraid to go up to the blackboard.

"There's nothing you can do," said Eliahu. "That's the nature of penmanship."

The nature of penmanship. Eli knows everything and that's why he likes going to the board. He raises two fingers. He raises two fingers and stands up, bows to the teacher, takes the chalk, quickly solves the problem, writes the answer at the bottom, underlines it, and then looks her straight in the eyes for a long time, and without any fear, to see if it's correct. She says it's correct and tells him to sit down, but Eliahu does not sit down. When she opens her grade book and writes in it with a red pencil, Eli looks over her shoulder. Eli is the top student in the class and has a fountain pen with a gold nib. Then Teacher calls Albino to the center of the room. A tiny little boy stands up near the last bench and says that he is present. White hair, a white forehead, white hands, he is just like an agile white mouse. He doesn't do anything at the blackboard; he just laughs. Teacher looks at him sternly, opens her grade book, and says out loud, so that everyone can hear, "Ernest Bierka—unsatisfactory."

When he returns to his seat the boys stick their feet out between the rows to trip him and call to him in a whisper, "Wipe your nose, Albino!" He stumbles and gamely smiles at his tormentors. Teacher coughs quietly and just barely restrains her laughter.

But in the gymnasium, skinny little Ernest climbs nimbly onto the rope ladder and from his high perch mimics Zyga, who is the strongest boy in the class.

Stone on stone,
Stone on stone,
And on that stone
Yet another stone.

And so on, without end. In his rough voice, which is horribly off key, Zyga always hums the same song over and over. He does everything with his left hand and that's why Ernest calls him "Sh'maya."

Albino is at the bottom of the class and Zyga says that he'll surely be kept back to repeat the year. It's embarrassing and a nuisance. Zyga is repeating the year and he's bored stiff. He's been playing naval warfare all winter long with Baruch Oks, who sits next to the wall, in the corner, in the third row of benches counting from the door. Once there was an uproar because Teacher heard one of them yelling, "Four d's!" And the other, "Dead." She ordered him to stand up at once and tell her what that meant. He answered glumly, "The last three-master."

Teacher didn't understand what was going on. There was quite a to-do about it and she ordered one of them to speak up. Now Zyga was called "Three-master" in school. He used to box with Baruch Oks during recess and go to the bathroom with him to smoke a cigarette. He wrote on the bathroom door: "Look to your left." On the left wall: "Look to your right." On the right wall: "Turn around." And on the rear wall: " . . . " And that was all, but Dyrko called them both into his office and asked what that was about.

They were sent home halfway through the school day and the janitor spent the rest of the day scrubbing and washing the wall.

The janitor was quite a guy: he sniffed like a dog, reported everything to Dyrko, and always rang the recess bell late. He would take their lunches from their bags, certain they would be afraid to complain. And on the Third of May, on Constitution Day, he would lead the boys out to the school yard and drill them. The janitor shouted, "Long live the Polish Republic!" And the boys responded, "Long may it live!" The janitor would hiss an aside, "May it rot, may it rot." Then Dyrko would hold an assembly, collect flowers from the parents, drink water from a thick crystal glass, and lead the cheer in place of the janitor. The Third of May was a historic moment. May was the loveliest month of the year, when the lilacs bloomed in Kazimierz Square. In the evenings, the girls called attention to themselves, standing inside the gates till late at night, and the statue of the Mother of God in the alley off Wronia Street glowed with the flames of candles. She was painted for spring: her garments were bright blue, her face and arms lilac, and her kerchief white. She stood barefoot, trampling on a snake and the moon. The snake held a blood-colored apple in its jaws, and the moon was crescent-shaped.

In May thunder rolled across the sky and at dusk there were short, heavy rainstorms. In May, Mr. Stankiewicz, a seasonal dealer in pigeons and owner of a large, cooing aviary on Kercelak Square, would sing out in his passionate, hoarse tenor voice: "Titina, ah, Titina . . ." Strumming the mandolin, he rolled his eyes up toward the windows; when he opened his mouth, his gold tooth glittered. He was called Gold Tooth in Kercelak, and his street orchestra was made up of real artists. In the summer they wandered from courtyard to courtyard; in the winter, they spent time in the lockup and the papers would write about which of them was arrested, and when.

When the mandolin falls silent a pedlar carrying a sack enters the courtyard and goes from door to door on the ground floor, the first, second, and third floors, and the basements; he buys cheap goods, an old wardrobe, brass coffee mills. Everyone trades with him, leaning out their windows. Later, a knife sharpener sharpens knives and hammers sheets of metal into circles, and in the afternoon a circus dancer steps onto a carpet, gracefully lifts her arms, turns around, and bows once more in the other direction. The man rolls up his sleeves, under which can be seen a dark blue, tattooed Scorpio and Libra. Their breath whistles, the veins are distended in their faces, darkened from their effort. Oh, won't she get hurt? It's dreadful, the woman is frozen in the shape of a bow! She leaps down lightly from the man's arms and blows a kiss to the first floor. A somersault, a bridge, and a split—then they roll up the carpet and go on, and in the evening a man with a wire hook can be heard rustling in a corner of the courtyard where he collects bottles and puts them in a sack, makes separate piles of bones, rags, and paper, rummages in the garbage bin without lifting his head, while the golden light of the streetlamp glimmers faintly in front of the gate. You can definitely hear that he is saying something. Is he talking to himself? You can hear the jingling of the glass, the scratching of the hook. But what is he saying? He is a mute and he babbles. Sometimes he appears in the gray hours of the morning, when the first yawns of Mr. Władysław, the janitor, can be heard through his open window.

He remembers: it was a very long time ago. Mr. Władysław's sons, laughing, dragged him into the janitor's apartment, where a Christmas carol with the monotonous, sweet melody of a lullaby, and words full of threats, floated in air that was saturated with the aroma of unfamiliar holidays. They were singing that fire gives strength, that the mighty tremble. And in the corner by the window stood a tall, pointed tree dressed in white, in sparks, in the glow of burning candle ends. It was the tree of knowledge. Of good or of evil? He didn't know. At any rate, it was the tree under which Adam and Eve, naked, sought shelter. He noticed an apple on a bough, wrapped in a strip of tinfoil. And a snake that coiled in long loops among the branches and encircled them like a chain. And he noticed a star, the star that showed the shepherds the path into the wilderness. And the big fish that still, after so many years, could not spit out Jonah was rocking carelessly and gently on a branch. And he saw a bird on the branch beside the fish, the dove that our forefather Noah had released when the waters receded. And angels, white angels with puffed-up cheeks, flaxen hair, quicksilver wings. The candles were burning, the golden nuts sparkled, bright sparks showered down, there was the sweet smell of the straw hidden under the tablecloth, the suffocating smell of candles, of poppyseed, of the damp fir tree. In front of him, right in front of his enraptured eyes, stood the tree of life.

Clang. The clanging comes from the bell on the shop door. Professor Baum enters and loudly greets Father, holding his arms out in front of him. David mimicked their voices when he was alone:

"How do you do, Mr. Fremde."

"How do you do, Professor Baum."

Professor Baum jabs his finger at the newspaper that is spread out before him. There's something in it. "And what do you say to that, Mr. Fremde?"

Father answers, "We don't know when we know too much."

Professor Baum, carried away, holds the paper high over his head: Europe in grave danger, Czechoslovakia annexed, Klaipeda occupied, Minister Beck and Goering, shaking hands in a photograph. Both of them had shotguns on their shoulders; it was clear they were on their way back from hunting. He shouts, "*Sturm-und-Drangperiode!*"

And Father replies, "*Schwein-und-Dreckperiode.*"

"What?"

When he worked, Father sang. He hammered away and the floor shook. He grabbed a saw and a song was heard. "*Der yold iz mir mekane mit mayn klayn shtikele broyt. Oy, oy.* The fool grudges me my little crust of bread. Oy, oy." He picked up a plane, there was a hissing sound, and golden, oily-smelling strips of damp wood fluttered to the floor. They clustered together, grew into a tall stack, and every single shaving glistened like sunshine.

And then, in the autumn, to the crashing sounds of collapsing walls, the first bombs fell from the sky and also a new word: *Jude. Juuuude.* Now he knew who he was.

Triumphant, he brought home his last prewar report card: conduct—unsatisfactory; religion—unsatisfactory; arithmetic—unsatisfactory; shop—unsatisfactory; zeroes from top to bottom. Mother and Father studied that report card for a long time, shaking their heads in disbelief. It was unheard of; how had he done it? Now no one will ever know, because summer vacation began right after that, and at the end of vacation the war broke out and Father was conscripted into the cavalry, and then there was the siege of Warsaw and the airplanes circled above the city, the population sat in dark cellars, and then Father was taken prisoner, escaped and crossed the Bug River, and by the time he came home everyone had long since forgotten about the report card. He'd gotten off easy.

"*Bitte schön!*"

A military soup kitchen full of German soup drove into their street and the civilians were jostling for places in the line. "Jesus, Mary, and Joseph, let me in, people!" A cook, wearing a white apron over his putrid-green uniform and a floppy three-cornered hat, dispensed smiles and goulash from the cart and, gesturing grandly, waved his shiny brass ladle in the air. Rubbish swirled in the wind, dust blew up and coated the cook's apron and landed in the cauldron and in the people's soup containers. Warsaw was under occupation.

"*Bitte.*"

He remembers: every evening police patrols passed under their windows, guarding the freight station; dogs followed silently behind them. Every morning under their windows two September beggars passed by, men without faces, two shadows. And he didn't know whom to fear more. A Jew with a box of glass on his back came here, right beside the walls of the tenement houses that still bore the traces of the September bombardments. His face was dirty, earth-colored, sunken, and sharp as a shard of glass. He looked at nobody and nothing as he walked. He would stop, raise his eyes to the sky, roll them, and cry: "Windowpanes, I install windowpanes." Then he would walk on, continuing his wanderings through the ruined city, stooped under the weight of the glass, his face hidden in the upturned collar of his jacket. He would be passed by a man wearing a coat pinned closed with a safety pin, and without a shirt underneath. White cloth armbands with the six-pointed Star of David fluttered on a hanger that he carried in front of him like a shop window.

"Rags, rags! Who needs a rag?"

Now he knew who he was — when his mother sewed an armband just like that onto his jacket sleeve. And one day masons appeared in the streets and they began to build the wall.

Is this what the Tower of Babel is supposed to look like? Is this what the Tower of Babel actually did look like? And had God already mixed up all the languages? He had always thought that myth murky, unclear. Probably because of the gloomy, blurred picture printed on cheap paper. It fused in his memory with the colors of the approaching storm. Probably he had looked at that picture at some dead time of day, in the winter, when the weak electric light was unable to vanquish the grayness of the gloom in the alcove behind Father's workshop where they slept, or to chase away the shadows of night from in front of his eyes. Srebrna Street was full of such alcoves, pierced by the clamor of the freight trains, pierced by the wind that blew through the outskirts of the city, enveloped in a pillar of coal dust. Blackness, darkness, and in that darkness a crowd of toiling shadows circles endlessly, and the thunder rolls. For a moment, the figures bent beneath their burdens, their mouths open and their teeth bared from exertion, can be seen clearly and sharply; you can see the stones passed from hand to hand. The thunder rolls, it hurls bodies down from the tower and stones and more stones tumble to the ground, the bowed bodies fall heavily onto the ground, and the clouds gather low, very low. That's it. The myth was somber, abruptly ended like the tower that was broken in half.

A large sheet of paper was pasted up at the entrance to his closed school, a black and yellow poster showing a huge upper arm encircled by an armband with a star. On this arm a Jew with a hooked nose perches comfortably, extending his own arms, astride which sit two Jews with the same hooked noses, on whose arms sit four Jews with hooked noses, on whose arms sit eight Jews, on whose arms sit sixteen Jews, on whose arms sit thirty-two Jews . . . The Jews who didn't fit on the black and yellow poster walked along the streets of the Ghetto. Swarms of Jews in the form of a pyramid that vanished somewhere high up, far away, climbed over each other, and all of them wore the armband with the star around their arms. *Achtung! Weltjudentum. Gefahr!*

The wall was already completed when Father said, "David, how long has it been since you've gone to visit Grandfather, eh? It's not nice. Let's go there for New Year's."

But they didn't go for New Year's; they didn't go until Purim. They walked along the streets, skirting the naked flame-blackened ruins that hung over their heads like the skeletons of enormous long-dead animals dangling from a butcher's hook. They walked in a crowd of crying pedlars, of women who guarded their barrels of herring and barrels of sauerkraut from dawn to dusk, of teenagers with wings on their heels and little boxes hung around their necks, who shouted while running and ran back and forth while shouting. "Ciii-garettes! Maaa-tches!"

They walked past an endless line of beggars who were sobbing for mercy and impudently showering the passersby with curses full of Polish words, Hebrew words, *zhargon*, and the soft German of the eastern border towns. They passed cantors who had been driven from the provinces to the city, to the streets, and here they were on the sidewalk, singing their hunger and their psalms. They passed stern old men in tattered black garments, rabbis expelled from their little towns and villages who, raising up loud prayers under the open sky, timidly stretched out their hands for alms, and those hands, always in motion, desiccated and frail, hung loosely and trembled in the air like leaves set quivering by a puff of wind. Alms, prayers, curses—the everyday music of those streets.

When they arrived they found everyone seated in his usual seat: Grandfather, Aunt Chava, Dora Lewin, Professor Baum, Uncle Yehuda, Uncle Shmuel, Uncle Gedali. At the head of the table, in the corner, was Grandfather, but where was Grandfather's beard? Unconsciously, David checked for it—that beard that was as carefully cultivated as a garden—where it usually lay, broadly spread out and curling over Grandfather's gabardine. Dry as a fruit stone, yellowed, unkempt, wearing a stained vest, the distraught old man pressed his pale fingers to his pale temples. When shouting could be heard from the street he grew smaller in his corner and his eyes tightened with despair. His bent figure sank into the gloom of the late winter afternoon, while Aunt Chava bustled about nearby and thrust little pillows behind the old man's back. Brushing the dust from his sleeves and yarmulke she tried to give him a straighter, more acceptable demeanor through the power of her despotic love.

His old eyes looked past them today; they were focused on a point on the ground. Purim, Purim. In the old days, Grandfather used to brighten the holidays with the light of his stern dignity. His eyes banished from the table and dispelled everything that was petty, insignificant, unworthy. A restrained joy would inhabit his face, hope supported by prayer, a pledge of humility before the Lord renewed throughout the holy days. That's what those days were like, days of destiny, days of the legend of victory, days both joyous and stern. Capable of instilling strength through good news, through cheerful spirits, from generation to generation. Grandfather had the legend fixed in his smile; with every gesture, every glance, he infused it with warmth for all the people gathered around his table. Purim, Purim, holiday of destiny, when the characters from the ancient intrigue stepped out of the pages of the Bible and enacted, as they had done every year from time immemorial, their ambiguous roles. There is Esther, there is Mordechai, there is Haman, there is King Ahasuerus, docilely obedient to the promptings of a beautiful Jewish girl.

David remembered the moment when, with fear and shame, he

felt on his temples the crown of golden oakum. Esther's gown was draped over his shoulders. Baruch Oks was Haman, the cruel deputy. Eli was the Persian king. And Zyga, because he was "Sh'maya" — the lefty, whom everyone in school feared, because he had a terribly strong left hand that he used for writing, lifting heavy loads, and giving beatings — was Mordechai.

Behind them stretched a paper Shushan and the royal gardens, and in front of them sat the audience, their parents, noisily blowing their noses. They were here, in the light, acting their parts, and there, on the other side of the proscenium, the rest of the world sank into the terrifying darkness. Slowly, slowly, in the black abyss of the auditorium, bright spots began to shine, faces, eyes, and tears glistened. From far away they sent them signs, smiles, sighs, while Dyrko ran around in the wings like a madman, looking for Ahasuerus's scepter. Meanwhile, they had to drop the curtain and there was an awful uproar in the hall before Eli found an apple in his lunch bag to hold in his hand. And the King and Haman came to Queen Esther's feast. Baruch Oks, in a terrifying voice, roared that he was going to murder all the Jews. That was required by his role. But he yelled a little too loudly. King Ahasuerus kept going outside to the fig tree in the garden in order not to hear him. Esther fainted. That is to say, David fainted, or rather, he forgot to faint on time, so Zyga kicked his ankle.

"Faint, right now! What are you waiting for?"

David fell down and lay there on his back. But Dyrko kept getting in the way, and just at the most important moment he pushed the janitor out onto the stage. The janitor burst on stage, shouting, "Here it is!" and handed Haman his sword.

Baruch Oks didn't miss a beat and said in his own words, "What does this mean? Yet another delay?"

The audience realized what was going on and burst out laughing, and the janitor stood stock still. Finally they managed to get him off the stage and the performance continued. Haman kept intriguing against the Jews, but nothing came of this because King Ahasuerus was wrapped around Esther's little finger and happily followed Mordechai's advice. Then the gallows was driven onto the stage, with the evil Haman hanging from it, and . . .

Uncle Shmuel is saying, "The Allies will declare war and it will all be over in a month." His left hand gestures expressively, all the way up to the elbow. "Go on! In the worst scenario," and, pretending to think, he leans over to his left, toward Grandfather, "in the worst scenario, it will go on until winter. The Germans will have time to send us to Madagascar in the summer, and that will be the end of it."

Father says, "I once heard a story about a baby that was born to a couple on Smocza Street, and the moment it came into the world it predicted that no later than New Year's, during Rosh Hashanah, all the Jews would be saved. And then it died."

Uncle Shmuel shrugs his shoulders. "During Rosh Hashanah itself? So what? The New Year has already passed."

Uncle Gedali asks with dead seriousness, "And the baby didn't have time to say anything else, Yakov?"

Aunt Chava absentmindedly places in front of Uncle Shmuel the tea she prepared for Grandfather. Grandfather, not even glancing in her direction, slowly and approvingly nods his head. An ambiguous silence reigns.

"Ersatz Herbatol? From a cube? No, I won't put that slop in my mouth," Uncle Shmuel declares grimly.

"Not a word," says Father. He looks sorrowfully at Uncle Shmuel. "Unfortunately, it didn't want to say anything else, but had it lived—blessed be the memory of that child," he interjects in a shaken voice, "—even one more hour, we would have learned unbelievable things."

"That's entirely possible," Uncle Gedali roars, and draws the rejected glass of tea over to his place.

. . . And that's how the Jews were saved. The gallows was supposed to be "fifty elbows" high, but they could never have managed such a tall one. And then the children took off their costumes amidst the applause and kisses and their parents took them home. They walked home at dusk, when the city was enfolded in a carnival tumult, colorful balloons floated in air filled with laughter and spring breezes, and Chinese lanterns extinguished the light of the stars. High above the crowds, Haman moved around on enormous stilts, with a gallows attached to his collar and a noose flapping freely over his head. In the many-colored, swaying light of the lanterns his grimacing mask was flooded with a dead, unnatural glow—green, red, violet. And as soon as those words issued from the king's mouth, a hood was pulled over Haman's face. The noise-makers rattled furiously. Purim, Purim.

Where should one seek fate? Where seek Queen Esther? Her voice will no longer echo from the pages of the Book, her beauty will not save her people. Mordechai will not defeat their enemies. On the table lies half a loaf of rationed bread and in front of Grand-father is the Bible, spurned, unopened.

Uncle Yehuda says, "Madagascar, Madagascar . . . Come to your senses, Shmuel. Hundreds of thousands of Jews are dying in *Arbeits-dienst* detachments, including most of the men over sixty, their blood drained by galloping dysentery. The Allies? In France they could barely get any action organized; the generals stuffed the gun barrels with their surrender documents. They signed a ceasefire agreement as soon as they could in order to avoid complete annexation. What else do you need? Now the Vichy government, that pimp in the employ of the Reich, is lying flat on its back before his whorish highness. And feverishly firing Jews in offices and firms, knowing only too well what the Reich prides itself on. Poor old France is under siege; she has to be saved from the Jews. The confiscations are mounting to hundreds and hundreds of millions of dollars. They've also expended just a little on supporting Vichy and on the costs of representation. Hitler himself put Marshall Pétain through his paces; isn't that enough? Ribbentrop is still telling his fairy tales about Madagascar, but Goebbels has the final solution to the Jewish question by now. On September 4, Jewish blood flowed in the streets of Marseilles and on the Riviera. Exhausted whores leaned out of the windows of the brothels, waving their tear-soaked handkerchiefs. They cheered the mobs, sobbed and prayed for the avengers' valor. The Jews are being driven from the towns and locked up behind barbed wire, and in the places where it hasn't come to that yet, their houses are marked so that no innocent persons should make the mistake of entering under their sinful roofs. Pope Pius XII has bestowed his blessing on the Brown Shirts, who are supposed to save the world from the plague and fulfill their mission until the end. This is a controlled conflagra-tion! Some snot-nosed kids from the Hitler Jugend, Baldur von Schirach's young followers, set fire to the Strasbourg synagogue and the SS men ceremoniously hurl grenades into the flames. In full view of the crowd that is gathered there, which applauds with delight.

Every street musician is blaring dashing Berlin marches instead of those melancholy Viennese waltzes. The anthem of the National Socialist revolution is resounding over Europe! *Und morgen die ganze Welt.* Very nice, eh? And tomorrow the whole world will be theirs. Shmuel, Shmuel, my foolish brother . . .

"In Hungary, during the period of bloody head-bashing, the Jewish representatives were expelled from parliament and Hebrew was strictly prohibited. In Italy, Mussolini banned the sale of books; in Holland, all the children were expelled from school, all the men from public firms. Everywhere, the property of Jewish families has been subjected to detailed registration procedures. What more do you need, Shmuel? Madagascar, Madagascar . . . On the high seas, in the vicinity of Malta, a transport of Jews en route to Palestine was stopped and all the passengers, together with their passports, their suitcases, their boxes, canaries, nursemaids, Aaronele who doesn't like to eat his cereal, and Benele with his whooping cough, were placed behind barbed wire.

"Where . . ., and if I tell you where, will you believe me? What nation equals ours in gullibility? Do I have to present you with your own death certificate to make you believe me? Do I have to show you the bill for the funeral, how much for the wreaths, how much for the coffin, how much for the tears of the professional mourners? But I'll tell you this: Franco has ordered the construction of a camp for thousands of people, and at night the dogs there howl with desire for kosher Jewish meat. In the meantime, you are free not to believe, but when you do come to believe, it will be too late and you won't have to believe a word I say. A dead man believes in nothing, not even in God, but the Bible says nothing about that. Not a word, not a single word. Maybe you'll find something. You can't take faith into the grave; faith is left behind for the living. That's what I was taught, and what about you, Shmuel?

"But that's not the point, rather that Switzerland, neutral Switzerland, that pasteurized corpse, that prig grown old in her vaunted virtuousness—even she has added her clean hands to the mess. In Switzerland, my dear brother, the press is forbidden to reveal even a single word about what the Germans are doing to the Jews in Germany. Their good example has quickly had an effect, because virtue is as contagious as clap in our times. A couple of weeks later Portugal, that nun gussied up in a habit, declared that refugees are to be refused entry into the country. *Judenrein*. Then Luxembourg, the mangy cardshark who isn't embarrassed at extracting half a dollar from any foreign lady, from her you-know-where, also suddenly experienced a revulsion toward Jews. And how many Jews could be living in Luxembourg? How many? One hundred? Two hundred? They were deported from there to the east, to the east, that is, to us, to the Generalgouvernement.

"Lately, a rumor's been circulating among the journalists. Who started it and who repeats it? Two ships—listen, listen to me—have been loaded with Jews to transport them to Haiti, presumably out of concern for their health. And closer to home? In Latvia, in Czechoslovakia, in Romania? Everywhere is *Judenrein*. Antonescu has closed the Jewish schools, frozen Jewish bank accounts, expropriated Jewish land, and ordered all Jews who entered Romania within the past five years to leave the country. Is that enough? In Belgium . . ."

"That's enough," Grandfather interjects from his corner. "Enough already."

Uncle Yehuda obediently falls silent, but he's so wound up that he still emits a couple of angry inarticulate snorts, like a horse reined in from a gallop.

"Listen to me, did you hear how he let his mouth run?" Grandfather reminds us in his singsong prayerful voice: "'And the Lord opened the mouth of the ass.'" And then in his normal voice: "May a boil grow on your tongue and make you mute, amen."

"Amen," Uncle Shmuel repeats passionately.

Grandfather regards him solemnly.

"And what's the climate like there, in Madagascar, Shmuel?" he asks calmly, with a poisonous sweetness in his voice. "Is it bearable?"

Aunt Chava pushes back her chair noisily, gets up, and goes into the kitchen. Uncle Shmuel nervously adjusts his tie.

"Tss, tss, tss."

David held the noisemaker, since he was the youngest at the table. His hand was wet with sweat. What would happen if the noisemaker rattled when it shouldn't? What would Father say? What would Aunt Chava say? Oh no. When Grandfather begins to read the Bible he will have to pay careful attention so as not to miss any mention of

Haman. Whenever that name is mentioned he will raise the noise-maker high, twirl it—"Harder! Harder!"—and obliterate the memory of that enemy with the noise. Yes, that's the way it's supposed to be. And in the synagogue he heard how at the sound of that name the Jews stamped their feet, jostled the benches noisily, opened and shut the doors with a bang. A heavy, choking dust was raised; the *talesim* flapped angrily. In the rustling of shawls, in the cloud of dust, the figures grow dim and dark. Prayerful faces. Angry faces. Anxious faces. Faces caught in a burst of passionate ecstasy. A great uproar was created, a wordless uproar filled with the agitated sighs, the vengeful labored breathing, the silent rebellion of the crowd. He remembers how frightened he used to be. And how the cantor's sharp voice silenced the anger with a single long and insistent refrain and kept the story moving.

"Dora, try some," says Aunt Chava, bringing in a tray. She has made a pancake batter out of grated rutabaga and boiled potatoes, a pinch of rye flour, a couple of grains of saccharin, and some ersatz powdered eggs, and fried the mixture in oil. What can she do? She remembers holidays, far-off holidays when, by the light of the candles flickering in the silver candelabrum, fish fragrant with saffron were brought to the table, and a goose with broken wings, sweet wine, nuts, cakes almost brown from an abundance of vanilla and cinnamon. What, Dora can't stand the taste of vanilla? But she can't imagine the holidays without it. And *kugel*? Does Dora make that without spices, too? No, of course not. She uses spices, but she doesn't eat it herself. It might as well not exist as far as she's concerned. Strange, isn't it?

"Let it be called a cake," says Uncle Gedali. He wiggles his ears at the sight of Aunt Chava's pancake, and he makes such a face that the boy immediately feels better. He looks quickly, stealthily, at Grandfather. Can Grandfather see him, or is he pretending not to see?

"It tastes like a cake from Gajewski's," says Dora Lewin. "Marvelous! Where do you buy your ersatzes, Chava? I haven't had a cake rise like this yet. Give me your recipe." And she nibbles elegantly at the pancake. Aunt Chava is laughing now, loudly, and with relief, at the sight of Dora eating. The nauseating, bitter smell of rutabaga and scorched oil fills the room. Aunt Chava is clearly waiting for additional compliments.

"What was it we were talking about?" Professor Baum asks in the silence. "Wait a minute, wait a minute. Aha." He picks up the rutabaga pancake with his spoon and breaks off a piece.

The holidays have flown away. Outside the window is a late winter sky, dark blue like a knife. Hail is falling and the sun is going down. The sharp glare of the nasty reddish light is smeared over the wall of the tenement facing theirs, and a windowpane glitters vacantly like a blind man's wide-open eye. Grandfather slowly turns his head and looks solemnly at David, solemnly and fixedly.

Uncle Shmuel: "People were saying at the council that the authorities have levied a contribution of ten thousand dollars on the Jews for an assault on a German. To be paid by the end of the year. Otherwise every third man between the ages of seventeen and sixty will be sent to a labor camp."

Silence. The cries of beggars float up from the street. "People, people, have pity!"

Uncle Gedali: "Not ten but one hundred thousand, and not dollars, but zlotys, and not by the end of the year, but by the end of this month."

"Let them take it," says Aunt Chava. "Let them take it and choke on it! Amen. Then maybe they'll leave us in peace."

"Until the end of the year," Professor Baum replies. "They can impose more than one contribution and not choke on them at all. And the council will extract the money from us." He pointed to the window as a passionate cry erupted from the street. "And from them, from the poorest of the poor."

"And that's how it will be," says Uncle Gedali.

"Who? Who? Who will give them anything? *You* will give, I can see that already." Uncle Shmuel dug into the pancake energetically and pieces of sticky rutabaga splattered all around.

"No, not I . . . I won't give anything because I don't have anything. But the Judenrat will dig that money out of the ground."

Uncle Gedali began counting on his hooklike fingers. "One, they'll steal from the kitchens for the beggars. They'll save a little on the bread ration, that's two. The rest they'll get by requisitions and that'll do it."

"Requisitions? Of what? From whom? People have been tearing the shirts off the backs of corpses in order to sell them for bread. Their shoes, too."

"You have forgotten where you are living, Shmuel. Sienna Street is a well-to-do street, well-to-do," said Uncle Yehuda.

"The merchants! If that's the case let them sell us alive to the Germans. And they call themselves Jews? They call themselves Jews, too?" Uncle Shmuel repeated.

The rutabaga fell to the floor under the blows from his fork. Grandfather sat nearby in his dark corner, his eyes closed, as if he were not there, covering the Bible with his hands.

"President Czerniaków himself."

Uncle Yehuda broke in, "Should he make a contribution out of his own pocket? He's negotiating with the Germans because that's what the Jewish Community Council established the Council of Elders for. What else can they do? No doubt they're consumed with the thought that they're defending the interests of the population, because they are official saviors. Mordechais, Mordechais. Only they don't have anyone to urge to take their Esthers. And the beauty of their young girls doesn't count for anything, Shmuel."

"God of Abraham, God of Isaac, God of Jacob. My Lord, Who in Thy goodness delivered the chosen people from the house of bondage in the land of Egypt and led them into the desert. Amen. Today Thou commandest me to watch as my sons quarrel with each other and lose their common sense. Thy will be done. Amen. Listen to me, Shmuel; listen, Yehuda. Feh! I'll say this: Everyone has foolish ideas but the wise man doesn't put them into words. Have some consideration for your old father, who is listening to you but does not understand. And no longer wants to understand. Amen, amen. Oh, again, again. They're coming. They're coming, and they're shouting."

Grandfather, in his dark corner, uttered his halting, hesitant words between one sigh and another, while a band of beggars drew nearer in the street. Their rhythmic noise was getting closer—the clattering of the tin cups they shook in their despair. The shouting and yelling of the hungry crowd approached: "People, kind people, people, have pity. Give us money for a piece of bread. People!" The plates and spoons of the alms-seekers rattled furiously.

"Oh, my ears. There are old men there, rabbis without bread or water. The shepherds, the shepherds are leaving. They are crying out. My sins are crying out to Thee, o Lord. Have I gone deaf? Why do I hear my own sons and why do I not hear the sons of other people? Forgive me, Lord, and don't make me see how Thou punishest others for my sins. Don't touch me with the heaviest of punishments. Don't let me see, don't command me to see. Don't let me see, don't command me to see."

Grandfather's whisper faded away in the late afternoon twilight, dissipated in sighs, and was replaced by his pained rocking.

"My children, my grandson. My children."

Professor Baum broke the silence. "What were we talking about? Wait a minute, wait a minute. Aha. So, what if the Judenrat refuses? Eh? You think the Germans can't manage by themselves? A little while ago I read in the rag that a certain American Express Company is offering its services to everyone in the GG who wants to receive support from their relatives in the USA."

"We need the support and the Germans need the foreign exchange," said Father.

"That's it, that's it! The idea is a good one. Only it's the first time I've ever heard of the American Express Company and I don't know who's going to be taken in by that firm."

"The American Express Company? Maybe somebody knows."

Aunt Chava pointed at the untouched plate of rutabaga. "David, you're not eating? Should I make you some hot chocolate?"

"No." He was awfully embarrassed that she had drawn everyone's attention to him.

"Even if you wanted it you wouldn't get any," said Father.

"But I don't want any," David answered quickly.

"Really?" asked Uncle Gedali.

Father began to laugh in a nasty, mean way. Meanwhile the conversation continued.

"Lice," Uncle Shmuel shouted. "Lice have built themselves a nest in the Judenrat. The lice are sucking our blood and they won't stop until we turn into dry skin and bones."

"If only that were the end of it. If only," Professor Baum said. "Skin and bones is a lot."

"Those flunkeys in the Kahal have gone over to the Gestapo's payroll!"

"I wouldn't bet that isn't so," said Uncle Yehuda.

"They're stealing money out of the pockets of Jews and using it to buy the Germans' favor for themselves." Uncle Shmuel's shouted words hung there in the thickening darkness.

"They wanted power? They set up a 'council,' they set up a 'police force.' They opened their own jails and their own tax offices. The Germans don't even have to lay a finger on the screw, it just turns itself and digs into the living flesh."

"Oh, come on. What are you talking about? This is nothing," said Uncle Gedali. "In a year or two the Germans will really show you."

"Madagascar," Uncle Yehuda interjected hastily.

"Madagascar," repeated Uncle Gedali and bared his teeth. "Then you'll see what ground you're walking on. All this is only Fiume all over again! Children playing at Haman. But one day the Germans will say, 'Enough! The Judenrat has done its thing. The Judenrat can go away.' And adieu, saviors. Adieu, Mordechais."

"Saviors!" Uncle Shmuel yelled. "Leeches in epaulettes playing at being saviors of the nation. Have you seen how they strut around, how they carry themselves? Have you seen their tall boots, their armbands with the seal on them, their nightsticks? For shaking under the noses of impotent old men. And as if that's not enough, they already have their own club on Leszno where they carry on their nightlife. That's a sight to see."

"Oh, go on. Nightlife. It's business, business. They're doing their crude business deals there," said Uncle Gedali.

"Who is he talking about? And what is he talking about?" Aunt Chava raised her hands to her cheeks. "My God, what is it all about?"

"About the Mordechais," said Uncle Yehuda.

"And this is supposed to be Purim . . . ," she repeated. "This is supposed to be a holiday."

"He's talking about the Jewish police," Dora Lewin explained.

"The Jewish police!" Anger and excitement had taken Uncle Shmuel's breath away and he screeched like a rooster whose throat has been slashed. "Dogs on leashes. Dogs on leashes attack the throats of Jews and the Jews pretend they are *their* dogs because they were bought with Jewish money, but those dogs serve the Germans, the Germans, and it's the Germans who will hold their leashes and direct them to sniff out every single Jew's business and lead them straight to it without thinking, by the shortest possible route."

"That's the holy truth, the holy truth. You shouldn't add or subtract anything," said Dora Lewin.

"The holy truth," Professor Baum repeated.

They nodded their heads in agreement, and united by the same worry they turned to face each other with a sudden motion. Yes, yes. Only Uncle Yehuda laughed bitterly.

"Apparently," he began, "during the first few weeks it cost three hundred zlotys to buy a post in the yellow police. Am I expressing myself clearly? Now the price has jumped to a thousand, and it will go even higher. Fear will have its way, I know what I'm talking about. Insurance. A Jew will pay any price to save his head. The time will come," he exclaimed forcefully, "that they'll pay gold for a stick. And sell another human being for a lousy grosch. That's what."

Aunt Chava grew so agitated that her wig fell over her ear, revealing the yellow skin of her scalp covered with transparent, limp clumps of hair. "How dare you!" She struck her fists together feebly. "How can you?" The jostled wig drifted lightly and gracefully to the floor, like a dried thistle flower. "I don't want to hear such words on Jewish lips in a Jewish house on a Jewish holiday!"

Uncle Yehuda bent down, picked up the wig, and handed it to her, his head bowed. She pushed away the blasphemer's hand with contempt. She looked terrifying now: bald, enraged, her eyes wild and opened wide with despair.

"God, why didn't You give me a different fate?" whispered Dora Lewin. "Why did I live to see these awful years?" Her hard rolled r's flapped around in the air like crows.

"Worse years will come," said Uncle Yehuda.

"Whaaat?" Now an inexplicable change came over her. "What do you want of me?" was all that Aunt Chava could say.

"Tss, tss, tss," Grandfather lamented. He dusted off the wig, slapping it against his knee. A clump of dead hair resisted his weak hands. "Children, what are you saying? You shouldn't talk like this, no."

The masks had dropped from faces, the lantern lights had gone out, and the holiday laughter had long since fallen silent. Mordechai, Esther, and Haman took flight from David's memory. The noise-maker remained in his hand. He raised his sweaty fist, in which he still held the the handle tight, and whirled it—*drr drr drr*—fast and loud. Father snatched the noisemaker out of his hand and angrily threw it down. In the silence that suddenly descended he could hear Aunt Chava's agitated breathing, her dry, heavy sobs. He felt uncomfortable and ashamed; he didn't know what to do. Her dry little body quivered in the deepening twilight, shaken by her sobbing. Could this powerful weeping really belong to her? Or were the others weeping in her voice, all at the same time, and was she just lending them her tears for this day? Her sobbing became more and more hysterical. She had been sobbing for thousands of years. Those sobs had been passed on from generation to generation, from Mahalaleel to Jared and from Jared to Enoch, and from Enoch to Methusaleh, and from Methusaleh to Lamech. Aunt Chava's pale yellow face gave off a mournful glow.

She wiped her nose and stuck her wig on crookedly. Unsteadily she walked to the sideboard, her arms stretched out before her. A fading howl followed her, the complaint of a beaten dog. It began abruptly and was over just as suddenly: a sort of scream or cry erupted from her and filled David with anxiety and nervous amazement.

"It's all right, it's all right, nothing happened. Give her some room."

Now she was herself again, until the next time. Exhausted, she lay down on the couch beneath the window, and Dora Lewin patiently unbuttoned her high-necked jabot, allowing her to breathe. Then Dora Lewin stood up and remained standing, expectantly, for a long, long time, her eyes fixed on the face of the woman lying there, as if she were tied to her post—a conjurer, a priestess calling upon holy voices.

Uncle Shmuel's cry: "If only the earth would swallow them up alive!"

And Grandfather's cautionary hissing: "Tss, tss."

Uncle Gedali slowly and calmly said a couple of words that immediately soothed everyone's anger. "It won't be long, Shmuel, before the earth swallows us alive. Don't yell like that, you'll break the windowpanes. You can see that they're cracked already and the paper barely holds them together."

No one said anything in reply and Grandfather stubbornly kept on fussing in his dark corner, shoving his chair back and returning it to its place. Groaning, he repeated, "Shmuel, Yehuda, do you hear me? When a deaf Jew descends into the grave and understands nothing, the angels shield his face with their wings. What kind of a Jew is he, and who has grievances against him, and how will he stand there at the Last Judgment? Ech! I'll tell you, Shmuel. He'll stand at the Last Judgment with a stupid grin on his face. He'll complain to the Lord that he wasn't given the time remaining to him before his death. And he'll start asking the Lord questions in order to hear the answers that he couldn't hear from the lips of people throughout his entire deaf life, because a deaf Jew thinks that he can hear only the Lord and that the Lord can speak to the deaf. I can already see how a deaf Jew ingratiates himself with the Lord and complains to Him about other Jews. How he wants to mend the world as soon as he has departed the world. And what does he care if in the meantime the end of the world has come? 'God,' he'll cry out, 'Thou punished Sodom severely, but I know that Thy anger was turned against her in time.' Such faith and such justice cannot be pleasing to our Lord. 'God,' he'll cry out, 'now I know everything and I curse the sins of others whom Thou hast cursed, but why me? Why me?' Such complaints and anger of the deaf man cannot be pleasing to the Lord, because there are no just angry men, even if they are carried away by a righteous anger. And what if that anger is successful? Is successful anger not a sin? 'God,' he'll cry out, 'everything happened as Thou wanted it to, therefore *it had to happen!*' Such wisdom of the deaf cannot be pleasing to the Lord, and in any case, what kind of wisdom is it if it did not save Sodom? 'God,' he'll cry out, 'from now on I shall remember Thy law: Thou separatest the mangy sheep from the flocks and drown them in order that the rest should not become mangy, too.' Such devotion and such love cannot be pleasing to our Lord, and what kind of love, what kind of devotion is it if the people did not seek them from close up? Should He strain His eyes and seek them from afar? No, no, such faith in God's judgment cannot be pleasing to our Lord. And who besides Him dares to know which sheep is sick and which is well? 'God,' the deaf Jew cries, 'and if the entire flock is sick it is a sign that there is no healer other than Thee, and no man has been born who—' Here the Lord will not restrain His anger and will drive the deaf Jew out of his sight. 'Deaf Jew,' He'll cry, 'your tongue is working but not your head, your head is working but not your heart, only your liver is working. You knew what you should bring to the Judgment Day . . . Don't make speeches when others are suffering, and don't suffer when others make speeches. Don't pray when others are acting, and don't act when others are praying. You have been busy your whole life ripping open other people's mezuzahs and were always able to find an error in each of them. For so many years. And for what? Why did I create you? So that you could distinguish the letter *hey* from the letter *het*? So you could shake your fists under other people's noses? Now take those clean, white fists out of my sight. You cannot serve people or Me with the cleanliness of your hands. I removed you from Sodom not so that you might be perfect . . . You said it yourself about yourself. *Did you hear it said about yourself?* Sodom burned many years ago and no one knows why. Even I don't know. But this one comes before me and says that he knows why. A deaf man wants to tell me how and why Sodom vanished in smoke? If I gave him a second and a third life he would understand nothing. If I gave him a fourth life he wouldn't be able to finish weeping over the sufferings of Sodom. If I gave him a fifth life, he wouldn't have enough time to say prayers for the dead. So then why should he have a life at all? To recognize the pain of the deaf? Did he recognize it? Good. Then he should know that that is how I always punish latter-day false prophets.' Shmuel, Yehuda, do you hear me? They have grown deaf, like beasts. Have they gone deaf or have I? They have gone deaf, I have gone deaf . . . Everybody is deaf."

Uncle Yehuda: "Sodom, Sodom! So God Himself has descended to earth in a German uniform and is punishing guilty Jews? When did Yahweh start wearing a uniform? Who has been saying such things? I ask you, who says things like that? *They* have had it on their belt buckles for a long time. *Gott mit uns. Kisvey Hakoydesh* and National Socialism? It's a mishmash; people don't know how to think anymore. Since when does an angel inhabit every uniform, weighing human sins? Sodom, Sodom! I don't want to hear a word about Sodom as long as there are people walking around barefoot and hungry crowds roaming the streets. Later we can count their sins, every last one of them. Later. But I'll agree to that only at the Last Judgment. Not now!"

"Yehuda, there are some things in this world that cannot be postponed until Rosh Hashanah. You could find yourself before the Lord at any time. Excuses will count for nothing then. The strong and the weak, the wise and the stupid are all of equal value there. You don't have to frighten me; you don't have to comfort me. I know what is coming. And I'm talking about the same thing as you, only in different words . . . To appear at the Last Judgment, you have to discard everything. A sack on your shoulder and ashes on your head are enough. Shmuel, Yehuda, can you understand me? And if what I say is true, does it mean that the fate of the Jews will be easier? And if it is not true, will the fate of the Jews be any worse? What will be will be. Words are one thing, life is another."

Uncle Yehuda: "Is that what the Last Judgment will look like?"

Uncle Gedali: "That's what a kosher war should look like."

Uncle Yehuda: "A slaughterhouse . . . But not every butcher shop is kosher, not every misfortune is a punishment for sins, not every extermination is for a Sodom, not every war is a sentence of divine justice. In this butcher shop anyone can become a slaughterer and anyone can fall under the knife. Why should the slaughterer have been sent by Him?"

"Yehuda," said Grandfather. "The world has already existed for so long, so long . . . There must be some meaning in this. And if not? Then what the hell can I, an ignorant old Jew, do about it? Tfoo. God forgive me for these words."

"Have you always spoken like this, Father?"

"I shall always speak like this. A sack over your shoulder and ashes on your head."

Uncle Yehuda sighed deeply and flung his hands wide apart. "There are no guilty people here and there is no guilt."

"But there are those who are living and those who are dead."

Uncle Gedali: "Am *I* living?"

Father: "You have been dead for a long time."

"Tss, tss," hissed Grandfather. "Such words are a sin."

"For a long time now I've been sinning in words alone. But it is not for my words that I'm being punished. And not for my sins. It's my very existence that concerns them. My guilt is that I exist. *Das nackte Leben.* Yes!"

"You know that very well, Father," said Uncle Yehuda. "Those who have everything else also have right and justice on their side. Power, power. And you know that, too, very well, Father."

Grandfather wriggled uncomfortably in his corner. "Enough of this. Give me my *tallis*. I am an ignorant old Jew and I know nothing. All I have is the Book and it's my whole life. Not much . . .

maybe it's not much. But my eyes don't see very far, and my mind burns with only a low flame. I used to tell myself, 'Let it be, it's not for you to dig deep into the Book.' What would the wise men, the rabbis, and the *gaons* do? And now this old man feels such regret, so much regret. And if I could live my life over again I would pull out one hair from my beard and burn one candle over each verse of the Book. The beard won't vanish and the light will grow and gather wisdom unto it. No, I never understood those words, let alone today . . . Who remembers them? Those words with which the Book of Esther ends?"

Uncle Gedali repeated the verses about how the king laid a tribute upon the land, and upon the isles of the sea. He stopped midway through his high, thin chanting.

"Why does the Book of Esther end like that? Are those holy words? No, those are the words of a merchant. Common, ordinary words. That's what I used to think. Why on the day when everyone is expecting salvation? On the day when the fate of the Jews is supposed to change? Because Purim, the holiday of Purim, is a sign that the fate of the Jews has changed. Has changed? Will change? It's all the same. My language knows only two tenses, the past and the future. The present isn't worth considering . . . But those words— about money, about tributes. My God, now I know. Contributions and more contributions. Ransom money. It seems I was listening to you. Now I know, but what good is my knowledge? What good . . . Light the candles, give me my *tallis*."

"Sha, quiet, hush," Dora Lewin whispered. She was standing beside the window near the couch that Aunt Chava was resting on, straining to hear something. "With all your shouting we can't hear a thing. There's a lot of shouting in the building."

They turned their heads, all of them. And now the uproar of rapidly shouted commands exploded close by and very distinct.

"*Leute auf! Auf, auf!*"

And a Polish blue policeman's shout: "Upstairs! Get going!"

They could hear the heavy steps of policemen running up the stairs. Gleeful words spoken in a foreign language.

"*Aber das Viertel ist doch reich!*"

A racket of impatient shouts and blows from sticks and boots suddenly erupted into the apartment. As if they had all been herded together by the same swift, sharp lashing of a whip, they retreated without a word into the corner where Grandfather was seated and clustered around him in utter confusion. The horrible waiting lasted for one endlessly long moment, filled with a sticky, suffocating terror and with the young, carefree voices from outside. Then the door gave way under their blows and the Germans, genially cursing and laughing at the uproar they had created, came crashing into the apartment in a cloud of dust, accompanied by the sound of the wooden door collapsing into the room, the tinkling of the shattered glass in the breakfront, and the lamentations of all the lares and penates who had sought to bar the way before these intruders.

"*Jawohl, das fügt sich gut,*" a young gendarme said as he used a spotlight to extract their figures from the darkness, while they, blinded by the bright light, hopelessly covered their eyes and faces. The hand-powered light emitted a measured groaning sound that grew progressively louder and louder: *sha sha sha sha.* In his other hand was an automatic pistol which he pointed at the terrified group of people, inscribing a broad, mocking gesture of blessing and threat with it. "*Festtag,*" he said.

"*Festtag,*" the second gendarme said indifferently and, glancing at the table, at the closed, abandoned Holy Book, the confusion of porcelain plates with their chipped rims, the glasses filled with a tea-colored liquid, the sorry remains of the pancake, the ruins of the rutabaga cake, he snatched at the tablecloth, dragging everything onto the floor. And then gently and carefully moving a chair out of his way, he rested his boot comfortably on the curved edge of the old chest and, with one kick, dislodged the drawer, spilling its contents onto the floor. "*Ruhe,*" he spat out, hearing some movement from Grandfather, who was only sighing hopelessly as he saw his prayer shirts and caftans, his books, his *tallis* and *tefillin* fluttering to the ground. Among the scattered holiday linens, white as snow, two many-branched silver Sabbath candelabra shone dully.

"*Jawohl, herzbewegender Festtag,*" the young gendarme repeated pleasantly, not hiding his amusement at the sight of the Jews who, holding their breath, huddled against the wall motionless, silent, as stiff as corpses. With a sigh of relief he transferred his gun to his other arm, the barrel pointing downwards, flexed his numb arm twice, and smiled openly and familiarly at Dora Lewin.

"*Das Schöne . . . es steckt im Blut,*" he said, and cast a long, somber, insistent glance over her dark face, her hair, her bushy, close-knit eyebrows, her large nose, her breasts, and young hips. "*Ja, aber wo ist mein Rassenhass?*"

Two crowd-control officers were standing not far from them. A Jewish yellow policeman was waiting patiently for additional orders. The German, suddenly roused from his gloomy thoughts, energetically ripped the mezuzah from the doorpost and began stomping on it, while the tiny scrolls with the old commandments and prayers concealed inside their stiff folds emitted hoarse, angry crackles beneath his heel.

"*Klatsch! Klatsch!*" the young gendarme repeated with delight. "*Klatsch!*"

When the gaping wardrobe finally revealed its bounty of old furs and coats to the policemen's eyes and all the dresser drawers lay beside their contents, amidst the scattered pages covered with the ancient, threatening script, the old and now smashed tableware, the linens that had been feverishly searched and thrown to the floor; when the bearded Jews in the family photographs had fallen obediently face down, leaving pale spaces on the dark walls; when the musty featherbeds, pillows, and quilts, all shaken, jabbed, and ripped open with restrained enthusiasm, lay on the floor, limp and emptied of the feathers that were still swirling around or descending silently onto their shoulders—then the gendarme in charge of the search sneezed loudly and, still not giving up hope, turned his attention to the couch near the window, on which Aunt Chava was lying motionless. He gestured curtly to the yellow policeman, and pointing to the Jews huddled against the wall, he ordered him to translate his wish.

"Ladies and gentlemen, please," the yellow policeman began, and abruptly stopped. The gendarme in charge immediately came to his aid and, contemptuously shoving him aside, explained what was wanted. "Place all knives on the table. Gold, gold. And dollars," he added, dignifiedly casting his glance over everyone present. At that moment a single word, repeated emphatically several times, resounded from under the window. The gendarmes whirled around, as if a shot had suddenly echoed behind their backs.

"Typhus, *Fleckfieber,*" Aunt Chava repeated maliciously, rolling over on the couch. Her wig, carelessly knocked onto her forehead, covered her right eye; her left eye, wide open and glittering with anger, expressed the vastness of her contempt. "They're searching my house for gold, the fools, for gold . . ." She coughed briefly and then, raising herself on her elbow, she spat at them. *"Das fügt sich gut, nicht wahr?"* she repeated with open satisfaction, seeing how the gendarme obediently put back on the shelf the candlestick he was holding in his hand.

When the flustered Germans, exchanging anxious and disappointed looks, had marched across the room and out the door, wading across old clothes on their way, crushing the shards of plates, tripping over the now feather-covered remains of the rutabaga, and trampling the faces of the bearded Jews in the photographs, who were lying prostrate on the ground; when they had finally left Aunt Chava and Grandfather in peace, and David and his Father, Dora Lewin, Professor Baum, Uncle Gedali, Uncle Yehuda, and Uncle Shmuel, all of whom, huddled against the wall, had listened in shock and horror to the impudent shouts coming from the couch under the window; when the yellow policeman, with a barely perceptible smile on his face, had followed the Germans out, his head bowed—then the last German stopped in the doorway and, frustrated, bellowed in rage, "You got away with it this time—but not for long!"

Not for long. He was right, because when the last commands had echoed through the building, when the last doors were slammed shut and the police patrol had completed its last hasty search for loot, they heard steps mounting the stairs outside their door and once again the young gendarme stood in the doorway, with a carefree smile on his face. They could see that now he was drunk.

"Jawohl, herzbewegender Festtag. Hier fühle ich mich heimisch." He removed his helmet and put it down on the empty table. *"Ja, ganz gut."* He bent down, picked up the noisemaker, and twirled it happily. *"Klapper? Das gibt keinem guten Klang. Nein."*

No, its sound doesn't carry far, it's made of wood. He hiccuped. Damn it, he can barely stand up straight. Vodka, vodka, he's had enough today. Not on your life; it's out of the question! *Haman, Haman . . . was ist für einer?* Aha, he's the one who with God's help drew up the plan that would make Persia thoroughly *Judenrein?* Yes, Haman and the Jewish question. He was an incompetent, senile, naive antisemite. *Nicht wahr? Aber jetzt ist seine Tat an den rechten*

Mann gekommen, jawohl. There's a lot to say about that. And how did he die? Treacherously assassinated, of course. By whom? International Jewry had its hands in that business, no doubt. *Nun ja, Haman opferte sein junges Leben, damit unser Krieg sein Ziel erreiche!* Haman sacrificed his young life; others sacrificed their young lives. And Esther, black-haired Esther, black-eyed Esther, the little Jewess, married the great Ahasuerus, the King of Persia. *Nicht wahr?* A clever little thing, eh? You could burst out laughing at the thought of those good old days.

"*Meine kleine Jüdin.*" He stopped in front of Dora Lewin. He twirled the boy's noisemaker, then silenced it. "*Klatsch!*" Then he addressed her: "*Fräulein, wie steht es mit Ihrer Gesundheit?*"

They were standing in all that mess. He made her a deep, ironic bow. He pushed her ahead of him. She went submissively, like a sheep. *Drr drr drr drr,* chattered the noisemaker. The door slammed shut behind them.

"And this is supposed to be Purim? Purim? This is supposed to be a holiday?" It happened before, it will happen again. Those words, that voice.

Arrested! She walked down the street, three steps ahead of the gendarme.

Those words again? That voice again? "*Das fügt sich gut. Schnell, schnell. Also wie gesagt,* hurry up, miss, hurry, hurry!"

Clack clack clack. The noisemaker clacked tirelessly on the other side of the wall. It would soon be eight o'clock, the curfew hour, the time of enforced darkness.

II

One day, in plain view of the people on either side, bricklayers started building a wall along Żelazna and Sienna Streets, on Wielka, across Bagno, along Próżna, Grzybów, and Graniczna Streets, and then across Żelazna Brama Square to Hale, thus closing off the southern district. That was the Little Ghetto. The wall continued down Chłodna to Ptasia, along Przechodnia to Długa, from Mylna to Przejazd, Świętojerska to Ciasna, down Koźla to Przebieg, crossing Pokorna, Stawki, Dzika, and Okopy, enclosing the northern district. That was the Big Ghetto. A wooden bridge was erected across Chłodna Street near St. Karol's Church to link the two districts, which were separated by a streetcar line.

"It's starting, Jews," shouted Mordechai Sukiennik, waving his arms in a cloud of dust.

Who could possibly feel threatened by him? When there was no more hay to be had, he came over to the workshop for eelgrass to feed his mare. The doors of the shop were wide open; the windows that faced the street had all been smashed. The wind blew in through the doors and windows, and the broken shutters, which it was forbidden to replace, lay on the sidewalk. Father stood in the street, bareheaded, with the key in his hand. Mordechai walked back and forth, heaping the eelgrass onto his wagon with a pitchfork, while passersby stepped in the scattered strands.

"They're building and building. On Ptasia, Przechodnia, Rymarska; there's no end to it!"

He gathered up what was left of the grass, using a broom to sweep up every last bit, while Father looked around distractedly, like someone who has just been awakened from a dream. He was looking for the janitor, to whom he was supposed to hand over the key.

"Should I take those sacks? Yes, what good are they to you?"

"Take them."

He took them and set off; he didn't have far to go.

"Długa's already walled off!"

Uncle Gedali carried out the old furniture and lumber for fuel. Everyone took whatever he could; the upholstery workshop was emptying out. Father threw up his hands. Ech, we'll all turn to dust, all turn to dust. He fingered his tools, pushed them away. He looked long and hard at the chisel, as if seeing it for the first time in his life, and then threw it into a corner.

In the autumn, smoke from the slag heaps hangs over the freight-yard loading docks. In the empty square behind the tracks, Zyga is walking in front of him, unwinding string. The wind is blowing. What a day! The wind is fierce enough to lift a cow. Everything will be ready when Zyga has the string completely unwound and they can get started. In the meantime, Zyga is sweating and hurrying. Who could have foreseen it? Damn it, a knot! Eliahu is racing toward them, his head bobbing and his hand jumping stiffly on the string with every strong gust of wind.

"Hey you! Hold on to the clouds! Hold on to the wind!"

He was coming closer to them, shouting. Above them, high up against the autumn sky, the kite swooped in the cold light of the sun.

They hesitated for a moment when the wind blew them over to the tracks. Eliahu was already way off in the distance. They could see him let go of the tail. He knelt down and screamed. They raced over to him, gasping for breath. Near the tracks, stretched out on its side, lay a corpse under a paper cement sack. Little shoes stuck out from under the paper. The girl's head, eyes shut, was lying next to her legs. Her long black hair fanned out over the ground.

Eliahu said quietly, "Two men must have placed her under a train."

"What makes you think that?"

"Her legs are intact. She wouldn't have placed her own head so carefully."

Zyga was pale. He couldn't look, even though he was the oldest. He walked away. It was growing dark. They separated and sneaked back home, and they never said a word about this to anyone.

But back there, at home, it was always the same thing: "They're walling in Nalewki! They're walling in Dzika!"

Professor Baum, in his torn overcoat, taps the newspaper with his finger, then reads aloud from it. What a dog! The dog's name was Auerswaldt. He was the German commandant of the city and it was he who issued orders, distributed bread ration cards, hanged people, and ordered them to move from one part of town to another. He rode around the streets in his car and watched the bricklayers building the wall. Professor Baum gestures despairingly and then tears out the item from the newspaper. He can't make head or tails of this; who would have believed this just one year ago? What is this? The Tower of Babel? Miracles, miracles! No, he will never acknowledge such an authority. He throws the paper onto the floor and stamps on it. Before they can get everybody relocated, the war will end happily.

They kept turning it over and over. Every evening they said something different. Uncle Yehuda came over, scratched his head, and said, "They're building a wall on Waliców." Now *they* had to move.

Mordechai Sukiennik ran over to the workshop for the last time and piled the remaining shreds of eelgrass on his wagon. By now, people were wandering around the city looking for new living quarters. When they wanted to speed things up, the Germans put up wooden fences around the buildings and barricaded them with iron sawhorses bristling with clumps of barbed wire. There were fences like that on Biała and Ciepła Streets, diagonally across Waliców, and near Ceglana, until they all were replaced by the wall. Placards proclaimed: *Verboten!* Signs on the wall near the guarded exits of these streets warned: *Durchgang verboten! JUDENVIERTEL REVIER IST GESPERRT EINTRITT VERBOTEN.*

"Give it here, Maniuś, gimme it, gimme!"

In the silence of the still sleeping city, that cry jerked him to his feet. He stole over to the window. The first trolley cars were moving along the streets, looming out of the fog like phantoms from some other, incomprehensible world, but their high-pitched screeching vanished around the bend, somewhere in the empty spaces of the Hale Market. The bells of St. Karol's were ringing, ringing. He saw the faces on the other side. They were pale, indistinct; they swam up out of the fleeting night.

Father was saying his morning prayers, his face turned toward the wall that was under construction. There, at the intersection of Żelazna and Krochmalna Streets, the boundary wall was rising right under the windows of their apartment house. From dawn to dusk they could hear the shouts of the bricklayers mingled with the sounds of water pouring into the street from the open hydrant. The jaunty squeaking of the wheelbarrows alternated with the wet slapping sounds made by trowels pressing mortar against bricks. They were erecting the wall. It reached first the knees, then the shoulders, of the bricklayers. They measured, laid the bricks, moved on. When it was twice as tall as a man, they fortified the top with chunks of bottle glass that they planted close together in the wet cement. The temperature dropped and the mortar thickened in the hods; the bricklayers urged on their apprentices, rubbing their cold hands.

"Give it here, Manius, gimme!"

Now the voices of policemen cut across the guarded end of the street. They were at their post at the intersection of Żelazna and Chłodna Streets, stamping their feet in their thick felt boots, walking in circles to warm themselves, chatting lazily for hours on end. When they raised their rifles, people took shelter inside the gate.

Gray, dark days arrived. And during those first weeks behind the wall, David wandered about aimlessly, frightened, in a daze, without the courage to imagine the coming day. What does "adjusting" mean? No one knows yet. Uncle Shmuel has taken up bartering and says that you have to adjust. Eliahu repeats furiously that the weak must yield to the strong, but he looks like a ghost himself, he just drags around, exhausted, coughing, and when he walks he makes a mournful shuffling sound with the torn sole of his shoe. Eliahu is too clever, and Ernest hasn't changed one bit. Only Zyga has been transformed: he has suddenly begun speaking in a coarse, masculine voice.

November, freezing cold and windy, swept the last loose bricks out of the ruins and onto the ground, and blew the courage out of one's heart. Rubble spilled noisily into the street. There wasn't much difference between the life they had led before on Srebrna Street and their present exile on Krochmalna, and it was thanks to that good fortune that they had a little bit of resilience, of strength to endure. David looked at his father with new eyes and slowly began to understand that the straitened circumstances to which entire generations now had to accustom themselves had made his father's eyes burn with a terrible feverishness and obstinacy.

Ever since the move his mother had been breaking down, sobbing pitifully.

"Walled up alive!"

Father shouted angrily, stubbornly, for days on end. Was he complaining, denouncing, or threatening? In a rage, unable to stay still, he paced from wall to wall. He raised his fists and lowered them, then prayed for a long time. David listened to him and felt frightened and ashamed. During that early period in their apartment on Krochmalna Street, no one dropped in to see them, and the short, empty days dragged on in the waiting for their skimpy meal, for the time when they allowed themselves some luxury and lit a tiny fire in the stove before going to sleep. Begrudging the fuel, they quickly boiled some drinking water to wash down the sticky rationed bread, which was made with large amounts of bran and ground chestnuts. There was also marmalade, which everyone agreed was a clever mixture of beet puree and a sugar derived from mangels. They didn't buy saccharin or ersatz tea because of Father's righteous anger at even the thought of that fabricated chicanery. He insisted that lies for the soul are more powerful than those that cheat the body. Mother kept her eyes shut in disgust and spent entire days motionless, with her face to the wall. He comforted her as best he could. But solace was to be found in the streets. Rumors that in the past he would have rejected with scorn—the blind, crippled fruits of hope distributed by beggars, wild reports that made the rounds of the city each day—he now set in motion himself. That was the cheapest medicine.

Only later would it turn out that his mother's apathy had been a secret way of conserving the remains of her energy, that she had not lost it all, and soon would be sharing it generously with them. She complained, she moaned, she broke out in a sweat after swallowing a bit of food, and they watched helplessly as she lost her strength from lying down all the time. Father spoke to her as if she were a little child and hid the newspapers. Once he walked out without saying a word, sneaked across the wall, and returned late at night, with empty hands. He had a black eye and a bloodied forehead and looked as if he'd been wallowing in mud. He tore off his soiled, wet clothing and fell asleep immediately. Mother cried that she would not survive this. But she got out of bed for the first time in a long while and began to bustle about clumsily.

"God Almighty, when will this all come to an end?"

But it had only just begun. David went to the store with the ration cards, crumpling them compulsively in his clenched fist. He had seen coupons stolen right in front of his eyes, and after a wild scene that had ended with a fight among some hungry women, he took precautions and carefully cut out the coupons needed for that day before he left the house and stood in the crowded street clutching them in his hand. Poor people who had no ration cards ran up to the line and, holding out a few coins in their palms, begged others to sell them a crust. Loaves of bread were already being divided into eighths, and people were fainting in the line. The aroma of freshly baked bread knocked them off their feet. The weaklings were revived, sometimes robbed, the crowd stepped back for a while and then formed a line once more, waiting for hours for the bakery wagon. The beggars lay in wait outside the store and surrounded people as they left. You had to be careful, because they would grab your bread without warning, and before the crowd could come to your aid they would gobble up its soft insides.

The first days of hunger are the worst; afterwards you can hold out. First comes exhaustion: your hands and feet feel heavy, every word swells to a painful roaring in your ears. Colors aren't soothing and light actually hurts. There were days of blindness when David's sight was unexpectedly submerged in a darkness that swallowed up broad daylight. Every movement made his skin damp; sweat poured from under his arms, and his forehead was covered with a thick coating that was sticky to the touch. He felt thirsty all the time; his cracked lips were dry. His jaws were clenched and he felt a pain behind his ears at the sight of a tin spoon lying on the table. Then thoughts about food began, horrible, excruciating hallucinations. His stomach pumped like a siphon. If he thought for just one moment about a piece of rutabaga, his teeth started ripping at the stringy flesh, and a juice that was vaguely reminiscent of black turnip, but milder tasting and sweetish, flowed into his throat and moistened his swollen tongue, leaving a bitter residue in his mouth. He dreamt about the large, round root with the yellow flesh and green top. The newspaper talks about pumpkins, but why doesn't it contain a word about rutabagas? It's good to scrape a rutabaga with a spoon and get those small, juicy shavings. To swallow it a little at a time. Mother taught him how to do it and warned him that if he stuffed himself with the hastily chewed raw vegetable he could get very sick. His thoughts moved away from rutabagas and soared.

"When are they bringing the bread?"

The question is asked repeatedly in the line in front of the bread store. Who can recall the taste of bread? Who among them will remember the taste of bread? They used to buy it on Wronia Street. Laban had a bakery on Wronia. In the mornings the heat rose from the freshly baked rolls and you could smell them out in the street. The dough, kneaded by the baker's wife and daughter, would be rising in the enormous troughs. And Laban's daughter was white, covered with flour, and her cheeks glowed; the customers saw her, too, as a rosy, crunchy roll. The aroma of caraway seeds wafted from the baker's apron. He laughed: "Laban sells, Laban bakes, Laban kneads the flour before his customers' eyes!"

Today there isn't any bread like that. The ration cards get you clay that sticks to your teeth and crumbles in your hand, because chestnuts and potato peels are added to the dough. Sand crunches between your teeth; sometimes you have to spit out a piece of string, and sometimes the knife grates against a rusty nail. Filth.

He distinctly recalls the taste of the top crust of a loaf and the different taste of the bottom.

"Don't push, people, there's enough for everyone."

"Sure."

The crowd is in an uproar. Shouting is heard; then a truck stops in front of the store and two bakers' assistants, wheezing from the effort, drag in the basket, watched by a member of the security police.

How much would a loaf like that weigh? The young green rye rose quickly and fermented in the trough, aided by a starter. He remembers the taste of that bread he ate in the countryside, the first bread after the harvest. Mr. Hrybko ground the grain in a mill that looked like two grindstones. And Mrs. Hrybko worked the dough, splashing it, kneading it, slapping it, until a loaf as big as a wagon wheel took shape beneath her hands. It was placed on leaves to rise, surrounded by coals and ashes, and after it was thoroughly baked it was left to cool on a beam, in a drafty spot in the attic. When the housewife cut open a loaf like that (first cutting the sign of the cross into it), the green center was exposed and the smell of coals rose into the air, along with the sweet smell of the young rye, damp and warm. They would smear the still-warm bread with butter that melted before their eyes. They washed it down with cold sour milk that had been chilled overnight in the well. And they ate that green bread while looking through the window at the sun-drenched orchard.

"Don't push, people, there's enough for everyone!"

He returned home, sniffing the small ration loaf, stealthily pressing his face against it and inhaling the dry odor of chaff. Emaciation had flung its first victims onto the sidewalks. With bowed head he walked by them, avoiding them, kicking away the black, outstretched hands. The dry, sunken faces of the dying, their angular skulls and their eyes fixed on his bread, pursued him in his sleep. Their long, bent necks protruded, expressing everything: hunger, fear, grief, curses against the living. Their necks stuck out and their eyes grew large; they surrounded him from all sides, drew nearer, enormous . . . "No!" He awoke drenched in sweat.

One day, their first-floor neighbor, Natan Lerch, who sold his rations door to door, appeared in the doorway. A weak, thin man in a dark suit and badly stained white shirt, he had on one torn shoe. He named his price quietly on the threshold, his head bowed. In the semidarkness, they could see his sad, thin nose and painfully strained lips as he tenderly caressed his bread. Father cried out in despair, "Have a heart, man. How can I buy this bread from you?"

They must have had enough ration cards. But Natan Lerch kept on bargaining; he was insistent; he was begging for a sale. He kept glancing sideways, humbly, his gaze wandering over the patterns on the rotting wallpaper. After all, he's no profiteer. Eh, he'll go down a few more groschen. You have to be able to put yourself in another man's shoes. Father, losing patience, breathed heavily, closed his eyes, opened them again, and looked up at the ceiling. And Mother, letting her hand drop, tried to stuff a few groschen into our neighbor's pocket. He backed off. His head hung even lower, but he would not accept alms.

"Excuse me, I'm not a beggar," he said mildly. And repeated, "Excuse me!"

Mother pressed her clenched fist to her breast.

The bread had to be toasted over a flame. The streets were full of sick people, typhus was spreading, and when they returned home they carefully searched their outer garments for lice that might have crawled onto them. At every intersection, young boys hawked, in addition to newspapers, an insecticide made of powdered chalk and some other ingredient, carefully packaged by crooks. Gullible people sprinkled it under their shirts. Father sniffed it just once and said contemptuously, "Mint-flavored tooth powder. That's all we needed."

They reverted to simple, tried-and-true methods: you searched carefully for the lice and threw them into the fire so they wouldn't crawl away.

Wearing the armband was a torment. David would forget to put it on when he went outside or would lose it in the streets. He felt vaguely ashamed. He could sense it pressing against his arm, encumbering it, even though the cloth weighed nothing at all. There were different ways of wearing the armbands: Father wore his negligently; Uncle Shmuel, with deliberate elegance. Some people sewed it to the edge of their cuff; others wore it around the forearm or above the elbow. You could discern people's disdain for the authorities or their fear and docility by the way they wore their armbands. Aunt Chava wore a filthy band that was twisted around her arm like a pretzel and was barely visible, while Natan Lerch's armband was pinned on, clean, starched, stiff, and visible from afar like a signboard. Once someone had been beaten up by a policeman for wearing his cloth band in a sloppy fashion, he would never be careless about it again. The women street vendors wore narrow strips of cloth, three fingers wide. The Judenrat officials walked around on Grzybowska Street with broad ribbons as wide as two hands.

Oh, those white armbands with the blue six-pointed star! During the next two years they would remember to put them on as in years past they had remembered handkerchiefs. The star on one's arm was a distinguishing mark, a proof of existence more important than any document. But there were people who laughed at that. Zyga never attached his armband permanently. Like the smugglers and those who stole across the wall to get food, he pinned it on lightly with a safety pin so that he could take it off at any moment and hide it, and then, in case of need, quickly pull it up around his sleeve again.

A Jew who is caught anywhere without his armband will be shot on the spot. That's what the posters said that were pasted up everywhere along the streets. Mother reminded him: "David, remember your armband."

It was the same thing on all sides. The campaign never let up. His ears were filled with nationalist bleating, the hoarse howling of the loudspeakers. The Jews control the world; death to the Jews. The Wall Street banks and the Comintern faithfully serve their filthy interest. And the dollar is their God. They have bought the people and extended their power to all the continents. They have Russia and both Americas in their pockets. The shame of civilization! The Jewish Communists in the East and financiers in the West long ago handed over their governments to the rabbis.

He knew they were talking about him. And he was amazed that his young life could be of importance to anyone. He was overcome with fear of the hatred that surrounded him on all sides. Would it always be like this? It had always been this way. In his daydreams he strode freely and bravely through the world, without a past and without a future, his hands in his pockets, and no stone or cutting remark could reach him. He walked straight ahead and . . . Here his thoughts broke off. Would he leave his mother and father? Here, behind the walls? And tear off the armband by himself? He suffered and was ashamed.

But the Germans will save the people. *Ein Volk, ein Reich, ein Führer!* Bow down, nations, the new order is approaching. Europe, Asia, America will be granted their freedom and not a single Jew will hide from the law wherever a German soldier plants his foot. But if someone should hand over his gold or dollars—well, that's another story. Whoever hands over gold and dollars, whoever displays contrition and obedience, will be allowed to go to the island of Madagascar. That's where he belongs. The Jews are multiplying like lice.

That is, there are too many of them. Long ago, after the first battle, he decided he would go to sleep a Jew and wake up the next day as someone else. The years passed and nothing changed. How can you change the world? He didn't know. (Only Uri knows, but he doesn't want to tell anyone yet.)

"I'm going to run away, I've had enough of this," Zyga said, and he was missing for five days. Eliahu laughed, and little Ernest asked in a whisper, "Did you run far, Sh'maya?"

Zyga didn't want to say where he'd been. He looked down on

them. He already knew that there was only one way out: you had to join the Gypsies. The image of Zyga stealthily following a Gypsy band, at night, among the naked, black, autumn trees, when dogs hide under the wagons, their tails between their legs, overwhelmed David with sorrow and pity, and he was close to tears. Somewhere, a rain-smudged light is twinkling. The windows and doors of the houses they pass slam shut, and the village watches the alien wanderers, distrustfully listens to their soft, melancholy songs, the jangling of the indifferently stroked guitars. The Gypsies are coming! To tin the cauldrons, fix the handles on frying pans, sharpen knives. And bringing up the rear is Zyga, pushed away by everyone. No, he couldn't imagine anything more pitiful. But Eliahu said they only steal young bastards. They don't need Jews in their bands; that's all they need! And anyway, now *they* are being locked up behind barbed wire, with their horses, and when the horses die the Gypsies roast their meat and die of typhus. They aren't telling anyone's fortune from cards anymore and they no longer steal chickens. Zyga got mad, called Eliahu a rat, and beat him up, but he never again spoke of running away to the Gypsies.

David used to walk aimlessly over to the *Wache*, the guard post, and look sorrowfully across at the other side, fingering his sleeve to check that his armband was in place. There were always crowds there and the hungry beggars would be running across the guarded street outlet. Occasionally a shot rang out and a man would lie in the middle of the roadway until someone shoved him over to the side. People would flee into doorways. The porters had a name for the policeman who was such a good shot: "Bloody Hands." He was a good shot and he was also delighted to accept bribes. He wore a *Zugführer*'s stripes on his sleeve, and he beat people for free or for payment, and when he walked down the street to his post, in his green uniform with the brown piping, the news preceded and followed him. Pedestrians panicked; they froze with their caps in their hands. The street vendors hastily folded up their stalls and hid themselves and their wares. After the shot, Bloody Hands would walk up to the person who was lying there, roll his corpse onto its back with his foot, and look at the face. Then he would go over to the gutter and dip his boot in a puddle to wash the blood off.

Long Itzhok, one of those who'd been resettled, would boldly latch onto the policemen from the post. He would point to the other side and pat his empty stomach, crying, "Guts with water!" They drove him away lazily and without anger. Bloody Hands would look on, amused, and laugh loudly. Long Itzhok's appearance could make even him laugh. He would take off his rifle, use the barrel to prod the ragged man through the *Wache*, and Long Itzhok would run away happily, his clogs flapping.

Facing the wall, Father began his morning prayer. The hoarse, resonant murmuring dragged on, slow and patient. Father's back swayed obediently, his lips kissed the edge of the *tallis*, his hands caressed the straps of his *tefillin*. His voice rose and soared in the air with the music of the sad and weary old melody. He said no word in response to Mother's remarks but drove her away with a short, angry wave of his *tallis* and a hiss. Completely immersed in prayer, he kept his eyes covered with the *tallis* for a long time. Hush, woman. This is the time when a Jew says his prayers and is one with his God—while he still has his eyes open and can see where the sun rises. While his body hasn't yet been thrown into a hole.

Is it going to take long? Haskiel the janitor was standing under the window, waiting for Father to finish and to stop pestering God. The soul he got from Him is pure. He banged the broom handle on the pavement. He is preserving it. He preserves it. He will take it back. Praise be to the King of the world. Done. That's good.

"Fremde, I have something to tell you."

Yakov Fremde leaned out the window, winding the long straps of his *tefillin* around his bent elbow and his stiffly retracted thumb. And time chased the graceful movement of his hand, a semicircular, fluid movement—at the height of the first floor, where he stood bent over, savoring the last words of the prayer—and the parchment scroll shuddered.

"What is it? Who's there?"

Haskiel gestured carelessly with his hand: "So they've fenced us in, eh? Like goats in a pasture!"

"No one is stronger than they are."

A black skullcap perched on top of Father's bald spot. Haskiel lowered his voice and warned him, "If something should happen, hide behind the curtains, because the porters have arranged for a little business and they should be here any moment now."

He stamped his foot at two snot-nosed little skeletons, his youngest treasures, who were running down the street with their noses dripping.

"Roizele, Surele, scram! Get out of here. In any case, I advise you to disappear from the window, Fremde."

That's exactly right. But when *she* asked him, begged him, not to stick his head out in the way of the bullets, he pretended to be deaf. Father slammed the window shut.

"It's starting now," he said, and looked unwillingly at Mother. "People can build walls, keep watch, smuggle, but a man can't pray in peace! Tsss!"

A long ladder rose high into the air, as in a dream. Shaken, it inscribed an arc in the air, and before it was firmly planted against the wall Kepele was already climbing the rungs to the top, and behind him came Aaron Jajeczny. Kepele quickly took off his shirt and carefully covered the sharp, jagged pieces of glass that were firmly cemented into place on the edge. From the first-floor window you could see the creased peak of his cap, the colorful scarf around his bare neck, and, as he climbed higher, his shirttails pulling out of his pants. In the meantime, porters came running out from everywhere and their short, muffled cries echoed in the empty street. From the other side of the wall came merchants with sacks of flour and salt. Dragging their bundles along the pavement, hunched over, they looked around cautiously and then threw down their goods beside the wall and ran off. Stacho Żeleźniak whipped his horse and drove off with an empty wagon. "Gee up, make way! Gee up, gee up!" A group of teenage boys, stationed along the wall as sentries, urged the merchants on by shouting and waving their arms like windmills. The porters on the top rungs of the ladder passed the sacks of foodstuffs down from hand to hand; a couple of porters stood on the sidewalk, inside the gate, catching the heavy bags tenderly and carefully. From the top of the wall, a rhythmic groaning floated over their heads and over their outstretched arms, straining against the sky, and then faded away, disappearing within the bowels of the apartment house.

The first whistle from an outlying sentry was answered by other whistles, closer, each one passing a warning to the next. Now the porters had passed the last sacks from arm to arm, and the long ladder had slipped into the courtyard on their backs. A patrol came running up, hobnailed boots clattering, and peered inside the gate. The alleyway was absolutely empty when, as if from nowhere, a desperate cry resounded in the silence: "The sack! Hold tight, it's spilling . . . The sack, the sack!" Laughing, the policemen headed off in the direction of the *Wache*. A little later, a quiet cry: "Fremde, Fremde!" And when Father went over to the window, Haskiel the janitor was standing in his place.

"All clear. You can show yourself now. A tempest in a teapot. Just so long as the skinny Jewish goat doesn't nibble any grass. No, they didn't nab anyone, but the porters are saying that some innocent guy caught it in the head just as he was walking by the *Wache*. And he had a pass!"

He leaned his broom against the wall. He hadn't managed to start a conversation. He anxiously scanned the intersection, which was alive again with people hurrying past. Roizele was standing beside him, pulling at his trouser leg.

"*Tate*, give me a little carbide. Yankiel's waiting."

"With a pass! He couldn't pick a better time? Oy, people, people, when will they wise up . . . ? Roizele, tell him I'm coming . . . Fremde, it seems there was something in the paper about our having to pack up, one-two-three, and go to Madagascar."

"What's that? Another move?" Mother was visibly upset.

"It's starting now," Father cried out and shut the window. "Madagascar, Madagascar. Has everyone gone crazy or what? I can't listen to it anymore! I've had it up to here." And he drew a finger across his neck.

"Heh heh, what a wet blanket. An intellectual! You can't even have a human conversation with anyone. Phew!"

"To Madagascar? When? Is it absolutely certain?"

Yankiel Zajączek came running out of the basement and stood next to the janitor, pinning a needle into his apron strap. Haskiel's voice reached them from the street: "Roizele, Surele, scram!"

The Ghetto, with its clamor and chaos, its aimless movement in the narrow, winding streets, depressed David. He wandered around Grzybowski Square, along Ciepła, Ceglana, Prosta, and Waliców, avoiding the streets that ended suddenly in guarded intersections. But wherever he turned, the wall rose up in front of him. The watchmen's helmets shook as they ran. A bell brushed against in haste could ring at an unexpected moment and betray those who were fleeing. That happened on Grzybowski Square, not far from the *Wache*, where the old chapel for Jewish converts was located, and where, in the nave and choir, the smugglers now hid, pursued by the police. The Germans fired blindly, whole series of shots, straight into the windows of the bell tower, and a flock of pigeons rose up into the air. The sky was clear, and a white cloud hung in one spot, unmoved, while the dry fluttering of wings resounded in his ears. He walked down the narrow, cramped tunnel of the walled-in street and came out into the open space of Żelazna Brama Square. He caught sight of the tops of the old trees in the Saxon Gardens—a view from another world. He came here often, without any particular reason. On his way home, he passed carts pushed by skeletons who were harnessed in pairs, their teeth bared, headed for Hale. Hale was where cloth goods and hides were loaded onto horse-drawn wagons every day by informal arrangements (secured by bribes) with the Germans and the police. The wagons left the Ghetto at nightfall while the buyers, concealed inside the gates, watched carefully from a distance. A quarter-hour before curfew sounded, the city lay dead and dark.

One day later on, mustering his courage, he stood on the wooden bridge. He saw the horse-drawn bus, a yellow and blue box on wheels that looked like a circus wagon—a new means of transportation in this part of the city. He saw the beggar who stood down there, always in the same spot, and threw himself in front of the rickshaws, wailing, noisily extracting alms from the passengers sprawled on the seat. Watching from above, he suffered, and his heart constricted with amazement and bitterness. From the bridge, he had an unimpeded view of the Aryan trolley cars traveling down Chłodna and Wolska Streets beyond the boundary of the Ghetto. Everywhere, near the police posts, there were gangs of smugglers, porters, shopkeepers, and, usually, emaciated youths waiting for a chance to race safely outside the wall where they could buy food or sell the shirt off their backs, which was worth less than a slice of bread, to the black marketeers loitering behind the line of sentries.

Mother greeted the day with the clanging of the cast-iron pan that she shoved around irritably on their sheet metal stove. "There, it's done," she said. "Eat! Stuff your belly and go to your converts on Sienna Street. How long does Counselor Czerniatyński have to call for your highness the upholsterer to fix his couch? To call you, to implore you? You won't get bread out of anyone, Yakov, by praying and standing in the window."

"Czerniatyński! The lawyer! What else? Czerniatyński has come back to his old haunts and once again goes by the name of Szwarc."

"Let him do what he wants. But that's not what I'm talking about. It's that you're not eager for work."

"Sure, work. I'm supposed to cover an old torn sofa in exchange for two rotten rutabagas that fell off that convert's table, and she tells me to my face that that's called work."

"The pope and the peasant each have their own work."

She scraped at the bottom of the pot with a knife, angrily turning it around and around in her hands, loosening the burnt-on crust.

"The value of work is the satisfaction derived from the work."

"Ech, pech. I hear that all the time; it's coming out of my ears."

Father greedily moved over to the rutabaga and shoved a piece of dry bread into it, then stirred it with his spoon.

"Yes. You produce something with your hands and you have money for bread, money for soup, money for a Friday herring. Then," he made a slurping sound, "it's worth praying a little so you should have enough work until Friday. But what if a Jew doesn't see a herring on his table even once a week?"

He was speaking to Mother but looking straight into David's eyes.

"Again. He talks to me like that crook the janitor."

"So now they consider me to be a crook in this house?" He clenched his fist and struck his breast with all his might. "Me!" Then he lowered his voice. "Me?"

"Yakov, Yakov, you won't get any bread by this endless praying at the window. Take off the *tallis*, close the Torah. Since when have you been such a good Jew? You don't understand? Then I'll tell you. You've lost your flair for work. But I didn't marry a rabbi; I married an upholsterer, and may I be struck dead this instant, right here, if I ever wanted anything more!"

"Ach!"

"What a mess. Why should I care? Don't you know? It's the end of the world, starvation is peering through the windows of every house, and the men have turned into priests out of fear. They're praying. They're praying and singing psalms."

"Ach!"

"Take a look at the streets and you'll see that it's a beggar's occupation. Those who can't earn a piece of bread by any other means pray. All the rest either work or steal. Steal or work. Amen. That's what the times are like now. Leave God alone, don't tug at His coat, because He's given up. He's not even dreaming of getting mixed up in this mess. Yakov, you're going to wait until I'm naked and barefoot. You and He. The lice will flee from our backs and take our shirts with them."

To this, Father said nothing. He hastily swallowed the last bites of cold rutabaga and pulled himself together. The rutabaga was cloying, sweet, frost damaged, and had congealed in the pot since yesterday. They went outside feeling the rutabaga in their stomachs like a stone they had swallowed.

"David, come back! Your armband!"

He stretched out his arms and the white band of cloth fluttered from the window and landed on the stall. Small piles of fuel were lying there: slivers of split wood, a bit of coal, a handful of coke, and on the side, covered with a tarpaulin to protect it from dampness, bits of grayish blue carbide, which people used for lighting their houses. The voice of Buba the street vendor, ensuring that the fires wouldn't die out on Krochmalna and Walicόw, resounded in measured counterpoint with the interrupted laments of the beggars.

"Wood for sale, coke! Carbide! Only from me! Wood for sale, coke!"

He took in everything at once: the armband, his outstretched arms, the vendor at her stall, rushing at him with a cry. Running after his father, who was disappearing around the corner, he smiled indulgently. "Carbide for sale . . . People, protect me! A thief, a thief!" Well, that's all they needed. Who stole fire? And who gave men the gift of light? That was long, long ago and naked men danced with joy in front of the burning pile. It was Prometheus who stole fire; that's what Professor Baum said. The oil lamp was invented by Łukasiewicz and the electric lightbulb by Edison, but who was more important? If Buba the vendor shut down her stall, no one here would be able to cook dinner.

Filthy snow spattered his face. Riding in an empty, speeding rickshaw, a porter yelled a warning at another porter who had passed him, bent over his handlebar. Enlarged veins, like cords, bulged at his temples, and his neck was swollen. In front of him, in the soft, deep seat, a passenger rested comfortably, smoking a cigarette.

"Hey you, watch out for those turns!"

Past the intersection, people were running around, spreading the latest news. "A German patrol's coming!" The warning came from a window on the first floor, and panic set in. In the meantime, a patrol appeared on Chłodna Street and quickly, expertly, knocked the hats off the Jews' heads as they marched down Żelazna Street, persuading them to get out of the way and step down off the sidewalk and, in accordance with orders, bow politely to the Germans. Utter terror washed over everyone: should they stay or run? They stampeded in a herd. A woman who was passing by set her child down in a bay window and began to shriek. If they don't open the window she'll break the glass! The child, smiling, kicked its little feet up on its perch.

Two open vehicles emerged from Prosta Street, turned into Żelazna, their brakes squealing, and drove slowly past the bricklayers. In the first one officers were lolling, their uniforms carelessly unbuttoned. Their glasses, their medals, the polished belts on their uniforms all glittered, and the silver of their epaulettes lay like freshly fallen snow on their shoulders. They were speaking audibly, pointing out the entrances of the Ghetto streets with curt nods of their heads and waves of their arms. They responded with laughter to the terrified bows of the passersby who were doffing their hats to them.

"*Getto sehen und sterben!*"

"*Nicht wahr?*"

Laughter, shouts: "*Hoch! Hoch!*"

"*Hoch, es lebe! Noch einmal!*"

"*Hoch!*"

Ribbons of smoke rose from between their fingers, and they turned back, amused. In the other vehicle, the driver, his fatigue cap tilted rakishly onto one ear, pounded the horn with his fist and shouted, "*Der König. Mützen ab! Jüdisch König!*"

Behind him an old man in a fur coat buttoned up to his chin sat rigidly, both hands resting on his cane, silent, pale, staring straight ahead into the depths of the gray street. The cars were moving more and more slowly.

"Look, David. That's Czerniaków, President Czerniaków himself."

That morning the city was white with snow and black with mud. A bricklayer was pushing a wheelbarrow along the sidewalk; he banged into a pedestrian and spilled whitewash all over his legs. The old Jew stood there, dazed, with a dirty towel wrapped around his neck. He raised his soaked trouser legs, revealing his skinny shins. He picked his way carefully across the mud, inspected his drenched rags, stood to one side and patiently shook himself to remove the wetness, and when he had decided that that was enough, he spat on the paving stones and walked off.

The cars passed them. "There's nothing to look at. Let's go." Father picked up his bag with his work tools and threw it over his shoulder.

The inspection of the walls continued. But the elegant old man who had attracted David's glance wasn't President Czerniaków; rather, Czerniaków was the middle-aged man who was seated beside the old man with the cane and trying to be inconspicuously useful. Father still hesitated; he retreated to the entrance gate, then came out again. And David saw his sensitive, quick glance, seeking a sign, a warning, when he stood in the middle of the street, carrying on his struggle with himself and calling in vain on his outmoded instincts to help him. But now what's going on? David could feel the cold, nauseating rutabaga making him sick. The patrol had come to a stop.

"*Mütze ab!*"

The woman snatched her child from the parapet and held it tight to her breast, covering its eyes.

"God in heaven, people, does anyone know why that German is beating him so hard?"

"The Jew didn't remove his cap."

A fresh bloodstain was spreading along the filthy wall. A deaf-mute stood in front of the German patrol and babbled helplessly, a frightful question in his eyes. Blood was trickling from his mouth onto his face and shirt. Shoved against the wall, he slowly extended his hand, and the policeman began to beat that hand as if it had its own life. A blue policeman, smiling, explained something to the

Germans and the punishing arm of justice hung hesitantly in the air. They surrounded him in a tight circle, inspected him curiously. Suddenly, with gleeful shouts, they began to pull at him, shove him, until they brought the deaf-mute down with one kick. He began to crawl around their legs, writhing, avoiding their blows with convulsive contortions of his body. When they stepped back, he was lying on the ground, groaning softly. "*Weg, du Schwein!*" Then he got up obediently and, limping, ran over to the crowd of people being detained in front of the *Wache*, wiping the blood and sweat from his face. Someone hidden inside the gate said quietly, "He was lucky. It could have ended badly for him."

The area in front of the *Wache* was an open-air circus with non-stop performances. It was an open arena in the center of the city, where pedestrians who had been caught in roundups performed punitive exercises in accordance with the fantasies of the changing guards. Old men in long black coats crawled around in the snow and mud while an eager young guard kicked their protruding backsides. With an angelically patient smile on his face, holding his gun at the ready, he inspected their ranks seriously, taught them how to obey orders and corrected their mistakes. Hopping like frogs, they ran away from him, gasping for breath. They collapsed in the mud and lay there, their legs flung any which way. Others sang psalms on command, and the words of the prayers floated over the street. They placed their trembling hands together and lifted them up, raising their eyes to heaven, squinting in fear as the policeman's hand yanked at a strand of their beards. This caught the attention of the patrols who stopped to see the spectacle, and elicited bursts of wild laughter from them.

Bloody Hands stood on the side and called to them gaily, pointing at the young guard, "*Kraft durch Freude!*"

"*Jawohl.*"

Yarmulkes lay in the mud. Jews lay in the mud. A teenage boy, energetically encouraged by the guard, tried without success to stand on his hands. He fell down, got slapped in the face for his laziness, and again waggled his legs in the air. Meanwhile, the old men were crawling over the wet stones alongside the gutter, throwing off their boots and coats on command. Terrified of being kicked, they had to dip their beards into the snow when the guard bent over them and shook his gun threateningly. Bloody Hands issued a new order and they all jumped up.

Sighs escaped into the air like white streamers. Bluish, contorted hands moved nervously; they trembled, pressed against the men's breasts. Their faces were covered with soaking wet strands of hair. Stretched out in a disorderly file, the men froze in expectation of a command, linked by their common trembling. A voiceless whisper flew among them as they repeated the words of the prayer. Among them were Reb Itzhok, Yankiel Zajączek, Avrum, the son of Haskiel the janitor, and Faivel Szafran, a deportee. Reb Itzhok fainted and slipped through their hands, his head hanging down. Avrum grabbed him around the waist and Faivel flung the rabbi's arm around his neck. Reb Itzhok rose higher and his bare feet hung helplessly above the ground.

Suddenly someone groaned, and that groan broke the silence. Riva pressed her clenched fists to her temples, swaying back and forth. Other voices could be heard and in a moment the crowd of trembling figures was shaken by sobs, groans, incredible laughter, and howls. The shouts of the horrified Germans couldn't be heard at all; their mouths were visible, though, open wide with shouting. Gesturing with their weapons got them nowhere, and quiet reigned again only after two shots were fired.

Bloody Hands removed his helmet and wiped the sweat from his brow. *"Genug davon!"*

The patrol marched off quickly.

On that December day the city was white with snow, black with mud. A dirty light drizzled from the cloudy sky onto the crowd of people who had been caught in the roundup. Faces dry as bone glimmered white in the gray light, hung in the foggy air. Picking up speed, the trolley screeched across the intersection and disappeared from sight, and when it had passed, three women were standing in the middle of the empty street.

Riva, Avrum's mother, timidly stretched out her hands to the guards. Regina Zajączek and Esther Szafran, painfully stooped, were leaning toward each other, discussing something quietly. Their olive-skinned heads touched, and sadly, fearfully, they raised their shadow-filled eyes toward the old men.

A crowd of children with yellowish little faces huddled against the wall, watching the detainees. And in the apartment house over the *Wache* a Jew was sitting behind a windowpane like a dead man, his covered head resting on his arms.

After the changing of the guard a policeman unenthusiastically herded the detainees together. He yawned, looking at them. The last ghosts got up onto their knees, sluggishly, with no strength left. Moving blindly, stiffly shuffling their bare feet, they came together to take each others' hands. The teenager who had been ordered to stand on his hands was lying on the ground exhausted, his legs flung wide apart like a puppet's.

Suddenly a soft, cautious cry was heard: "Mr. Policeman, can I get up now? Mr. Policeman?"

The policemen were standing with their backs to the group, watching the street with their dead, glassy stare. A blue policeman pointed out the teenager to a yellow policeman, laughed uproariously, and tapped his finger against his forehead. *"Man spricht davon. Es fällt mir schwer das zu glauben."*

"Eisernes Kreuz? Ihm geht alles nach Wunsch. Eisernes Kreuz!"

"Mein Gott, jeder hat sein Kreuz zu tragen."

"Ja, ja, mit Eichenlaub."

"Ach wo!"

The voices of the gendarmes floated past in the foggy December air, to the outlet of the guarded street.

Father looked carefully at the wall and the *Wache* on the corner of Żelazna and Chłodna Streets, which had to be passed very carefully on such days. He looked at the policemen's circus and the rounded-up Jews, who, knowing that no one would hurry to their aid, were writhing resignedly on the pavement, trying to keep the necessary distance from the guard's boots. He looked at the signs of warning that had recently appeared on this section of wall and at the identical posters pasted up all along it, posters that silently ensured the security of the citizens of the GG: *JUDENVIERTEL REVIER IST GESPERRT EINTRITT VERBOTEN.* He looked at the now empty bridge, its wobbly wooden scaffolding dripping mud, which no one would dare to pass at such a time. And then he drew David to him with a quick movement of his hand on David's shoulder, on his neck, and with this cold touch ordered him not even to breathe.

❖

III

Inside the courtyard, in the bluish light that seeped onto the snow from the blacked-out windows, Baruch Oks's gang was giving a beggars' concert. Long Itzhok and Baruch Oks circulated through the apartment house, hats in hand. The chorus, a collection of rags and lice huddled close together, stamped their wooden clogs to the beat, and wheezed, coughed, and swayed to the rhythm of the fading melody. Moishe the Crip limped along in the frost, warming his withered arm by blowing on it. His hand was stiff and bent at the joints, with stunted, crooked fingers. Saliva spurted from Henio the Herring's wet lips. His neck was swollen from hunger and his head was as enormous as a clay pot; both head and neck swayed heavily, in time with the beat. Henio's mother was an elderly herring vendor, the owner of a herring barrel which she dragged over to the brewery winter and summer, waiting there with a long, jagged fork in her hand. Five-Fingers Mundek groaned over and over again, mooing in his indistinct bass voice. A slow-moving, strapping fellow with the broad back of a porter, he was Baruch Oks's right-hand man. He'd always been a rotten apple, and as a young child he was already considered a thief by his own family because he had stolen his parents' wedding rings. Where have those days gone? Where are the golden rings? Where are Mundek's parents? They are lying in the earth. In front of Mundek, his eyes closed, little Mordka the Ram is daydreaming. He joined Baruch Oks's gang when they were still living on the other side of the wall and typhus was sweeping through his family. He and Kuba the Gelding, who crowed in a quavering, rapt voice, ready to levitate with the melody. Yosele, known as Egg Yolk, was puffy from hunger; he moved his lips silently, with a look of suffering in his protruding froglike eyes. Those eyes ran in his family; Laban the baker, his father, had died of a thyroid condition.

Laban used to measure his customers with those same eyes as he handed them their bread in his bakery on Wronia Street. Chaim the Orphan, who had no other nickname, only stretched his neck. There were seven of them, that's all. Seven who stuck with Baruch Oks, following him through fire and water.

"Not like that, no," Haskiel the janitor scolded them. "Draw out the notes, draaaw them out!"

They shouted out the old rollicking songs that once had made the bright candles shake and wink merrily on the tablecloth. David, who was walking behind his father, closed his eyes for a moment.

Holiday songs! The fragrant boughs and leaves of the *sukkah* rustle, and a star peers in through a chink in the roof. Aunt Chava brings a potted palm tree out of the house. Everything is green, festive. Everyone visits everyone else and they all crowd, laughing, into the little booths. A candle drives the shadows out of the corners. Flowers, garlands, and paper chains hang from the ceiling. Grandfather sits on a shaky bench and puts his hands together, applauding silently. Uncle Shmuel sings in his thin voice; Father and Uncle Gedali sing bass. The melody echoes in the warm twilight, melancholy and slow, swaying in their throats, and then repeated humorously with a juicy smacking of the tongue. "Chiri-bim, chiri-bam, chiri-bim-bam-bam-bam, ai-ai!" With hoarse, crackling voices, Baruch Oks's gang was singing now in the darkness.

Father stopped for a moment, reached into his pocket, and shared a smoke with the janitor.

"They're destroying everything, cutting everything down. They're all the same," Haskiel complained. "Bing bang and they're ready to fight."

Mordarski the merchant, who lived on the first floor, quickly slammed his window shut. And on the fourth floor a plaintive cry could be heard: "Buba!"

The old furrier, Judah Papierny, ordered his daughter to move his armchair, in which he napped all day long, closer to the window. He'd had his legs amputated.

"You lazy good-for-nothing!" The janitor pointed his finger at Chaim. "You could bellow a little louder and make an effort when you see that others are tearing their throats out for you."

"You brat, you," Judah Papierny scolded from above.

Chaim the Orphan only stretched his neck.

"Enough, brats," shouted Mordarski the merchant. "Too much of this good stuff!"

There was the sound of a window being thrown open, and dry crusts of bread, wrapped loosely in newspaper, dropped onto the snow from the first floor.

Mother's face floated out of the darkness of the hallway, partly concealed by a fold of her kerchief, which had slipped over one eye. A small flame flickered and straightened up again. She set down the bucket, lifted the lamp, and carefully shaded it with her hand.

"Finally, you're back." Naum was sitting there in his coat, his feet tucked under the table.

Father stooped, cranked the handle, and without taking off his overcoat poured water into the lamp. The white flame flared up with the hiss that wet carbide emits. He adjusted the flame, corked the reservoir, and wiped his brow distractedly. Unconsciously he clenched his fists. He covered his face and rocked lightly back and forth. David knelt on the windowsill; he hung the blanket on the hooks, blacked out the window, and got down. They all sat together in silence behind the window that was open just a crack, breathing heavily from exhaustion, and swallowing at the sound of the pots being moved around on the stove.

"It can't go on like this anymore, Yakov. It's either you or me."

"Who are you speaking to, Naum? Is everyone in your home still with you?"

"Yes. They are."

"Then give them my heartfelt regards."

Mother came over to the table with a pot of cooked beets and looked carefully at Father. Sweaty strands of hair were plastered across her forehead. She tucked the hair behind her ear. "First have something warm to eat. Here!"

Father carefully avoided Naum's gaze.

"But it's all over. Tell me, how much do you want for the cart?" Naum insisted. "Well, how much?" He paused, waiting.

"No," David squealed.

Father raised his head from his plate. He looked at him in silence for a moment. And then he said, "Children should be seen and not heard. Quiet."

"Listen, friend." Naum turned his hands palms up and shook them, and every finger was crooked.

"Hmm. All right."

"You have eyes and ears. You can see and hear what is going on."

"I am deaf and blind. I see nothing. I hear nothing."

The door opened and Yankiel Zajączek slipped inside, walking with his shaky, spidery gait. He was wringing his long hands in a timid gesture of supplication.

"You have a trade and a crust of bread, and I have empty hands," said Naum. "You know very well how it is."

"I don't know."

The sound of a throat being cleared.

"May I? What's that? I've come to see you." Yankiel Zajączek took two tiny steps and entered the circle of light. Quick reflections from his glasses crossed his mobile face. "What's new, eh?" He stuck the needle he'd been holding into the lapel of his smock. "Nothing new? I don't have any news either. I've forgotten, I've clean forgotten, why I came to you. Aha."

Behind him, smiling, stood Uncle Gedali, laying his coat on the box that stood beside the door.

"But what business would I have with you? It's obvious." Yankiel took off his wire-rimmed glasses and blew on them noisily. "A little piece of carbide." They remained silent and he kept on painstakingly polishing his glasses. His naked face grew longer. "It would be so helpful. My good people, lend me one tiny lump of carbide."

"One? Are you sure just one? Yankiel?"

"Well, two lumps. All right." He looked at Naum with a timid smile. "There I was sewing and all of a sudden the lamp goes out. What should I do? I say to Regina, 'Regina!'"

Mother sighed. She turned away and rummaged for a while in the corner behind the box where they kept what remained of the fuel—a bit of coal, some splinters to start the fire, a handful of carbide in a small darned sack.

"So I say to Regina, 'Regina, add some water.' And then it turns out that there's nothing to add the water to. Oy, what a problem. Oy, what a shame." He clutched the carbide to his smock with both hands. "I'll sew the boy new trousers for this. May he have them and wear them in good health."

"Which number will they be?" asked Father. He asked the tailor but looked at Uncle Gedali, who was standing quietly in the doorway.

"Eh?"

"The trousers."

"The trousers? They'll be new ones."

"New?"

"Completely new. Twill."

"Yankiel, better you should sew a patch on his elbow. Take a look at him with a professional eye. Everything's sticking out on him."

"I'll do it. Absolutely."

"Because I could open a store with all those trousers you've promised me. Your promises are as great and as empty as a bag full of holes wrapped around eternity, Yankiel."

"Full of holes? Did I say they'd be made of whole cloth? If they're full of holes, let them be full of holes. In fact, they even ought to be slightly torn. Sometimes at night you can see the stars through those holes."

Mother wiped off the chair with a damp rag and stood nearby. The tailor's elbows were flapping as he held tight to the handful of carbide. Uncle Gedali grabbed him by the arm and sat him down at the table, carelessly knocking his hat off his head. He picked up the pot that was resting on a brick and looked inside it. He smacked his lips. And put it back on the stove.

"Yes."

Then Father said, "Yes, that's the way it is."

After a minute of silence Uncle Gedali answered, "It's the same all over."

"And there's no future."

Uncle Gedali made a vague gesture. A long sigh escaped him.

"If only we can hold out till spring."

"That's easy to say, Gedali. By now I can barely make it from one Friday to the next."

"Pray some more, pray," and Mother flung the wet rag into a corner. "I can light the stove with your prayers. I'll put them in the pot and then stuff your empty belly with them."

"Sha, quiet, woman." Father cleared his throat angrily. This was followed by a silence broken only by Mother's heavy breathing and the sound of pots being angrily moved around. "How's Shmuel? What's new with him?"

"He's doing fine. He's trading." Uncle Gedali stopped and leaned over his chair.

"Trading what?" Father frowned.

"You know him. Shmuel can thread barbed wire into a pickle in the evening and sell it as a porcupine the next morning before it rusts."

"You see, you see," Mother said hastily. "Everyone can do something; you're the only one who pulls his ragged *tallis* over his eyes."

Uncle Gedali glanced at Mother and repeated in a tired voice, "Shmuel won't die, don't worry. He'll catch butterflies and turn them into pigs."

Butterflies add color to the green of the garden with their soft, soundless flight. They swoon, and their light wings lie motionless; the delicate calyxes of flowers bow beneath their weight. The insects' antennae poke around amidst the shaggy stamens and golden pollen. That was in Mr. Hrybko's garden. Over there, near the fence, Mr. Hrybko is chasing a hog that has dug up the rotting fence posts with its hooves and snout and is filling the vegetable bed with its joyous snorting.

But David knows that they're talking about something else. Butterflies are soft. Pigs are hard. And Uncle Shmuel buys and sells dollars. He trades banknotes for gold rubles.

"That's good, too. A real business." And Father says gloomily, "Before leaving."

"For a warm climate. In the meantime, while waiting for the good news, he's in business and he won't come out of this badly. But only until the time comes."

"Good news," Father repeated angrily. "Good news; he should only be so healthy."

Yankiel Zajączek's hands were occupied.

"News, rumors. Your head can burst from all of this. The beggars carry who-knows-what from street to street. And who's making them do it? Yesterday Haskiel comes running up to me. Why beat around the bush; you know Ajzen yourself. And shouts that he has good news. Signed passports are lying around in the Judenrat offices. One for every Jew—men and women—and a half for each child. If you give them a bribe, you'll get to go first. He says I don't have to spend any time thinking about it, all I have to do is arrange the passport and the place through him and before the hard frosts hit I'll be able to leave on the first ship out, in a deluxe cabin with running water and steam heat. 'What are you saying, man? Bite your tongue. Where were you told all these things? What self-respecting Jew would dirty his hands with this?' And he tells me that it was in the Judenrat. The most respectable Jews are employed there and they are engaged in polite discussions with the authorities. 'What respectable Jew conducts discussions with those dogs? Don't you know?' That's what I said to him. He can see that nothing will come of it. He turned, ran up to the first floor, to the Lerches. Your neighbor, the musician; maybe he can be hoodwinked. What person with an American passport would come to see his family right before the war? At the very last moment? And they locked the borders right under his nose. Now what? He's going nowhere. A musician? No, an ass! Who knows, maybe someone like that will believe those dogs. And pay."

Silence reigned again and the white streamers of their breath crossed in the green light of the carbide lamp.

"And what will I give them? A louse from under my collar? I could, why not? The only question is whether those dogs would accept such currency."

Naum spoke up. "The big *makher* drags the little *makher* on a string. And the little *makher* jabs the deaf man in his sleep and wakes him up."

The lamp was slowly dying down. Uncle Gedali said, "Where there is great fear there must also be great hunger, and where there is great hunger there must also be dirty deals. The Judenrat provided a skinny goat for the city—the community kitchen for the poor—but its teats are drying up and every day more and more hands are stretched out to milk it. Those people who take their pots there for soup are running around creating an uproar in every street. They have to believe in something by now! Before Easter a man went out of his mind from hunger and began shouting that he was Elijah the Prophet. A Jew from Leszno. He insisted, he had become Elijah and now we have a new prophet. And how many people in Leszno have died of hunger since Easter? He's still alive, probably living on alms.

Everyone knows him, but the rumors are still circulating. The end of the world is coming when Elijah the Prophet walks among the living. Who is supposed to derive comfort from rumors about the end of the world? The Germans photographed the madman from Leszno a couple of times and leaked the joke to the press. The next day, people were tearing the newspaper out of each other's hands. A Jewish prophet in the Diaspora. Not bad, eh? They gave him shoes, so in one of the pictures he's wearing shoes. *Im Winter.* But not in the other. *Im Sommer.* A Jewish prophet in winter and summer; that's what he looks like. For those shoes . . . Nothing's free! For those shoes he ran around and pointed out the places were Jews were praying illegally. And what more could the Germans want? Now, when they catch a Jew at prayer, they pour water over him and order him to dance in the snow. And if he doesn't, they beat him up."

Yankiel Zajączek flapped his elbows. "Ach, it's no good."

Naum began to squirm and said, "It's gone on for so long that it can't keep on like this much longer."

Father's hands wandered distractedly over his face. He pulled them away from his temples, shook the lamp, and the carbide flame grew brighter, the released gas hissing audibly. He began to speak in a whisper, "The people who have fled here are talking about what's going on in the towns. You don't want to believe them; it makes your hair stand on end."

David looked at his father's yellow bald spot, surrounded by clumps of short black hair.

"Can one believe the very worst? Everyone grasps at any rumor, like a drowning man at a straw. Believe? Specters, walking specters. Naked, barefoot specters. They nest in dark corners, and horrifying cries reach us from there. In hallways, attics, and cellars. In the dark. Without proper registration cards or ration books. They are afraid of their own families and of strangers, of everyone. They run away when they catch sight of someone. It's impossible to look at them. They are dying before anyone can find out the truth from them."

From the courtyard came the cries of Avrum the janitor's son: "Eh, you there! The first floor—Fremde, Lerch, Mordarski! Second floor, Drabik! Fourth, Papierny! Check your blackout." After a while, he yelled again: "Isn't that too much light? Sura, Faiga, the whole third floor has to cover up. More, more! It's shining like it's

Hanukkah. And I don't want to have to tell you again."

Father got up and walked over to the window. He peered carefully through the crack. He ran his hand over the blanket and adjusted something. Then he came back.

A cry: "Blacked out?"

"Yes, it is, it's covered!"

The gate slammed.

"They're saying, but don't say a word about this, sha . . ," and Yakov lowered his voice, while Gedali, Yankiel, and Naum craned their necks across the table. "A prophet can walk freely around the city and announce the end of the world to people, but it's forbidden to let slip even a word about what those thugs are doing all over the country . . . People say synagogues are going up in smoke, entire villages, towns, and that Jews are being driven out into the fields without their things or even a rag to cover them. The rabbis are ordered to collect the Torahs and the *talesim* themselves, and to lay them in a pile, pour oil over them, and set them afire. They set dogs on the rabbis to make them leap through the flames. The old men are arranged in a circle and ordered to recite psalms in front of the fire. They stick burning fuses in the little boys' *peyes* and laugh uproariously." Father clawed at Uncle Gedali's sleeve. "That's what they call wiping out injustice."

Yankiel Zajączek placed the carbide on the table. He held out his empty hands and cried, "What's happening? What's going to come of this?"

"*Sonderaktion.*" Naum moved again. "The world is topsy-turvy and a madman is in charge."

Father calmed them down, gently raising two fingers. "Shh."

"And who's to say," Yankiel suddenly exploded in anger, "that that painter wasn't crazy a long time ago? A house painter, phew, what filth! I said it from the very beginning, but no one wanted to believe me. Not Haskiel, not Mordechai."

Uncle Gedali sat up straight in his chair and looked at the tailor, then at the ceiling. "How can one identify a madman in a crowd of murderers? I don't know," he said and gestured helplessly.

A swarthy forehead glistened and an arrogant broken nose slid forward. "That Hitman has organized quite a spectacle in our beloved Europe and the Jews are paying the cost," said Naum. A thick strand of his woolly hair, rough and curly, fell over his temple.

"Sha, quiet," Father repeated, and gave him a stern look.

For years he had come over to the workshop and discussed politics with Father while picking over the eelgrass. Will it be peace or war? The dust rose up to the rafters that rested on steel girders and the sun just barely penetrated the chaos of sacks, tools, and eelgrass heaped in steep piles along the walls. Naum used to point to them as if they were stacks of dead bodies. Don't intervene, let Spain bleed until the bitter end. But not a single Italian soldier crossed the Pyrenees while Franco was carrying out his butchery. Don't intervene, let Hitler occupy the Rhine lands, annex Austria, invade the Sudetenland. It's all right to lend a hand in the partitioning of Czechoslovakia. To create a disturbance on the border while the German navy is steaming across the Baltic and seizing Klaipeda-Memel.

"Shh."

And who's next? After the Rhine lands, Austria, the Sudetenland, Klaipeda? Oh yes, by now a child could understand this. What is it newsboys shout in the street? It's obvious. At such a moment the leader proclaims to the entire country that he won't give up a single button from his shirt. Oy, that button. But maybe Poland is worth more than a button? We shall see; Hitler hasn't had the last word yet. In the meantime life is gay. Neither guns nor butter. But the Polish cavalry will enter Berlin in forty-eight hours. That's a good one, isn't it? Who does Minister Beck think he's fooling? And Chamberlain, why did he sign the Munich agreement? Tomorrow England and France will meet the same fate, but by then it will be too late.

"Shh."

Briand showed the Germans the road to the east in Locarno. And what if they should want to go west tomorrow? Treaties? Pieces of paper that fascists can tear up at any moment. Ribbentrop has them all in his pocket and he's playing for time. He won't let them out of his clutches. He has time.

They used to go on and on about politics; the dust rose from the threshed eelgrass and flew out the windows, and Mother was placing dinner on the table. Peace or war? September was approaching, the month of good weather and clear skies, the month of a sudden invasion that passed over the earth with the earsplitting noise of bomber attacks and the chaos of flight, the babble of helpless radio communiqués, and the darkness of the cellars where they sought shelter. Mother sewed anti–mustard gas tampons by candlelight. When the siren wailed, the motorman stopped his trolley and the passengers scrambled out, ran into the nearest courtyard, and looked for the outhouse. They urinated on their handkerchiefs and held them to their noses; no one used those tampons. The level, dead voice of the loudspeaker came in through the broken windows and resounded through the silence of the emptied upper stories. Fat rats crawled out into the city from the pulverized apartment buildings. *"Warschau kaputt!"* Leaflets, bombs, dry leaves fluttered down from the sky into the square. Then the city capitulated, the Germans marched in and organized a parade with a band. They cut off the beards of Jews, published a newspaper, and issued orders. Ration cards for bread and other things. Is this peace or war? Some people said the war was over; others said the war was just beginning. But until Father came home from the internment camp nothing would be clear.

The dollar climbed; bread became dearer. But human life grew cheap and every day there were more victims of pogroms. Beggars spread the pathetic news of the deportations, and there were people who believed the rumor. Imagine: across the sea! Everyone lost his head. Father wasn't there, and instead of Father, Naum rubbed his head behind his ears. In the confusion, he repeated the rumors. Are we going to Madagascar? It seemed like a joke; David looked it up in an old geography book. Madagascar, Madagascar . . . there! It is inhabited by Malagaysians; the climate is hot and humid; the capital city is Tananarive. In the meantime Father returned and said that Naum had been duped. Naum, Uncle Shmuel—he, too, believes every idiocy. Who would want to transport Jews over such a long distance, and in winter to boot? The same fate awaits us all. He'd been hit in the ribs by shrapnel, had somehow broken out and escaped from a POW transport, losing his bandages along the way. He was at the front; he knows what he's talking about. But the whole city was repeating anything at all in their panic. Believe the Huns yourself if you want to. Oh yes. Naum stood in the doorway and pulled a silver onion out of his pocket, checking the time. He was always out of breath. Pack up! There's not a moment to lose. Mother packed their nightclothes into a suitcase, knelt on the wicker basket to press down the linens in it, and locked it with a little pad-lock; later, feeling anxious, she reopened it. As for the rest of their things—clothes were worn, food went into a rucksack. What about the washbasin, brushes, and the primus stove? What a fate. When Naum went out Father poked at the bundles. She'd better untie them all immediately. But Mother didn't want to.

Now the whole building was packed up. People sat on their suit-cases before the sudden journey across the sea. The kids ran into the street to see if it was time. Oh, how bitter it was. Father gestured dis-gustedly: What's happening to all of you? Mother repeated what she always said: Every husband who returns from war has lost his head. Even if he hasn't been shot, he's no longer the same man. Father drummed his fingers on the windowpane for a long time. The Ghet-to walls were rising outside the window. So, it had happened. One man believed this, another believed that, but what was fated to hap-pen came in its own way, in its own time. And who was right in the end? No one.

The wicker basket for the linen reminded David of all the moves they already had behind them, and the island of Madagascar was shrouded in clouds and despair. If they could only travel without baggage! The last move, from Srebrna Street on the other side of the wall, took place on a rainy September day, and they'd been detained in the city from early morning to late at night, and when they finally reached their destination, the bundles, clothing, and household arti-cles had to be wrung repeatedly and hung to dry. Their ancestor Noah hadn't gotten that soaked in the waters of the Flood. Their route was marked beforehand and the streets they had to walk along were guarded. They walked down Towarowa to Pańska and, after running across Żelazna, they marched down Twarda, turned into Ciepła, then followed Grzybowska Street in a tightly massed crowd, one behind the other, until they reached Graniczna, and in the after-noon they stopped en masse in Żelazna Brama Square. A blue policeman opened their suitcases, spent a long time feeling their pil-lows and tearing at the featherbeds. After a couple of hours guards herded the mass of people into Grzybowski Square to make room for newcomers. They waited patiently, putting up with the down-pour of water from the sky and the flood of frenzied, confusing commands and curses; they were driven forward by the Germans and shoved back by pedestrians and vehicles. Their household goods rested on a two-wheeled cart that they'd rented from Sura, the fruit seller; it had a shaft and a leather loop on a chain. Father doggedly hunched his back beside the shaft, with the strap across his back and shoulders. There were drops of rain on his yellow bald spot (a policeman had knocked his hat off in the morning at the corner of Pańska and Wronia), his jacket collar was raised stiffly, and his bare calves were white under his rolled-up trousers. The wicker basket, tied with coarse cord, had popped open, and the red corner of their featherbed stuck out from underneath a blanket; the cast-iron pots on top of the load filled up with water and the flour-streaked bread-board on which Mother kneaded dough was wet. The three of them kept the cart propped up so that everything wouldn't go tumbling into the gutter. David looked on with disgust as his mother fussed with the linens, smoothing and pressing them under the blanket, pulling the rope tighter in an effort to keep her belongings from getting soaked. He pretended he didn't see the way passersby looked at them. He was suffering; he felt uncomfortable and embarrassed. The sun shone weakly through the clouds; then the sky again became overcast amidst the soldiers' curses. It poured as if on command. Their belongings got drenched and seemed to curl up in this rain, under the careful observation of the convoy guards.

They entered their new home at night and Mother clutched her head. The door had been chopped up with an axe and the window frames lay about in jagged splinters, the floorboards near the walls had been pulled up, and all that remained of the stove was a pile of broken tiles. David picked his way carefully and gloomily through the rubbish, through the pieces of brick strewn around the decrepit building, through the crumbling chunks of plaster knocked off the walls by someone's vengeful hand. The kitchen was a shambles, and Mother stood there with her teapot, complaining. If a Jew is supposed to move in, then it's all right to burn everything. If a Jew is supposed to move in, then you have to chop up the doorway and destroy the stove. Let the veteran of September take a good look at this and remember! Father was patiently sweeping up the rubble and smashed tiles and throwing it all into the hallway. A cloud of dust rose above him. Coughing and spluttering, they went up and down the stairs, carrying out the rubbish, which just wouldn't disappear, and the next day their devastated nest looked even worse than it had at night. Exhausted, Father walked over to the sink to wash his hands, but all the faucets had been torn out and the pipes twisted and smashed flat with a hammer; standing there with his shirtsleeves rolled up to his elbows, filthy, with clumps of dirt and soot in his hair and on his beard, covered in a shroud of ashes, he cursed without stopping for breath.

"Shh, quiet, sha!"

Yankiel Zajączek stands on tiptoe and shakes his tailor's fists at the window. Who knows whom he's threatening; he's deaf to any warnings. He shrieks, "They're warmed by the fire in which other people are burning. People! And they're not afraid that they'll be burned?" His black tailor's apron, raised on his crooked shoulders, hangs down loose to the floor.

"Shh."

But you can't get to Madagascar in a cart rented from Sura the fruit seller, Eliahu's mother. You go there by boat. First by train, and then by boat. The sirens whistle, the engines wheeze, the chimney emits smoke, the captain walks up and down on the deck, smoking a pipe. Captain Silver, an old acquaintance. How do you do, Captain? "Fifteen men in a dead man's boat, yo ho ho and a bottle of rum!" Which way to Treasure Island? David stands there, leaning on the rail, and looks at the sea; he clutches a stamp album and two triangular Zambezis. No baggage, no suitcases. The wicker basket and the unfortunate red featherbed, thrown overboard, rock on the water. The ship moves and he tears the white armband with the blue six-pointed star off his arm and flings it behind him, because he doesn't have to wear it over there. Only Naum can say what it will be like there, on the subtropical island, and that's why David loves him.

"To make fun of death and then to deal death out. That," Uncle Gedali covers his eyes and speaks in a stifled voice, "I just can't begin to understand."

Father stands up. He opens the box, takes out a letter, and hands it to Uncle Gedali. Under the propped-up lid David sees the covers of old books, prayer books. He sees the white of the linen shirts and caftans worn on the holy days.

"There. Read what Hrybko writes."

Naum raises his head and you can see his Adam's apple moving slowly in his throat. Yankiel Zajączek repeats, "German humor is crude humor."

Uncle Gedali reads the letter, holding the paper at a distance from his eyes, and the little sheet trembles in his heavy hands. Without saying a word, he and Father go out into the stairwell. Naum follows them with a long, solemn look. Through the open door indistinct voices can be heard in the hallway and a short, rough shout from Faiga the vendor, while inside the lamplight is fading on the table, the faces are growing darker, and the elongated shadows jump about on the wall in a vain attempt to escape, while Mother adjusts the flame. The tailor's elbows move, his mouth silently chews over some hopeless words. Naum sits hunched over, his head bowed low, his hands on the table in front of him. A thick strand of woolly hair has fallen over his ear.

In which of Naum's pockets is the silver onion hidden and ticking? Tick-tock, tick.

A long time ago, when he was little, he had grabbed Naum by the trousers. There's also a clock on the church tower. The hands on its face move rapidly, although they measure the same time. And Grandfather always removes his watch before he prays because you can't measure time that is dedicated to thoughts about God. He prays and meanwhile his watch ticks quietly in the chest of drawers in the other room. There are thousands and thousands of watches in the world, but time is the same everywhere. Here and there. When the noise of the siren reached the cellar a man said, "Fourteen zero zero. How punctual!" That was the all-clear signal. Did the flyer who dropped the bomb also look at his watch? He dropped it and flew home, his load lightened. In any case, the all-clear was sounded, the bomb destroyed the building only down to the first floor, and that man ran up the stairs, slipped, and broke his leg in the darkness. He screamed something awful; they couldn't take him to the hospital until they had dug out all the people on the block. If only he'd waited a little, maybe he wouldn't have broken his leg, but someone else might have. Sometimes a watch is fast and sometimes it's slow, and you never know how long an air raid will last and when the all-clear will sound. And if the siren had sounded just a little later, would that man have broken his leg? And if it had been earlier, would the bomb have fallen? How long does such a bomb fly through the air? Is time passing now? And what about at night, in our sleep? They talk and talk without end. They talk and they forget that time is passing. They forget, and that's probably why they talk so much.

Naum has business to talk over with Father. He's waiting. Father doesn't have a big silver watch like Naum's. But he has a uniform that he keeps hidden. And when he returned from the front he was wearing knee-high sapper's boots.

David remembers that day. He was alone; a hammering on the workshop door suddenly broke into the noise from the skirmish that was just beginning, because a tribe of redskins had gone on the warpath. Before him lay the open book from which the last voices had just resounded. The desperate hammering stopped and then started up again. He was afraid to ask who was there. And when he caught sight of the hairy face, the gray and sunken cheeks, he couldn't say a word. Which way? Why that way? They concealed Father's presence from the janitor and the neighbors for another half a year, until the day when they had to load their household goods on the cart and set out across the wall. The uniform lay on the bottom of the box, among the old books and holiday linens. But when he'd heard the banging at the locked workshop door, he'd thought the police were coming and, driven by fear, walked into the stuffy, damp darkness, full of the odor of eelgrass, sweat, and wood, of resin, moldy furniture, varnish, and glue. He went into the room where for months there'd been no sound of a hammer, file, or saw, and stumbling over the overturned stools, getting up and falling onto his face again, overwhelmed with terror and with the noise, he felt his way straight ahead, right up to the door that was barred from inside with heavy iron bars. They were high, a little too high for him. He yanked them out of their tracks with both hands at once, then set them aside with some effort. The blows from outside the door resounded nearby, loud, right next to his face. The last blow was the one that burst open the solid wooden door so suddenly that he fell down, and then he felt himself being lifted up into the air, and his nose was being tickled by the beard of a soldier who looked wild and strange in the gloomy light. Tatters of a rotten green overcoat hung on the man. The coat and his face were dusted with snow, and his breath was cold, cold, and he smelled like discarded iron that has been rusting for a long time in the open and gotten wet in the rain many a time and been stiff from cold again and again.

What kind of day was it? There was snow underfoot and it crackled joyously when he ran to the bakery. It was white and sky blue everywhere. The air trembled and crackled with frost. The sky was high and clear and, before it bent down to spray the light of the first star onto the streets, the roofs, the petrified trees among the snowdrifts, everything was peacefully and slowly turning blue. He ran down Towarowa, along its lengthy blind wall of bare bricks, as if he had wings. The porters used to call out at dusk on the other side of the tracks. What was it Laban said in the cold, darkened bakery? "David, my boy, this bread will cost me my life." And he handed him a loaf that was turning green with mold. Later, the moon floated over the city, over him, when he was returning home, skipping along, looking back at his footprints in the young snow. It shone brightly, like a white tablecloth illuminated by candlelight.

Father ripped off his stiff black footcloths with some effort and groaned with pain. He sat there barefoot and ate the bread, not letting go of the knife, and his head kept drooping from exhaustion. His swollen feet dangled in the air, covered with an extra skin of blood and filth. It took a long time until he slept off his escape. A night, a day, another night and then a second day. Mother set up a folding cot in the workshop, and when their neighbors knocked she opened the door unwillingly. She kept dropping things. David stood over the sleeping man: the defenseless hands, flung wide apart, moved restlessly, clutched at the shirt he was wearing. He tore at it in his sleep. He tossed and turned, and an inarticulate rumbling surged up in his throat. Mother placed her finger on her lips, warning him. Be quiet; don't tell anyone. David, keeping watch beside the sleeping man, saw a transport moving down the tracks into the distance, the rumbling of the wheels fading in the snow-covered emptiness, in the noisy barking of the convoy, in the murmur of weak voices: "Water!" In front of him lay his father, babbling in his sleep, while his mother tenderly dried his overcoat by the stove, caressing the worn cloth. In this overcoat, which was the color of rotten hay, Father had gone to the front, been placed behind barbed wire, and escaped from a transport. He had escaped and returned to them, when they had thought he was dead. This was where he had come back to be.

But the Germans say that the place Jews should be is on the island of Madagascar. Why did Mother unpack the trunk? Meanwhile, the sirens on the ship were emitting their last weak blasts, the captain had finished smoking his pipe and had given the order to raise the gangplank. He opens his stamp album, takes out a long blue stamp on which slender palm trees cluster in the bright sand and, leaves fluttering, wave to the far-off ships. He carefully wipes his fingers on his trousers and smoothes the slightly curled edge of the stamp. A notch is missing; it's imperfect. And when he holds the flimsy scrap of paper away from his eyes he sees a tiny, foggy cloud of light. A tiny tear; it's not worth anything. He'd better trade the damaged stamp for a brown Australian with a kangaroo as soon as possible. Eli has one like that. A kangaroo mother is carrying a baby in her pocket and running as fast as a train. Almost anyone could have a fifty-cent Australian stamp. But it would be best to get rid of the damaged stamp, especially if they're not going to Madagascar. Eliahu will be happy to trade. He's been trying to persuade David for a long time, since before the war.

There was a cold draft from the hallway and the flame of the carbide lamp dimmed in the sudden burst of air.

"Shut the door, there's a draft," Mother shouts.

Faiga's footsteps and the thump-thump of a table being dragged carelessly upstairs to the third floor fade away. Uncle Gedali says, "On Easter night he got up from the table midway through the Seder and couldn't finish saying 'L'shono habo-o bi'Yerusholayim.'"

"Next year in Jerusalem, but close the door to this hole right this minute! I can hardly sit still in this cold."

Uncle Gedali and Father take their time coming in.

"He's drying up, he's wasting away. He can barely drag his legs and he's only reading the prophets now."

"The prophets! As long as he reads the prophets, nothing will happen to him!"

"You're so certain, Yakov," Mother says, looking straight ahead, "that nothing will happen to him.

He sits sideways, stiffly erect, with a black woolen scarf around his neck, and the flame paints a bright spot on his temple. Uncle Gedali grimly holds the letter that he still hasn't given back. Father, bent over, shoves rags into the crack between the threshold and the door.

"For the boy," and Uncle Gedali puts a little package on the table, a small *tallis* in a cloth bag. "He told me to repeat this," he says about Grandfather, smiling sadly. "He told me to repeat that you should send the boy to the other side, across the wall. Don't keep him with you until the Judgment Day."

Father clenches his fist on the package. "I should throw him out into the street? With what?" He shakes what he's holding. "Have you read Hrybko's letter? Then tell him from me that I won't let the boy go. Until the Judgment Day! How's Chava?"

"Chava's coughing. She groans, she moans. How should she be? A skeleton. Everything hangs on her, like on a hanger. That skeleton stays alive on her nerves alone."

Mother bites her lip and covers her face with her kerchief. Uncle Gedali quickly turns his face away.

"I'll be going now," says Yankiel. "It's time. To the needle, to the needle!" And he disappears, taking the carbide with him.

David quietly turns the pages of his stamp album and looks at the old stamps with the new overprint. A GG and the black crow of the Huns, under which almost nothing can be seen. Trash. He keeps his worthless stamps separately. Who knows; some day they might be a rarity. He knows that it can happen. He and his father bought this album on Świętokrzyska Street and spent a whole day lazily prowling around the little shops full of books and globes and dusty maps, where old salesmen picked up their rare items with metal tweezers. A globe set spinning on a counter showed the country that the stamp came from. The earth turned obediently in honor of the young customer, and a blizzard of islands, bays, seas, cities, kings, animals, and machines fluttered out of translucent envelopes and blinded them with their bright colors. He shuddered with excitement and felt feverish. Look, it doesn't cost a cent to look.

There weren't many such days, and he remembered every one of them. Father took him along and said, "Look!" He felt carefree and jubilant. Time vanished in the interval between the hippopotamus's yawns, but they walked along freely amidst the fluttering of birds, the cries of monkeys, from morning till nightfall. Walking in the garden, in the sunlight, among the trees, David looked at his album of postage stamps. A polar bear was cooling off in a pool, his head protruding from the water; his paw was carefully stamped by the post office in Nordkap. It was burning hot that day; the parrots were screeching and their sharp thirsty tongues protruded from their beaks; a flock of these parrots fluttered on the cheap Brazils that were sold by the hundreds, practically by weight. A red fox was digging up the earth in his cage; only his tail protruded from the hole. A thirsty she-wolf bent over a trough with a rusty liquid in it and, sniffing cautiously, carefully lapped at the water. A lone flamingo stood in one spot, its wing drooping feebly toward the shallow puddle in which its tiny leg was planted, fragile and slender as a bamboo shoot. Snakes slept coiled beside radiators; fish flailed the water with enormous fringed tails, and a lightbulb was always on in the aquarium. Father said that those animals were in captivity. Meanwhile, the elephant waved its trunk jauntily and generously sprayed the curious spectators; bouquets of withered flowers flew into the air together with clusters of rotten bananas, bunches of carrots, watermelons; he snatched them all and, waving his supple trunk, thrust them between his jaws. Triangular Indias with an elephant wearing a golden caparison cost as much as fifteen groschen in the used-book store and lay in the place of honor under the glass on the countertop. Nearby, a velvet panther hunted softly, moving silently behind the bars, back and forth until dark. Feathery little clouds on long sticks shone pink; they were held aloft in bunches by a vendor near the gates of the zoo. He stealthily poured a drop of denatured alcohol onto the sugar to give it color. At sundown his joy passed. "Cotton candy! Cotton, cotton!" Set in motion, the spinning machine grated. The first streetlights began to glow; crushed tickets littered the grass. The pony galloped nervously; its trainer stood beside it with a long whip in his hand and a leather bag for money. The lion stretched and angrily shook its pale blond mane, cut from a tall block of concrete. David, worn out, dragged himself along beside his father, stiffly planting his feet after dismounting the elegantly saddled pony, who had shaken him unmercifully in the crowded riding ring. He heard the evening clamor and fluttering of the caged birds, the sad cries of the monkeys, and the lion's farewell roar.

He remembered the lion's farewell and also that other day. The air was dusty from the cinders on the railroad tracks, and they were walking down Towarowa along the blind wall of bare, unmortared brick, passing the posters that announced the mobilization. His call-up papers in his pocket, Father was taking David for a last walk before the war. Together, they dreamed up a slender bicycle, silvery, draped with sky blue cables for the brakes, with thin, dependable tires, with gears that made a pleasant noise — sh-sh-sh — when shifted down. They put that bicycle together piece by piece from David's dreams, and on the next day Father was gone; called up, he had left for his mounted heavy artillery unit near Modliny.

He remembered the lion's farewell and also one other day. In the first week of September, outside the city, on the highway in the shade of tall trees, the batteries were drawn up in formation. The wheels of the guns rested amidst piles of horse manure; the animals, covered with coarse blankets, snorted peacefully, and their neighing was like a sudden burst of wind over a river, like the fluttering of sparrows in the tops of roadside trees.

"Go to Berg and collect what he owes me!"

David saw his father's sunburned neck in the regulation linen shirt, his legs in Russian leather boots laced up to his knees. A battery of heavy guns was moving along amidst an uproar of commands and the wild shouting that people used in order to get the animals moving. He heard the creaking of the harnesses, the slow and heavy footsteps of the Percherons. The horses' hindquarters glittered under the setting sun, the river glittered in the sunlight, as did the barrels of the silent guns; and suddenly the quiet singing of the soldiers could be heard, singing full of a bitter bravado, and David dragged himself along in the dust at the edge of the ditch. Mother was running now, frantically clutching Father's uniform. When their column moved out, Father shoved her away from him with one strong blow, and without looking back, he ran after his carriage, and the tin box of his gas mask bobbed up and down below his shoulders.

"Go to Berg!"

Later — in '40, '41, '42 — the rubber tubing from these masks was slipped onto the handlebars of bicycle-powered carriages: the city was crowded with unemployed coolies, and three-wheeled rickshaws came into use. The rubber grips had deep, wavy indentations; they rested comfortably and securely in one's hands without making them sweaty, and therefore they were sought by everyone. Anyone whose arms and legs weren't swollen from hunger could drive at the cost of a great deal of sweating, pushing both passengers and cargo. What of it; people were cheaper than horses. And so David's dream, like all the others in his life, was realized: the light racing bike that he longed for was changed by fate into a heavy coolie's vehicle that dripped grease, on which his father transported loads in partnership with Naum. Their rickshaw, assembled from a low bike frame that was wired to a box suspended on stiff springs, served valiantly until the end, only its old tires used to go flat on turns and had to be continually retreaded, patch upon patch, though that didn't help much because they were as worn and threadbare as sweat-soaked socks. Naum brought to the partnership two spare wheels with thick Dunlop tires. When the inner tube exploded in the middle of the street with a sound like a rifle shot and the passenger started shrieking, Father would pull over and change the wheel, patiently enduring the passenger's verbal abuse. Every day more patches were added to the inner tubes and more calluses to his hands. They took turns; Naum would come over to their place one evening to calculate their earnings and the next day Father would walk over to Naum's place after finishing his last trip. That was their routine for the time being.

"David, are you asleep? What's the matter?"

"No, nothing."

Ashamed, he rubbed his eyes. Uncle Gedali was already saying good-bye to everyone. Stand up, click your heels, shake hands. But a weight is pressing on his neck; he feels his numb cheek on the clammy table. His ears are burning and his feet are cold. Father's face, green in the light of the carbide lamp, bends over him, as large and sad as the moon. He can hear their voices, but what are they saying? He hears his uncle's footsteps. In the hall, in the entranceway. But here in his ears there's the noise of sleep floating away, his mother's terrible sobbing.

"And what can I put in that pot? Should I cut up my head and put it in?"

Father puts away the letter, slamming the lid of the box. Naum pushes his bowl away and spreads out the dirty, sweaty banknotes on the table. His stiff, heavy hands move slowly.

"Yakov, have you heard a starving man crying in his sleep?"

Silence. The carbide burns down with a stormy hissing noise. Naum puts his hands over his eyes and sits there, his face covered.

What? David strains his eyes and looks for their household monster on the wall near the door: a huge, frost-covered, damp stain that changes its shape from day to day.

"I have two cases of typhus at home." Naum slowly lowers his hands. "And the only thing that wagon gives you is trouble."

"Okay, that's enough," says Mother. She noisily moves the pot around on the stovetop. "All you do is buy, sell, and trade rainbows."

Naum gathers up a roll of crumpled banknotes and the *młynarki* tumble all over the table. That's what those worthless bills are called in honor of Feliks Młynarski, director of the Generalgovernement's treasury.

"I'll drive for a week or two myself . . . and I'll buy out your share, Yakov. We can't both live off these groschen."

Mother thrusts a poker into the bucket. "Hurry-scurry! He's in a rush."

"How much? I'll pay."

"No," David whispers despite himself. He can feel sleep overwhelming him again. Is it he speaking or someone else? Father turns to him, "Children and fish don't have voices. Shush."

Naum walks over to the door. He hesitates at the threshold, his hand on the door handle. "Groschen, groschen. This whole business is on springs."

"On broken springs," Father adds.

"I'll buy out your share and soon you'll find an easier way to earn your bread."

"No, Naum, no." His voice rises. The windowpanes rattle. "No! If I find an easier portion of bread I'll let you know!"

He pushes Mother away from the sink. He puts his mouth under the faucet and drinks some water. He gulps it down for a long time. The drops roll down his gray, unshaven face. Finally he turns back, calmer. He yawns, pulls off his shirt. Tomorrow, at daybreak, he'll have to drive into the city.

Mother bends over. She tucks freshly laundered thick socks into his shoes. She extinguishes the carbide lamp with her wet hand, as if it's a candle. She carries the dissolved, hissing carbide, together with the lamp, into the hallway, so it can be thoroughly aired overnight.

She groans. "Buba keeps fuel and carbide in the cellar. It's damp there. Yesterday she found two dead rats."

They were yawning, falling asleep; quietly, without even creaking, the door opened. Just one word; it's absolutely necessary! The front left tire has to be covered with a thick coat of tar and the axle has to be greased. The chain has already gotten shorter by one link. The chain might not move. Father answers him back. It'll get done. He has grease. And some tar can be found, too.

Naum leaves. Mother says, "Do you see what a partner he is? Sell him the button off your shirt since you yourself, thank God, are walking around naked."

Father turns over impatiently in bed. "Shh!"

David slept like a log. The wheel turned; gray dust whirled. The streets slipped by like open graves. Whose load he was carrying he did not know. He covered the corpse with a newspaper; a louse crawled out from under the paper and slowly, slowly came closer to him. Down Żelazna to Żytnia; then he got lost. There was a black pit in the street and figures bowed over it. In one gust of wind their raised arms and faces turned toward the dark, cloud-swept sky. Everywhere, on every corner, there was a blizzard of street signs. "Madagascar." Which way to Okopy? The louse was growing, and he couldn't escape, he couldn't stop the speeding rickshaw. "You, watch out for the turns!" A yellowed arm slipped out from under the newspaper and Naum pointed at the wheel. And there, under the wheel, Mother had fallen, wrapped up in a bundle of rags. Her head was striking the stones, banging against them. "Don't leave me here by myself, son, in the darkness of night." Had she crawled to Okopy by her own efforts? Everyone was heading there, in a crowd. Now he could see clearly. The louse was growing, it loomed up like a yellow glimmering, it shone with an enormous glow. "No!" No, that's the sun, the sun flooding the earth with a corpselike light.

"No!"

He screamed; he heard his own scream; and then he woke up. He lay there in the darkness and the silence broken by the loud beating of his own heart, and he couldn't hear his mother breathing. Father slept the sleep of an exhausted horse. Mother's sleepless nights roamed the streets like the laments of the hungry beggar who cried out for bread outside their locked gate. He raised his head. *Gite mentshn, rakhmunes!* The cries and groans of a specter dying on the stones in the darkness.

Bang. Bang. The crashing of hobnailed boots; a shot. Footsteps, as of a patrol marching into the distance. Silence. That voice no longer horrified the sleeping people; now he himself slept without complaint.

He heard his mother tossing cautiously from side to side, and sighed. The last thought sneaks in, when he's no longer fighting off sleep and it's too late to drive it away. Can she hold out for long? She's skin and bones; she's shriveling up from hunger and terror, and that lying awake at night watching will finish her off, one-two-three . . .

He ate. He ate without stopping and without restraint. He'd already swallowed two Dunlop bicycle tires, Naum's silver watch, and a handful of carbide. Yankiel Zajączek pulled out a needle. Was he threatening him? Blood dripped from his finger, drop by drop. Whose scream rose above the city? The Jews were moving in a crowd toward Okopy. Again he was standing next to the cart, and in the cart sat Naum, comfortably reclining. He shook hands with everyone; the passengers got in. "There's not a moment to lose!" Move; keep going. David was sweaty from fear; he was scratched and jostled by the crowd. He was dreaming, he thought he was dreaming; and there would be no end to their flight into the pits at Okopy as long as this dream, this nightmare, this life, continued.

Abandoning the rags of the dead, the lice, the lice, are fleeing in swarms from the cold, stiff bodies, and crawling over his face.

IV

He could barely make ends meet and now they were going to take away his fodder.

When there was no one left for him to drive around in his cab, Mordechai Sukiennik, following Zajączek the tailor's advice, hitched up his wagon and drove straight to the Judenrat, to President Czerniaków himself. President Czerniaków shouted at him that he was busy, that he had more important matters to deal with, that they shouldn't be letting people in to see him about just anything. Just anything? But it was about Saba: she might roll over and die any day. They sent him away and he came back. He had time; he'd wait. And then he started going to the Judenrat every morning. He sat in the waiting room and waited patiently for the president. With his whip in his hand.

If not today, then tomorrow. He'd sat on the coachman's seat for thirty years, the whole city knew him, he even used to drive the Lewin girls along the boulevard—Anielcia and Dora Lewin, imagine that. A spring day, the streets have been swept clean, Dora Lewin is wearing a suit with light-colored accessories and a white flower pinned to her jacket. The world is smiling; fodder is cheap. Anielcia Lewin sits beside her sister, and it's good to be alive. She's wearing the sheerest stockings, the color of a suntanned ankle, a flowered print dress of French silk, seventeen golden meters of it, chamois gloves, and a straw hat with a rolled brim. The sun is shining, the cab moves at just the right pace, a humming sound fills the boulevard. Everyone turns to look at old Lewin's daughters. Anielcia's light dress flutters over her knees and Dora snaps open her alligator purse and pays the two zlotys for the trip without batting an eyelid. Lewin was a doting father and his daughters didn't want for anything. They wore the most expensive shoes, always from Kielman's.

He used to drive his passengers to the railroad station, to weddings, to the cemetery in his elegant black cab. And now what? Nothing. Czerniatyński the lawyer would drop in at Kleszcz's for just a moment and give the cabby fifty groschen just to wait for him outside the café. And how long does it take to drink a cup of espresso? Czerniatyński stopped at Kleszcz's every day for twelve years. But now you can't find a single individual in this lovely city who feels like going for a little drive. What's going on? It costs more to live, although life has gotten cheaper. The cost of living is going up, the dollar has skyrocketed, and everyone who has an arm and a leg gets up on a bicycle and makes like a Chinese coolie. There's no more room for a horse in this world. People are draft animals for other people. It's the end. Tfoo!

So they hired the cabby to haul rutabagas to the Judenrat soup kitchen where the beggars could buy slops for a pittance. The president himself handed him the official papers: a requisition for feed for Saba and a pass stamped with a crow. The next day the mare stood up and allowed him to harness her. Once again she tossed her head gaily when she felt the cold bit in her mouth, and Mordechai shouted in the open doorway of the stable, groomed the mare till she shone, and plaited a red ribbon into her mane. The old nag neighed amidst the ruins of the destroyed outbuilding inside the dark courtyard, calling to the horses who were beyond in the green meadows.

"Mordechai, you can see me, toss it here!"

Dry, charred trees, like umbrellas with holes in them, protruded from the sidewalk. A group of skeletons were dying there, their hands outstretched, but Mordechai Sukiennik stood up on his coachman's seat and forced his way through their wailing. In the summer, when the sun was warm, the old cabby hauled young vegetables; in the winter, he carried frozen, rotted rutabagas.

Oh, he's got her in harness, he's driving again.

"Mordechai, Mordechai, slash your whip!"

Clop, clop, clop, clop. Tiny skeletons covered with sores came running down from every floor, attracted by the sight of the animal in the courtyard and wheezing, squealing, joyously waving their stunted arms. Impetigo was already in bloom in the summer warmth and their skin was overgrown with its luxuriant tendrils. Their scabs oozed and their lips, ulcerated with canker sores, smiled broadly, jaggedly. Red blotches grew on them like weeds. The stigmata of abcesses, scarlet stains on necks and torsos, persistent thrush infections, and an assortment of rashes covered the frail, swollen little bodies that shunned the bright rays of the sun. Hunger had placed its filthy mask on them, deforming their faces with old men's grimaces, gnawing at their chapped skin. They squinted in the blinding sunlight and their festering eyelids squeezed shut involuntarily, lending them a cunning expression, the hint of a cruel, sly smile.

"Oy!"

They came running, running. Roizele and Surele, the janitor's littlest treasures, and his son, Avrum, too. And Leibuś, the apple of Faiga's eye. Running to see Mordechai harnessing a live horse. The white kerchief on Surele's head concealed her bald scalp. When the boys pulled off the scarf she burst into heartrending sobs. Leibuś was terribly scaly; the faster his blisters dried up, the more he was covered with fish scales.

Now a corpse-gray skeleton with a puffy face stole into the barn. His nose, ears, and neck were decorated with creeping erysipelas. Long Itzhok lay down on the straw while Mordechai hitched up the wagon.

Baruch Oks and his gang fingered the feed bag. They crept into the manger behind Long Itzhok and pulled the fodder out from under the horse's head. The mare emitted a loud grating sound and snorted as she tore into something with her teeth. A hum escaped her velvet nostrils and then a loud, high squeal: "Eehoooo! Eeheeee!"

The coachman shouted good-naturedly, stamped his heavy boots at the pale-green brats to chase them away, and put the bridle on his nag, thrusting his fist into her mouth. The mare snorted like a dragon. When the harness was fastened and the whiffletree in place, Mordechai cried out, "Gee up!" and drove out through the gate, and the stallkeepers moved their tables and stalls out of the way. The Krochmalna Street gang ran after the wagon, hanging onto its boards and axles, trying to reach the bag of chaff.

One day they launched a coordinated attack on the wagon and in just one minute they had grabbed a quarter of the oats. They gulped down the grain and the chaff, searching for scattered bits of bran, while Mordechai Sukiennik, cursing, flailed at them with his whip, knocked the skinnier boys onto the ground, and wrested the remains of the torn sack from them.

Should he go closer, right under her hooves? Leibuś, scratching his blisters, kept his distance.

"Leibuś, my boy, be careful. Stand back, my little fishy!" Faiga the stallkeeper hollered at him, leaning out her fourth-floor window. She was wearing a pink shirt and clung to the broken window frame.

"Gee up!"

Mordechai Sukiennik stood high in the driver's seat, wrapped in the graceful folds of his whip and surrounded by the sparks that the horse's shoes struck from the cobblestones. He shouted his commands, and once again Saba clopped into the roadway lined with beggars, stepping carefully among the starving bodies whose dimming gaze followed the coachman as he drove toward the other side. The clatter of the horse's hooves faded away, along with the squealing of the axle and the creaking of the harness.

"Mordechai, Mordechai, slash your whip!"

Saba's lips were thin, black, and moist, and her front right hoof was cracked. She was an old horse, a prewar horse. Before the war she used to pull the black lacquer cab. At night, two lanterns shone next to the coachman's seat, as large and bright as two moons. That's what Mordechai Sukiennik's cab was like, and its number was 315. One could still go and see it: it was parked in the stable with its shafts raised. Inside was a flowered featherbed, two flat pillows, and a blanket, because that's where Mordechai slept.

Leibuś was standing pensively beside the green mounds of manure, wallowing in the rotted straw in which he sank up to his ankles. David climbed onto the running board and set the dead cab rocking with a sweep of his arm; the glass lanterns with the candle stubs inside rattled, and the raised shaft jiggled up and down. Suddenly the proud, grotesque landau came to life. The blackness of its upholstery and lacquer covered it like a yashmak; it was shrouded by the dust that lay behind its veil of sticky spiderwebs. Leibuś clambered onto the other step and with unconstrained, wild glee began hurling black curses. *"Une, due, rike, fake."* Be quiet, take a deep breath, and get on with it. *"Orbe, borbe, osme, smake."* Take another deep breath to last a long time. *"Eus, deus, kosmateus."* And now hold your breath and: *"Bakst!"*

Malka used to drive to the Roxy movie theater on Wolska Street in this cab. Count Grandi, with his little moustache, would sit beside her, dressed in riding breeches. The hooves clattered on the asphalt; suntanned boys were walking back from Kercelak, carrying the pigeons they had bought there and feeding them seeds from their own mouths; the lilacs were fading to a rusty color behind the fence of the Hospital for Infectious Diseases at the corner of Młynarska; and on the other side of the street, Rudolf Valentino was smiling with his eyes. Two times he took her to the movies and already she was his. In the cab, under the raised hood, his little black moustache carelessly brushed against her brass earring. Count Grandi was the son of Papierny the furrier, who lived on the fifth floor and had lost his legs before the war; he was Buba the stallkeeper's half-brother. On Pawia Street everyone knew him as Count Grandi; on Krochmalna, as Loniek Papierny. When he put on the yellow arm-band of the Ordnungsdienst and clutched his billy club, they could see what a scoundrel he was—a Jewish policeman, an OD man. Despite his paralysis, Judah Papierny rose up in his bed and grabbed a heavy crystal vase. Loniek escaped in the nick of time. The vase broke the window and smashed into the courtyard, and the furrier's son fled from the house. Buba was sobbing; curious neighbors lined the stairs. Judah Papierny screamed that the lout shouldn't be allowed to cross his threshold, because he no longer has a son and doesn't wish to know him. He made quite a scene; the shattered glass lay on the asphalt; and Count Grandi was already on his way to the Roxy with Malka.

That was the beginning of their romance. The end came one year later, when Malka was bitten by a typhus-carrying louse and was admitted to the Czyste hospital for a kilo of lemons; she left the infirmary without any hair, her head shaved clean, and Count Grandi no longer wanted to know her. And who did want to know her? She emerged at nightfall, like a moth. The darkness mended the holes in her stockings and concealed the smeary splotches of rouge around her lips, her broken heel, her shaken gaze, her little ears pierced with brass earrings. She stood watch in front of the gate and then moved on; a policeman was posted at the corner to keep order. The darkest spot is under the streetlight. And there she stood, one hand resting on her hip, the other holding a cigarette. The toe of her dainty shoe rested carelessly on the sidewalk and you could see her torn-off heel.

"*Eus, deus, kosmateus . . . bakst!*"

There was a small stove in the stable on which the coachman did his cooking. Also hay, old leather straps, a fancy harness for special occasions, and a coachman's cape with metal buttons. The leather of the old straps smelled of pitch, tar, hay, and something else he couldn't name, and the hay smelled like a real meadow.

"Don't you know what a meadow is?"

"No, I don't," said Leibuś.

"But I remember."

He closed his eyes, and the courtyard resounded with the cry: "Scraps! Crusts! I buy stale bread, moldy bread!"

"What else do you remember? Tell me."

"Pine trees."

"What are pine trees?"

The pines were still there, on the sand dunes. Also the sky, buffeted by the wind, and the blades of grass against the background of clouds, looming as large as pine trees when you pressed your face to the ground. And summer, the first summer that he remembered. The meadow would come to life before it rained. Brightly colored toads, no bigger than hazelnuts, were everywhere. He picked one up; it was cold, clammy. Starlings swooped down; they rested on the ground, strutted about, and searched for food in the grass. A long, mild summer. He remembers. His mother was standing over him and in the bright sunshine her body cast a huge shadow in which he could hide, and it felt so good. The trees in the orchard and the clouds. A single thicket; green, whiteness, all so very far away. She asked him, "David, what's the matter with you?" But he didn't know. It was a bright, clear morning. Dew dripped from an apple on a branch. Were those tears? He didn't know. And then it was night, night scampering away with a terrifying cry at the sight of the rising day. Pure drops furrowed the lusterless skin of the dangling fruits and diffused the light like cut crystal. Pure tears dripped from the fruits that no one's fingers had touched. What could the name of that village have been? In the woods . . . Where could that village have been? The village of his childhood was in the woods, encircled by ribbons of sandy roads, tiny, isolated, cast onto a plain between two rivers, full of the fluttering of birds and the rustling of boughs, the sleepy voices of animals and people. It must have happened at dawn. He also remembers the pure cold of the wind among the quivering leaves when he heard her clear, kind voice. And he remembers the sparkling of the rising sun in the wet orchard.

But what he says is, "Pine trees have needles."

"Needles?"

"Yes, needles. And milk comes from a cow."

Leibuś didn't know what a cow was.

"Crusts and stale bread! I buy crusts and stale bread!" First he heard the chant; then a man with a sack wandered into the street.

Apples, brown and rotting, were buried in the hay that was piled up beside the stable wall. Stealthily, he dug out a fragile, forgotten fruit and covered the hole he'd made with wisps of hay. Leibuś took the fruit from him with both hands, carefully and respectfully, held it up to his nose, and sniffed it. Yum. They wolfed down the stolen apple, covered as it was with gray mold, and the bitterness of the nasty, fermented pulp bit into their stomachs.

Long Itzhok, who was lying under a horse blanket, woke up without making a sound. Suddenly he yelled from his pallet, "Get out of here, rats!" He patted his empty stomach till it rumbled loudly, and announced, "Guts with water." He emptied his bladder onto the straw, yawning mightily.

In a panic, they ran from him into the courtyard and scrambled over the precipice formed by the ruins of an outbuilding, straight into the raging sunlight of those summer days, into the broiling heat of noontime, into the very center of the hungry crowd's shouting and yelling. They took off their hard wooden clogs and spent a long time wandering around in the ruins. Entire families of displaced persons were roaming about over there. The people were wrapped in scraps of blankets, tin cans dangled from their belts, and they carried on their backs whatever belongings they had not yet given away. From here a passageway led into a tiny street that had been sealed off by the wall. It was filled with noisy beggars. Curiosity commanded them to look, and shame forbade them to avert their eyes. Warmed by the sun, the boys made their way along Waliców, past the bodies sprawled helplessly on the pavement, covered with lice-infested rags.

"Do Jews die on Saturday, too?" Leibuś asked. "And what day is today?"

The naked skeletons shook their begging tins, cried out, and stuck their legs out in front of the passersby. They were rotting in the sunshine, and blue flies kept landing on their sticky wounds. Here, people became carrion while they were still alive.

He felt a gnawing sensation. He knew it was hunger. Nothing in his mouth since morning except for those slops, the slops from the Judenrat kitchen, a watery soup that was almost free, just fifty groschen. Children got a special rate. Manna from heaven is watery and that's why it costs fifty groschen. At this time of year the dying gulp down that *Wassersuppe*—half a liter of a murky fluid with beet shavings and traces of kasha, garnished with green nettle leaves. Their final memory. Raw vegetable matter, just barely blanched by boiling, floats on the surface. And the beggars' ragged clothing, the paving stones beside the wall, and the street where they lie lethargically, stretched out flat on their backs with their tin cans beside them—all are splattered with the vomited green stuff.

Into the tin cans splash the watery slops, a gift of coerced compassion. A skinny goat, the Judenrat's offering, hovers and kneels above the city, and everyone, lamenting, stretches out a hand to its generous teat. A skinny goat, milked by the poor, hovers over the city, and the Judenrat broth squirts from her udder. The great heart of the wealthy has been cooked in this broth. It has scraps of meat for everyone; you just have to be able to detect the taste of those scraps. Those who are lying on the sidewalk can no longer gorge themselves on this broth; it runs right out their noses. They vomit the slops, then sleep all day in a green puddle. They are delirious, torpid, exhausted by the scorching heat, and the flies crawl into their mouths, big, blue, sated flies. Who sent the flies? Who sent the hunger?

When the Jews were murmuring in the desert, God sent them manna from heaven, He sent them quail. The quail fluttered obediently into their encampment and the hungry people caught them with their hands. That was in the evening. They caught them with their bare hands and in the morning grain covered the ground like frost. Their cry rose to heaven. *"Man hu?* What is it?" They ate without knowing what it was. They ate and they praised God, without knowing what they were praising Him for. For six days they gathered the *man hu,* and then came the seventh day, the holy day, the Sabbath, and there was no grain in the fields.

"Rakhmunes, gite mentshn, rakhmunes, rakhmunes!"

Don't hear that cry for alms. Grow deaf forever. But how can you walk around, day in and day out, with your ears plugged? His head feels as light and empty as . . .

"Look, a soap bubble."

Who's that in the window? Pale blond hair, white hands and face, and a straw between his teeth. David shouts, Leibuś waves his clenched fists joyfully at the sight of him, and Ernest puffs up his cheeks, blows carefully, and releases soap bubbles through the straw. They flutter lightly down to the street.

"Hey, Albino, where'd you get the straw?"

A rainbow-colored bubble grows, sails away, rises on the air. It flutters, carefree, above the beautiful, horrid, impossible world, and in its glassy, transparent center it reflects everything it meets on its way.

"Do Jews die on Saturday?"

Struck by a fist, a mirror will crack. A stone thrown into water sinks. The rainbow soap bubble blows apart in the wind.

"In a little while we, too, will be dying in the streets. The same end awaits us all."

That's what Father says, and Mother begs him to stop. She begs him to have pity. Her words. David has heard them more than once and they make him uncomfortable; probably he feels ashamed. Shame is when a person doesn't want to sleep on the pavement, to become exhausted and delirious in the sunshine, when he doesn't want other people to see the flies parading all over him. When a man is hungry, it's not right to look him in the eye. But then you have to gobble your own bread on the sly, and to eat like that is also shameful. The hungry have no shame and they prefer to whine and hold out their empty hands to people walking by, rather than die without help inside their four walls. They'd rather demand that good people have pity on them. Good people walk down the streets, and the poor lie beneath the wall. Good people throw them a coin and walk on, but the hungry remain on the pavement that belongs to them.

"Rakhmunes, rakhmunes!"

You have to hear that all day long. The Germans promised they would burn down Waliców. And burn down Pańska, Krochmalna, Ciepła, and Prosta Streets, too, because that's where the epidemic is raging. The worst epidemic and hunger in these back alleys of the

Little Ghetto. Who sent the hunger? The typhus? The lice? They were even crawling all over Professor Baum and the old man couldn't get rid of them. And since the disease is spread by lice, Professor Baum will come down with typhus like so many others before him, and it will turn out that the Germans were right when they ordered that posters be put up all over the city with the warning:

JEWS
LICE
TYPHUS

Leibuś sat down on the ground, dejected. "My feet are asleep. Let's go home, there's nothing here."

They returned home from their walk.

"Please read me the paper, David. Just one little article."

The newspaper was written in colored pencil on pages torn from an accountant's ledger—lined sheets of paper with a thick red line at the top. Above that line it was perfectly clean; he hadn't scrawled anything up there. There were ten pages in all. On the first was the title printed in block letters, CHRONICLE, and below it, in smaller letters: of our courtyard. He had scribbled his first work in secret, embarrassed by what he was doing, and when it was ready they had all gathered to look at it. They turned the pages, looked closely at the drawings, found sentences here and there that had special meaning for them, read them out loud, and nodded their heads in recognition.

"You really did a good job this time. I should be so smart," said Zyga.

And Eliahu asked in disbelief, "Did you do it all by yourself? Just like that, without copying?"

David remained modestly silent.

Ernest couldn't understand one thing. "What's a chronicle?"

Eli also had some reservations about that word. "You mean you can't change it now?"

Zyga answered definitively, "Newspapers don't change their names. *The Courier* doesn't either."

"*The Courier* doesn't either?"

"No. Once something has been written down, you have to stick with it forever."

Ernest said meekly, "All right, but what does 'chronicle' mean?"
And David replied, "I don't know."

There were ten pages in all. The first installment of a novel, a complicated adventure story ending with a hail of gunfire, written in the style of Westerns such as *Sergeant King of the Royal Canadian Mounties*. That took up a little more than a page. Beneath it were the unknown bookkeeper's blurred debits and credits, which made a terrible mess. Next, a scene from a play that he'd dashed off in a fit of inspiration about trappers lost in some vaguely sketched region called the Wild West. Then a poem, held together by forced rhymes, that was the disgrace of the issue. News from the apartment house; rumors from the city; a letter from a friend on the other side of the wall. Jokes that began: "Once Hitler went to see a rabbi . . ." A lot of space was taken up by an article on Madagascar that he had copied from the encyclopedia: "Madagascar is located on the Mozambique Channel off the southeast coast of Africa near the Cape of Good Hope. It is 590,000 sq. km.; its inhabitants are called Malagaysians; it has a hot, wet climate. The major city is Tananarive. Madagascar has plains and mountains, Brazilian rosewood, ebony, sugarcane, manioc, cacao, vanilla, coffee." Finally there was sports news, without commentary. The results of the championship playoffs in the mumbletypeg match: Eliahu 3, David 2; Eliahu 5, Ernest 1; Zyga 2, Eliahu 1. That was the contents of his *Chronicle*. It also contained illustrations. No talent at all. Father would shake his head mournfully. He can't do anything well; who does this child take after?

No, it was unheard of.

The article on the island of Madagascar, the fruit of his passionate devotion to facts, was preceded by a motto from his beloved poet:

Will there be room at sea?
Enough for us, good sir.

He read his smudged creation. Carried away, Leibuś dug his finger deep into his nose, his eyes wide open. What does that snot-nosed kid understand? His pockets are stuffed with pencils that he puts to use at every opportunity. He draws whatever he sees. And his clogs are worn down because he plays hopscotch with the girls all day long.

When they hear shouting outside the window it means that Haskiel the janitor is sweeping the kids away in all directions with his broom.

"A zloty's a pile!"

"A pile is dirt!"

"Dirt is the earth!"

"The earth is our mother!"

"Mother's an angel!"

"Angels are guardians!"

"And guardians are janitors!"

Haskiel stands in the courtyard, waving his birch broom, deafened by the shouts. Up we go! The pale green kids hop noisily up to heaven. Skinny braids and bare knees flash by, the words of cabalistic children's chants float on the air. Torn shoes confined inside a chalk circle. Potholes filled with scribbles, numbers, dark signs, and incantations retreat before him. The walls sway and rock, the earth sways and rocks underfoot, and a black and blue bump swells on his head. Go back to the beginning; the whole game's ruined.

"You're out, you're out," Surele shouts, and takes the piece of glass away from him. One's not supposed to let that foot touch the ground, but the other foot's asleep. A warm drop gathers under his nose; dust collects on his face.

"We'll have to draw hell all over again," says Roizele. She bends over, dragging her foot, which is swollen from hunger, through the dust, and draws seven diamonds. At the top: heaven. Below: hell. The green piece of glass from a broken bottle is supposed to sail past all the boundaries.

Hopping on one foot, you can wind up in "seventh heaven" or go crashing into the tailor's basement. When a pebble hits his windowpane, Yankiel runs out of his shop and starts screaming.

"They've broken my window," he yells. "You stinking brats! I'll give it to you now!"

They run away and hide in a corner of the courtyard behind the garbage bins.

"Yankiel, Rabbit Fur, sew yourself a cabbage burr!" the girls yell, rhyming. But the boys don't bother with rhymes: "Yankiel, sew up the hole in Regina's wig."

The tailor, spitting, runs down to his shop and slams the door.

Leibuś peeks out from behind the shelter of the garbage bin and sticks his purplish tongue out all the way down to his chin. Hey!

When Faiga locks him in the apartment he pulls his chair up to the window and stares sternly out into the courtyard. He puts circles, lines, blots on the paper; he wants to draw the street, but it is hard to draw Krochmalna Street so that it seems to come to life before your eyes. Leibuś spits on the pencil point, wets a paintbrush in his mouth, sighs. A small, lonely, gray cloud remains on the paper. It has already gotten caught on the chimney. If the paper were larger there would be smoke coming out of the chimney, but as it happens the building is tall and blocks the entire sky. Windows, windows. A building like ours has to have a lot of windows. The panes should be sky blue, the house yellow. A little circle in front of the gate: that's a head. Two lines: arms. Haskiel the janitor stands with his broom in his hand and looks at the wall. From one end of the paper to the other stretches that horrid wall. Where there's an empty spot on the sidewalk he places a kitchen stool. Tall, like the apartment house. Faiga stands next to it, selling candy. Otherwise what would Leibuś eat? He could eat up all the candies. He looks at the sad drawing for a long time and searches for something. The wall takes up so much space. He picks up his pencil and with a broad sweep of his hand he draws a tiny cross and a zigzag. There, a bird is flying over the wall. Could such a little bird carry an olive branch? Leibuś thinks about this and then he leaves everything as is and pushes the picture away. It's ready; now it has to dry.

> A bird is flying up and down,
> Seeking crumbs on city ground.
> But there's not a trace of wheat,
> Nothing for that bird to eat.
> Tweet tweet tweet,
> Tweet . . .

He picks up a second sheet of paper, he makes two spots with green ink: a big egg, a little egg, and a neck between them. The big one is a head and the other is a body. There has to be hair, eyes, a nose and mouth on the head, and the body has to have a dress. The mouth has big gold teeth; you can see them clearly. Without giving it any thought he quickly draws a brown nose, black eyes, dark blue eyebrows. A careful glance at his mother: what else is missing? Red legs should be added to the blue dress, so Leibuś dips his brush into the red paint. Faiga was standing behind her stall, and under the stall you could see large, loosely fitting shoes.

That's not enough for him. Now Baruch Oks's whole gang rushes onto the paper, with Baruch at their head. They are marching toward the *Wache*, straight at the policeman. Baruch Oks in his black leather jacket, Moishe the Crip behind him, with one arm shorter than the other, behind him Five-Fingers Mundek with his square head on his oxlike shoulders, behind him Henio the Herring with his swollen lips, and finally, bringing up the rear, thin little Chaim the Orphan. They're walking. In the second rank are Yosele Egg Yolk, Mordka the Ram, and Kuba the Gelding with his paper face, pale as a ghost that's been sprinkled with flour. There was still a little room in the upper right-hand corner of the paper, and into the gray shadow there he fits Long Itzhok.

His eye wanders over the crowd and, detecting a space, he hangs a round sun high on the paper and two little sparrow clouds floating in space. The sun's rays go right past the figures. Inside the round sun he draws a nose, eyes, a mouth, and he laughs his timid little laugh because that's him, Leibuś. Right there.

Should he draw something else? Okay, Mordechai Sukiennik. Uh oh, how do you draw a horse? A horse has to look like something: four legs, a mane, and a tail. He begins with the ears, and Saba, whose profile kicks up its heels and flees from his memory, slowly and painfully enters the piece of paper, subdued by his patient, dirty little hand. The cabby's clumsy nag tosses her head, paws at the ground, snorts. She already has three legs visible and a fourth that is concealed by the traces and crossbar. Behind the horse is a wagon, and behind the wagon stands Mordechai in high-topped boots; he has to give him reins and a whip; when he tugs on the reins the horse will turn left. And how does a horse know it has to turn left? If it doesn't, it will trample the people lying on the pavement.

There are so many of them, and they all have to fit in here, propped up against the wall, stretched out on the pavement. Mordechai's wagon has to go in that direction, across this one small sheet of paper, and not jostle anyone. It's hard to do that when you're five years old. He scratches out and smears, completely covers the little drawing with paint. Yellow as the sun, red as blood, green as grass, black as night. The spots of color, interrupted by the white of the paper, become alive and powerful, the flush on his cheeks burns his scaly skin like fire. It's finished; he squeezes all the pencils into his fist at once.

They can go over to the inner courtyard and hang around near the shed. No one will bother them there. Leibuś, Roizele, and Surele look into each others' eyes. Leibuś is going to scratch his blisters. And Surele will carefully adjust the white kerchief on her head with her little fingers and gravely plant her dry, skinny doll's legs in the ruins. Roizele, wheezing from the effort, will drag her swollen, deformed foot, covered with horny, thick skin, through the dust. And this is how they'll play:

"Are you hungry?"

"Tomato."

"How much marmalade do you get on your rations?"

"Tomato."

And then he'll finish the game with a cunning question, "Will you eat a slice of bread?"

"I'll eat it, I'll eat it."

"Now you owe me a forfeit!"

He'll stretch out his hand for the white kerchief, and Surele will squeal and push him away. Roizele will kick the wooden clogs off her swollen feet with a feeling of relief and softly say, "Do it again. With me."

The swelling feels like it's burning inside the stiff clogs and the skin, rubbed raw, is covered with a sticky fluid that oozes from her foot onto the ground.

When Leibuś suddenly came down with typhus, Faiga couldn't find him. He had run away to Mordechai's stall and hidden himself there in his fever. He fell asleep inside the abandoned cab, under the raised hood, on the coachman's flowered quilt with the feathers coming out of it. He was asleep, and the horse was noisily ripping something with its teeth, snorting, tossing its head, and emitting piercing cries. It rubbed its neck against a plank in the manger for a long time. The hissing and buzzing of the circling flies, sated with the horse's blood, filled the green damp darkness, and liquid shivers flowed down the horse's back from its ears to its tail and from its rump to its hooves. An angry snort issued from its nostrils, and then a sad "Eeeeee!" That was the beginning of his typhus delirium, but who could have known that? Haskiel the janitor looked for him on Grzybowa Street, Faiga ran along the wall to the *Wache*, losing her shoes on the way, and Mordechai returned home at sunset, watered his horse, and found the delirious little boy. He carried him in his arms, across the courtyard, up to the fourth floor; Leibuś whimpered and the coachman whispered, "Sha, my little angel," and the tailor came running out of his basement apartment, sticking a needle into his lapel, and shouted, "Mordechai, where did you get such a big colt?"

The stamping of the excited mare could be heard from the dark stable. Rearing up on her hind legs, she strained against her tether and the chain jingled; she tossed her head and sent a piercing whinny from the inner courtyard.

Ernest says that Leibuś is good for nothing since he's had typhus, but Zyga has a knife with a corkscrew on it, can do everything with his left hand, and has promised to supply some jokes for the next issue of the *Chronicle*. He scatters witticisms about as if he's got a sackful of them, without cracking a smile, his face stony.

"Why isn't there any flour in the city?"

And after a moment's silence the answer issues from Zyga's lips: "Because lately the Germans have begun adding flour to the bread."

Empty, blind eyes watched them from the walls—advertisements for Zeiss lenses—and a blinding sun on a poster: RADION DOES YOUR LAUNDRY BY ITSELF. They were wandering around in the cellars of the old soapworks—Maria and Max Leder, Pharmaceutical Supplies, Laces, Soap, Dyes—to which Zyga had proudly brought David and Ernest when the shop was already closed forever. Descending into the extensive caverns in the underground of the abandoned warehouse, they passed recesses where water dripped and mold was growing; in the semidarkness they banged into vats that emitted deep bass echoes, casks from which dark blue and gray powders were spilling, and demijohns the color of green glass, nestled in wicker baskets. Some of these gave off the odor of resin, the aroma of flowers, honey, herbs, pinecones in the woods, while others gave off a hellish stench of pitch and sulphur.

"Phew."

"That's a strong poison, Albino."

Zyga had long since divided everything in the caves of the old warehouse into poisons and medicines. Ernest inquired in a matter-of-fact way, "Sh'maya, is that for rats or for people?"

Zyga thought a while and answered, "For rats, but it could be used for people, too."

Their voices resounded in that dungeon like shouts aimed into a deep well.

"Does it work?"

"And how!"

His hands stained with the sticky fluids, Zyga opened jars, flasks, bottles, and ominously hissing demijohns. He shook out a pinch from each container into their hands. He poured out whatever there was. They sniffed at it, hesitantly tried it with their tongues, sneezed in the clouds of dust. Zyga was having a ball in the rainbow of colors; he was covered with powder like a butterfly. He shouted from the ladder, "Well, how's it going?" He was all different colors.

"Listen, you guys, don't touch anything. You mustn't. There's wood alcohol, carbide, acids over there. They'll suffocate you, burn you, scald you."

Shuffling footsteps muffled a lisped, unclear complaint, a rebuke preceded by the knocking of a key against a wall. A clumsy shadow descended the stairs; in the semidarkness they could make out a figure in a gabardine approaching them with outstretched arms, shakily counting off the barrels it passed with an iron key. That was old Zelda, dragging her swollen legs. The demijohns hissed venomously. Her gray face and loose hair, the gabardine tied sloppily with a piece of string, the shuffling of her felt boots approaching them in the darkness, filled them with a more intense terror than the contents of the abandoned warehouse.

"Bing, bang!"

Headlong, pushing the helpless old woman out of their way, they ran up the stairs into the light of day, while she moved something around in there for quite a while still, feeling her way. Zelda had been the sole guardian of the cellar since Mania and Max Leder had fled the city in 1939 and crossed over to the other side of the Bug River.

"She's touched." Zyga tapped his forehead. "She's loony."

"Don't say that."

"She is. She gets up at night and wanders around the cellar, groaning, 'It's escaping, escaping. It will poison us all . . . the gas, the gas . . .'"

"What?"

"Barrels of carbide have been stored in this dampness for a year. Prussic acid, denatured alcohol." Zyga listed the chemicals.

"Don't say that."

"Do I feel like jumping," and he opened the door to the cellar. Taking a deep breath, he shouted into the darkness that was filled with old Zelda's groans, "Bing, bang!"

Driven away from there, they set off for the Westerns. Tom Mix, Ken Maynard—hey, those were the names of their crazy, unrequited, boyish love, a love that was serialized from week to week, and whose price in the marketplace was five groschen. Every adventure inside its blood-colored binding had thirty-two pages. In the frenzy of a headlong gallop along the desolate trails that the mail trains stealthily traversed, or on the range among herds of cattle, under the glaring sun of the Wild West, the law was upheld. A Colt drawn too quickly shows who's guilty; a Colt drawn too late means death. A free cowboy fires only once and always draws his gun last. The bullet pierces a barrel of water or the fetlock of an escaping horse; the warning shot knocks the hat off the bad guy's head. A cowboy fights with a bandit with no witnesses. And what if the sheriff's people come to the aid of the gang? The cowboy disarms the sheriff and pins his star to his own leather vest. Ken Maynard is a free cowboy. The broad brim of his stiff Stetson casts a grim shadow on his brow. A red scarf covers his face up to his eyes. He hides in the plains or wanders alone in the Rocky Mountains, saves the women in an ambushed stagecoach, and without warning frees prisoners who are under arrest. The sheriff organizes a posse and loses the trail; the horses are dropping from thirst, and the great Ken cannot be caught. His spotted mustang gallops to West City; at the bar stands a rider in a hat shoved defiantly down over his eyes. There's a commotion; the rescued ladies rush to hug him. An old farmer opens his mouth wide in amazement and stops chewing his tobacco.

"The great Ken is back!"

It was getting dark. They put down the old, well-worn Western from years ago. Ken Maynard was dying in the ruins on Waliców.

Outside the window the rough singing of Baruch Oks's gang could be heard, and Baruch and Long Itzhok were going from door to door in the apartment house with their hats in their hands. David heard the song breaking off in breathless wheezing, the squealing of hoarse throats. Coins wrapped in scraps of paper fell softly at their feet.

At this hour the pale green, snot-nosed little skeletons would run over to the inner courtyard outside the stable to watch Mordechai unhitch his horse, cover her with a saddle blanket, and give her water. He leaned a tin bucket against his knee, and the horse would carefully sniff the coachman's hand. She lifted her head and water dripped from her mouth. She was tearing something apart with her yellow teeth, and Mordechai carefully tilted the bucket for her. He tilted it, then poured the rest onto her cracked hoof, and the old mare turned around and walked off to her stall, audibly catching her horseshoes on the high threshhold. Will Ken Maynard succeed in escaping from the sheriff's men on this horse, with Malka in the saddle in front of him? The posse is approaching with fetters. Don't leave her, Ken! Ken Maynard smiles a carefree smile and pushes back the brim of his hat with the barrel of his gun. He turns in his saddle and his first shot hits its target. Mordechai's horse weakens, breathes heavily, stumbles, and falls. Ken Maynard stands over it, loosens its saddle girth, throws the saddle over his shoulder, but the dust is rising under the hooves of the pursuing horses and they're drawing closer, and the second bullet hits its target. Now they have all fallen; Count Grandi, too, has rolled over dead. Under the pine tree on the hill the farewell of the cowboy and the girl from Krochmalna takes place. Ken walks off into the distance and from afar a shout can be heard: "Eh, everything got screwed up like that because of those damned policemen!" He has to flee, but the hard-ridden nag is barely breathing. He won't be able to escape from the sheriff's men on Mordechai's horse. That horse was meant for pulling cabs; it could haul a passenger with a suitcase to the station, or Czerniatyński the lawyer to the café, or the Lewin girls along the boulevard, but only a wild mustang can gallop at full speed across the prairies.

When the horse was taken care of, Mordechai would sit in front of her stall on a pile of harness straps and wait for night to fall. His sad, pale gray eyes stared into space. The coachman's and tailor's voices circled lazily in the evening grayness of the inner courtyard.

"Yankiel, why did you come back?"

"For my needles!"

After listening to the radio broadcasts that urged all men to leave the city in 1939, the tailor had hastily bundled up his things and marched out to the highway with Max and Mania Leder. Swallowed up in the wave of refugees, they had marched eastward; and then, having reached the border, he ran away and returned to Krochmalna, behind the wall, embarrassed, as if he'd been out on an unsuccessful stroll.

Behind Mordechai's shoulders the mare's gentle snorting could be heard.

"Yankiel, you are incapable of crossing the border. In your place I would have crossed it three times back and forth with a lighted candle in my hand."

Yankiel opened the doors of the workshop and skillfully threaded his needle, squinting at the gold and gray sky.

"Let's say you would."

Mordechai, resting his gray head on his hands, mused, "A cherub with a fiery sword drove the Jewish tailor from the Gates of Paradise because the tailor did not know where he was going and did not know what he was returning to."

After it grew dark, Mordechai began throwing bricks out of the stall and carrying out rubble in a large bucket. He was secretly digging a passageway to the cellars of the destroyed outbuilding that lay under the pile of ruins; Haskiel the janitor was working on extending the passageway by breaking through the cellar walls of the neighboring apartment building and the laundry's storehouse. People said they had dug all the way through to the deep cellars that connected Krochmalna Street with the warehouses in the sub-basements of Hale.

The tailor disappeared into the depths of the basement, from where his voice could be heard: "Let's say you could. Regina, add some water!"

He shook the dying carbide lamp.

"Ach, this is a twentieth-century discovery. Hitler should be so healthy. Can you imagine what he's thought of? The painter! He tells you to sew by such a light; is it possible to sew by this? You can't even pray by the light of such junk. It's worse than *shabbos* candles. Feh, it's an insult."

Amidst the chaos of torn-up rails, pipes, coils of cables swaying in the wind, and the broken scarecrows of the chimneys left untouched by the flames and stretching now up to the clouds, the annex, gutted by fire, bent its convulsed, naked, dry skeleton over the courtyard, shedding plaster and sunlight-bleached wallpaper, story upon story, held up by fragments of severed, ruined staircases that climbed to nowhere. On the second level a mirror dully reflected the glow of the setting sun and a young birch tree dipped its roots into a pile of smashed bricks. On the fourth, an iron bedstead hung suspended with one leg over the abyss, under a lonely chandelier. Beside it, in a wide-open bathroom, against a backdrop of shattered sky blue tiles, a bathtub stood in its normal place, its rain-rinsed enamel gleaming. And in the basement, with a view into Mordechai Sukiennik's stall, the master sat at his tailor's table, pulling on his needle. A flying bomb had pierced the annex right down to the ground floor in 1939 and no one knew how the workshop had survived unscathed in the depths of the inner courtyard. When the ruins were partially cleared away, a twisted sign was revealed: TROUSERS VESTS SUITS TO ORDER ENTRY THROUGH THE COURTYARD AND DOWN THE STAIRS. It had been blown upwards by the blast and was hanging from the second story.

Yankiel Zajączek had a self-heating coal iron. When he touched it to damp cloth it filled the basement with noise and hissing. Steam billowed out of its open nozzle. The master would appear outside to catch a breath of air. He would grab the iron with both hands to heat it up. The iron flew from wall to wall, shaking the tailor with its weight, and he'd hang on comfortably, his wispy beard trembling. When the master's wife cooked beets for dinner, his beard was the color of amaranth; when she cooked rutabagas, it was the color of yellow flowers; when she cooked spinach, his beard was as green as a meadow. And on days when there was nothing for dinner, his beard returned to its usual mousy color.

"Before a man can even use his needle it gets dark. So when can he do his sewing?" The green flame of the carbide faintly illuminated the corners of the dark cellar. "Regina! Regina, add water," Yankiel hollered and shook the dying lamp. By its light, with the ruins of five stories over his head, David could barely read the letters that the tailor thrust into his hand.

They were old, well-worn, posted long, long ago.

V

They sleep and they beg.
Fumbling hands grope blindly for a tin can; withered limbs tense in vain on the paving stones. Unkempt hair touches the ground, pressing into the dirt of the dens where they sleep, into the dust of the ruins, tangled from sweat and matted with feathers; lice swarm over them.

Dried-out skulls with sunken eye sockets and sallow orifices set in yellow skin turn timidly to look at the people passing by. They reek of the fevers that are consuming these fading, helpless, mute skeletons. Life is departing from them, quietly burning itself out like a handful of damp carbide. They drag themselves along clumsily, clinging to walls for support, and when their brittle leg bones can no longer support their emaciated, starving bodies, they lie down in rows on the paving stones. Their skinny bare feet, covered with ulcers, protrude from under a sheet of dirty paper or an old newspaper. Their glassy eyes, turned toward heaven, are covered with road dust, burned by the sun. They shake their tin cans feebly, crawl over to the passersby and rub against their legs, stretching out their empty hands to them. Callused, filthy, oozing skin covers these gray skeletons like a rough, stiff shell. Clusters of swollen blisters spread over their faces like wildfire, eating into the skin.

"Cursed be the day!"

A contorted, greenish face, the mouth and beard stained with smudges of dried egg yolk. The chapped feet and arms are covered with rags, and a huge sweat stain is spreading across the man's gabardine. The holy man's yarmulke lies near him on the sidewalk; pedestrians throw alms into it, averting their eyes. He prays in the sunshine until he feels faint, grows quiet, and slips down onto the ground, and when he regains consciousness he gets up again and the street is inundated with the wailing and chanting of the swaying old man who incites all the beggars to join in his lamentations.

"Mister, toss me a five-groschen piece!"

Baruch Oks shouts as he runs past the holy man, "Rebbe, let me tell you the words of a woman who saw her husband covered with ashes and holding a crust in his hand. 'Enough, curse God, and drop dead!'"

He brushed against the man's rags in the crowded passageway and heard him answer mournfully, in his weak, groaning voice: "My legs are being kicked by . . . who are you, son of a Jewish woman?"

And Baruch Oks sang out in a falsetto, "I am an eye for the blind, a leg for the lame."

"That's good, I congratulate you." The holy man screwed up his eyes; he continued the conversation with sly clumsiness, weighing his slim chances. "And who was your teacher, my God-fearing boy?"

"Reb Itzhok Kohen."

"That's good, I congratulate you. Reb Itzhok Kohen? My, my, my, he's a pretty good rabbi. And who was your father that he wanted to have such a learned son?"

"No one in particular, a Jew."

"So throw a five-groschen piece into my hat and save an old man; I can't stand with my head uncovered in the sunshine for too long."

"Tell me, Rebbe, since when is it permitted to have your head uncovered?"

"Throw me a fiver," the holy man repeated, shaking his arm. "Throw it, son. It will be counted."

"Sure thing. I'm off."

Merchants walked by, stopping every now and then. They kept walking to the corner and back, bargaining out loud. They walked back and forth, looking at the porters. Stretched out lazily in the ruins, their sacks scattered about, the porters were napping, yawning, waiting for the smuggling hour. Mordarski spoke in a sharp, raised voice: "Things aren't going so well. I'll give half, and if the jump is a success and the porters return with the goods, Felek Piorun will get the rest."

"Pack it up, corpses!"

"Everything has to be figured out beforehand, how much for the porters, how much for the police. How much graft, how much profit. Am I supposed to hire people blindly for two whole days and risk my money, my hard-earned money, for a couple of sacks of meal? Who I am going to sell it to? To them, to the men lying in the street?"

"Pack it up, corpses. Bowls on your heads," shouted Henio the Herring. "Elijah is coming with his caravan."

There was a commotion among the beggars, a protracted rustling. Faces turned blindly, their eyes shut. Elijah's wagon, bumping along on the uneven pavement, emerged from Krochmalna Street and slowly moved through the alley, rocking from side to side. The rotten cart was transporting its dead load through the city. An OD man with a yellow armband on his sleeve, shouted, "Make room, don't sit all over the middle of the street. Make room, make room!"

The wagon plowed into the people lying in the street, and immediately an ugly, panic-stricken howl rose up, a beggars' chorus of eternal lamentations.

"Where are you going? Over cripples? Watch how you're driving!"

"Wait a minute, let me get up first."

"God Almighty, a person doesn't have a moment's peace. I just settled down, and now look!"

"Hit him with a tin can, with a can, that son of a gun!" A rusty tin plate flung by a weak hand flew up into the air, not very high, missed its target, and landed in the wagonload of naked corpses. Elijah stopped the wagon, not knowing what to do in that crowd. The little dead-end alley, blocked off by the wall, didn't leave him much room to turn the wagon around.

"Eh, move it, pick up that corpse. It's your uncle? Big deal; take your beloved uncle by his legs and drag him up onto the truck. One-two. Don't spare your arms. You owe him something, you young squirt. What's the matter? You think only the deceased should lie in this good spot with a view of the street, where you can always beg a few groschen? Your customers close their eyes and run across the street. Move it, one-two. What are you, a beauty queen? He's been sticking that swollen stump out in front of people for a week. It's a bore to watch him. You're drooling, you bungler! Your pus-filled eyes are popping out of your head! And who is going to be touched by that nowadays? You have to know how to beg. Listen to me, you SOB. Get hopping, move it."

Elijah kept on talking, dragging his load without haste, and with him was Avrum, the son of Haskiel the janitor, and an OD man who came to their aid. They had to lift the stiff corpse up as high as the wagon, swing it, and heave it onto the top of the pile. Its head and arms fell back heavily over the edge, so the youngest of them, Avrum, climbed into the cart and made room for the newcomer by stamping down the dead load. They moved on, then stopped again.

"Let the day perish wherein I was born, and the night in which it was said, 'There is a man child conceived,'" wailed the ragged holy man, extending his skinny, dirty arms to heaven.

"Greetings, honorable servant of the Lord!"

"Greetings, guardian of the morgue! Greetings, corpse bearer!"

"You have entered the house of the dead in your priestly robes?"

"Benighted drayman, the entire world is a house of the dead. Where am I supposed to move? From where? Here? Do what you have to do and don't waste my time."

Baruch Oks and his gang violently shoved their way to the front of the line formed by the crowds waiting their turn with basins and bowls and old cans, with whatever they had available—up to the head of the line that led to the Judenrat kitchen and stretched into the alley in a shapeless column. Beaten by the OD man, they scattered, screaming and whistling; they came back a moment later and pushed through to the cauldron, stoically enduring the blows, protests, and outrage of the crowd. Directly across from them—you could hit him if you threw a stone across the little square in the middle of the ruins—Moishe the Crip was guarding their bucket in an alcove inside the scorched gate. Baruch Oks returned.

"We've got to live!"

Henio the Herring followed him across the street, running after him and stopping to rest, eyes fixed on the can of soup he was carrying in his outstretched arms. They bent over and carefully poured it into the bucket, but Moishe the Crip shouted at them in rage, "That's all? Is that all?"

"I spilled a little," Henio the Herring confessed sadly.

"I'll spill you. You gobbled it up on the way back, you sack of bones. I saw you. Go back for more. Quick, march!" And Henio the Herring ran back to the line with his tin can, and his shadow flashed crookedly across the sunlit square. The Crip turned away and, holding his withered arm close to his chest, he used his healthy arm to chase flies away from the bucket. He kept his eyes fixed on the holy man's yarmulke, which was full of alms. The holy man was mumbling to himself; then he fell silent and put his head down. A beggar was crawling toward it, slowly and deliberately slipping along with his back pressed against the wall. With careful, precise movements, he searched his rags for lice.

"And what good things are the people of Israel eating today?" Elijah shouted across to David, who was standing closer to the cauldron.

But it was Baruch Oks who answered him, in a singsong voice, as if reciting a verse: "The people of Israel are eating vegetable soup with sour cream and dill. Do you like that?"

Henio the Herring pushed past David and barked, "Shove over. Make room."

"Today?" yelled Zyga. "Corpse soup. And for the entree, consumptives' phlegm."

"And tomorrow?"

Bored, Zyga patiently threaded the handle of his pot onto his belt. He freed his hands, stretched, and sighed loudly. Scorching heat billowed up from the ruins. David stood behind him, holding his aluminum canteen. It felt burning hot in the sunshine. It was the last usable item from his father's army equipment; they had kept it hidden for a long time.

"Tomorrow? Wounded patties with pus sauce."

Zyga's voice was swallowed up in the tumult. The crowd suddenly parted and then regrouped as a tight mass, having cast out into the middle of the street an old man and a little girl in a pink dress.

"She fainted! The poor thing, standing in the sunshine for so many hours, in such a crowd, I wouldn't wish it on anyone."

"She got heat stroke."

"People, why is it so wet over here?"

The old man waved his hat in front of the girl's face and begged for some water. A little cup of water! People must have stepped on her in the crush, because her pink dress was dirty and trampled on.

"Soup, sure thing," said Zyga. "Before you get to the counter the only thing left will be coffee brewed from used grounds. And for the guys, extra oaten beer. Why did you let Herring get in ahead of you, David? Kick him out of there, right away."

"You jerk," Henio the Herring hissed. "Don't be such a big show-off."

The holy man's skinny, filthy arms waved in the sunshine, casting fragile, quick shadows that the passersby stepped on.

"God of Abraham," he began. He pushed away the living skeleton that had come too close to his yarmulke. "And Jacob."

The beggar blinked his lashless eyelids. His hands, convulsively clutching a crumbled piece of bread, did not open; they were covered with a husk of sticky sweat. Smeared filth filled in the wrinkles in his loose skin and covered his torso, as skinny as a snake's body. He lifted the crumbled bread to his mouth and sucked on it. He crept away to a safe distance and turned to watch the holy man.

"God of Abraham, Isaac, and Jacob. Thou . . . Thou, who spake with the smoke of the burning bush. Thou, who secretly, behind the backs of the Jews, entrusted Moses with the tablets of Thy laws."

People walked past with full bowls, on their way home. The line edged forward step by step.

"Where's Egg Yolk?" shouted Baruch Oks. "Just let me get my hands on that creep."

Five-Fingers Mundek shouted across the square: "He's hotfooting it over! He'll be there in a minute."

Baruch Oks stepped out from the shade of the alcove. His leather jacket was slung over his shoulder. He put his hand on his forehead, looking sternly ahead of him, like Moses on the mountain looking down at the Jews.

"And what about that thief Herring?"

Five-Fingers Mundek swayed heavily down the other side of the street, approached the curb, and spat. "Everything's okay. Herring's getting close to the counter."

"Did you give him change?"

"I gave him, I gave him."

The merchants reached the end of the alley and turned back, gesticulating with tight movements of their hands, and stopping every now and then. Kepele the porter emerged from the ruins.

"Kepele, he's a little stinker who thinks he can frighten me with the hump on his back. That'll be the day! Tell him to look into his own heart. I spit on his lousy word of honor. *I* didn't rent two rooms and a kitchen. I rented two rooms and a kitchen for myself and one room on the next floor up for Kalman . . . If Jajeczny wants to meet him on the back stairs at night, let him; he can come, but he should remember that I'm the one who's feeding his bastards out of my pocket. He's such a good jumper? Oh, come off it. I sell people like him by the bushel and buy them back for half the price."

The cadaver hesitated a moment and then put the rest of the breadcrumbs on a saucer next to the low wall, and again, sliding slowly along the wall of the building, he tried to get close to the holy man's yarmulke without being observed. Moishe the Crip was waving his stump around gently, like a fin, driving the flies away from the pot, and didn't take his eyes off him.

"How many of you are there? First! Tell Jajeczny not to blow at the sun. And not to spit at the wind. Those are my last words. Tell him right now."

The holy man lamented, "Thou hast lifted me up and cast me down. Thou hast covered all my paths with dust and ashes. Hey you, scoundrel, don't you go throwing garbage into my hat! And I was made to wander about, exposed to the abuse of strangers—hey!"

The holy man bent down and began crawling on his knees, chasing after a coin that was rolling down the pavement. Then he stood up. "Lifted up, I was cast down. And all Thou wanted was to show others the reproaches of fate that fall upon the just, when they forget that they are made in Thy image and deserving of mercy, that they are guests among the creations of this earth, a crowd of coxcombs in the dust. We, Thy entire people now—hey!"

The holy man took aim with his withered arm, knocked the persistent cadaver out of his way, and got lost in the complexities of his psalm. Another holy man, who was standing near the first, took advantage of this and, lifting up his red beard and his torn shirtsleeves, spat out the verses in rapid-fire order.

"We, Thy servants. We, Thy children. We, Thy flock. We, Thy chosen people."

Baruch Oks ran out into the middle of the street, waved his black leather jacket in the air, and hollered, "Mundek, make a deal! Take the whole lot and have done with it. We've got to live."

Shouting, whistling, laughing, the gang descended on the cauldron inside the gate, mercilessly hooting at the OD man who was drowsily standing guard in the square.

Mordarski the merchant came to a dignified stop, thrust two fingers into his vest pocket, and dropped the loose change he found there straight into the holy man's yarmulke. Kalman Drabik did the same.

"It will be counted! It will be counted! We, Thy people . . ."

A porter was running after the merchants, clutching his trousers to keep them from slipping down. He was shouting, "Mordarski!"

"Not with me."

"He should be so healthy. He's a crook, not a merchant."

"Jajeczny, count your words. I have a feeling you've let fall one too many."

"I dragged those sacks like an ox and I risked my neck for him. There's no such thing as free labor!"

Mordarski the merchant spread his arms wide and humbly bowed his head. "Your own lips condemn you. Not I. And your words bear witness against you. Don't blaspheme, Jajeczny."

"Murder me. Go ahead and murder me, a father with children."

"I have time."

"Mordarski, don't be a capitalist. You're sucking my red blood like a louse and pulling in your own direction."

"You all live with me and each one pulls in his own direction." Mordarski lifted his hands as if in prayer. "What can I do? Losses today, profits tomorrow. The Lord giveth and the Lord taketh away, and there's no sense talking about it, my dear man."

"Did you see that? Look at him! Oh, oh, oh, that crook!"

"If I, a just merchant, I, Mordarski, who all my life, I, can be called a crook, then what should we call Him who created this world? And governs it with impunity from on high?"

"A crook! You greased the blue policeman's palm without blinking an eye, but you paid for my sweat with a slap in the face."

"Jajeczny, when my goods come back into my hands, I pay up. When my goods fall into someone else's hands, my porter pays. There's no two ways about it. Jajeczny, don't try any of your rabble-rousing against me in broad daylight."

Mordarski's constrained, measured gestures quieted the porter's rage and his irritation faded noticeably, burning itself out in impotent complaints as he walked behind the merchant, treading on his heels.

"Mordarski, be a mensch."

"To please you?"

A wave of consternation ran through the group of porters gathered in the ruins of the brewery. They stood up, feigning indifference, warming their faces in the sunshine, while they stole glances at the merchant. The scene on the street was still going on, lazily coming to a head like an inflamed boil that will burst eventually but not soon. The cowardly eruption of anger did not lead to a rebellion.

"Kepele, tell me what happened. Everything, in order."

"In order? This is how it was, in order. Mordarski wakes me up on Saturday at four in the morning like a dog and says he's got a deal for me. I open my eyes and already I'm wondering why I've opened them, because I've known him for fifteen years. What does Mordarski say? Mordarski says what he always says. This jump's guaranteed. I'm supposed to run and get Jajeczny; only the two of us will be in on the deal. What am I supposed to do, since I already have one eye open? I open the other eye. And I look at the street. It's gray, rainy, wet, my Saturday, and Mordarski's standing over me with an open briefcase. Do I know him or not? And it's the same thing every time. Okay, we'll go. I take my old quilt, Jajeczny has his ladder, and Mordarski vanishes on the way. You have to understand. I spread out the quilt, cover the glass, climb onto the wall, and I see Piorun's gang, in full strength, on the other side. There's no one he didn't bring along! From Kercelak, from Wronia. He had goons there he'd rounded up from all over Siberia. With sacks, spread out, waiting. Żeleźniak's wagon was waiting around the corner. And Felek himself was inside the gate. He didn't even look around carefully. Bam, the first sack. I take it from him, drop it, Jajeczny lugs it over to the gate. The second sack comes and then the pipeline's plugged up. What's going on? I give a look, and I see a cop running toward us at full tilt. Oy, was it hot; Jacob didn't sweat as much on his ladder when he counted the rungs to heaven as I sweated on mine. Felek Piorun shouts at his men: 'Retreat! The archangel's trumpeting!' It was as if a watchman was dragging me down onto that cop's head. There I was, watching that archangel from above the whole time, while he was moving around among them. There were so many of them . . . Me, I've got one leg on the wall, the ladder is creaking under me, I'm holding a sack a meter long, and a sliver of glass has poked through the quilt and is slicing into my knee. I can't get down and I can't stay up there. I don't know what to do. I bellow: 'Stand still!' Piorun's gang freezes. They stand there. With sacks in their hands. I'm here, the wall's here, the sacks are here, and the cop is beating on them. Piorun doped it out that he wasn't a regular sneak, just an innocuous fellow with a blue backside who'd stumbled across a watchman who showed him the way—and came at him from behind! Now the cop was as humble as could be. 'Gentlemen, what's going on here? They'll take my uniform away because of you. They'll throw me off the force, put me on trial.' Just like that, I swear. I yell from my perch, 'If only that's as far as it'll go.' And Felek chimes in, 'Never mind the uniform, I'll rip your skin off.' The cop looked at the gang. Such eyes. Bums, thugs, hoodlums, rounded up from all over the city, wherever they could be found. He can swallow one pill, but he can't cram them all into his gullet. By himself? With that tiny pistol? 'Gentlemen, if the gendarmes find you with those sacks, what am I supposed to tell them?' The headcheese went soft, it's our gain. One sack, another, my hands are numb, Jajeczny drags them over to the gate, and Felek hollers, 'Hang in there, chief! Stand guard and warn us!' And he took off."

"A blue policeman?"

"What else? A blue! A Pole! He went to the corner, stood guard, and sounded the alarm. How long did it last? A few seconds. And the sacks were on this side of the wall. Meanwhile my knee had puffed up, and the next day the archangel and the cop presented themselves to Mordarski. Mordarski panicked and paid them off for no reason at all."

The porters' laughter rose above the square.

"And he paid you off by screwing you? Eh, Kepele?"

"Oh, he's a skinflint!"

"Yeah, he screwed us. He didn't want to pay the gang. He smacked Jajeczny in the face, the quilt got torn to pieces, and that's all the good that came of it."

"Everything's fine. Couldn't be better."

The porters roared with laughter, rolling around on their sacks and pawing the air, like horses on a fine warm day.

"This jump's guaranteed!"

The line inched slowly forward, step by step, closer and closer to the coveted cauldron. The aroma of boiled cabbage leaves and sandy vegetables in a thin cream sauce wafted toward them—the daily summer menu of the Judenrat soup kitchen.

The skinny, filthy hands of the holy man fluttered in the air; his words were drowned out by the shouts of the other holy man, who ran into the middle of the square in a beggar's ecstasy. He lifted up his red beard and thrust out his short, torn sleeves, singing right in the merchants' faces. "Reveal to us the land of Canaan. Let me lay my weary head on the stones of Jerusalem. Transport us to the land of our fathers. Amen." And he stopped.

"Mordarski, I have witnesses," the porter yelled. He blocked his path and stood in front of the merchant.

"Jajeczny, I'm telling you, you don't have any witnesses."

"I do!"

"Ugh, the worst thing imaginable is when an idiot loses his mind!"

And the first holy man kept on, tirelessly: "We, Thy people, are like a tablet of the laws whose fragments I cannot piece together, nor can I decipher them. Therefore . . . It will be counted! God of Abraham, Isaac, and Jacob, have mercy on me, Thy priest and a priest for Thy people. Here I stand, a priest, imprisoned behind a wall just like my entire people, in the center of this city and the center of the world."

There was a third holy man, too, with feather-covered hair and a gloomy beard that grew wild like a forest that has never been logged. He was sitting hunched up on the pavement with his arms wrapped around his knees and his head bowed, staring at the ground and muttering rhythmically as he rocked back and forth.

"*Adoynoy*, the words of my prayer will not lighten the death of the Jews nor make them more worthy of Thee. Thou hast no punishment for our enemies."

"Jews, he's got all of us under arrest," Elijah cursed. He stopped his wagon in front of an impassive skeleton who stubbornly refused to get out of the way. "I work like an ox, I break my neck for a few coins, and someone like that lies down in the street, rolls up his long johns to expose a walnut-sized boil on his leg, and in a minute his hat is full of money!"

"Then change places with him, Elijah!"

"What do you think? It won't be long."

"I'll wait for you. I'll wait and I'll even make room for you beside me."

Long Itzhok shouted across the street, baring his rotten teeth. The second holy man began to sing out loud, moving even more brazenly into the middle of the street, and tearing at his red beard.

"Disperse the clouds. Disperse our enemies that burn our bones like dry straw. May a six-winged angel descend with the news. May he come and visit us."

The spell ended, he crowed and fell silent, and his short, torn sleeves dropped and hung on his breast, trembling slightly. The merchants passed by without stopping. He looked around helplessly at the third holy man, yielding his place to him.

The third holy man was lamenting, "*Adoynoy*, my prayer falls back to the earth, it cannot rise up to the heavens. For Thou hast no power in Thy right hand and no volunteers to sit on Thy left side. Amen."

"Phew," the second holy man whistled, astonished.

Kalman Drabik shouted across the street to a man who was leaning despondently out an open window and making some kind of signs.

"What's doing today? Beef, veal, or mutton?"

The man in the window gestured dismissively.

"I have no patience with his petty deals, and since he's still standing there why don't you cry from the rooftops that he can talk to me face to face at any time. I'll be on the wooden bridge at eleven and I'll wait for him. Yes, yes, on the wooden bridge. Even on Saturday!"

The window slammed shut and the merchant walked on, followed by the watchful eyes of the porters.

And the first holy man kept on, tirelessly: "Lord, dost Thou see this wall? This is one side of it. And over there is the other side. And Thou alone canst change this. The north and the south face each other, but they are far apart. Only a bird can fly over this wall. A bird can see the entire wall from on high. And Thou. And Thou, amen."

The second holy man began chanting mockingly: "But why? Why should a bird fly across it? What tree would it alight on? Under whose window? And to whom would it bring news? And who . . ."

The first holy man stared at him glumly and said, "All right, all right, go on."

"And who . . ."

"Well, go on, keep it going."

In the meantime, the merchant, who was closer to the redhead's begging tin, passed him by. They stared at each other; their beards stuck out and they looked like goats who might begin butting each other at any moment. The third holy man lamented without looking up: "Women give birth to dead infants and devour them. Brothers brandish knives against brothers. Fathers drive their sons in front of bullets, saying, 'Go, go and bring back bread to my house or spill your blood on the ground.' Old or young, people are dying like cattle on the thresholds of strangers. *Eyli, eyli shebashomayim!* Thy people are dying and Thou lookest on and givest no sign. Dost Thou find naked life unpleasant? Is our death unpleasant to Thee?"

The first holy man wheezed and got his voice back. "Here am I—," he began, and broke off.

A passerby bent over the redhead's tin can, fulfilled his obligation, and walked away with a light heart. Then a second passerby did the same. The first holy man shook his tin furiously with his thin, filthy hands.

"Here am I, Thy holy man, lifting my hand, and even if Thou must smite in Thy righteous anger, now and forever, whenever a Jew lifts his hand against Thee and blasphemes . . . Here am I, for those who have gone, for those who will come . . ."

The heavy, unuttered blasphemy hung in the air.

"And where do you grow those cucumbers of yours, little boy?"

"In the ruins."

His head shaven after his bout with typhus, Leibuś was pushing a small four-wheeled cart full of scraggly, yellowish-green seedlings down the middle of the street, oblivious to the obstacles in his way. Eliahu shouted delightedly from his place in the line, "Cucumbers grow better in a dump!"

"You can laugh. I know."

"No. No."

Sweat stains spread over his coat. The first holy man coughed drily and again got lost in the intricacies of his psalm, hoarse, exhausted by his hours-long lamentation. His voice broke off.

"I say. I say and I thunder . . . Didst Thou wish to extinguish the world with Leviathan?"

"Sss," the second holy man hissed. A passerby let a coin drop. He swiftly slipped it into his pocket. "It will be counted!"

The first holy man fell silent, bowed his head. He gently shoved aside the cadaver, who, having thrown down his bread and tin bowl near the wall, was crawling enthusiastically toward the pile of alms. Then he returned to his blasphemous prayer. The skeleton, pushed away, suddenly shrieked, and began moving around like a blind man with outstretched arms, collecting dust from the paving stones. The bread thrown near the wall was already gone. Moishe the Crip turned away, disappointed. And Long Itzhok sat on the curb, digging his teeth into the last crusts.

"Chaim, take the pot and come back," yelled Baruch Oks. Flies circled intently above the full bucket, and sticky streams of slops seeped into the dust of the street.

"I'm coming!"

A shot was heard and a man screamed. Suddenly there was the stuttering of an automatic rifle and bullets were whizzing in the ruins, raising clouds of dust. The holy men fell flat on their faces. The wall that barred the end of Walicόw concealed from them the crowd of running soldiers who, shouting and stamping, continued to pursue someone for some time. There was a commotion. First the merchants fled, trotting laboriously, flinging their legs in front of them; behind them, the porters disappeared into the ruins. Elijah hid behind the corpse wagon. The crowd waiting in line began to seethe, it swayed anxiously, but it didn't move away from the Judenrat kitchen. The chase vanished in the direction of Hale and Żelazna Brama Square. In the silence that now reigned, Baruch Oks's mocking voice could be heard. He stood in the center of the little square, his black leather jacket flung across his shoulder, squinting in the bright sunlight.

"Ay ay ay, now that's some Leviathan!"

Five-Fingers Mundek, his broad shoulders swaying, ambled away without undue haste from the spot where the holy men were prostrated on the ground. With a slight, rapid movement, he slipped the coins into his pocket and tossed the black yarmulke behind him.

Empty, lightweight, it fluttered in the air and fell softly to the sidewalk.

"It will be counted."

He bowed his head and winked at Baruch. His lips stretched wide.

"A scandal," shouted someone in the line.

"Guard! Over here!"

The beggars lifted their heads. The redhead opened one eye, closed it, opened it again. The shots could no longer be heard. He flung his short, torn sleeves in front of him and carefully moved one knee. He thrust out his red beard and wagged it from side to side. And sobbed, "Thou hast no Jerusalem for us."

The third holy man sobbed, "Be Thou stern but just, our Lord."

The first holy man sobbed, "Be Thou merciless but not cruel, our Lord."

The second holy man sobbed, "Be Thou our executioner, but do not lend support to our executioners."

The third holy man sobbed, "Be Thou our torturer, but do not lend support to our torturers."

The three holy men began wailing in unison, like children. "Be Thou our eternal torturer, but do not rejoice with our torturers."

Baruch Oks's gang gathered around the full bucket. They knelt down, inhaling the faint aroma of the gruel in the dust of the ruins. Moishe picked up a ladle made from an old jam tin and dipped it into the bucket, convulsively pressing his deformed arm to his side. Kuba the Gelding shoved Chaim aside and held out his bowl first, then bent over the bucket, his face tense. Henio the Herring licked his wet lips, which were swollen and ulcerated from psoriasis, while Mordka, squinting, inhaled the odor of rotted, year-old cabbage. Yosele Egg Yolk watched Moishe's hands greedily, as if his protruding frog's eyes would leap out and splash into the watery gruel.

"Give it to him." Baruch Oks pushed Kuba out of the way and dragged little Chaim forward by the nape of his neck. "You bunglers! He should be first today. He went there and back four times."

Five-Fingers Mundek gloomily smoked a cigarette behind Baruch Oks's back. Long Itzhok sidled over to them, drawn by the smell of the Judenrat gruel. His eyes were glassy and his forehead soaked with sweat from stuffing himself with the clayey rationed bread. He stumbled heavily, fell against the wall, and hiccupped.

"That's enough for today. You've had enough, Itzhok." Five-Fingers Mundek shoved him so hard he fell down in the dust like an empty sack, his face on the paving stones.

The tin cans swayed, passing the living cadavers lying against the wall. The crowd was returning from the Judenrat kitchen, pursued by their cries.

"There is no Jerusalem for us, none!"

The tin cans swayed uncertainly in their hands and the gooey gruel ran over the brims, scalding them. David, Eliahu, and Zyga, exhausted, were returning late in the afternoon, carefully carrying the containers from which the gruel splashed onto the sidewalk. They left behind them Waliców Street and the uproar from the wailing, imploring beggars.

"We are perishing, and the hangman walks around free among the living who sing his praise. We are perishing, and the strong revile our death. We are perishing, and our names vanish with our lives, for Thou dost not desire that we should have witnesses. We are perishing, we, the ancient guardians of Thy laws and faith, and with us perishes Thy faith and Thy law on this earth. The branch will never turn green again. The mature fruit will not yield seeds, the grapes will wither. Lord, henceforth Thou shalt rule over a wilderness . . . The earth is naked. And every trace of Thy creation shall perish, amen. Amen. *Rakhmunes, gite mentshn. Rakhmunes, rakhmunes! Gite mentshn, hat rakhmunes, varft a shtikele broyt. Broyt, broyt . . .* You dead men, cast some bread for the departed."

The mangy, skinny nag strained and pulled the wagon full of stiff skeletons, and Elijah walked beside her, holding the loose reins. The road from Waliców to Okopy was long and sown with corpses.

"Where are your eyes, you brat? Get out of the way! Can't you see?"

Ernest comes running, waving his shoes at them. The air is drenched in bleeding, darkening sunlight. Ever since his feet began to swell, he'd been trying to sell his shoes in town, but he couldn't find a buyer; then the swelling subsided on its own, but he walked around barefoot because he was more comfortable that way. Now he was glumly waiting for them to return, and the sunburned skin was peeling off his reddened nose.

"Do you know what happened?"

They don't let him speak. Zyga punches Ernest's frail muscle so he'll feel it. Eliahu energetically exclaims, "Gentlemen," and puts his tin of soup on the ground. "I've got a deal in mind. A golden deal, only you have to trust me. Well, what do you say?"

But Ernest insists, "Do you know what happened?"

Zyga interrupts him raucously, infuriated by Ernest's mournful voice: "Baaa, the goat is bleating, baaa. Say what's what, Albino, and leave me in peace. Is the Vistula on fire?"

"Well?" asks Eliahu. "Is it standing?"

"The wall," David interjects.

And Ernest repeats after him, but it's obvious that something else is troubling him, "The wall."

It's not at all clear what's on Ernest's mind. It is dark inside the gate and silent, the silence broken by a loud yawn that suddenly escapes through an open window; somewhere nearby a carbide lamp hisses poisonously; Nathan Lerch is calling to someone from his second-floor window; on the fifth floor, Judah Papierny sighs painfully, propped on his elbows on the windowsill; in the courtyard, leaning against the far gate (which frames in an arc the red sea of the ruins and the distant, brown silhouettes of people walking across it), stands redheaded Estusia, with her hair hanging loose in the sunshine, raising her eyebrows and hesitatingly, questioningly, pointing a finger at herself; somewhere a door is slammed shut; and from below, from the cellar in the second courtyard, the tailor's despairing cry can be heard, "Regina, Regina, pour me some more water!" A dull rumbling can be heard from Mordechai Sukiennik's stable.

A face that had been blotted out of memory emerges from the shadows and Uncle Yehuda stands above them, his arm slightly extended. The last, low rays cast the color of pale dust onto the blond growth on his face. They gently stain his pale forehead, cling to the white shirt that can be seen under his open overcoat.

"Little scamp." He warmly draws David to him. "You're still alive? How are things with Yakov, at home?"

David looks into Yehuda's face, into his bright, drily squinting eyes, and feels no joy. He points out a rickshaw that is lying on its side, parked in a corner of the courtyard, resting in its usual place with one wheel in the air. It's a sign that his father has come home and taken the other wheel with him so that no one will ride away with the cart during the night.

"Oh, he must be home already."

"And you? What are you up to, scamp?" Taking in at a glance the pots standing on the ground, he adds only, "Ah yes," and disappears into the stairwell.

Ernest, who had kept quiet in his presence, says, "Do you know? You don't? Then you'll find out . . . The janitor hacked Mordechai's horse to death!"

"Into pieces," Leibuś repeats after him softly. His gray little head, shaved bare during his bout with typhus, sways on his frail neck, and his protruding ears look enormous.

"Whaaat?"

"Yup. With an axe."

"With an axe, an axe," Leibuś repeats.

"Quiet!" Eliahu cries.

And it became quiet.

"It was like this," says Ernest. And then he starts telling them the story. In the afternoon, while they were standing guard near the Judenrat kitchen on Walic101w, Surele, the janitor's littlest treasure, died. At first, it was completely quiet in the janitor's flat, but then suddenly Haskiel charged out into the courtyard and started flailing with his axe. Too bad they couldn't have seen him. He ran around in the courtyard and shook that axe in broad daylight. Running and hollering. Everyone come on down, he'll organize matters right away and feed the entire tenement. Bring a cleaver, a knife, whatever you have. Come on down. And so it started. Mordechai Sukiennik and Żeleźniak were drinking on Grzybów Street, and the horse had spent the whole day at its empty trough. And Haskiel knew this very well. He went there and whacked her with his axe! On her head, but his arm was already weak. On her neck, on her back! The mare was tethered with a chain and could only kick her heels, and blood covered the stable. The horse collapsed. In the meantime, people stood around, head to head, and waited. They were watching what would come of this, and Haskiel exhausted himself. Then Kalman Drabik came home, the butcher who lives on the third floor. He doesn't do any butchering anymore and he closed down his pork-butcher's shop a long time ago, but once a butcher always a butcher, and every week a smuggler comes to him with a cut of pork and kielbasas. People, what is this? A butcher shop or a slaughter of innocent creatures? Imagine bungling a job like this, beginning it and not finishing! He yelled and he yelled. And Haskiel the janitor said excuse me, he begs this Kalman's forgiveness, but there's abject poverty here, typhus and dysentery, the kids are dying like flies, and there's no end in sight. Others could say the same thing. That's how it is! Tell him. They all said the same thing, horse meat or not, *treyf* or kosher, you have to put something into your pot. Mordechai? They'll pay Mordechai, they'll take up a collection now and pay for the lost horse. For the meat. But that's not what bothered Kalman, who was a guild butcher. It was just that that's not how horses are slaughtered.

He showed them how, and he had golden hands. First he clubbed the mare between the ears with a wooden hammer, and next he took a long, sharp knife, ran his finger down its cutting edge, and drew the edge once across her throat. Then he drew it across once more and the job was done. No one even knew exactly when it happened. That's how quick he was. Done. And before the meat grew cold the people surrounded it. Kalman Drabik the butcher said, "Carve it up." And they all flung themselves on the mare and began cutting her up, using whatever they had—a knife or a cleaver. They went at it for about ten minutes until all that was left on the ground were her front legs with their hooves, the head with its mane, a red ribbon, her tail, and her intestines, but Nahum Szafran ran over to the intestines, scooped them up into his wheelbarrow and, straining against the weight, wheeled the whole thing into the ruins where the deportees were camped. And when Mordechai Sukiennik came home, only a bloodied hide was lying in the stable. He pounded his head with his fists, ran from floor to floor, hammered on all the doors shouting that this would be the death of him. He'll hang himself, he'll go and drown himself in the Vistula in a moment. He'll run over to the *Wache*, stand in front of the gendarme with his cap in his hand, and beg him to take pity and shoot him, because there is nothing he can do on this earth without his nag, with a wagon but without a horse.

"Me, the last coachman on Krochmalna? That such a thing should happen to me!"

Mordechai survived his horse; he didn't die of grief, he didn't hang himself after his loss, he didn't drown in the Vistula. He chopped up his wagon, he chopped up his cab, and he used the wood to keep warm all the next winter. But he continued to work with horses until the end, almost until the end. He worked as a Judenrat employee, driving the blue and yellow omnibus through the Big Ghetto—a horse-drawn Jewish tram with a Star of David painted in front and in back. Down Żelazna, Gęsia, and Nalewki Streets. "Mordechai, Mordechai, snap your whip!" The old cabby once again sat up high and towered over the crowd on his coachman's seat; from there he shouted encouragement at his moribund nags in his peculiar, forgotten, ancient language, while inside, on the hard benches of the omnibus, a crowd of lice-infested passengers jostled and bounced. "Mordechai, Mordechai, snap your whip!" And when in that July, the famous July of nineteen hundred forty-two, the police vans invaded Krochmalna and a policeman stood in the courtyard and yelled, "Jews, come out! It's time!" and began translating the Germans' orders, and urged them to come downstairs because nothing was going to help them in any case and the same fate was awaiting them all, and he would drag them out from their corners by their beards if they didn't come down at once—then Mordechai locked the stable with a padlock, threw the key into the rubble, and was the first to come out and stand in front of the building.

Under his arm he carried an old feed bag, and in this bag he had a knife, a strap, and a piece of dried bread. On his way across the courtyard he stopped once, knocked on Zajączek's basement door, and shouted, "Yankiel, are you coming?"

❀

VI

In the corner of the gray envelope is a little two-shilling stamp, as blue as the sky above the Promised Land. On the stamp is a stooped-over farmer and an upright menorah. The farmer is cutting back a vine to form a grape arbor. The menorah lifts up its arms to the sky; the crippled plant will raise its new growth to the sky, survive, and produce fruit.

There are seven days in a week, a menorah has seven flames, and seven shoots climb up the arm of a grape arbor. The two-armed grapevine and the menorah both grow from a single trunk. On holy days the arms of the silver candelabrum glitter with the flames of candles, and the clusters of the fruit-bearing vine glitter with bunches of sweet berries.

Ela's letters were written under the desert sun. One of her postcards was so strange and incomprehensible that it frightened him. The glossy picture postcard depicted a city full of color and life, huge, as full of movement as Babylon, and on the other side were a couple of obscure sentences. Paris tears her heart to pieces. Autumn makes it even more melancholy, and life is beautiful! What does that mean? The postcard was a quiet disappointment to the Zajączek family. Her letters had made the rounds before, and there were sad holes where the stamps had been, because David had torn them all off. He knew the words practically by heart. Greetings and wishes for good health were in the first lines of the letter: to her noble father Yankiel and her good mother Regina, who brought her into the world. It is very hot here, dry. When you work in such sunlight, sweat pours over your eyes. But she is well. She sent spectacles for her father and a scarf and slippers about three weeks ago. Has the package arrived yet? She wants to know, so please write. Soon the lemons will blossom and the happy holidays will be here. When will they be able to sit down and have a Seder together? Be of good cheer, good cheer.

In the second letter she had gone to the city, rested her head on the Wailing Wall. She often thought about her beloved parents. Why has fate (a streak of black ink, censored). But it's nothing. They will celebrate Sukkoth together; all her hopes are focused on this. They will take their tents and set them up in the vineyard. The holiday will come, and with it, true joy; the young girls will dance, the boys will sing, and her beloved old folks will look upon all this, clap their hands, and sip wine. Does Mama still remember that silly little bower that Father constructed from flowerpots in the hallway? She can't forget it. The beautiful, dear memories of childhood. Our life (censored). So they should keep warm. She sends greetings to the whole family, to everyone, and will stop for the time being. When will they write again? A thousand kisses. Be of good cheer! This letter was marked with black ink, and the black German crow sat on the envelope. Yankiel Zajączek had a thick gray envelope full of stamps and seals from the foreign department. Whose hands touched those letters on their long journey? Who will decipher the inked-out words? The tailor turned the letter over and over, helpless, then thrust it into the boy's hands. He was always calling David to come over, as he had when the letters were still going back and forth. How many times? And he would beg, "Come here, you'll read to me a little, boy." He shook his beard, wiped his hands as if he wanted to grab him, the wire-rimmed spectacles slipped low on his nose, and pure, bright tears gathered in his eyes.

"I don't want to," he said, and looked indifferently at the rain-splotched mirror that dangled from the first floor amidst the ruins.

"Come, David, I'll sew you a pair of trousers. Nice ones, made from twill."

"With suspenders or a belt? A belt, Yankiel, a belt!"

"So be it, my good little boy, and you'll read me my Ela's letters for a while? It's the last time I'll ask."

Yankiel reached out stiffly to touch David's face with his coarse hands with their pricked, black fingers.

"I don't want to anymore," he said. "No, no," and he ran to Mordechai's stable, and from there, cutting across the ruins, he raced over to Walicόw and the Judenrat kitchen, passing the dens where the deportees lived.

Long Itzhok had already left the stable, driven out by the cabby on the eve of the green holidays, when, as was his custom, Mordechai Sukiennik cleaned his dark stall. That year, Baruch Oks's gang was terrorizing Walicóws and Krochmalna with their songs. In broad daylight and with horrifying self-possession they would attack the stalls; the beaten merchants dispersed silently and then came back. They prowled the length of the wall, setting upon the smugglers and fighting them fiercely for their goods. They had grown fangs and claws, and their hands reached out automatically at the sight of bread. Long Itzhok would run up to a passerby on the street, grab the loaf of bread from under his arm, and right in sight of the man whom he'd just attacked, he'd gulp down the rationed black bread, coughing and spluttering under the man's blows and turning blue in the face in his haste.

Whenever David was on his way to the Judenrat kitchen with his tin can or to the store with his ration cards, he was filled with fear of the long black fingernails, the dry arms, the pus-infected eyes in the pasty dead face distorted by the grimace of hunger. The only thing the man owned was the louse-infested shirt on his back. He also had wooden clogs and denim shorts that he had begged or stolen, and that hung down to his knees. Long Itzhok had turned up here on the first day in a transport of deportees. The first to arrive were Faivel Szafran, his two sons, Nahum and Shulim, and his daughter, Esther. Long Itzhok followed them; they came from the same region. During the winter of the first year of the war, railroad cars filled with bodies which had been stripped of their clothing, the dead and the living embracing each other, frozen as stiff as stone, were opened up on the outlying tracks of the freight yard. They came back to life only inside the wall, on the streets of the overpopulated city—and they died in those streets, in the ruins, in the hallways of the tenement houses, in attics and cellars, wherever they managed to squeeze in.

An enormous crowd flowed down these streets, and Faivel Szafran, Esther, Nahum, and Shulim stayed on Walicóws. Standing on the alien pavement, Nahum handed Shulim his heavy load and kissed the fringes of his *tzitzith* or perhaps the torn strips of the rags that were falling off him. Shulim had *peyes* on his temples, wisps of sticky, dirty hair growing over his ears. They spent that first day wandering helplessly along snow-covered Krochmalna Street, humble and quiet, lacking the courage to stretch out their hands for alms, shunned by the people in the street for whom they had suddenly become beggars. Soon the news spread through the alley that they had fled in the night from a burning house of prayer, escaping with their lives and the Torah scroll. They had sought out their relatives behind the barbed wire of a nearby town, had stayed for a while in the attic of the community center, and then had fled onwards, leaving the embers behind them, until they reached a tiny provincial town from which the Germans were deporting the ghetto population to Warsaw by train.

The four of them knocked at doors, lamenting as they stood in the hallway. Nahum and Shulim struggled with the heavy scroll that they had carried with them in their flight.

"They're clever ones; they've latched onto something," Haskiel the janitor said when he saw them. "They knock at your heart, hiding behind the Torah. Who could do more?"

The fire illuminated their dark faces for a long time; its wild glow was reflected in their eyes.

In the ruins of Waliców a crowd of beggars camped day and night, and the deportees found places among them. They slapped some bricks together to make stoves and spread their sleeping mats in the shelter of bombed-out rooms. They got their water from the apartment house and on cold nights they slept in the stairwells; as time passed they began to occupy the apartments that were vacated by those who had died of typhus or starved to death. Reb Itzhok took them in at the illegal synagogue on Ciepła Street, where they spread out their trophies on the platform of the *bima* and the ark amidst the crowding and the tumult, dropping their lice on the crumbling old tapestries. Reb Itzhok lobbied the Judenrat for ration cards for the deportees and used the contents of the synagogue collection box to buy meals for them from the Judenrat kitchen; a certain baker on Grzybowska Street, on the other side of the wall, sent his children over to Ciepła Street twice a week with bread so the old rabbi could distribute it. Many people preferred their dens in the ruins to the crowded conditions in the little synagogue and went back to Waliców, taking along whatever rubbish and junk, mattresses and broken crockery they could find.

Sweat-soaked clothing was hung out to dry on lines. Linens,

quilts, and blankets fluttered in the wind. When Reb Itzhok appeared among them, they gathered around him in a circle.

"My lambs," he would say. "My louse-infested lambs. Who is better off? You celebrate the Sukkoth holiday all year long."

They laughed, whistling, hawking, coughing. Reb Itzhok removed his black hat and brushed off the yellow dust that seeped out of the ruins.

"And I? What can I do for you? I don't know the difference between dysentery and typhus. Better I should bring Obuchowski to you."

And he did bring Dr. Obuchowski, who trudged through the rubble heaps of the ruins with a stethoscope in his ears and a white lab coat over his overcoat. Using force, the two of them pulled apathetic specters out from their dens and dragged them to the medical post, accompanied by the sobbing of their families.

"Typhus shots. Everyone downstairs." Haskiel the janitor hammered on a piece of rail as if sounding an alarm.

An open satchel with the doctor's instruments. In front of it, a long line of people, all skin and bones, all with their sleeves rolled up. Dr. Obuchowski stuck them, looked at their abscesses, listened to their complaints. He put his stethoscope between the ribs of skeletons, sighed, and, distracted, stared straight ahead into the swaying ruins from which the yellow dust was rising, thought for a moment, and wrote a prescription. The skeletal men took off their shirts reluctantly, averting their eyes; the children who were brought to him watched the doctor's movements disapprovingly.

Estusia Szafran came out of the janitor's room with a basin on her hip, stepping gracefully across the rubbish heap. Dr. Obuchowski made a face, dipped his hands in the basin, regarded the gray towel with a pained expression, and called out, "Next!"

Swollen Riva appeared, and behind her came Roizele with her pinched, dark little face. Dr. Obuchowski wrinkled his brow and pushed his lips out with his tongue to make himself look like a gorilla. Roizele began to laugh in a quiet little voice. Relieved, he took Riva's hand. She towered above the seated man like an enormous vat. From head to foot she was covered with ulcers caused by malnutrition, and every time she moved, her whole body shook with fine tremors. She had an emerald-colored woolen cap on the back of her head that covered her disheveled black hair. The smile vanished from Dr. Obuchowski's face.

"Abdominal edema? Everything for the people, Mrs. Ajzen. It happens. Nothing raw, please. Gruel. That means recook the Judenrat kitchen's *Wassersuppe* at home. Take the vegetables out and press them through a sieve. Add a bit of flour to the gruel and feed it to her with a thoroughly dried rusk of rationed bread. It will be delicious! And if you should have a bit of horse meat, oho! Grind the meat. Thank you. Next!"

The skin had pulled away from the suppurating calf, revealing the hollowed-out muscle. Shulim Szafran waited with his trouser leg rolled up, barefoot, displaying his foot, which would not fit into his wooden clog. With his pincers Dr. Obuchowski tore away a strip of the abscess. Shulim gently turned to look at him.

"What is it, my dear? Phew! Come to the clinic with this. From ten to twelve in the morning, daily. Don't poke at it, don't touch it with your dirty hands. Next!"

Long Itzhok, hunched over, held onto his trousers with a pained gesture. Dr. Obuchowski pulled down his eyelid, pressed his abdomen.

"Stupidity plus galloping dysentery. You've stuffed yourself with rutabaga again, you good-for-nothing. With your delicate tummy, raw vegetables mean death. You could have cooked them. And don't tell me you didn't have any fuel. No one will believe you. Where did you get so much food from? Ten healthy men would have rolled over and died in your place. Nothing raw. At all. Thank you. Next!"

"I'm wounded! Let me through to the doctor!"

There was a commotion in the line and then Five-Fingers Mundek pushed to the front, wearing an outsized sling around a bundle in which he'd wrapped his injured finger. Dr. Obuchowski smiled at the sight of him.

"At last, something worth looking at. Show me. A torn nail? I understand. A potato peel, a rag on top of that, then a red thread, and keep it wrapped up like that for two days. You can tear up your bandage. And if you don't recover, I'll kill you. March! Next!"

Faiga turned Leibuś's face toward the doctor without saying a word. The boy smiled timidly, rubbing his cracked lips with his fist. His shaved skull, bald after his typhus bout, swayed on his thin neck. Dr. Obuchowski removed the stethoscope from his ears.

"Go immediately to the pharmacy on Chłodna Street, you know where, don't you? It's a few steps from here. Tell them to give you a bottle of cod-liver oil. It costs a few groschen, perfect for what you can afford. One tablespoon three times a day. You can dip rusks in the oil, color his soup with it or even his potatoes. I have never tasted that disgusting stuff myself, Leibuś. They had to hold my nose and force it into me. But nowadays? There's no choice. Thank you. Next!"

They were standing behind Mordechai Sukiennik's stall, deep in the second courtyard, on the spot where the cabby used to throw out piles of rotten straw and manure. A patch of light earth lay like a hump over the hastily smoothed-over rubble. Eliahu was hammering stakes into the ground. The line in front of the doctor was growing smaller, and his crackling shouts echoed ever more quietly through the nooks and crannies of the ruins.

Next . . . ext . . . ext.

The wind snatched whirling dust clouds into the air. They floated back down in a lazy, spiraling dance. Eliahu grabbed his spade.

"You mean I owe you a perfect Australia with a kangaroo and three Luxembourgs for that damaged stamp that's missing a corner and has such a worn-out spot on it?"

David stubbornly repeated, "It's a Madagascar," and wouldn't lower his price.

The ill and decrepit were dispersing, and the armchair stood by itself in the ruins of the nearly deserted square. Exhausted, Dr. Obuchowski, smoking a cigarette, leaned back and stretched his stiff muscles. Haskiel would take back the chair when he left. Chaim the Orphan raised clouds of dust as he shuffled over in his sandals and bowed politely. A frozen, still face; the eyelids held partially closed with great effort. He waited patiently; stretched out his neck. Dr. Obuchowski looked at him attentively, wincing while he smoked.

"You're still alive? I wouldn't have thought so. The worst mistake in my career. Chaim, you're going straight to the hospital with me. Just wait a few minutes. Next!"

He threw away the cigarette.

Next . . . ext . . . ext echoed through the nooks and crannies of the ruins.

Eliahu shoved his spade into the ground and wheezed. The blade was wedged in the rubble of bricks lightly dusted with earth.

"I'll give you the Australia with the kangaroo. *Or* three Luxembourgs."

"I won't take it," David insisted. "The Australia with the kangaroo *and* the three Luxembourgs."

"Keep talking."

Eliahu waved his spade. David hunkered down on his heels, rested his elbows on his knees, put his face in his hands, and watched him attentively.

"What are you going to plant here in your garden?"

"Tomatoes," Eliahu wheezed. "It's just the spot for them. It gets sun all day long."

"What about the seedlings?"

Eliahu had gotten hold of seedlings, but for some reason they hadn't done well. Their skinny, leggy stems had begun to droop and the leaves fell off, and then they dried out beyond all help although Eliahu spent entire days in his garden, watering them nonstop until the thin layer of dirt he had brought there became saturated, was washed away with the mud, and the dry brick rubble showed through. The damaged Madagascar was sold for three Luxembourgs, the dried vegetable corpses lay out in the sunshine all summer long, and the two of them continued to come here to sun themselves and to kneel on the little field, carefully fingering the few clumps of black turnip and onions that came up. They gnawed at the pale green leaves, sucking on their bitterness. In Haskiel's garden, which was next to theirs, grew the vegetables that the janitor and his daughter were raising. Roizele's little skeleton was shedding its skin in the searing heat. David and Eliahu looked at the luxuriant feathery tops of the carrots and celery, the patches of blossoming potatoes, the rows of sturdy limas and green beans. One night they sneaked into the garden and ran wild like calves that have been let into the yard. A light breeze caressed their faces; waves of warm dust swirled up from the ruins. When somewhere near the wall a beaten Jew began groaning and complaining, a brick fell next to them, knocked down in a panic.

"Get going; get out of here this minute!" A specter in rags stood frozen at the shop door; the wakened cabby grumbled. "Look at me. And then at yourself, Itzhok. There's not a single louse on me. But on you? An entire regiment is on the march, complete with band. Lie down. But at a distance."

Eliahu put his hand on a board and greedily pressed against the wall of the shop, listening open-mouthed. Mordechai fell asleep and he could hear his rhythmic snoring: "Feeyoo-hrrr!"

"Awful green stuff. I crammed down a little too much," Eliahu whispered.

David felt himself becoming sick; he was nauseated and his teeth were chattering. Eliahu stuck two fingers down his throat and threw up everything. But David was choking on his own hand and sweating. Like before the war, long ago, when he was half-awake, running away from his dream, from a horrible nightmare. A technicolor nightmare for elderly morons and their little moron brats, full of bearded dwarves, with a knight on a white horse and a princess in a forest. A raven was sitting on her shoulder and a black cloak streamed out behind her. There was a single little poisoned apple in a huge cauldron. The girl bit into the fruit and fell down, singing at the top of her lungs. David's head ached as he watched the shadows on the screen, the sentimental and cruel intrigue that was filled with evil and with naive colors and morals, and accompanied by sweet songs. Terror overwhelmed him: first in the movie theater, then in his dream. He screamed, woke up, and began to choke. His father asked, "What's the matter with him?" But his mother grasped his head firmly and tilted it backwards.

He sat there in the ruins, in the vegetable garden, his back against the shop wall. Eliahu stood over him, pale, scared, not knowing how to help him. He slapped him on the back between his shoulder blades and the nape of his neck. He knew why he had fallen ill: Disney's movie had nauseated him and brought on his childish terror, and he had seen that technicolor mess in the Joy cinema for fifty groschen. For fifty groschen the queen died, the white steed came galloping, and the bearded dwarves hummed in their bass voices. The girl's corpse came to life amidst sighs and her lips sang in a joyous soprano. The duet ended in a gallop across the screen. The end. The sound of the projector ceased. But why had he seen the same thing a second time in his dream? Out of fear, undoubtedly.

David and Eliahu visited the vegetable garden all summer long, and their sunburned skin peeled off their bodies in big strips.

Walicòw exploded with noises, with ear-splitting lamentations.

The cemetery wagon made daily trips, and the sidewalks, denuded of corpses, kept filling up again with the new walking dead. Shameless, they pulled off their rags in the hope of touching the hearts of passersby and coercing them into giving alms; they displayed legs that were eaten away with suppurating ulcers from their hips down to their ankles. One day Elijah walked behind the wagon calling out, "Kiev has fallen!"

The walking dead leaped up. In the silence that followed his cry, Faivel Szafran came out of his den and approached the porter, clutching his tin bowl. "What about Minsk?"

"Conquered."

"Kharkov?"

"Taken."

"That's how the front's been evened out."

The red-haired cantor waved his short, ragged sleeve and you could see him clenching his dry fist.

"A curse on fascism, a curse," he muttered. "A curse. May they drop dead. Now and forever. Amen."

They dispersed in silence, making way for Elijah's loaded wagon. In the line in front of the Judenrat kitchen the news from the front was passed from one person to another, and before Faivel Szafran could return to the ruins with his bowl of soup, the apartment house on Krochmalna Street was fully informed. People spoke in a whisper. Long Itzhok came running toward them and shrieked, "Malka, Malka, lift your fancy skirt!"

She was standing in the middle of the alley, dressed in a filthy white frock over a lilac slip that showed through the transparent gauze. A moth-eaten red fox was draped around her neck and across her bony shoulders, its snout pointing toward the ground. She walked stiffly over to Leibuś, thrust her canteen into his hand, and stroked his gray shaven head.

"Do me a favor, little fishy? Stand in line and buy me some soup. My legs hurt so bad."

Leibuś made a face and said drily, "And what will you pay me, Malka?"

"The change from a zloty."

He traipsed off to the line and Malka stood there, keeping her eye on the street. A sound like hissing arose from the beggars. The red-haired cantor shook his short sleeves in a rage. "Begone, unclean woman, begone!"

Long Itzhok shouted, "Malka, where's your man? Count Grandi sends his regards. Where'd you get the flowers?"

David looked stealthily in that direction, blushing, and afraid that someone might see how red he was. Eliahu smiled weakly. She was holding a couple of crushed, drooping flowers in her sweaty hand. The flowers, her dress, her face, were all powdered with dust.

Long Itzhok took the pitiful bouquet from her, flung it to the ground, giggling, and then crushed it with his wooden clogs until all that remained of it was tiny fragments and a damp green stain on the paving stones.

"Tfoo! I love flowers, animals, and children. I hate people."

She grabbed the tail of the moth-eaten fox and rotated it so its snout lay on her shoulder.

Malka is a common name. But in our ancient language it means "queen." The poorest woman beggar might be named Malka and not know that she has a royal name; and all the street urchins call out to every ragged-looking Jewish woman, "Malka!" Felek Piorun would stand still for a moment on his unsteady legs, take off his hat, fling it down in front of him, and cry, "Everything for you, my Queen!" Malka would climb into the cab, he'd give her a light, she'd take a drag on a cigarette that she dangled between her fingers, unsmoked, for the entire evening, and the cab would head for Bagno. They went there to drink vodka and sing songs until the morning. Did Felek Piorun know that "Malka" means "queen"? That's what he called her. For a drunkard, any street girl can be a queen. Drunks have their own language and they combine it with all other languages.

Long Itzhok giggled like a ghost and pointed at her while she waited for Leibuś to return with her canteen. The line in front of the Judenrat kitchen crept forward like the walking dead snaking along the wall.

Coming back with his pots, David set the burning-hot cans down on the bricks and sat with the deportees from the eastern territories, listening to their singsong voices.

"I lived my life the way one is supposed to live."

Esther was standing on tiptoe, hanging the family's wet rags out to dry. She wrung out the linen, splashing water around. Flat-nosed

Nahum was chopping up a chair for firewood. Faivel Szafran muttered, "I lived my life like you're supposed to live and now I have to look at this sinful city. Tfoo, it's disgusting, a Babylon . . . Shulim! Where is Shulim? Did he go to get the soup yet?"

"He went, he went," said Nahum.

"Did he wash the bowls?"

"He did."

"Tfoo. It's God's punishment. *Treyf* slops in a *treyf* pot, and I have to swallow this in my old age. And whose son are you?"

His lion's beard pointed at David. The old man's yellow eyes looked him over.

"Shaved like a *goy*. Where are your *peyes*? Maybe your family doesn't wear any? *Peyes* aren't fashionable anymore, is that it?"

"*Tate*, don't pick on him." And Esther smiled at David.

"Nu, nu, so that's how you speak to your old father."

"It's not the village here."

"I can see. Tfoo. It's Babylon."

Esther hung out the linen, stepped out of her sandals, and dipped her feet into a basin. She bit her lip; with graceful motions she rinsed her foot, her calf, her knee, lifted her skirt and moistened her thigh. She spent a long time looking at her heel with her head turned and her hair tumbling down over her back.

"Nu, a troublemaker, just look at her! And who's going to follow you to the *mikva*? Go, that's where you should go to wash your flesh. Even if they stamp your ration book."

The water in the basin grew dark, but the girl lowered her glance and her face grew calm. "To the *mikva*? *Tate*, the only thing you can get at the *mikva* is typhus."

She caught up her red hair in her wet, rosy hand and twisted it into a thick knot. She bent over and rubbed the soles of her feet with a piece of coarse brick.

"Shameless hussy!"

She blanched and her green eyes flashed. Agilely she removed her wet foot from the basin and pulled the wooden sandal over with her big toe. A wind blew up and scattered dust on the broken shells and garbage; it tugged at the old man's beard and the skirt over the white knees. Up above, over their heads, the naked ruins of buildings were swaying and rocking peacefully. They could feel the gritty sand between their teeth.

"Who's there?" asked the old man. "Is it you, Shulim?"

The sound of falling rubble could be heard. At the sight of Long Itzhok, who was creeping toward him, David snatched up the now cooled can and fled, running home without a backward glance, across the yard and under Zajączek's windows.

During the day, Long Itzhok used to steal, beg, and hang around with Baruch Oks, lying in wait for the smugglers from Żelazna Brama Square; at night, he crawled into his den beside the Szafrans'—a sloppily excavated cave in a pile of rubble. He had surrounded it with a heap of loosely scattered bricks, sealed it off with the doors from an old wardrobe and a piece of corrugated metal sheeting, and stuffed the cracks with bits of tar paper that he'd stolen from a roofer. He'd gotten it all together before Sukkoth, when, just as they did every year, the streets and houses suddenly turned green with the shabby tabernacles that the Jews hastily, clumsily threw together at that time. Since there were no branches, the holiday booths on the balconies and in the courtyards and entranceways were decorated with green rags, blankets, flowered tablecloths— with whatever household goods people still owned. The tattered, drooping cloths flapped about for a long time after the holidays were over, like huge bats.

"Holidays again," Mother complained.

She was standing near the open window with her back to him. The gray and golden light gently enveloped her black silhouette, her head, arms, hair. She raised her elbows and knitted her fingers together. Her arched hands made a dry cracking sound. She turned around, and the dying sun shone red in her eyes.

Peering into the can he'd brought her, she complained, "It's Sukkoth again. New Year's barely passes and you have to put up the *sukkah* just a couple of days after atoning. Oy, Jews, Jews, couldn't we do without this just for once? What's it supposed to mean? Mordechai, who sleeps in the stable all year long with the animals, also has to put up a *sukkah*. Haskiel the janitor took his kids to his vegetable garden in the ruins. He planted Roizele and Avrumek in one of the beds. And Riva walks back and forth from their quarters in the courtyard, carrying bowls out to them and bringing them back. She's as proud as a peacock. Yankiel, with four stories collapsing onto his head in his basement, has also put up a holiday booth for himself! There's a resplendent *sukkah* on Mordarski's balcony even though he eats enough bacon for three and has forgotten the words to the prayer. Natek Lerch set a cactus in a flowerpot on his windowsill in place of a *sukkah.* Sura the street vendor carried two chairs into the courtyard and covered them with a flowered table-cloth. And what is that supposed to be? A *sukkah!* Faiga gives her Leibuśś a candy inside the tent. A tent—a rag stretched on a clothes-line! Attorney Szwarc, that convert who called himself Czerniatyński for forty years, as if he were a magnate with five bars on his coat of arms, and who had stuffed hares and deer antlers hanging on his walls, went and ordered an elegant *sukkah* for himself this year so he shouldn't forget that he's a Jew. Why go so far to find examples? Papierny also demanded that a green branch and painted eggshells be hung over his bed. And where are you going to get a branch these days? But Buba brought him one. She dug it up from under the earth and brought it to him, so that the paralyzed man could eat his rutabaga in a bed decorated for the holidays. The herring vendor with one urine-soaked shirt on her back and the richest of rich men who sleeps on a featherbed all year long both seek holiday discom-fort in a crowded *sukkah.* Everyone wants to observe the holiday properly. But no one asks is it proper for Jews to observe it now at all . . . A holiday commotion. What's it supposed to be? Sukkoth? A crazy, topsy-turvy mess! The deportees have their Feast of Taberna-cles under the open sky all year long."

"It's only for a short time. On my word of honor, it'll only be for a short time!"

"Don't interrupt when I'm speaking. I'm always as silent as the grave; you're the only one who can talk. Once a year after the Day of Atonement I can also say something out loud in this house."

"But you don't shut your mouth, woman, from morning till night."

Father put tension on the spokes of the wheel with a key he held near the rim, testing them with his finger to see if they were properly seated.

"So, didn't I say that it would boil over? And it did! Whenever I heat the milk you have to make a scene."

"Me? A scene?"

Father rested his hands on the rim of the wheel.

"The house is in an uproar, the pot's boiling, and I don't have any more tears."

Mother had bought a bit of milk somewhere for the holidays. When milk boils over it makes a terrible stench; you sprinkle a pinch of salt on the stove top and that helps.

Angry, resentful, she keeps sniping at him. "There's never a kind word for me in this house! Whatever I say is bad. Whatever I do is wrong." She wipes her tears, takes a deep breath. "I'm so sorry about that milk."

Father lifts up the wheel and rotates the rim through his hands, checking under the light for any warping. He says, "It's only for a short time. On my word of honor, it'll only be for a short time! Who dreamed it up? Probably a Jew who was putting up a *sukkah*."

"Humph."

"The tent will shelter us for a while. Oy, let us rejoice."

"Hmm."

"Today I'm here, tomorrow there. Oy, let us rejoice."

"Ech, it's absolute craziness!"

"The world is arranged in such a way that a small, quiet place can always be found for my miserable *sukkah*."

"That's how it used to be. But now we have *Judenrein*. I'm talking to you about the deportees who have to spend their nights under the open sky in summer and winter, and you want to expound on the meaning of the fate of the Jews."

"That's how things were divided between us. Have you forgotten? What Reb Itzhok said? When I stood with you under the red canopy our whole life was before us. Our whole life was as bright as day. You were supposed to worry about the big things, and I was to worry about the small ones. You were supposed to take care of *our* fate and I was supposed to agonize about the fate of the Jews as a whole. Now tell me, with your hand on your heart, could the whole world have been divied up between us in any better way so that in this divided world we might always remain together? Didn't Reb Itzhok have a light hand? Can you say that he had a heavy hand? Today, after so many years . . . 'It is what it is. And there's nothing to discuss.'"

Mother laughs.

"When the canopy fell down on our heads everyone began to shout, 'Is it a bad omen? A good omen? A bad omen!' But Reb Itzhok said, 'It is what it is. And there's nothing to discuss.'"

Mother is laughing, and Father steals a look at her face.

"You haven't forgotten?"

"When the canopy fell down, I was horrified. I thought I would sink into the ground." Mother puts her hand up to her face and bows her head. "And . . . and I'd baked such a dark bread for that day. When I cut it open it was just a soggy dough. I was terribly embarrassed, ashamed. I didn't know why myself."

"Shmuel teased you and complained in that way of his, 'What kind of challah is this? Is this supposed to be a challah?' But Father defended us: 'When there's a challah on the table, don't ask what kind of flour went into it. Eat, Shmuel!' And he had to eat it."

"Everyone ate a little piece of that soggy mess." She looked up. "But there's one thing that I won't forgive you for for the rest of my life."

"What's that?"

"How much time passed before you proposed."

"Hunh?"

"You hesitated and hesitated, and I waited like a fool."

"That again? After all, I was doing a job for old man Lewin! I had to take care of that first. Did you want me to make an entire dining room suite in five minutes?"

"Yes, yes. Eight chairs, two armchairs, a table."

"And a settee! Sycamore veneer, bentwood oak. Sycamore was very, very fashionable then. I can see it as if it were today. The upholstery was red brocade with gold trim! It's not often that work goes so well. And then—"

"And then we had our wedding."

"Wait, not yet. Then Lewin paid me and gave me a second order. I was to furnish the maid's room for Ceśka. Everything was coated with white lacquer, even the picture frames. Can you believe it? I couldn't get my hands clean. The damask alone was about twenty meters."

"Everyone said that old Lewin was head over heels in love with her."

"Ah, it's just talk."

"But she went behind the wall with them. You know, my dear, she's not a girl."

Father repeats, "Eight chairs, two armchairs, a table with a serving cart, and a settee. I can see it as if it were today."

They are silent for a while.

"And then I was caught up in a whirl. I didn't have a moment to look around. And it all," Mother makes a vague gesture, "seemed so insignificant to me. As if my life was always worse than I myself was. Not identical with me."

She stops.

"Go on, go on."

"I probably sinned. Pride."

"You and your pride! It was good for you."

"But now I know that you can lose even that. So little." Her chin trembles and suddenly there's an obvious dimple in it. Mother clenches her teeth, shuts her eyes tight. Her mouth, eyebrows, temples, forehead are all wrinkled. She stiffly places her hands against her face and tears run down between her fingers.

"You see, everyone has the same fate prepared for him."

"Is it all right . . . if I think . . . that . . . it's a punishment . . . for me?"

"It's all right, but don't give yourself more grief. Just because the milk boils over you don't have to reckon with your conscience."

"When a blind man stumbles does it mean that he's being punished for his sins? He was already punished long before with his blindness. We Jews are small retailers and that's why we can't make peace with God. But the Lord is a wholesale dealer and doesn't worry about details. Only a wholesaler could have created such a world in six days."

"His hand didn't even tremble. But what about that milk? Is there any left?"

Mother doesn't answer. Sobbing, she presses her hand against her cheek and bows her head.

Sukkoth, the harvest holiday, the celebration of a year's worth of memories and quietly concealed wishes, transformed into a carefree holiday of nomads, when potted palms are carried outside and late foliage, foods, and flowers are piled up, along with garlands, wreaths, and other flimsy decorations. When the household furnishings are moved outdoors amidst shouts of joy, little tables taken out of corners, boards and windowsills removed, and the doors lifted off their hinges in order to construct the temporary, funny-looking buildings. And under their unreliable roofs, in the shadow of their swaying walls, wine is drunk and bread is broken, raisins and fruit are eaten.

To inhale the air deep into your lungs, to raise up songs under the naked sky, take gulps of freedom, waiting without a care in the world until the hut collapses on your head. To gulp down the freedom that doesn't exist, to rejoice while remembering the sorrows of the endless road, to play out the annual comedy of expulsion and exile. That's what the Sukkoth holiday is about, the holiday that comes during the time of the first autumn winds.

What does it matter if year after year passes and there is no end in sight to that road? Such is the fate of a Jew. If they drive him out of one place, he'll cower in another. If he runs away from there, he'll wander on. And wherever he happens to stop for a while and catch his breath during his flight, he sets up his temporary, shaky house that falls apart with the wind.

There was a craftsman who used to go through the streets on the eve of the holiday, shouting, "I put up *sukkahs*, I build huts! *Sukkahs!*" And when people stuck their heads out the windows, he added, "Guaranteed for eternity."

But can the Feast of Tabernacles last all year long? Long Itzhok slept in his *sukkah* until the sleet drove him out of it. When it rained and his den filled with water, he would crawl inside a dry metal tar barrel that lay on the ground, and when the cold weather came he would try once again to sneak into Mordechai's stall and warm his bones in the warmth from the stove. The old cabby let him in reluctantly, because Long Itzhok had more lice than hair.

"Enough, enough. You're here again. A bundle of rags has no other place to shake off his starving lice but here in my room? Go on, scram!"

"Mordechai, where was it written that the Feast of Tabernacles has to last all year long for me?"

Long Itzhok glumly rubbed his skinny back against the wall, scratching his protruding, pustule-covered shoulder blades. He stood patiently near the door of the stall, across from the straw-fed fire sputtering in a squat iron stove that glowed red from its short-lived heat, blinking his suppurating eyes in the glare, unperturbed by the cabby's shouting or his whip slashing the air. He waited until the storm passed and he could creep into a dark corner on a pile of sacks, near a stack of straw and hay. "Thief!" That's what the inhabitants of the tenement yelled at him, all of them, from basement to attic, while Haskiel chased away the ragged, corpse-gray specter with a single sweep of his broom. He would come back stealthily and hide in the dark stairwells, unexpectedly snatching rutabagas from old ladies as they passed him. His victims would run around in the long entranceway, squeaking softly like mice.

In the middle of the courtyard he took a carrot out of a little boy's hand and gnawed at it indifferently.

"Give it back, there's a dear," Leibuś begged him. "Even a teeny-weeny piece. Like this." And he pointed to his finger.

Sure he'll see his carrot! He's more likely to see a flowering cactus right here in his hand, last year's snow on the roof, the old mare harnessed to Mordechai's cab, and Mordechai himself on the coachman's bench wearing his cabdriver's cap. When Long Itzhok swallowed and took aim, Leibuś fled to the inner courtyard. Since his illness, his skin had hung loosely on his thin little wrinkled scaly face.

"Horsey, horsey," he whispered in the empty stable. "My diamond horsey, I'll give you some sugar. I'll give you a meadow. I'll give you a palace . . . I'll give you everything."

Through the open doors Leibuś could be seen standing there for a long time, his head resting against the empty manger.

"Buba! Buba, my darling daughter, what's taking you so long?" Papierny, the man whose legs had been amputated, called from his bed and rattled his tin mug with the spoon in it.

"I'm coming, I'm coming."

In the gathering darkness you could hear the insistent, cloying murmuring of the women vendors as they closed up their stalls in front of the gate.

Buba was complaining, "What a day. Again nothing. How can I do business here? Twice they overturned my table and came to change bills into coins—my entire earnings."

At that hour the gang, concealed in the dark gateway, would quietly launch an attack against the women who were on their way home, snatching whatever they could from their hands. But what is there to grab from such a merchant, even after an entire day of trading? Those were stalls for beggars. They were guarded by dried-out shadows, who begged from dawn to dusk in order to buy some wood, rutabaga, turnip.

"Thief! Hold him, catch him—my goods, my money!"

Baruch Oks's gang was undertaking a short, quick battle with the tradeswomen under cover of darkness. The hard tables fell on their shaved heads; hungry hands tugged wildly at aprons and pockets. Moishe the Crip spat and wheezed inside the dark gate. Herring's head, round and swollen like a clay pot, knocked against the paving stones. Yosele Egg Yolk was the first to take to his heels, and his wooden clogs clacked loudly along the pavement. Kuba the Gelding was groaning in the corner behind the rubbish bin, lying belly-down on top of his loot, like a rat that has been painfully impaled on a piece of wire but still guards its bit of cracklings, while Faiga showered blows on his skinny bones with her shoe. Five-Fingers Mundek could scarcely defend himself from the enraged hags, and walked off with whatever he could carry during the uproar the gang had initiated.

The vendors were disheveled, frenzied. Haskiel the janitor, who had been sworn in as the building's mediator and judge, shrugged his shoulders from a distance.

"Sweetness itself, honey and fat," Faiga sang out the next day when the beggars' market, that pure exchange of money for calories, started up once again, amid a cacophony of hoarse voices and the feverish noise from the newly energized specters.

Buba, sporting a black eye from the previous night's free-for-all, primped her elaborate hairdo. "Hey, young man, let me earn a bit of cash. Start the day off right."

Zyga was hanging around near the stalls. Ernest tagged along after him, greedily eyeing the the displays of sweets.

Sura, who sold rutabagas, turnips, and beets, was crying out, "What am I doing, I must have gone out of my mind, I'm giving it away for nothing. People, come here."

Faiga repeated her singsong cry, "Turkish sweets! Look them over, take what you want! By the piece or by the kilo."

The sweets lay on the little table inside the gate. Faiga had put on display a fresh carton of pressed poppyseed with sugar, shelled nuts coated with a dark brown syrup, sugared almonds, taffy, and nougats. What witch had cooked up those disgusting concoctions in what cauldron, with the help of what curses and charms?

"Sweetness itself." She stamped her feet behind the table, and the men's shoes she wore, wide and worn down at the heels, drifted in the puddle like ships with holes in them.

"Faiga, what do you fry your doughnuts in?"

"Do you think I know?"

She took her foot out of her shoe, and under the table you could see her rubbing her hairy, thin calf with her toes.

Zyga stood in front of her, dirty, with a smile on his face.

"In louse fat? In rat lard? What, Faiga?"

"You runt," yelled Buba from her stall where she sold charcoal, carbide, and coke. "You're a petty thug, your pockets are empty, you've got lice all over your head, and you stand there sounding off!"

Faiga thrust her foot into the loose shoe, leaned over the table, and hissed, "Fish scales!"

"Whore on cat's paws!"

From her cart with the rutabagas, turnips, and beets, Sura said softly and pleasantly, "Sh'maya."

"What?"

Zyga turned around, disarmed. A crooked smile lurked behind her gray, widely stretched lips.

"Sh'maya, tell me, my sweet, do you steal with your left hand, too?"

"Oh, kiss me you-know-where and crank it up from the other side."

"What?"

There was a chorus of laughter from the vendors.

"Surele, Surele, I can't help it."

Buba squealed with delight. Shaking her head and disrupting the tall pile of hair on her head, she signaled to Sura. Faiga wiped the tears of joy from her eyes with her apron, and blew her nose onto the ground, pressing it between two fingers. Sura, stiff and unmoved, stood there silently, with that same crooked smile on her gray lips.

"What's the matter, Sh'maya? Ah, I understand. I understand, but I can't comprehend it."

Eliahu, drawn by the shouting and the loud laughter, came running up to help, and said, as if there were nothing amiss, "What's new?"

"The vendors don't want to drop dead."

Taking their time, they walked arm in arm to the other corner of the little street. The hawkers returned to their monotonous cries, calling to the passing beggars.

"This is all a charade; it's watery glue and pretty wrappings. You're wasting your time there," said Eliahu. "And for what? That old toad Faiga fries starch and molasses in turnipseed oil and wraps it up in shining paper! It's disgusting. Come with me, instead. We'll hunt cats."

"Don't tell me: with our bare hands?"

They whispered for a long time. Eliahu shook his finger at him. "Albino, are you going?"

"I'm going."

"Sh'maya, are you going?"

"No."

"So don't. We'll take a sack, a crowbar, and a shovel. Let's get a move on."

They walked towards Przebieg with a sack, a crowbar, and a coal shovel. Ernest held the crowbar with both hands, Eliahu carried the shovel on his shoulder, and David had the rolled-up sack. There was no one here; a graveyard silence reigned, and the muffled noise of the distant market district barely reached them. They marched briskly past the abandoned shanties and patiently meandered among the dismal tenements that had been overwhelmed by pestilence and condemned to quarantine and were now still, emptied out by death, where the odor of carbolic acid spilled into the street and the rats said *Kaddish* over the corpses in the emptiness.

They lingered near the rubbish heap for a long time. The day dragged on, like someone dying of hunger on the paving stones.

"Hit him on the head once with the spade." Ernest energetically demonstrated how to strike with the spade.

"And the crowbar."

"With the crowbar on the head, too."

Eliahu advised them to throw something out as bait. Anything at all; they'll come right up to you at once.

"But what?"

They swallowed their saliva.

"Here, kitty, kitty," Ernest said enticingly. "Kitty, kitty."

He put his hands innocently behind his back, trying to hide his intentions and the iron pole. He breathed heavily and peered impatiently through the window into the cellar. Eliahu hunkered down in a posture that promised no good. He had a knife with a corkscrew that belonged to Zyga, and both blades were bared.

"I see it, it's there," said Ernest, sticking his head into the cellar, but it was as dark as a black man's pocket there and he probably couldn't see a thing.

Eliahu picked up a discarded bottle. "With this," he said, and shook it menacingly over his head, but he still held the sharp knife in his other hand.

David held the sack. "Uh oh," he sighed when a child's weak, drawn-out cry was heard from inside the entranceway behind them.

Then they went down slippery steps to the cellar, wading cautiously through a thick layer of scattered feathers as if walking through snowdrifts. They walked around the basement and the ground floor, which was full of abandoned, blackened corpses, still seated rigidly in armchairs, stretched out on mattresses, or grown stiff along the walls, naked or clothed in clumps of sweat-stained, stinking rags. They tiptoed out of there as if someone were chasing them.

"Here, kitty, kitty."

A sudden clatter of milk cans rolling off the rubbish heap, the groan of a rail that someone had touched—and all three turned back. In the cloud of dust that hung over this spot, in the storm of loud noises that showered onto their heads and echoed endlessly from the bottom of the deep well of the courtyard, a familiar specter in rags glided feebly toward them, swaying and limping, clattering over the cement in his wooden sandals, noisily trampling the piles of broken crockery, rustling through the newspapers, and kicking aside the scattered bottles with a loud clinking. They fled—with the sack, the crowbar, and the coal shovel. But the enraged skeleton, emaciated from starvation, ran after them for a long time, bellowing so that the echo resounded through the ruins of Przebieg.

"Hey, you rascals!" He bellowed and threw a bottle that he picked up from the ground. "I'm gonna get you!" And he threw an empty jam tin, and hurled a shard from a large pot. They fled, and the skeleton ran after them, shedding his lice in his haste.

They stopped to catch their breath only on the wooden bridge — from where it was just a few steps to their homes — among a crowd of frightened pedestrians who were hurrying along with their heads tucked into their collars. The thin boards bent and creaked; the policeman under the bridge walked slowly back and forth along his beat. From there, from that elevated spot above street level, they could see the crooked, crowded back alleys of the Ghetto, the spacious jaws of the Hale market all the way to Żelazna Brama and, closer to them, in the square, the massive white building that was St. Karol's Church and, behind it, in the distance, the tops of the old trees in the Saxon Gardens.

"Oh, over there," Eliahu pointed. With longing and sorrow they looked straight ahead, yearning to see the banks of the Vistula River.

Behind them, in the Wola depot, the trolleys were clanging their bells. Eliahu screwed up his eyes, quickly bent over the railing of the bridge, and spat onto the peak of the red, white, and black booth of the policeman who was now standing with his back to them, busy checking people's papers.

A passerby in a gabardine and black hat screamed when he saw this. "Jews, run away!"

And when the bridge emptied in a tumultuous panic of fleeing people, the policeman turned around, straightened his helmet, looked up, and called out without anger, *"Juden, was ist los?"* astonished by the unexpected commotion.

But there, on the bridge, the three Jewish brats stood unmoved near the railing and looked into the distance, where the river flowed, hidden from their view.

"Eli, what if you see one now?"

"They ran away a long time ago," said Ernest. "Beyond the wall. To the Aryan side."

That's how it was. The animals had moved out to where the garbage heaps weren't disturbed by starvation-crazed people who hid behind the rubbish bins and suddenly threw themselves on cats and dogs, strangling them with their bare hands. The animals succumbed first, while people continued to endure their fate for a long time.

"Aha," Eliahu said indistinctly, resting his head on the railing. "Do you know who it was that chased us all that way? Itzhok."

"Itzhok. But what is he doing there? He should go to Waliców, he should lie down on the paving stones, the goner."

"To Waliców. It's amazing that he hasn't been buried yet."

✽

VII

Rosh Hashanah, the New Year, passed without hope or the sound of the shofar; Yom Kippur, the Day of Atonement, was celebrated without repentance; Sukkoth, the Feast of Tabernacles and the Harvest, dragged on without bread. Faces grew black from hunger. During those autumn days the sun hung over the city like a typhus-carrying louse threatening everyone.

Those who were supposed to die had died already. Those who were going to die later were still alive, waiting their turn. Driven out by hunger from their dark, unheated dens, they ran around freely at night through the emptied streets, crowds of them crying out, making a racket, jangling their empty metal jugs. They dropped clumps of rags and lice in the streets. Dried-up skeletons, staggering weakly inside loose scraps of clothing, collapsed on the ground, whimpering pitifully. Their cries and helpless lamentations beat against the windows. In the morning the janitors covered the corpses with paper. The epidemic was spreading inside the walls, and the threat of an outbreak in other districts of the city moved the Germans to increase the number of guards at the outlets of the streets, along the gutters at the edge of the boundary wall, wherever a rat or a small smuggler with a sack for bread and typhus fever in his eyes could squeeze through. The orders were a warning against both the living and the dead.

Corpses were removed out of fear for the community's health. Janitors broke into locked apartments and dragged out into the streets bodies that had been gnawed by rats. The cemetery porter, circling the city with his cart for days on end, would come upon them and cram them in among the other corpses on the stinking, Lysol-sprinkled boards of his wagon.

"Grave Digger!"

The cry resounded. It was old Elijah whom they called "Grave Digger" and that's how he was known until the end. He was greeted with nasty words, curses, insults whenever his cart drew up, always in the nick of time. He would drive past the gates of the tenements and his hoarse cry would ring out: "Bring out the corpses!"

He'd wait a few minutes, glance at the closed windows, then turn away and drive on. The horse that used to pull his wagon had long since fallen, and now it was Jews, straining their leg muscles, who harnessed themselves to the wagon in order to carry the bodies away from the auspices of the municipal authorities and perform their last service for the miserable wages paid by the Judenrat. Hurrying, they dragged their load through the ruins amidst clouds of rubbish swirled up by the wind, while the filthy tarpaulin that covered the wagon flapped above the stacked-up dead.

"Greetings, your honor, greetings, Mr. Corpse Bearer," yelled Zyga when he spotted the wagon, which had stopped in front of the gate on a cold, cloudy morning.

Dressed as usual in his ragged undertaker's outfit, with the sorry remains of its brass buttons gleaming and the hem of his unfastened overcoat flapping, wearing one boot that came up to his knee and a bundle of rags secured with a string on his other leg, Elijah raised his head and howled, baring his black teeth as he let out his cry. Avrum was with him and two unknown young porters who stood there with nothing to do, looking around the street, coughing, spitting, panting from exhaustion. Avrum, the son of Haskiel the janitor, gestured broadly and hitched up the trousers that hung on him like a sack, with pants legs that had been trampled in the mud though the pants were tied under his armpits.

"Just a minute, I'll be right back. I'll just check out everyone in the building."

Clattering loudly in his wooden clogs, he snatched up little Leibuś and, with one jump, sat him down in front of the gate. He'd been lying there quietly for a couple of days. There was a patient, sad smile on his dirty little face. Faiga had already died beside him; her uncovered remains lay stiffly on one side, her knees drawn up to her chest and her head in the dust of the street; she was shirtless and there were tattered slippers on her feet. But when a fly landed on the dead woman's forehead, the brow still twitched. Haskiel the janitor stood there for a long time that morning, bending over the little boy and holding a pot of water. His lips opened but the water trickled out. Leibuś's huge black eyes stared vacantly at the passersby and he didn't even stretch out his hand. During the night he had still cried out softly before the locked gate, but no one had come out to him then.

"Hup to! Get going, Avrum," one of the young porters shouted. "It won't take us long."

"Take the feet. Get moving," Elijah said, and the space on the sidewalk beside the little boy was emptied.

He looked in that direction, lowered his head, and then crawled over to the wagon. The weak little body dragged enormous, elephantine legs behind it, and the child's heavy skull swayed on the thin neck, as fragile as a withered stalk. When he stopped for a moment, emitting a weak sigh, and raised his head, his eyes closed from exhaustion, the old porter said sorrowfully, "Don't be in such a hurry. Where are you rushing to, my little angel?"

David and Zyga stood motionless, watching as Leibuś tensely followed the wagon and porters with his dead gaze. The porters were silent and did not avert their eyes. And suddenly they distinctly heard him say, "Take me away from here. Me, too . . ."

Avrum turned around. He had a dry crust of bread between his teeth. His free hands were pulling up the loose, baggy trousers. He stopped, gauged the distance, took one step back, and leaped in a graceful arc across the little boy lying there on the sidewalk. Then, his clogs clattering, he walked up to the wagon.

"Let's go. No one's calling for us," he said in a vibrant voice. And that's how it started.

"Avrum. One more time. Show us how you jump."

Those loose trousers got in his way, however, and his feet tripped in those slippery wooden shoes. When David grabbed him by the back of his shirt, Avrum's hands were no longer free. A light shove and he stumbled clumsily against the wall. "What? What?" was all he could say, and bread stuck out from his shirt.

The porters were walking over from the wagon with their heads lowered. Zyga ran out in front and spread his arms wide.

"Let them fight. Leave them alone," he screamed wildly, and suddenly burst out crying.

"What's the matter? Are you blind? You creep!"

And Zyga punched him in the ear.

"Leave them alone, one on one," said the old porter sorrowfully. He solemnly regarded the little boy, who had crept back to his place near the gate. Leibuś crawled over with his head hung low. Over to where he had to remain.

Avrum swung a punch. Once, and then a better blow. He grabbed David around the waist and, wheezing from the effort, tried to throw him over his shoulder. He swayed on his stiff, slippery wooden shoes, and each foot slid out from under him in a different direction. They both fell down. Avrum jumped up in a fury and began pounding David in the face. And when that didn't help he again grabbed David around the waist and dragged him around, cautiously feeling with his clogs for a foothold on the pavement. Suddenly tilting his head back with a swift, sideways movement, he gave David a couple of quick blows like a bull. David bent his knees, collapsed in a heap, and, his elbows working furiously, escaped from his grasp.

They stood a couple of steps apart, breathing audibly and carefully watching each other's movements, waving their clenched fists in the air like professional fighters. Now David leaped behind the wagon while Avrum moved forward. He heard the porters laughing. Avrum's shirt, which barely clung to his back, got caught on a board and tore loose with a loud rip.

"Avrum, Avrum, don't give up. Punch him in the mug! Slash him with a knife!"

Rags fluttered along the street. Avrum lost the bread. Together they fell against the wall, tearing at each other's ragged clothing, colliding feebly and thrashing at the air with their wooden shoes; they tumbled about, knocking their teeth against the paving stones, then rose to their feet again. David grabbed Avrum by the ears and started banging his head against the wall until it flopped from side to side. He was wheezing; everything grew dark before his eyes and from out of the darkness he could hear the porter's laugh and his accusatory voice: "What for? What for?"

A crowd gathered, and the old porter stood there, propped casually against the wagon shaft.

"All right, kids, that'll do. It's good enough."

Riva ran to the front of the building and began yelling, "Jews, do you stand there calmly and watch while that bandit murders my Avrum in broad daylight?"

Riva's cries, her disheveled hair. The porters leaning against the wagon shaft, laughing unconcernedly. David looked around as if he'd just awakened from a dream. Is it he standing here? He was ashamed and he didn't know why. Avrum was on his knees in his torn shirt, his hand over his mouth, from which blood dripped onto his ragged clothes.

"Beating my Avrum while his health is hanging by a thread— what am I saying, by a hair. And now Avrum is lying there and not moving. Lying there and not moving." Riva wiped her eyes with the back of her hand, then dried her hand on a dustrag. "I gave birth to him, I carried him under my heart. I fed my little sunshine with my own blood. And a bandit like that had to appear, without mercy, without a conscience . . . Wait, just you wait, I'll tell your father!" Her shaking hands fluttered in the air, grabbed the dustrag and again returned to her puffy, wet face. "A tragedy, a tragedy! Listen to me if you have a heart."

Sura the street vendor came out of the building carrying a stool.

"My Avrum is so gentle, he wouldn't hurt a fly. He sits in a corner and reads or writes. Such a good, smart child, oo-oo-oo . . ." Her wails became sobs and Riva sat down on the stool that someone brought over for her. "You, I'm talking to you! You thieving brat!" She sat on the stool, her knees spread wide, and rocked back and forth. Tears flowed from under her reddened eyelids into her open mouth.

The wagon started off and the porters moved away, laughing. He set off in the direction of the *Wache*, wiping his battered face with his cap. His heart pounded against his ribs; he could hear it. He felt exhausted and his legs were giving way beneath him. Huge drops of sweat trickled down his arms. There was a noise in his ears, as after a sleepless night. As after an entire day without a piece of bread. He saw Avrum's face in front of him now, white and blotchy. He saw his eyes, opened wide in amazement, the carefree pug nose. The blond hair that grew thickly around his neck and ears, the *peyes* on his temples, thin as mouse tails, twisted into curls with a saliva-moistened finger. Haskiel the janitor says that Avrum his son spends his days walking about with the porters but spends his nights sitting over a book. By the light of a carbide lamp he casts his tired eyes over the ancient verses, rests his feverish head on the table and wakes up again, tugs at his *peyes* till it hurts in order to keep himself from falling asleep, and repeats the words without stopping for breath . . .

"Don't run so fast. Wait up."

Avrum sits over the Bible and blood flows from his mouth. And who made that blood flow? He was ashamed, and he knew why. By day he has to bear the burden of the dead who are falling now, and by night he has to bear the burden of the dead who fell a long time ago. It will never be any different, so why did he strike Avrum? Leibuś will turn up his toes in front of the gate before night falls and no one will care. Because Avrum kicked the dying boy? Yes, that's why. And in his memory the image of Avrum jumping over the corpses in his rush to sit down with the Bible assumed enormous proportions.

"Hey, don't run so fast. Wait up. How long do I have to carry your sack for you?"

He could still hear the words long after Zyga was no longer beside him. Oh, now he is running on the other side. He passes people stealthily, without the armband on his sleeve that the friend waiting for him had hastily stuffed into his pocket.

The gate that seals off the street, a cast-iron grate on which rust-resistant red paint has been splashed, opens wide when the trucks roar outside them. On command, OD men rush to set the heavy gate in motion and to pull it into its open position. When the grate seals off Żelazna Street, traffic on this side comes to a stop and the trolley runs along Chłodna Street, slowing down under the wooden bridge. When the grate seals off Chłodna, traffic stops on the other side, and rushing pedestrians and carts and rickshaws pushed by porters hurry along Żelazna Street. There's a rule that the coolies and their passengers have to run alongside their bicycles on this stretch of road. You can get lost in the crowd of smugglers who noisily conduct their negotiations across the street, gesturing at each other behind the guards' backs; you can lose your bearings in the shouts of the zealous policemen, in the commands of the gendarmes who keep their eyes peeled for potential victims, waving on pedestrians who have passes or stopping them with a single movement of the head, checking the papers of the columns of people marching to work with their convoy of guards. Here, at the outlet of this guarded street, Jew, every step may be your last.

The Jews are watched by the yellow police, the yellow police are watched by the blue police, the blue police are watched by the gendarmes, the gendarmes are watched by the SS, the SS are watched by the Gestapo, and at the very top Heinrich Himmler watches over everyone while he himself reports to the Führer that no one will escape across the wall today. No Jewish boy will run across to the other side with a sack, *mein Führer*, it's out of the question! The *Wächter*, Bloody Hands, who is on guard duty at the intersection of Żelazna and Chłodna, shoots without warning. The other one, who is on duty in the morning, shoots into the air. Shooting into the air is a traitor's job. The Germans would have achieved order a long time ago if ammunition weren't wasted . . . And if there is frost? If there's frost, *mein Führer*, a German soldier shoots with his gloves on, according to orders. *Ah so, selbstverständlich*. In that case, change the order of the guards. From now on, that guard will be on duty in the morning and the other one in the afternoon. It's an order, but how can you tell them apart when their faces always look the same in those iron pots? So they shoot, shoot all day long without a break and their hands don't even hurt?

POLIZEI DEIN FREUND UND HELFER. Pedestrians, be alert! If you should brush against a Jew as you pass by him, you will put your health at risk; if you hide a Jew, you risk your life. Value the quality of your race. You are duty-bound to bring to the nearest police station every tramp who goes outside the Ghetto walls. *Achtung, Achtung! Vor Juden wird gewarnt. Halt! Warnungsstimme. Juden, Läuse, Fleckfieber.* David stared without thinking at the flyers, the warnings, the posters that were put up everywhere on the other side. Remember, Jews and rats carry disease. Black figures with curly beards against a yellow background, and on their arms, rats whose wavy tails spell out the contents of the slogan in expansive, decorative script. Next to them, on another poster, an enormous insect lies in wait above a column of laconic signs. This insect has drunk diseased Jewish blood, beware! The Jew in the poster has a louse in place of one of his pupils, but the other eye is normal—it squints slyly, ominously.

"Halt, Ratte!"

Chaim, whose face had turned black, was running straight at the guard with his eyes closed and his armband still around his sleeve. The specter's ragged clothing flapped as he ran. His feet, wrapped in blanket strips, moved noiselessly across the mud, quietly and softly, and his black little face glided towards the *Wächter*, who beat a hasty retreat before the ragged apparition. Chaim stopped in the middle of the street and opened his eyes after the first shot. He stood there and didn't run away, he only stretched out his neck and looked at the German with his dull and stubborn eyes. After the second shot, he began to scrabble at the air with his fingers. He staggered with his head still held high; his mouth was open, dumbly, making no sound, as if all he wanted was to take a deep breath. Bloody Hands retreated and fired, again and again. And then he put in a new clip.

"*Polizist, Polizist, komm hier, aber schnell! Nimm den Dreck weg und schmeiss an die Seite.*"

The police quickly dragged the emaciated skeleton over to the sidewalk, and the blood flowed lethargically into the gutter.

That's how he spent his time near the *Wache*. But he could barely stand on his feet and he thought with bitter envy and a guilty conscience that Zyga had managed to run across and back, to bring bread to his house and return by a circuitous route. He's next to him again, out of breath, ready to jump once more. It's noon, the best hours have passed. After the changing of the guard they can't count on anything. And David knows that today he will not conquer his fear. He already knows that he's a coward. They are waiting there and he will return politely and show them his empty hands. Hesitantly, with his indecision showing in his eyes, David attempted to run across the guarded street, hiding behind a truck that was driving out of the district, but before he could pass the red, black, and white sentry booth, a blue policeman lazily hit him with his stick and forced him to return. Zyga observed him sympathetically.

"Oy, I can't do it! Nothing will come of it. He died with his shoes on."

When someone talks like that, someone else immediately responds, "With high-top boots."

And David, eager to conceal his confusion, his shame, repeats, "He died in shoes with high-top boots."

Hey, don't be an idiot. Look at what's going on. Mordarski and an OD man are having a quiet chat on the side. That means he's buying him off. But the OD man shakes his head: not yet. Kalman Drabik gestures to the blue policeman on the other side of the street, bends down two fingers and makes an inconspicuous gesture that all thieves and deaf men understand. Watch out, the blue policeman is coming inside the gate, they're going to deal. In the meantime the porters have come a little closer. Oy, too close, now they're standing behind the gendarme's back and the gendarme doesn't like that. A line of wagons moves down Żelazna and messes everything up. The OD man returns to his post, the blue policeman returns to his post. And Kalman Drabik stands inside the gate and calls over Baruch Oks. You see, Zyga points. If *Herr Wachtmeister* has allowed himself to be bought off, there'll be an opportunity to run across with the porters. But take it easy and be alert, because Bloody Hands doesn't like disorder and will shoot you like a rat. Well, well, is he going or not? The porters are coming back. Nothing doing. You have to stand so as to see everything. You have to wait, wait, always wait.

It's easy for him to say that; he jumps across to the other side like an old-timer. He knows all the guard posts in the area, on Grzybowa, on Żelazna Brama Square, on Leszno; he remembers each *Wächter,* both the blue and the yellow police, when they go on duty and who they are. He recognizes those faces from afar, all of them. When they are drunk and when they are sober. He has tried different passageways, times of day and times at night, he's gone over the top of the wall and crawled through sewers sealed with barbed wire, he's spotted places no one will ever squeal on. He knows the smugglers' dens where camouflaged openings that lead straight to the other side have been cut through the walls, from one building to the next, from attic to attic. Not everyone can find those addresses that are a smuggler's holy secrets; for betraying them you risk getting spit in your face and a knife in your back, and if the Germans should discover them, everyone caught in the place could be lined up against a wall and shot. Zyga knows what's going on around him, he sees everything with his little slanted eyes. He moves goods to be traded; he's been admitted to the gang that works for Mordarski, and there isn't a day that he hasn't made a run across the wall. As for David, what a joke, he is supposed to run across to a shop and get bread and a couple of kilos of rutabagas. But he still doesn't know how he'll manage to do it today. He's lost his head. He was always lacking in cleverness, quick wits, and courage.

The December sky hung as heavy as smoke above the city. He stood helplessly near the guarded crossing point until twilight fell, feeding his fear, his impatience, and his bitter pangs of conscience. Once again the *Wächter* fired into the crowd of Jews who had stubbornly gathered around. Everyone ran to the nearest gate in panic and David ran after them to hide. A porter from Solna Street who had been hit was walking near him, beating a slow retreat, swaying on legs that could barely support him, and groaning like an ox when the butcher has botched his job. His shoes left wet spots on the sidewalk. He turned around and stretched out his large, wet, red hands toward the Germans.

The man cried out, "Aaron Jajeczny, 12 Solna Street! Jews, call my . . ."

The *Wächter* raised his rifle, aimed carefully, and prevented the curse for shed blood being called down upon him. The wounded man's hands dropped. The guard stood with his feet firmly planted on the ground, leaned forward, and with a slight motion of his hand removed the shell and then, with the same motion, only in reverse order, inserted a new cartridge into the chamber. The rifle slipped downward and Bloody Hands confirmed the accuracy of his shot with strained attention. A faint smile curled around his clenched jaws, around his eyes, and immediately died away on his broad, almost swollen face, which was tightly crammed into the helmet that he wore pulled low onto his ears.

"His cap, his cap . . . Jews, toss him his cap!"

If not today, then tomorrow. He will keep trying until he conquers his fear. But that's only what people say; he doesn't believe that fear can be conquered. David thrust his fist into his pocket, tucked his head between his shoulders. Before him in the gathering darkness, the guarded city stretched out into the distance, and its ugly clamor filled his ears. The beggars' cries frightened the horses, and the omnibus was stuck in the sprawling crowd that moved down Żelazna Street and kept on going, climbing onto the wooden bridge like a swelling wave, while a long column of coolies alongside their incapacitated rickshaws dispersed in the darkness of the nearby side streets. In the depths of Chłodna Street, surrounded on two sides by the walls of the Jewish district, the white mass of St. Karol's Church rose from the square; amidst the thundering music of the organ and a chorus of angry prayer that suddenly burst into the night, the flickering flames of candles shone brightly for a moment, vanishing when the doors were shut again. The guarded outlet of the street sank into the dark blue light of the street lamp, and the blackout colors reminded him that the darkening sky above the city was pierced in all directions by tracks along which trucks had not yet driven, caught in a net of traces from the swift and graceful searchlights that had not yet been turned on, hollowed out by the bright sheaves of explosive shells that rested silently in the chambers of the anti-aircraft guns. There were night and silence under the sky, but, installed in their nests under the roofs, the sirens were waiting for a sign, ready at any moment to resound with the roar of a thousand tubas. The stormy organ music, the muffled words of the mass prayer, awakened the day's anxiety, its bitterness, to which he now surrendered, passively, with a sense of relief. A torrent of overwhelming sadness, of yearning—for what, he did not know—washed over his helpless impatience. He stood stock still, clenching his fists until they hurt, and forgave himself his terror, his dishonor. It was late, he had to go home. Reluctantly, he thought that he would come here tomorrow. A cold wind wrapped around his emaciated body, biting him to the bones, directing his steps as he walked back to the tenement after an entire day of hopeless watching beside the *Wache*. The recollection of his home, where the green flame of the carbide lamp hissed on the table and colored the faces of his loved ones with its corpselike light, filled him with inexpressible warmth, it raised his spirits, and his humiliated, cowardly heart beat with joy.

The next day, as soon as the curfew was lifted, the crowd again gathered in front of the *Wache*. The Jews spoke in whispers.

"The porter from Solna who took a bullet in the head—have they taken him away yet?"

"Yes, they took him away. His old woman came and the *Wachman* made an exception and allowed her to take him while he was still warm."

"Warm? What a merciful *Wachman*; he's got a heart. Usually it's forbidden. He's shot, so let him lie there."

"Let a cold corpse lie there like a scarecrow. Whoever was born a Jew has to die a Jew."

"Yes, yes, that's the holy truth . . . But how did she take him away? The woman is skin and bones."

"You know, on a cart."

"A cart?"

"She came by cart and she took him away by cart."

"I'll never believe that. How could she manage all by herself? Jajeczny was like an oak."

"You know, she had her son with her, her son took care of it. He drives a rickshaw around town; don't you know him?"

"So Jajeczny had a son? Aaron had a son? I didn't know."

Chaim still lay on the same spot on the sidewalk, black and shrunken like the remains of a dog that has been run over. At a distance of a couple of steps the gendarme, resting his rifle against the guardhouse wall, rubbed his hands together in the dying heat rising from the bottom of a charcoal burner. The morning fog hung low over the street, wrapped itself around the wires, slipped heavily over the wall. It dragged past the *Wache* like a hideous beggar. It was gray and empty outside as the reluctant day slowly rose in the faint light of the gas lamps. Coughing, a street sweeper quietly pushed his heavy cart in their direction; a Jew removed a paper-wrapped packet from the metal box and immediately walked away. The gendarme assiduously attended to building up the fire, pretending he hadn't seen anything. The street sweeper went up to the sentry post with his poker and tongs, boldly raked the dying coals, shook the burner with both hands, and the charcoal, crackling loudly, began to give off smoke. The guard wiped his hands and gave the sweeper a friendly pat on the back.

The pyre is raised up, in a moment the fire will catch. The sacrifice will take place, but how is that possible? Abraham, Abraham.

Standing in a crowd of young boys, David bitterly recalls the humiliation of the gift that is his life. He presses deeper into the shapeless assemblage of mothers' kerchiefs, scarves, and sweaters, fathers' long cloaks, the dragging trouser legs of gaiters that move in all directions over the icy paving stones of the sidewalk. Visored caps fall low onto noses, warm breath hangs in the air, eyes shine with amazing courage or fever, and trousers drag on the ground. They will stand together like posts, driven into a single herd, with their sacks for bread and potatoes, waiting patiently for that moment when the *Wächter* magnanimously waves his hand and allows them to run across to the other side of the wall, to scatter among the neighboring shops. They will wait, stamp their feet in the frost, clap their hands together to keep them warm.

In a moment the lamb will come running up, the angel will avert the blow, the son will escape alive, and the sacrifice will take place without bloodshed. But now there is no angel, and no voice sounds from on high. The pyre is already burning and Isaac's hands are bound. It is happening now and it shall never pass. That moment, that fire, that fear. So Abraham restrained himself; so what? What if the voice did not resound, or what if the voice came too late? The bound body continues to lie on the ground, helplessly cast down, the heavy hand of Abraham lies upon Isaac's face and he does not see it. He waits; perhaps he does not even know what he is waiting for. Isaac's head, shoved onto the stone, the straining throat and the raised knife. That's how it was and that's how it will be forever. Good, so be it. Let the offense against the son take place, but whosoever has heard that cry will never forget it. And Abraham, who held the knife in his hand, must have heard the cry. Whose cry was that? Who ran up and tracked down the lamb, since the servants were standing at a distance? Who carried the wood and built the pyre? And who said to Abraham: Behold the fire and the wood, but where is the lamb for a burnt offering? They were alone, Abraham and Isaac, because the servants remained at a distance. It is hard to think about, but Abraham did not raise the knife against himself . . . and why not?

"*Woran bin ich? Also wie gesagt,*" the gendarme drawled in a cheerful voice, and halfway through his sentence he reloaded his rifle. He carelessly fired a shot into the air and then, pointing the barrel toward the ground, emptied the shells from the lock with a graceful flourish of his hand.

The loud clattering of someone's wooden shoes reached them as he fled along the paving stones. And the *Wächter*, stuffed inside a shaggy sheepskin coat and shod in felt boots, continued to stand at the intersection of Żelazna and Chłodna Streets, turning heavily in place, as if a view of all four corners of the earth stretched out into space from this spot.

"*Der Wolf ist satt und die Kitze ganz,*" he repeated with pleasure. His partner on guard duty laughed uproariously, and the OD men sleepily rubbed their hands against the cold.

David stood at the outlet of the street in the crowd of young boys and did not run away. As if his hands and feet were already bound. Why he didn't run away from there he did not know. It had to be, but why it had to be he also did not know. He had gotten up early that morning, and Father went with him, pedaling his empty rickshaw in silence; then he rode off without waiting, washing his hands of the business. He rode effortlessly and it looked as if the wheels were turning by themselves; he took every turn easily, and David regarded him enviously and with a sense of pride. He kept smiling sadly, turning around on his saddle to look back at him, until he disappeared in the distance.

"Bloody Hands isn't here today. Pass it on!"

The cry was repeated. Today he was standing in the crowd at the outlet of the street with Mordka the Ram, Moishe the Crip, Zyga, Yosele Egg Yolk; they all had sacks. The gendarme shouted energetically but without anger; the blue policeman ardently beat up every Jew who approached without holding his pass high over his head; the yellow policeman waved his stick under their noses. But sweat was running down his arms and ribs from fear and because he was so tense his legs wouldn't stop trembling; he couldn't control them. He walked away, ran over to the ruins to warm himself, came back, and squeezed himself in among the others. But now what's going on over there? The crowd of boys moves forward without uttering a word, heads hung low, pressing close together, shoulder to shoulder; it picks up speed, sweeps along everyone in its path, and in a single, enormous, indivisible clump rolls past the guards, who cry out, somewhat belatedly, *"Halt! Halt! Zurück!"* And as he runs, David, sensing with relief that the dense crowd is sweeping him forward without any difficulties, notices the twisted faces of the blue and yellow policemen whom he has safely passed in the tumult and commotion, who circulate inefficiently around the crowd and, tied to their sentry posts, tear at the rags on the people who run past them, striking feeble blows with their sticks. In a flash he sees a gendarme who in his haste leaps onto a curb in front of the running crowd and then nervously tries to take aim, but this takes a while, the safety catch won't release, finally his discarded glove flies onto the ground and . . . He was already on the other side when the first shot was fired. The gang dispersed in the twinkling of an eye, and he ran straight ahead, without looking back, among people who had no signs on them, and his first thought was astonishment at not seeing any white armbands on people's sleeves.

The quiet, empty street stretched out ahead of him in the sleepy silence of a winter morning, and the few people who were out walking passed him with calm, even steps. He noticed that he alone among them was running, like a madman, down the middle of the street. He slowed down and raised his head higher. In a strange city one's gaze has nothing to focus on. Space, the appearance of freedom. But after he crossed the wall the unexpected view became even clearer in his eyes: while over there a gray little street sank in the cloudy light, here the air was full of mist, and he heard the guard in front of a gate yawn broadly at this early hour. It seemed as empty as a holiday and he was afraid it might be Sunday. But it was not Sunday. He noticed a perceptive glance directed at him, saw someone's hand touch his sleeve, signaling to him in despair, and he realized that he still had not removed his armband. Feeling faint, he entered a courtyard. He stopped inside a dark stairwell and pressed his forehead against the wall, listening to his heart beating rapidly, unable to collect his thoughts. "It's only this hard the first time; later you get accustomed to it a little." He recalled Zyga's words. Easy for Zyga to say. Why had he come here? To buy a little bread? It was all so absurd and he fervently yearned to go back—immediately, there, to those little streets, where everyone walks around openly with their armbands on. He was alone, and the thought that he could be back home with his own people, surrounded by their faces, overwhelmed him with longing and with a bitter, intense loneliness such as he had never before experienced. Having removed his armband, he was an outcast; no longer was there a place for him in that world. The dark, empty hallway seemed to him to be his final shelter.

"Zosia, the jug, the jug—take the milk jug!" He heard the sound of a slammed door and clattering footsteps, and he ran out into the street.

He tried to walk calmly, with an even gait, restraining his suspicious haste. A loud shout made him jump aside in panic; he decided not to look around and lowered his head. Only now did he remember the advice that he had never been able to understand. Don't raise your head, Jew. Don't look anyone in the eye, don't draw attention to yourself when you walk down the street. If you are stopped, don't run away. Walk as if you aren't there at all, Jew. He used to laugh when Zyga said that. A lie, a bad joke.

He moved onward in a daze, holding his breath, with a helpless determination that might change his fearful march into a panicky flight at any moment. He knew he had to get away from the wall and then enter a store, enter a store where he saw the fewest people. He had to say what he wanted in a confident voice and put everything into his sack while the saleswoman watched him. That sack didn't look very nice. And what if they should chase him out of there? That wouldn't be the worst thing that could happen. *"Polizei dein Freund und Helfer."* Oh, yes. He walked on, looking down at his feet. In his panic he lost his way and didn't know where he was. He saw a sign on the second floor advertising Singer sewing machines; he knew the place and felt confident that it was Złota Street. But when had he crossed Marszałkowska? He couldn't remember. Inside a gate a streetwalker was straightening her stocking, slowly gliding her hand over her thigh, and her pale face was turned toward the street, where on the other side two Krauts were marching along.

"Na Kleine, na Puppe! Komm, komm."

She stuck out her tongue in response. The Germans roared with laughter.

Suddenly, the stones came to life. He noticed colored stains underfoot, signs, words painted in haste that he couldn't quite piece together. He kept walking and those signs followed behind him and wouldn't let him go. The insulting inscription trailed across the squares of the sidewalk in thin, crooked letters. Next to it was a wordless threat. A skull and crossbones. He trampled on the sign as if it were a judgment against him. Something moved inside him, some unbearable burden fell from his shoulders. Now he looked for those words on the stones, caught them at a distance, and repeated them in his thoughts. Whose hand had placed them here, who had walked here before him? Who had looked fearfully from side to side in order to give him courage? *"Victoria!"* It was crossed out, but under the capital *"V"* someone had written *"Verloren!"* His heart beat with joy at the sight. German slogans that had been painted across the asphalt slipped under his feet, and next to him were sentences hastily chalked onto the walls. Slowly he began to notice even more; the writings were repeated in some places, then disappeared under swirls of deliberately scattered gravel only to crop up again unexpectedly. Someone had been moved to scrawl in charcoal on the wall of a building a heartfelt *"Hitler kaputt!"* But no, that wasn't much to boast of. Someone else had added, *"Hitzler, darling, Hitzler, Hitzler."* To write about Hitler like that, in the middle of a street in broad daylight? Impudence can also engender courage. Later he noticed that the walls, the electric poles for the trolleys, and the trolley stops, were also covered with writing, but he didn't dare stop and look at them. Now he raised his head and saw a gleaming polished sign above a shop window: *"Nur für Deutsche."* He quickly turned around and noticed a drawing on a lamppost, a swastika hanging on a gallows like a spider on a thread, and beneath it the words: *"Nur für Deutsche."* He stopped still in his tracks.

He was in front of Meinl's shop; Krucza Street stretched into the distance all the way to Piękna and his heart contracted with sadness at the sight of it. He didn't know what to do. He could scarcely drag himself along. All this senseless wandering in circles seemed like a dream journey. The dream would end badly. How, he didn't know, but definitely badly. He slogged on in the uncomfortable, tight shoes that he had had to wear so that his wooden clogs would not reveal the difference between him and the people on this side. But he was betrayed by his clothing, which smelled of carbolic acid, his shaved head, which was poorly concealed by his ragged peaked cap with its earflaps. And the even, faded stripe on his sleeve in the place where he usually pinned his armband.

And his nose? They say you can easily tell a Jew by the shape and length of his nose. He thought about Aunt Chava's sad, black eyes and Naum's hair as curly as a sheep's fleece. Eyes, hair, everything can betray a Jew, but the nose is the worst. The Germans have meticulously measured and counted and the truth has come out. That's what's called science; he hadn't really known before what science was all about. They had had science in school, too, but a different science, a science from books. At the beginning of the school year Dyrko would always end his speech by pronouncing words that evoked their silent laughter: "Forward, youth, to the steep and towering heights of science!" When the Germans entered Warsaw, they arrested Dyrko and closed the school. Nothing had been clear since then. When someone resembles a Jew people say he's bad-looking. And if not, they say he's good-looking. Is he so very bad-looking? He didn't know and he stealthily rubbed his wet, unfortunate Jewish nose with his dirty hand. What else can they tell Jews by? Their walk and their hand gestures. It seems that a Jew plants his feet differently when he walks, and he waves his hands when he talks. He recalled the lovely, eloquent motions of Grandfather's pale hands when he folded and unfolded them in prayer; Uncle Yehuda's abrupt gestures that could convince a deaf man; the humorous movements of Uncle Gedali's fingers with which he could make everyone laugh without recourse to words. Father doesn't gesticulate because he has a heavy hand and it forms a fist of its own accord. But his accent is terrible; it's easy to mimic him. Mother says that as soon as he opens his mouth to say a word you can hear the Jew in him. That's why she doesn't allow him to go beyond the wall. You can be silent on the street. But if they can recognize a Jew by his movements, his walk . . . From a distance. Just thinking about it made him feel abandoned and helpless. He tried not to shuffle his feet, to walk evenly and with a springy gait, but such a walk looked even worse in the rags he was wearing.

He remembered the small, out-of-the-way, dark little shops on Mokotowska Street and set off in that direction, walking straight ahead. Only when he saw a patrol did he jump inside a gate. He waited a while, read the list of tenants, then came out. That man with the raised head who was moving freely down the street without a shadow of hunger on his face and without rags was not at all like a Jew, no, and yet he knew him very well. Fresh, clean, with a narrow-brimmed hat tilted jauntily to one side and a white scarf around his neck. New gloves, a little too bright, perhaps, stiffly sheathed his hands. He had a folded newspaper and a lit cigarette in his left hand. Is that Uncle Shmuel? It's hard to believe. But it was Uncle Shmuel, because when he saw David he turned his head and immediately crossed to the other side of the street. He noticed his narrow, screwed-up eyelids. Yes, it was Uncle Shmuel. What was he doing here? No doubt he had to do it because of business. Uncle Shmuel always had a head for business and hands filled with money. Grandfather says that Shmuel will support us all and arrange a grand funeral without grudging the cost, but he'll forget to go to the cemetery to say Kaddish because he'll have some really good deal to take care of on just that day. What deal? Everyone knows, dollars fly straight to his head, his neck, and Shmuel puts all his paper money into circulation to work for him.

On the opposite sidewalk Uncle Shmuel had opened the newspaper and, shielded by the paper, was walking more slowly. He passed by some people and was passed by others without paying any attention.

"Just imagine, a search! She didn't show up for three days."

"At work?"

"At home; where else?"

David didn't look around. Wilcza Street, a red light. David stopped at the crossing in a crowd of pedestrians; an empty space formed around him. "Phone Halinka, do you hear? You must phone her!" A green light. Uncle Shmuel carefully crossed the street and, hearing a shout behind his back, sped up. David followed him stealthily.

"And do you believe him?"

"I haven't gone mad yet, what do you take me for?"

"They're the worst kind."

Uncle Shmuel folded his paper. He stopped for a minute, lit a cigarette. Distractedly looking for his street, as if he were in this part of the city for the first time in his life, he turned into a sidestreet and disappeared.

"I went to lay flowers as I do every year on his birthday and the grave was all torn up." An old lady dressed all in black held her deaf friend's arm and screamed into her ear. "There was nothing left."

In a state of total numbness, David caught the fragmented words of people as they walked by, snippets of conversation, voices.

He tried mightily to imagine Uncle Shmuel's life, but he couldn't. It was incomprehensible, how people lived on the other side. But the words of a song that young Shmuel had sung in his bachelor days came to him: "Such a cold-blooded cad . . ." A summer morning, the sun peers into the workshop and the grizzled eelgrass turns green in the strips of light. Shmuel with his shirtsleeves rolled up, barefoot, is pouring cold water into the wooden tub. The tub, smelling of soap and starch now that the laundry's done, stands in the middle of the workshop. David plunges his hands into it and gives himself a sponge bath while Shmuel sings in his carefree voice, splashing and spluttering. After Mother cleans the tub, Father will open the workshop; but now he's praying, hunched over beside the window. Shmuel repeats with pleasure, "Pray and work and you'll grow a hump." David laughs, Shmuel laughs, Father hisses impatiently and keeps on praying. That's a memory. A memory from those years when, with his tongue protruding, he used to climb laboriously on all fours up the steep, sky-high stairs that led from Laban the baker's cellar, not knowing what to do with the paper sack and rolls. Laban would kindly carry the rolls for him. "David, this roll is costing me my life." At that time, in those days, Shmuel was taking his first steps, living in a corner of their apartment; he was a completely different person.

"Hey you, where'd you disappear to?"

Mordka stood in front of him with open mouth and dreamily closed eyes. His empty backpack dangled on his arm. As if everything were okay, he smiled broadly. David approached him and said, "Let's go inside a gate."

They found a gate and he said, "Mordka, I can't take it anymore. Let's go back."

Mordka the Ram only laughed.

"Not so soon."

"Let's go!"

"Take it easy." He slapped his empty backpack. "I have to load up my sack. That's one thing." He slapped his belly. "Empty. That's another." He looked at him closely. "But you've really had it. Well, well. The first time is always the worst. Let's go together."

After they had filled their sacks, a blue policeman came running up to the store at top speed, supporting his huge belly with his hands. He smelled of bad liquor, like a vat of mash. He raised his clenched truncheonlike fist and thrust it under his nose, breathing hard. Behind him came two civilians; they were moving fast and they didn't raise their voices. They wore *Volksdeutsch* lapel pins on their overcoats. One of them pursed his lips, forming them into a pig's snout, and his pallid moustache bristled. The other, with a scarf draped across his shoulder, smiled ingratiatingly and flashed his golden tooth. David saw how Mordka clutched his bread bag to his breast, but he didn't struggle with them and he didn't run away. The civilian with the blond moustache opened the sacks and peered inside with great interest. He pawed the potatoes greedily for quite a while.

"What have you got there, *Jude?*"

He plunged his hand deep under the bread, digging and feeling for something. He pawed through the sacks but didn't take anything out and returned both of them. The civilian with the scarf over his shoulder asked him, looking deep into his eyes, "And where did you hide the gold coins, *Jude?*"

"You'll find them," said Blond Moustache. "But there are lice under his collar. Go on, harvest them!"

"They swallow everything, the lousy creatures, even gold five-dollar pieces. They have a healthy appetite. I'll get them yet. I'll rip them out with their guts!"

"Sweetheart," said Blond Moustache in a voice tinged with regret, and his bristly snout turned in David's direction, "poor sweetheart, why do you traipse over to this side if you don't have any loot? I'm wasting time because of you."

Blond Moustache asked, "And what am I to do with you now, you snot-nosed brats?"

Mordka the Ram answered him in a fawning, falsetto voice. "You're a good man, sir, you wouldn't wrong a Jewish lad."

And he got it straight in the teeth for that.

"There, that's my kind heart," said Blond Moustache. "I've treated you generously."

"I know," said Mordka.

"Then thank me nicely, *Jude.*"

"I thank you from the bottom of my heart. I won't ever forget this, sir."

"You'll forget, you'll forget. I know you Jews only too well."

"No, sir."

And Mordka got it in the teeth for the second time.

"You'll forget?"

"I'll forget, sir. I'll forget everything. I've already forgotten."

Mordka bowed his head low and stealthily pressed his hand to his swollen face.

The blue policeman caught his breath and straightened his twisted holster belt around his belly. His polished boots creaked under his weight as he shifted indecisively from one foot to the other. He sneezed and the vat of mash overflowed.

"Fertig!" he said. "Take them to Hell and come back. Antoś and I will wait here."

They walked in front; Blond Moustache followed them. Mordka skipped boldly, stretched, patted his loaded backpack, and walked ahead without asking where he should go.

"Where is he taking us? Is it far?" David whispered.

"No, it's right here. Not far . . . There, you see, Hell is already surrounded."

On Hoża Street a loosely lined up patrol of the Feldgendarmerie, with brown facings and ribbons on their breasts, was on guard near headquarters, stopping traffic and pointing out the detour in absolute silence, while inside the courtyard a ragged crowd of smugglers pressed against the walls. Policemen made their way through the crowd, checking the papers of the Jews who were caught in this spot and waited with their hands up and their sacks at their feet. Hell was already full; the gendarmes' voices and the policemen's commands blended together in a nightmarish hubbub; in the corner of the courtyard, next to the corpse of a smuggler who'd been shot, a small generator was running, rending the air with its fearful roar and drowning out people's shouts and words. A woman's thin scream suddenly sliced through the uproar of the crowd to reach them at the guard post.

"Where are you from? Street, house number."

He questioned the civilian sharply and wrote it down.

"It's there," Blond Moustache added. "As much as your heart desires."

"Bartecka again! She's a plague, not a woman. If it's not moonshine, it's Jews. I'm going to give it to that whore."

With a mighty kick they were shoved into the center of the courtyard. Blond Moustache vanished like a dream, and a gendarme loomed up in front of them.

"Kinder von zwölf Jahren und darunter—an die Seite!"

Among the group of young children were Yosele Egg Yolk and Moishe the Crip, each holding a sack. Zyga, bigger and older, paced restlessly, glancing cross-eyed in their direction. In the back of the courtyard, against the wall, a corpse-white Uri held a green backpack in his outstretched hands, awaiting the gendarme who was moving slowly down the line of men. The gendarme snatched the backpack and flung it away, then turned Uri's pockets inside out. Behind the German's back Zyga kicked the backpack even farther away. Yosele Egg Yolk planted his foot on it and winked at Zyga. Uri, who'd already been searched, stood next to the others, facing the wall, his forehead resting against it. Moishe the Crip waved his stump when he saw them.

"Ram, is that you? Who is it I see? *Kess-uh-koo-say?* The count's here . . . The count who mounts dogs!"

"The prince who minces curs!"

A policeman with a sour look immediately ran over and ordered them to be silent, kicking out at them blindly. His shoe hit one of the boys who was standing near them and hadn't so much as opened his mouth. Yosele Egg Yolk's protruding frog eyes popped out and he clutched his ankle, unable to breathe from the pain. He collapsed and exhaled loudly, *aaach*, and with one motion threw the green backpack into the Crip's capacious bag and got up from the ground just as a military policeman stuck his head out a second-floor window.

"Form ranks!"

Pushing and shoving the rounded-up people, the policemen began to count them, but more smugglers kept coming in from the street and the count got all mixed up; every so often someone new was shoved through the gate and passed from hand to hand, accompanied by yells, until he found his place in the ranks. One Jew, whose buttons were all torn off and who had to hold up his trousers with his hands, distressed and at his wit's end, was suddenly led out of the crowd and thrust inside headquarters; then several other men were selected from among those who had been rounded up. Those men resisted and the police rushed them en masse, beating them with sticks and boots to drive the resisters into a corner of the courtyard from which, submissive and hunched over now that they'd been kicked and shoved around, they were led upstairs one by one.

A roar reached them from above, *"Ruhe!"*

There was absolute silence, the Jews froze, the policemen didn't move, and Bloody Hands came out into the center, without his gun. He pointed and a motor roared to life. He kept quiet and he listened to the silence.

"Auf die Knie!"

And they all dropped to their knees. He walked among the kneeling people, who curled up with their heads bowed as low as possible. He stopped here and there, gently touching someone's chin with his leather-gloved hand, and the head rose of its own accord, revealing a rigid face with tightly shut eyes. Suddenly he turned to face the people being held. He looked them over, walked on. Mordka the Ram nudged David with his elbow and hissed softly, "You, don't sleep. He's talking to you."

And David held his breath when he heard repeated above him, "What are you smuggling, Jew-boy?"

"Life."

He opened his sack with trembling hands, lifted it, and shook out its pitiful contents.

Then he heard the command, *"Ruhe! Judengebet!"*

And Bloody Hands led it himself, *"Ich, Jude . . ."*

And the crowd repeated after him in a disorderly chorus, *"Ich, Jude . . ."*

"Ich, Jude, bin schuldig am Krieg und Übel und Verbrechen in der ganzen Welt."

"I, a Jew, am guilty of war and evil, and crimes throughout the whole world."

Bloody Hands continued, *"Heute, morgen, in alle Ewigkeit."*

The crowd repeated, "Today, tomorrow, for all ages."

"Ich, Jude, bin ein Mörder."

"I, a Jew, am a murderer."

"Ich, Jude, bin ein Fresser ohne Menschenwürde."

"I, a Jew, am a glutton without any usefulness."

"Ich, Jude, bin ein Kriegshetzer."

"I, a Jew, am an instigator of wars."

In a raised voice Bloody Hands now let out a shout: *"Es lebe Judenrein!"*

The crowd shouted after him, "Long live *Judenrein!*"

"Fluch über mich, Jude. Tod für mich, Jude."

"Curses on me, a Jew. Death to me, a Jew."

Bloody Hands listened, smiling, to the last cry they repeated after him on their knees, and then commanded, *"Noch einmal."*

The kneeling crowd of Jews repeated the choral recitation without his help, and Bloody Hands listened in silence for a long time, until the last, lagging voice was heard. After a moment he turned away and said with a smile, *"Na ja, gut. Das Judengebet ist beendet."*

And he vanished into a hallway and soon afterwards leaned out of the second-floor window. "Bring me ten upstairs right away," he yelled.

"Yes sir, ten," the blue policeman repeated downstairs. "Pass it on, ten heads."

The police, energetically circulating among the crowd of smugglers, passed on the new command from mouth to mouth, "Ten heads!"

When the rest of the people were formed into a tight column, the counting began again and the gendarmes went out into the street to join the patrol. A woman whom they shoved outside the gate fell flat on her face on the sidewalk and groaned. She raised herself on her elbows, sat up, and holding her swollen, black-and-blue face in her hands, rocked back and forth in a daze, staring unconsciously at the crowded space. Her bag, which was thrown out after her, bounced on the paving stones, and the potatoes started rolling away. The mob, as it was driven out of the courtyard, managed to avoid her, but scores of feet trampled the contents of her basket. People huddled together briefly inside the gate, and then ran by threes into the street where the barrels of machine guns in the middle of the roadway pointed the way. They hurried along: a blue policeman ran in front, blocking the road and waving vehicles aside; after him came the column, and alongside the column, at a distance, the gendarmes; closer to the ranks, on both sides, were the rest of the blue policemen. They left Hell in this formation, moving in the direction of Three Crosses Square. Snow was blowing in from Aleje and the trees in the square were blue. As long as they walked down Bracka a deathly silence reigned in the ranks; on Złota, they were made to go faster; when they caught sight of the wall they took heart. They counted their losses in front of the *Wache.*

"*New Warsaw Courier* . . . A great victory at Kaluga! The Germans have stormed a piece of peace!"

The newsboy walked around with his pile of papers, shoving them at the returning people at the last moment. The convoy moved away and then stopped not too far off; a gendarme walked up to the *Wache* and negotiated with the guards; the police scattered slowly and the column of smugglers waited across from the guarded exit under the unwilling eye of the blue policeman, who didn't seem to worry that one of the gang might want to run away. Traffic was stopped every so often and the first group of workers returning from their jobs outside the wall were allowed past the *Wache.*

They could hear a cry from over there, "Uri, did you find an easy piece of bread for yourself?"

"Oh, dream on! An easy piece of bread, an easy piece of bread! You should live so long!"

"They took three kilos of salt pork from Drabik. Kepele was caught with a carton of Hungarian cigarettes. And Biała Ceśka, the woman who works for the Lewins, they pumped her full of Epsom salt and seated her on a porcelain chamber pot like a *tsaritsa* and after three hours the first diamond burst out of her."

"Nine carets, no less!"

"Old Mrs. Lewin's wedding ring, two gold cuff links, and a signet ring with a carnelian."

"And when they finally told her to stand up, she said that she couldn't yet because she still had pressure on her liver from yesterday's dinner: Anielcia Lewin's Swiss watch, a souvenir from her grandfather, with seventeen jewels, a chain, and a gold locket."

"Well, since they've robbed the whole Lewin family going back three generations, it's entirely possible that they'll win this war."

"Not necessarily!"

"What's to talk about? Even in the camps they don't fool around with that kind of nonsense. One-two-three and they're done. A haircut, a tooth pulling, a bath, and they're done with you. Give your hair for mattresses, your gold fangs to the pliers, your rags into the steam, and run downstairs!"

"When one person steals, it's kleptomania; when a whole nation steals, it's Germania. *Sieg um jeden Preis. Heil!*"

"Everything for the army. They're already sending trainloads of caracul coats east in order to thaw their frozen innards, and it's only the beginning of the Russian winter. Oof!"

"Caracul. What else do they need for victory?"

"Ermine, fox, chinchilla, seal, beaver, Persian lamb. Warsaw is removing its coats!"

"The Fritzes in the trenches are going to have a large selection of furs. The lice will be warmer in the Kursk district. Why worry your head about it?"

"That's it. They weren't able to enter Moscow in their tanks, but they think they can leap in there on my old lady's Persian lamb feet!"

> *"Deutschland siegt an allen Fronten.*
> *Deutschland liegt an allen Fronten."*

"Quiet there, Jew, are you angry that you've still got your skin and you're returning home with a piece of bread?"

"Hey, cop, go and translate, hurry. *Herr Wachtmeister* is curious."

> "Roosevelt plows,
> Churchill weeds,
> Stalin threshes,
> Hitler bleeds!"

"A poem? I don't translate poems, Jew."

"You, Uri, don't wag your tongue. *Herr Wachtmeister* has been walking around in a funk since morning, he can't sit still because he's being sent to the front. He's already killed three people, and you'll be the fourth."

"Gentlemen, don't quarrel. A curse on such politics! A man still has a few miserable zlotys inside his lining and if they start frisking us again he'll go home naked!"

"They don't take lice; those goods they leave. You won't go home naked; at the most you'll have offspring."

"My dear, beloved lice. If only my 'little ones' could be turned into capital I'd be a capitalist."

"Oh yeah? Rubbish. And how has a poor, lousy, Jewish porter like you offended the Krauts?"

"I'm still alive."

"This is life? Wake up, Germans."

"Deutschland erwache!"

"It's easy for you to say, but the Krauts are scared out of their wits. Uri, tell him how it is, because he doesn't believe me, the scoundrel."

"You're right. I don't believe you."

"Then go to the eastern front and see for yourself!"

"I'll wait."

"Who's waiting? Show me who has that much time."

"Gentlemen, let me read today's newspaper in peace . . . As a matter of fact, they're scared out of their wits."

"An offensive in the summer, now a counteroffensive in the winter: a man can get confused in all this. Eh, to see Berlin destroyed and die."

"To see the Krauts turn tail, losing their shoes on the way, and then to return to Abraham's bosom for a mug of oaten beer!"

"Don't be in such a hurry, Kepele! Do you have a bit of imagination? An Abraham's bosom that would receive such a crowd of lousy Jews—what a sight that would be!"

"Life is lousy, death is lousy, and Abraham's bosom is lousy, too!"

"Everything's moving, everything."

"Who's got something moving under his collar?"

"Here, in the newspaper! Here, the front is moving, here, between the lines. I'm telling you, the winter counteroffensive has begun. In a while the Russkies will chase the Fritzes out without their pants."

"Stop it, stop it. Don't scare us with your Russkies, because *Herr Wachtmeister* and the cop will both faint from the idea and there won't be anyone around to let us cross the wall."

"Gentlemen, pay attention to orders!"

"Gentlemen, pay attention to the blue policeman. If he goes home with news, his old lady won't recognize him."

"He'll have the worst possible memories after the Jews are gone!"

"He has to have something, after all. His pants . . ."

"He'll wash them! He'll forget about the rest. Gentlemen, have you heard the new joke?"

"They keep collecting jokes. Hurry up, don't waste any time, the second front is on the move and it will soon be out of date."

"It's not about the second front. The entire second front, you should excuse me, is a joke to amuse fools."

"Out with it, Uri."

"This time it's an international train. A mother and a daughter, and two officers. A German and an Italian. A tunnel. In the darkness there's the sound of a passionate kiss and a slap in the face. What does the mother think? 'I've brought up my daughter correctly.' And the daughter? 'I never would have thought it of her at her age; she always has all the luck.' The German? 'All right, the macaroni eater is making a play for the little one, but why did she have to slap me?' The Italian? 'Not good enough. When it enters the next tunnel I'll kiss my hand even louder and slap the other cheek!'"

"As a matter of fact, you told us the same joke last week."

"Naum, it's possible that you know my last week's jokes, but other people will repeat them next year when the green grass is growing over you."

"Ceśka, did you hear?"

"I heard. Ech, old folks. When they sweep you out of Warsaw, I'll buy a phonograph with a tuba."

"What for, *shiksa?*"

> "Sometimes she sold barley
> And sometimes she sold parsley."

"Don't trouble your head about it. Now, everything is cheap. But once the Jews are gone, then life will begin!"

"But in the meantime, you cross the wall and risk your stupid head for old man Lewin."

"I do, I do, because I like watching a Jew stuff himself with pork!"

"You'll come to a bad end, Ceśka. They'll ship you and your Lewins by freight train straight to the pit. You won't escape from under the shovel, *shiksa* . . . Yesterday a railroad worker from the freight yards told me in strictest confidence that transports have been rolling in from the Reich, four thousand Jews, in the direction of Biała Podlaska. And all the cars, every single one of them, is sprinkled with quick lime."

"Lime, lime! Well and good, let it be lime. Then only lime-pickled eggs will arrive at the place."

"You there, Kepele, wash your mouth out!"

"May a stick put out your eye, a stick as long as my leg from here to Tokyo and back!"

"Kepele, don't throw eggs or you'll go home empty-handed. Your kids are hungry, they're crying for Papa."

"Gentlemen, live and let live. She got caught with Lewin's goods and is still going back to him. The old man will put a bug in her ear, oy vey . . . Your face is swollen, Ceśka. You should see what you look like!"

"Lewin emptied only his middle drawer. He still has the hole under his floor, the leg of his armchair, and a fake brick in the wall."

"That *shiksa* already knows everything about the Lewins."

"And who doesn't? The whole city knows. Oy, they're going to get your master, Ceśka. And they'll pluck him, they won't leave a single feather on him."

"Gentlemen, quiet, the gendarme is returning."

"What? Are we going? And I completely forgot to buy mustard. Oy oy! Now everything is ruined."

"A blue policeman. At ease! Drink to my health and to the next time. Let's call it a day and be damned."

The convoy guard walked across the street, pointing to the guarded exit with the barrel of his gun; the group of workers from the outpost had already marched past that point, and the smugglers fell silent in expectation of the next opening of the *Wache*. There began a hasty search for crumpled armbands, and the six-pointed stars, extracted from their hiding places, again hung in place. Finally, they were on their way back. Moishe the Crip reached into his sack, his face glowing, tore a large chunk of bread out of a loaf, and hurriedly gnawed at it.

"To live, not to die."

The blue and yellow policemen were waiting for just this moment: they fell on the smugglers, barking at them and knocking their caps from their heads. Punching and kicking and shoving, they drove the first ranks of the column to the other side of the wall at a run. The crowd surged forward, and everyone ran at breakneck speed, knowing full well what would happen at the next stage of their run. The *Wächter* stood there with his legs wide apart, a patient smile on his face, tossing his gun from one hand to the other as if it were a tennis racket; it was obvious he'd been waiting a long time for this moment. He smartly threw the gun across his shoulder and whistled softly through his teeth.

When a finger rests on the trigger of a gun, fate has only six bullets in the magazine. A civilian who feels the muzzle of a gun behind his back runs straight ahead; a crowd runs straight ahead, and everyone in the crowd can hope that the bullet will pass him by. The *Wächter* fires into the center, into the mass, and his target doesn't have a face. The first one chosen is the best. Fate does not ask his name, death does not look into his eyes, and everything depends on this. Moishe, with his heavy sack, could scarcely keep pace with David, but they ran side by side, their heads drawn down between their shoulders in fear, keeping their eyes on the approaching dark tunnel of Żelazna Street, its roadway sliced in half by the wall, where, once they had passed the first bend of the side street, Krochmalna, a bullet could no longer reach them from behind. When he heard the shots, David automatically shut his eyes.

Moishe the Crip said in great amazement, "He fired without taking aim. Take this," he added, and handed him his sack.

He looked back only when he was already turning into the side street, running all the while and not noticing the weight of the two sacks. He saw bodies lying on the pavement and above them, on the wall, a huge yellow poster that he always avoided looking at. *"Achtung, Achtung! Vor Juden wird gewarnt. Halt! Juden, Läuse, Fleckfieber."* Moishe was already on the other side trying to get up, crawling down the street away from the spot where he had fallen in a puddle of blood, and his jaws were still moving, still chewing his bread.

Uri, minus his cap, was standing beyond the bend in the street, desperately crying out to the people running toward him, "Who has the Crip's sack? Who has—you, Gelding?"

"What do you mean?" Kuba countered him.

"*He* does," Zyga called out as he ran. "*He* does." And he pointed to David.

"Give it here," said Uri and jumped at him.

He was breathing heavily and couldn't close his mouth, as if his pounding heart were about to leap out of it. He threw the sack to the ground, and Uri immediately pulled from it a small green backpack. He opened it, looked inside. He fumbled in it feverishly until he pulled out a small scroll of thin printed paper that he slipped inside his shirt; then he hurriedly fastened the buckles and slung the backpack over his shoulder.

"That you can keep. It's yours." And he gave him back the sack.

They watched as he calmly walked away, buttoning up his shirt.

"What was that, Zyga?"

"You mean you don't know?"

"That little scroll that the Crip had in his sack. You're the one who flung the green backpack at him in Hell, you and Egg Yolk. Tell me, is it an illegal paper?"

"You mean you don't know?" Zyga replied, and he burst out laughing loudly, with relief. "It's a mezuzah. A scroll people put on their doors."

Baruch Oks's gang came to the courtyard to claim the sack that had been Moishe's property. Summoned from all directions, they assembled at the same time. Five-Fingers Mundek picked up the sack and mooed with pleasure. Henio Herring licked his wet lips. Kuba the Gelding, who always had to be first, elbowed him aside. Long Itzhok stamped his wooden shoes to warm up and circled impatiently, waiting for the sack to be opened. Mordka the Ram and Yosele Egg Yolk, arm in arm and exhausted, brought up the rear. This time they'd been successful, and how! Mordka straightened up to his full height, lifted his head high, half-closed his eyes. But Yosele was already gray: he was thoroughly depressed and looked like a dying frog.

Baruch Oks peered around uncertainly, almost furtively, turned up the collar of his leather jacket, and rubbed his hands.

"Bribe them! Bribe them! And bribe them once again," shouted Yosele Egg Yolk. "You'll be able to bribe the *Wache*."

But Baruch Oks turned pale, a twisted smile contorted his face, and his eyes narrowed as they did before a fight.

"Egg Yolk, if you didn't get enough in Hell, I can give you some myself," and Five-Fingers Mundek raised his fist.

"Beat me, beat me!" Yosele Egg Yolk squealed breathlessly. "What are you waiting for, Mundek? Beat me, only you can do it." Mordka the Ram had grabbed him by the hair and was holding him, but he wriggled out of his grasp.

A terrifying scream could be heard in all the outbuildings at once. Windows slammed, fists hammered on windowsills. A bucket of slops splashed into the courtyard.

"Beat me, beat me!"

Dusk fell and the first lights wiped the night from the air. In the center of the courtyard lay the discarded sack. Everyone was waiting.

"When it gets dark," said Baruch Oks without raising his voice, "I'll go get him. Is he lying far away?"

David answered, "Not far. The Crip's on this side."

That day he did not return home with empty hands. When he placed the lightweight bag on the table, a green face covered with hair rose from a mattress, and a bundle of rags, shivering convulsively, crawled out from the bedding, complaining in his mother's voice and asking why he was so late. Smelling the aroma of freshly baked bread, the dry aroma of flour and ground meal, she cautiously, disbelievingly, touched the loaf with her fingers. The bread was still warm.

❉

VIII

The wind blew in through the shattered windowpane and a star plunged earthward through the black sky. Darkness swallowed up the short day almost as soon as the noon hour struck. Winter, winter . . . When would this winter finally be over? David blew on his hand and rubbed his frozen, stiff fingers. Heavy icicles hung from the gutters and the edge of the roof, like beards severed by ice from the skeletons that lay scattered about the courtyards. The column of mercury fell relentlessly, degree after degree. And here life was flying away with every breath. In front of the windows of the tenement, which grew more deserted every day, a mound of garbage, furniture, and books was piling up, while the snow covered the rags on the street, the traces of the beggars' forced march. Papers flew out through open windows and doors, blew into the stairwells, swept from the stairs out into the courtyard and kept on traveling, and away we go—Leibuś with a smile on his face dashed through the city on Faiga's knees, holding a flag in his little hand, all the way to Żelazna Brama Square, where the holiday photograph froze in the mud. An apple crowned the flag and in the apple was a colored candle . . . Swollen tongues protruded like stones from between bared teeth, and the faces of the dead turned dark blue.

Discarded clocks lay in the snow, recording a time that had passed. Torn prayer books scattered their verses; mute curses wandered about aimlessly; yellowed, moldy pages flew off in all directions to the four corners of the earth. The eviscerated quilts in which they wrapped themselves when they went out into the streets loosed their feathers in the frozen air, and Jewish specters glided through the city like plucked angels.

The wind blew the stars from the black sky through the shattered windowpane.

"I set the constellations, the planets, and the moon in the void. I extend the Milky Way," said Professor Baum, diligently scratching himself all over.

A louse crawled lazily down his sleeve.

"These are the heavens."

He raised his open hand with the fingers pointing upwards in a meaningful gesture, as if he were lifting a priceless goblet, and his bluish eyelids closed of their own volition over eyes tearing from the cold.

Professor Baum's heaven was empty, swept clean of angels. The voice of God did not echo in it and no overturned throne barred the way to those who yearned to enter there. Light, space, harmony. The heavens were the first clock. A mechanism composed of mass and revolutions measured the flow of the centuries without error. It was the clock, the calendar people had read for centuries. The scales and the measure according to which they constructed their own small weights and measures. The source of energy that had never been diminished from the moment when man stood up straight and took in the stars with a single glance. The Hunter, concealed behind the tree, observed the movement of the Great Bear, at which the Hunting Dogs were barking, so that he might be at his station before dawn, when the Wolf follows the Bear to the dried-out watering hole. The Fisherman, making haste by night to reach his outlying fishing grounds, watched his Stern and steered his Sails and Rudder by the Pole Star, waiting for the rising of the sun and the first star of Pisces. From there, from under the vault of the world, indistinct signs reached him that he learned to accept and understand as if they had been sent directly to him. The succession of day and night, the seasons of the year—everything, he found, was permanently inscribed there.

The sky was direction, energy, motion. Motion and the location of motion, energy and the direction of energy. Here, down below, space was enveloped in silence and motionlessness. But you only had to prick up your ears, focus your thoughts, and you could hear the reverberations of an exploding star, the dull thunder of a burning mass, the hissing of a nebula that, struggling with the icy abyss, amasses energy over the course of the millions of millions of light-years of its birthing, in order to eject into black space the still unborn body of a young galaxy. In the immeasurable void that is prepared to receive it, in the concentration of accumulating energy, transitory matter congealed and life came to an end, scattering its glow in the darkness.

In this world, when the earth began to move from its place and revolve around the sun at a set speed of 209 kilometers per second, the harmony of freedom reigned, supported at a distance by the power of the heavenly bodies. The suns, planets, moons dived in space like agile fish in water, passing each other with dignity in the circular motion of their endless orbits. They emitted light, marking the place of their stay in the void, and absorbed light; they fed upon it as if it were interstellar plankton. Everything here had its order, place, and path—for a day, a month, a year. Eternity stretched out before the world like the calculations of a mathematician who is just closing in on a proof. Some stars died, others were born, and nothing appeared to perish here. Concealed white dwarfs grew smaller in hiding so that, years later, they might explode once again with the energy that had been hidden within them until the time was ripe. Enormous concentrations of fire gathered streams of nimble light on their journeys and whirled around like gigantic conches in order to give back to the world the offspring of many suns. The Milky Way, the fatherland of visible stars, stretched out in the nothingness among the distant nebulae that dispersed in their flight with unimaginable speed and, filling the universe, breathed life into space.

Professor Baum raised his arms in ecstasy, paying no attention to David, who sat huddled over his notebook.

The frost will not last forever. In January the days will get longer, in March the equinox will come, the ice will break up. He felt a surge of hope as he thought about the coming of spring and he was overwhelmed by emotion at the sudden recollection of summer, as if he could already feel the warming sunshine on his face. Frozen, shivering, waiting for Mother to build up the pitiful fire in the middle of this winter of 1941–42 that had descended upon the living and the dead, burying life under the snow, David asked, "So the world has its own goal?"

And Professor Baum answered, "Its goal is thermal death. The earth is heading toward extinction."

On the surface it seems that nothing can escape change. Winter precedes spring, spring precedes summer. But the stars squander energy, they die in a blaze of light, freeze, and are extinguished. The planets move away from the stars into darkness and cold. With every revolution of the earth the sun pulls the earth in an unknown direction; with every revolution of the sun the galaxy pulls the sun in an unknown direction. The forces of gravity grow weaker, the orbits enlarge. The universe rushes into nothingness, growing ever more immense with the speed of light, and perishes. A sphere of fixed stars does not exist . . . Geometry is thought cast into space, the motion of a stick in Euclid's hand, the sketch of a road that vanishes in the sand . . . With every revolution the parallax of a star must change until the sum of the angles equals zero and the triangle buries its apex in infinity. Tense as a soap bubble, fettered for an instant by lines of binding forces, the universe concentrates on straightening itself out.

Professor Baum closed his eyes as if by doing so he could see the flight of the nebulae.

And David asked, "So where is hell?"

Professor Baum unfolded a map of the starry heavens, gave a barely audible laugh, and, bowing his head over the cosmos, pointed with his finger.

"Here."

So it was here, where Scorpio sways its abdomen and lifts its poisonous stinger above the world, that Jews intentionally situated hell. Isaiah called it the worm that does not die. The heart of the worm, concealed among the segments fumbling across the sky, the alpha of Scorpio, the hole, the hole without water, the pit, the grave. Here the lost, the victims of all faiths, fall through eternity in a multitude, cackling demonically, *Ha, ha, ha, ha!* From here the gluttonous locust, unclean vermin, cockroaches, bedbugs, lice, emerge into the world in order to multiply on the blood of the living and fly away to hell. It is the kingdom of reptiles, serpents, and insects, where evil, disgust, and fear breed, and all of man's afflictions, which Jehovah scooped up from this pit with his generous hand and shook out onto the earth. Bats, spiders, snakes, lizards, moths that blind you just by the touch of their wings, toads that inject their poison, salamanders that copulate lazily in fires, vampires that suck blood, and apparitions that smother people all find shelter in this pit. They entangle themselves in hair, inflict furtive bites at night, gnaw on the fingers of sleeping people.

"Aha, it's here."

The fire Mother was laboring over flickered weakly. With a smudge of soot on her forehead and traces of ash in her hair, she waved a dust rag near the open grate and smoke seeped out. She stirred the barely smoldering trash with a poker. The evaporating moisture hissed at her. Father was in charge of the carbide lamp; its green light flooded his face. A coarse gray patch was visible on her skinny raised elbow—a sign of severely desiccated skin. Her black eyes glowed with the reflected light of the fire and grew dim when she turned her head away, choking from the smoke. It crept over her neck, her hair, and she started to cough, fending off the smoke with her hand.

"Give me that lousy shirt, I'll take care of it right now—ehem, ehem."

He was not afraid of hell although he knew it existed. Priests of all religions frighten people with hell and with the threat of eternal torments. Hell, hell . . . The slow cooking of human meat on an open fire and the continuous basting of the roast with tar. Sulphur, oil, all this feeds the flames, but can you burn forever? How long can you burn before you're completely burned up? How long can you cook before you're cooked into nothing? He tried to imagine such suffering and couldn't. He tried to imagine fear of such suffering and couldn't do that, either. It was cold; maybe if it weren't so cold it would be easier and the image of hell fire would terrify him? In any event, this is what it looked like on the map: from the constellation Libra, where the Scorpion's pincers used to be located, the arched body of the fiery worm that does not die stretched its abdomen all the way to the forking of the Milky Way. Professor Baum's finger stopped and pointed to a star of first magnitude. It was Altair. Can there be a fire that does not die out?

This fire is depicted by the star called the Altar. You see—oh, right there, it shines in the forking of the Milky Way. That star of the first magnitude glows in the shadow of the cosmic tree, the tree of life. O tree, tree, great tree! It has already been a fir, a cedar, an olive, a fig, a maple, a grapevine, a miraculous herb. The Bible says that the tree arose from the waters. Long, long ago people thought the earth was surrounded on all sides by ocean. That is why the tree in whose shade all the beasts and all the peoples live arose from the waters.

"In the words of the Prophet Ezekiel," Professor Baum laughed weakly.

In general, the whole expanse of heaven is an incomparably fascinating conceptual sphere. The Arabian Garden full of old, ancient mysteries. Heaven, hell, all so far away. Professor Baum sketched a circle on the map with his hand, uniting the distant constellations with a single motion. Oh yes, it is full of old mysteries.

Heaven. His imagination always came up with the same desire. When the war ends, he will set out five loaves of bread in a row, a basket of hard rolls and a basket of crescent rolls, and he will smear them all with butter and eat every one of them. Until he's too full. Since that will tire him out, he'll then lie down in a nice warm bed, stretch out, take a nap, wash up, and sit down at the table again. He'll gobble up the crescent rolls sprinkled with poppy seeds, washing them down with coffee and milk. He never used to want to drink coffee and milk and now he regrets that. Better not to think about food; the end of the war is so far away. If he can manage to get to the other side of the wall again tomorrow, he'll go to get bread. He'll succeed this time, too. All gates must open before the hungry—and all gates do open before the hungry.

But how can he say anything about this? It's a shame, a disgrace. Whenever he is on the other side, he buys a separate quarter-kilo of bread and eats it furtively, by himself, because he buys that quarter loaf secretly, just for himself. In the entrance hall of the nearest house, where he hides after he leaves the store, he swallows it in a couple of bites and keeps quiet about it; he swallows it with a sense of shame, closing his eyes and giving himself over to the extraordinary delight of stuffing his belly. But after all, he could bring everything home, grit his teeth, endure—yes, but when he thinks about the return trip that awaits him, a voice says to him mockingly, "Gobble it up, it's the last time!" He obeys the voice, the voice of reason, that always leads him into temptation, because each time is always the last time. Is that right? He knew it wasn't right. Now he was trembling, partly from the cold, partly at the sound of Professor Baum's words, which evoked something like fear in him. But fear before the vastness of the universe is something completely different from terror before Bloody Hands, the gendarme. Fear, awe, fascination. Would he never be able to express it? About his terror of the gendarmes he wished to speak to no one.

"It doesn't want to burn at all today, what a fate," complained Mother. "Give me that lousy shirt, right now."

Father moistened a rag with a couple of drops of furniture polish and threw it into the stove. It flared right up. Furniture polish contains oil, resin, flammable alcohol; whatever disgusting food they have is fried in this diabolical mixture and it does burn, and the warmth of the burning rubbish flares up into their faces as a soothing, transient rush of air. Father corked the bottle, pounded in the cork securely with his hand, and put it away in the corner behind the box where he kept the rest of his tools and half-empty bottles of dark upholsterer's fluids: varnish, stain, polish, lacquer.

"Die, pestilence," and Mother shoved the louse-infested rag deeper into the bowels of the stovepipe with her poker. She groaned, took the kettle from the stove top, and placed it in the firebox.

"Die, scorpion!" And man in the wilderness throws the poisonous death into the fire together with his own coat. There is nothing else he can do. David has his own explanation of how the fire of the Altar burned in the heavens and the constellation of Scorpio appeared in that fire.

"My altar is this kitchen, this house is my grave. Ehem, ehem," Mother coughed. "You can choke to death in this smoke, ehem, ehem. What is left of my life?" She grabbed the whole set of red-hot damper lids by the hook and held them up like glowing hoops. "My whole world has shrunk to this bedbug-infested hole, this firebox, these damper lids. Hell, indeed . . . All I see is lice, fleas, bedbugs, cockroaches, and other vermin. I can't even remember when was the last time—ehem, ehem. I never see God's world—ehem, ehem."

"The world," Father shouted from behind the mattress he was straightening out. "What world are you dreaming of? It's cold, empty, dark. Bloody Hands is running around out there drunk and breaking windows. Whoever he sees, he shoots. Bullets whistle around every corner. What are you dreaming about?"

"That's also true."

Mother walked into the entrance hall, groaning and carrying the steaming black kettle.

The lice suffocate and float to the surface in the boiling water, lightweight, swollen, yellow. Their nits somehow survive a bath in boiling water; in order to eradicate them, you have to iron every single seam after laundering the clothes. Oily stains spread into the folds of the shirt, the collar, the sleeves under the heated iron. The linen becomes gray and full of ugly smudges, but fewer insects nest in it. Once a month Mother soaks the dirty linen in a cauldron and steams the lice. With her own hands she is conducting a war against creeping vermin in all the corners, cracks, holes, seams in clothing, folds in linens, in hair, everywhere. She wrings out the rags, presses her hand to her liver, complains. In the summer she paints the beds with turpentine and ammonia: May the bedbugs die. She pours boiling water on the floor and scours it with a rice-straw brush: May the cockroaches drop dead. There are many varieties of cockroach if you look closely. They run easily on their energetic, long legs; there are loads of them everywhere, they trot about in squadrons in search of crumbs, they mop the floor with their long, thin little moustaches in their panic and confusion. When the light-colored cockroach scouts abandon the field, dull-headed, dark-shelled ones appear instantly, one by one; like heavily armored tanks, they lumber about hesitantly. Where did they get the name "German roaches"? In winter there are fewer bedbugs and cockroaches, but with every passing day there are more and more lice in their heavy clothing. Only incantations can help and Mother does employ incantations; she practices strange, dark rituals, grasps at ancient methods, inspects their ragged clothes. When she runs out of patience with some tattered piece of clothing she throws it into the fire together with the insects. Let them burn. They have fewer clothes but the lice keep on multiplying. They gather on the wall in a prominent place, fall onto the bed on their backs and clumsily paw at the air with their little feet until they turn over onto their bellies, and then, slowly, indefatigably, they come closer seeking warmth, shelter on human skin, and blood.

"It's amazing," said Professor Baum, "but since the freezing weather set in I don't have the strength or the courage to turn my shirt inside out. Big deeds, small deeds. But what does it all mean? For example, this doing the laundry without soap. You have to be a saint. Where does one find the strength, Mrs. Fremde? Where do you find it?"

Father sliced at the air with his stiff finger. "From big deeds, great deeds, and the greatest deeds, this world has gone to the lice."

Mother defended herself with a feeble smile. "Soap is so expensive. If I didn't do all this, the lice would have eaten them alive a long time ago."

"I have two world wars behind me," Professor Baum said proudly. "In the infantry, in the gray infantry. And after much thought I can say, my friends, that history passes over the truly heroic deeds in silence."

"Don't give up as long as you're able. That's what's important," said Father. "But don't look for heroes on our street, Baum! Their stomachs are full and they walk around brandishing a big stick."

Mother sighed. "There's only a little bit of kerosene, just enough for medicine."

Father asked, "Head washing again?"

David let out a loud, snorting laugh. "It's easy for you to say; the lice run away as soon as they see your bald head!"

And Father laughed.

"Yes, yes, the war. The second world war against vermin."

"Help me carry the tub to the entrance. When the rags cool off you'll help me wring them out, Yakov."

Professor Baum slid his hand over the table as if he were erasing a dirty and no longer needed chart that had been traced on it.

One motion, one glance—and the eternal world collapsed, but its fragments circled outside the window in distant space, whirled among the stars like astral admonitions, like moldy signs of the zodiac, like myths that had returned to their original locations. Noah will not save the species, the Flood will happen not just once but many times, and the distant mammoth will bypass the Ark. Poor mammoth, it is going to freeze in the ice of Siberia! The ladder on which Jacob climbs to the clouds leads nowhere, the ladder is missing a final rung, the dream has no end, and Jacob's hands are growing weak. Blind Moses, minus his stick, dies of thirst and the shattered tablets turn to sand, the sand of the desert. Jonah doesn't reach Nineveh in time. The fish loses its way among the waters and dies, and its great body breaks apart on dry land. Esther sobs eternally in the garden of the king and does not save her people. The wine glass is empty and when Elijah the Prophet comes to our street he will gather scattered bones. The Bible collapsed into the ruins; all of Grandfather's teachings became barren. David's ears burned, his eyes were glittering, feverish, and his thoughts caused him to break out in a sweat. In all that upheaval he yearned for the illusions he had long since abandoned. A part of his being was sinking into nothingness and clung to his memories with its last bit of strength, crying for help, but he felt no faith, only a shapeless longing. So there is nothing anymore, nothing definite, nothing lasting? Professor Baum said no. And gave examples.

He had only a hazy idea of what it all meant, but what emotions those examples awoke in him!

A man who is riding in a train throws a ball out the window and the ball returns to his hand. What was the ball's trajectory? A passenger in the car says it travels along a straight line. But the train is already thundering past a tiny station, and the stationmaster who is standing on the platform can guarantee that the ball is traveling along an arc. How can that be, David pondered. He rubbed his finger over the dirty, sticky wood of the table until it squealed. And if you could travel above the train at the same speed and in the same direction, you would be able to see the ball moving along a straight line parallel to the tracks. That is, differently from the passenger in the car, who threw it straight up into the air. You can choose a point in space from which the trajectory of the ball will follow the circumference of a circle, of an ellipse . . . You can imagine the same ball traveling along a curve that is a section of any figure you choose. Everything depends on what point we select in space and in what direction, at what speed we are moving in relation to the train, the globe, the configuration of the land. Hopla! — and the ball is dancing. It is everywhere and nowhere. It easily sketches triangles, squares, cubes; free and lightweight, it vanishes into space, outdistances the lumbering locomotive and shoots into infinity. Its motion has already carried it beyond the environs of the crowded car where the sleepy passenger, bored by the slow pace of the local train on the Skierniewice–Koluszki run, yawns and picks up a ball, weighing its dead weight in his hand.

All this took place at dinner, without bread, over a bowl of beet-root soup, three times a week, every other day. Mother said it was cheap. And Father replied in his characteristic fashion, "Even so, it will turn to dust; even so, it will turn to dust."

"Yakov, he's a good teacher, he knows something about everything, and he could even lecture in a university."

"Baum? A professor of what? What an idea! That conductor of fresh air!"

The remnants of a vest over a filthy, rumpled shirt, a blanket in his hand instead of a coat, and a tin can at his waist. Gaiters, and under the gaiters slippers with holes in them, and bare feet. And when he walked down the street, first he raised a chamois gaiter, then a dirty instep, and finally the loose heel of his torn shoe. And that was the whole of Professor Baum. In the summer he arrived punctually at five. In the winter at three, while it was still light out. He removed the blanket that was slung across his shoulders, folded it, and sat down on it. Before dinner he rubbed his hands together: What do we have today? David winced when he heard his own voice, courteous and alien. Words that belonged on paper rose in his mouth, sticking together like wet dough. Professor Baum swallowed the watery soup while David recited his assignments from the previous day. When the bowl was empty, the spoon licked dry, Professor Baum put it back in his pocket and then David straightened out the rolled-up pages of his greasy, shabby notebooks and undid the dogears. He laboriously conjugated verbs in a foreign tongue.

"I am, you are, he is, she is."

"Go on. The past tense!"

Who cares what it is? He wrote clumsily and kept making gross errors. Professor Baum picked up a pencil and with great dignity placed red checkmarks in the notebook. Lice dropped from his sleeves. When they fell to earth from under the stars, a slow, laborious, unbearable dictation began.

"The ruler of Paflagonia deigns to sit down to breakfast . . . Reading the letter so absorbs his attention that he does not see before him the noble soft-boiled eggs and the brightly illuminated rolls that are lying on the table."

Professor Baum dictated, giggled maliciously, and kept glancing at David. The refined cruelty of the school lessons was aimed at him; they were all stories for the well fed. He felt like throwing up but he didn't have anything to vomit. How do they say "king"? And "egg"? Is it possible to read a letter when there are rolls on the table? Well, but King Valoroso is a hero. Everything entered his head with such difficulty; it depressed him and he always misspelled "hero." He had had a lengthy break from all that; the lessons were set aside. He was moved to tears by thoughts of summer and his lost freedom. Recently, after a couple of months' reprieve, Professor Baum had

started up again with equations with one unknown, and David had
to bend his neck over his book after an entire day of wandering
about in the city. The dim light flooded Professor Baum's face,
glowed gray in the bristles of his wildly overgrown beard, rumpled
his rags and the blanket he threw across his shoulders like a shawl.
His voice boomed out. And David listened patiently, quietly. When
the dictation is written down and the hateful nonsense about roses
and nightingales finished, then Professor Baum will fold his hands
on the table, blow his nose promisingly, and begin to tell the story of
how the heavens are organized. There were noises in his head from
hunger after his meager dinner, he was dizzy from the effort of solv-
ing an equation with one unknown, and the words for which he was
waiting dropped into that noise.

"They're calling for you, go over to the window," said Professor
Baum.

Mother objected, "I have asked you over and over not to associate with him. Or with just anyone who happens to cross your path."

"Just anyone," Father repeated and noisily banged his hammer.
"Associate! That's a good one. All our lives we associate with just
anyone. Who else should we associate with?"

"My God, my God," Mother complained. "When will this be
over?"

"Soon enough," Father answered and deliberately banged his
hammer. "Just a little longer, and it will be the end of it!"

Eliahu was standing in the courtyard and the snow was melting
on his face. He waved his arm imperiously, whistled by sticking two
fingers between his teeth.

David shook his head but continued to lean out the window. He
was silent, looking reproachfully at the sky like a prisoner deprived
of freedom, and he thought about the Count of Monte Cristo. He
watched as Eliahu turned away, his fists jammed contemptuously
into his pockets, and vanished through the dark gateway, loudly
shuffling along on his ripped soles. He felt sorry for himself, sorry
for Eliahu, and sorry that he didn't know how to whistle through his
fingers like Eliahu.

In the meantime, Professor Baum had put his cigarette butt into
his tiny vest pocket, thrown the blanket over his shoulders to protect himself from the cold, and was saying, "It's time for me to go."
But he stayed.

That was enough for today.

David pulled out the drawer in which he kept his notebooks and all his books. The drawer was on the floor under his bed. He thumbed through the dirty, yellowed, loose pages of books that were missing their covers. A paper fell out of one of them. It was a letter. The letter began: " . . . For Christ's sake, man!"

They are living as if they're at the front. The Germans can burst in at any time, drive them into the field to shovel, everything has to be kept wide open—the sty and the stable—and they go to bed without taking off their shoes. The Jews in town were fenced in with wire. That was called the *Judenstadt*, and then a lot of Jews from all over the region were driven behind the same wires. They are dying practically naked and out in the frost, because the buildings are flimsy and can't hold all the people.

Earlier, people used to throw them bread over the wires out of compassion, but the punishment for such a piece of bread is death by hanging.

Those who hadn't died yet went to the field. People dug holes for their dear ones and buried them in those holes. And then lay down on top of them. There was almost no one left inside the wires, but the Germans wracked their brains and ordered them to open up the holes again. And to take whatever was left there and transport it into the woods and burn it. During the day a pillar of black smoke rises up to the sky; at night a huge fire blazes.

It can be seen throughout the district. The bones are ground up and thrown into the river. You can't look at it and your heart contracts. There's a bitter taste in your mouth from the smoke and the stench of burning, and your bread tastes like hemlock. You can't eat, you can't sleep; everyone walks around in a daze. And they also drive them by horse and cart, fifty kilometers there and back. The poor Jews who are still alive inside the wires are driven to the woods and straight into the fire. They don't even shoot the weak. Alive and naked, without even a shirt on, just as they are. And that's it—one after the other. They've used up all the Jews. You don't want to live, there's nowhere to run to, you lose your mind. In the village, brother is afraid of brother. People say it's like that everywhere.

The letter ended like this: "I hold no grudges against you; don't hold any against me. I will pray for you till the end of my life."

And that was that. He thought about the letter. He knew that at one time Father had wanted to send him to Hrybko in the country. It was nice there, quiet, green; but where did that fire come from and what was all that smoke? He understood each word individually, but they scurried away from him immediately, one after the other, and he could not put them together. Who started a fire in the woods and why is it always burning? There is a similar place in the Pentateuch, and a long time ago, when Grandfather was teaching him their ancient language, he made him repeat after him: "And the Lord went before them by day in a pillar of cloud, to lead the way; and by night in a pillar of fire, to give them light; to go by day and night." Grandfather believes that's a prophecy about the future, and Professor Baum believes the Holy Bible conceals astronomical observations. People say that someone is following his star; the Jews, too, were following their star until they reached the Promised Land, there's no doubt about that. He closed his eyes tight, making a great effort to imagine his own star, but the words from the letter forced their way into his thoughts and something terrible and suffocating fell onto his face.

He asked Professor Baum about everything and he received an answer to everything he asked. In the past, unclear verses had been a problem for him and he had had his knuckles rapped because of them, but he didn't believe it was possible to explain them. Professor Baum said the most extraordinary things with a gleam in his eyes and he didn't put his finger over his lips like Grandfather. The cloud was not a cloud and the fire was not a fire. The star Altair shone from within the dark words and the golden nebula of Praesepe was blurred by the light. Moses had lost his gift of interpreting the divine signs, so the Jews who were with him followed more reliable signposts, and when they lost sight of Altair they directed their gaze to the constellation of the Crab. Jehovah no longer covered the altar they were carrying with clouds nor did he light a fire on their path. Altair was that pillar of fire and the nebula Praesepe was the pillar of smoke. A cloud that leads them by day and a fire that leads by night? In the past he had had to interpret that sentence more simply and it hadn't made sense; it was only from Professor Baum that he learned that in the sky spring and summer extend from Aries to Virgo, and autumn and winter from Libra to Pisces. Spring and summer, the biblical day, placed a nebula before the Jews; autumn and winter, the biblical night, allowed them to orient themselves by a star of the first magnitude. They were walking through the desert in search of the right direction, and astronomy, not Jehovah, came to their aid; they chose different signs during their sojourn according to the seasons of the year.

How hard it is to concentrate. Thoughts fly away and circle high above the notebook, repelled by the difficulty of the problem in which two unknowns terrify him with their unfathomable mystery, like two apparitions whose faces are veiled. He wrote down numbers, crossed them out and corrected his answer, crumpled the paper and began all over again, and at the height of his efforts a clean sheet of paper lay before him once again. In a daze, he stared fixedly at the unblemished whiteness and his pen hung hesitantly in the air. He grew bored easily and was ashamed. He longed to conceal this from Professor Baum. Does everyone always have such difficulty learning things? He struggled to remember the students he knew from the school on Srebrna Street, the way they glanced hurriedly and anxiously at the blackboard, their sparkling eyes and inflamed cheeks during the math lesson, their mechanical motions as if they were asleep, the buzzing of a fly that raised an alarm in the silence of a written test as they anxiously listened for the bell, counting the minutes separating them from the moment when they could place their notebooks on the teacher's desk. They wrote expansively—introduction, development—and never had enough time to write a conclusion. Only a few managed to make it all the way to the end; concentrating, without lifting their heads from their desks, they carefully organized their outlines and then filled them out, point by point. He still saw some of them from time to time in the street.

He bit his fingernails and recalled in a jumble everything that his memory had preserved from those years. Nothing can compare with the terror of a cloudy day like this when he has to sit over his notebook and knows that the time for fulfilling his obligation is approaching. He could feel the dull resistance of inertia welling up inside him as he tried to concentrate. He complained and wallowed in self-accusations until he reached bottom. He was nothing, a speck of dust, the last creature under the sun; he didn't deserve any kindly attention (he had long since noticed that not even Professor Baum bothered to show him appropriate strictness). He looked sadly and unthinkingly at the open book, turned his bored gaze to his note-book, made another feeble effort, and was overcome with an inde-finable fear. In that case, if he wasn't capable of anything, what would become of him? He saw a barren, empty future ahead of him, long days filled with equally gray boredom. His fate lay concealed in terrifying images: without a doubt he'll become a miserable tramp, a lazy good-for-nothing, and he'll complain disgustingly, obstructing other people's paths as they hurry to their human occupations; he'll end his poor life downtrodden and neglected, unable to discover his life's goal because he cannot make the effort. He imagined, with sor-row and pride, the last day of his life, when he would grieve pitifully for all the past days; when, filled with remorse and excruciating grief, he would recall the vast emptiness, the squandered time, the wasted life. It was over, everything was over. He would die and whatever he had proved too weak and untalented for would become someone else's fate.

His misgivings about himself aroused his imagination. But his imagination suggested images that fed his laziness and soothed and paralyzed his will. It had happened. A coward's fall is lamented by no one; he should accept the sentence he deserves and bow his head before the indifference that he deserves. He felt his heart filling with tenderness, with a humble admiration for others; he recalled his father's deliberate, confident movements as he moved around in his workshop, concentrating on what he was doing; the distracted smile with which Uncle Gedali greeted him and timidly cheered him up, the bright forehead and sternly compressed lips when Uncle Yehuda became angry in a discussion, the attentive gaze of Grandfather's narrowed eyes when he straightened up and emerged from his thoughts as all heads immediately turned toward him—each of them had a quality that was hidden from him, and none of them had passed on to him even a fraction of those qualities. It's awful that he has to be the person he is. After all, a person who has a strong char-acter and will can correct his life and begin a new life; he believed that, he believed it all the more strongly the more he became con-vinced that he himself was incapable of such a deed. A pitiful weak-ness, a fitting end for such a cowardly existence. He'll never change, never; tomorrow he'll be the same as he was yesterday.

In the past, before he fell asleep he used to obsess over an idea he could never share with anyone. Stripped of words, it was clear and distinct enough to sink into his memory and remain there for a long time. *Is it possible not to be*? Not to be means not to exist. After all, it is impossible to not exist or to imagine the existence of someone else instead of oneself. And what if someone hasn't been born yet? If he could not be born, then he could also not exist. Really, what does it mean when you cannot imagine nonexistence no matter how hard you try? Not to be the person one is means to be someone else. But then, maybe one should not be at all? He who exists tries to go back in thought to the moment when he does not yet exist. Millions of possibilities and a couple of awkward questions. A small thought lost once again in the whirlwind of the world. If he had not been born, he would not exist. But his mother might have given birth to someone else. Could David's mother have brought into the world someone else instead of him and who would that someone have been? Maybe he himself is that someone else? And so he has to exist? The vague, disturbing thought melted away at that point; it dissolved in a feeling of anxiety, of disappointment that no one would be able to explain this to him and that he could not express it in words.

He was somewhat ashamed of this secret worry. He would fall asleep and his identity would fall asleep with him.

He noticed that just when he had remembered his first dream, he had a daydream in broad daylight. In the daydream he was himself, because it was his own dream about himself. When he was awake he didn't know such freedom; no one cared who he wanted to be; what was important was his genealogy, and anybody could ask him about it. He was a Jew, because a Jew is a person who is born of a Jewish mother and a Jewish father, whose grandfather and grandmother were also Jews, and the grandfather's mother and father and the grandmother's mother and father, too, were Jews, and since those Jews had ancestors who were Jews, therefore their descendants and the descendants of their descendants are cursed for ever. The farther into the past he reached in his thoughts, the larger was the multitude of ancestors that he envisioned. The tree forked into infinity and had more and more branches that had perished far away and long ago. How many of them must have had to live, procreate, and die in order that one despised individual might come into this world! They were all already lying in the earth and were irretrievable, dispersed in their lonely graves, scattered along the distant roads down which they had fled through the ages. He was assailed by impotent pangs of guilt and a gloomy sorrow at the thought of what had once taken place. He knew there was no salvation for him; the past was being played out.

The darkness that enveloped his mind, the cold that made his body stiff, the gnawing in his stomach merged into a single entity: hunger. First comes fear of expending any energy, then nervous rage, and finally apathy, quiet, blissful indifference, and the first signs of starvation. He huddled in his corner, where the semidarkness and cold pressed in from all sides, feeling, as he anxiously guarded his strength, the tiny bit of warmth inside him diminishing and disappearing with every breath; bundled up in a pile of damp rags, he felt his life dying out with every breath he took. Gentle feelings, bold intentions, courage, persistence, and daydreams all require light in order to be awakened; and at the thought that some day the sun might once again warm his face, he experienced a surge of quiet emotion. Light, where are you, light? He peered furtively out the window, cautiously drawing back the blanket. Life was bogged down in the dark, icy back alley of the universe; it seemed to him that he could see the dark, dead segment of the orbit along which the planet was sluggishly moving, approaching closer to the sun that was ineluctably awaiting it somewhere in that emptiness. Spring, summer; just a short curve of the arc and there, at last, the bountiful, blazing fire will approach in the center of this great revolution. He remembered that savages pray to the light by touching their heads to the earth, and that no longer struck him as funny. He remembered that birds call to each other when night is about to lift and the first pale rays of light glow among the trees. In the darkness evil apparitions emerge and joy vanishes. Horrid, deformed faces cast crooked, monstrous shadows, and terror grips your heart. It's gloomy, oppressive, awful. Thin, blackened little snouts with gaping mouths, protruding eyes, and dried-up little sticklike arms and legs attacked him like a swarm of bats: Leibuś with the fish scales on his skin; Roizele, dragging her swollen foot in the dust; Long Itzhok, Moishe the Crip, Henio the Herring . . . How many of them were there? Living, dead. They surround him relentlessly, watch him greedily, with pained attention, as if he were a piece of bread that had been thrown to them. He sits over a piece of paper with nothing written on it, where to the left of the equal sign a steep fraction, bristling with difficulties, piles up, and on the right side is a long product of squared parentheses linked to each other like freight cars. Is he sleeping? In his delirium, the faint, repulsed figures move about, circling timidly, hanging over him, and he feels they are poised to pounce on his neck.

He shakes himself awake; it's no use. Oh, he will never be worthy of them. Of them, and of the others.

He hunches his shoulders and watches as the flame in the lamp gutters, flares up, gutters. In the air, on its own, high above the burner, a thin strip of carbide glows like a flare. It dies back with a hiss, doubles and triples before his eyes. It is surrounded by a swarm of small greenish-blue flames—faces that are burning out. Guilt: what does guilt depend on? Existence itself is guilt. Someone may be dying on the other side of the apartment wall right now; in every nook in every house on every street someone is dying now and will not last until the break of day. Darkness fills his eyes, lulls his thoughts to sleep. His lids grow heavier and his head drops to the table. Perhaps tomorrow he'll have more energy, he'll gather his thoughts and finish the equation, find the solution. Tomorrow anything can happen.

Tomorrow: always and everywhere there is a tomorrow for someone, even if it is his last.

Sleepiness caused by hunger overwhelmed him completely and he could feel only his diminishing strength, the weakness of his arms, and the stiffening in his neck; he felt his feet swelling in his wet foot rags. Lethargic, somnolent, condemned to disintegration into nothingness, he drew no connections between his fears about himself and the annihilation that he saw around him every day. He did not know what to think about that and how to compare himself with other people. His deterioration also aroused fear in him, and shame. The great evil worked apart from him, but the small evil was within himself. He felt guilty that he was still alive. Annihilation had spared no one and had swept multitudes of beings out of every corner. By chance one bitter individual, of no use to anyone, insignificant, and astounded by his own insignificance, was still alive—he, himself.

As long as he heard Professor Baum's words, he felt strong emotions, his heart beat firmly, and in his imagination he saw himself walking erect and free through a world of erect and free people, but that world looked like a different world. At times it seemed to him that all he had to do was to run out in thought to greet a different future. He saw it and he lost the vision; but of all his unattainable desires, sleeping and waking, one clear thought, unsullied by dreaming, remained in front of him, always present and faithful to the end: one day, he will take off the armband with the star and from then on no one will ever exist who will force him to wear a sign. That will be a different world . . . And all the apparitions that hatched in terror, fever, and hunger descended once again, attacked his feverish head from all directions, and lay down to sleep in his heart.

IX

A short nail with a big, flat head stuck out from between his clenched teeth. His shirt sleeves were rolled up to his elbow and he had twine wrapped around his hand. An open, gutted mattress lay on the sawhorses in the middle of the room. The dust rose to the ceiling and it was dark inside the apartment. Light clumps of eelgrass fluttered in the air. Father spat and coughed. He cut the rusty strings that rested on the coils of the brass springs, throwing away the old, blackened knots.

"Another day or two. And then what, Baum? Who needs this and why am I doing it?"

There was the sound of someone clearing his throat softly, cautiously, and then Attorney Szwarc appeared in the doorway. He screwed up his eyes in the smoke and dimness, twisted his neck inside his tight shirt collar, said as he crossed the threshold, "Good, good, working away, working away. My best wishes. Oof, I barely made it here. Krochmalna is hell!"

Father spat out the nails. Attorney Szwarc started unbuttoning his coat and announced, "I'm here on business."

Father moved the sawhorses and pushed a flat block of wood toward him. Clouds of dust swirled into the air with every move he made. "It's coming."

"No," said Attorney Szwarc. "The mattress can wait. I'm here on urgent business!"

He cleared his throat, sat down carefully on the hard chair that had been pushed over for him, and undid his last button.

"Oho, someone else is here," and Professor Baum turned toward the door while Mother wiped her hands.

Uncle Yehuda didn't even greet them but immediately launched into a confused explanation: "I'm telling you. One Jew just has to pass another Jew and immediately a crowd of Jews gathers who have

to take advantage of the exceptional occasion to say something pro-
found about everything. So, what's new?"

He was propelling a bloodless apparition, a snow-covered shadow, before him. Grandfather entered, supported by Uncle Yehuda,
his trembling hands resting on his cane. His soft boots shuffled cautiously across the floor as he clumsily moved along, step by step.
Father embraced him, and he and Uncle Yehuda seated the old man
on a broken sofa, which he sank into. He looked about with a distant, clouded gaze. Apparently he didn't recognize anyone. Uncle
Yehuda and Father exchanged glances over his head; Attorney
Szwarc squirmed uncomfortably on his seat.

"To talk. And what is left to talk about?" Professor Baum
wrapped the blanket tightly around himself.

"When one simply has lost the desire to live," said Mother.

Uncle Yehuda motioned with his head to remind her that Grandfather, who had closed his eyes and was napping, was sitting there.
Mother sighed and went into the kitchen.

Father slowly wound up the twine and, head bowed, without
speaking a word, listened to what Attorney Szwarc had to say.

"It's common knowledge that I own one thing and another. What
is it that I own, Fremde?"

"What a Jew must hide," Uncle Yehuda interjected with a mocking smile.

"What a Jew must hide well in these lamentable times," Attorney
Szwarc repeated. "And my wife undertook to do the hiding. Where
does a woman hide her jewelry? Among the linens. And where does
the man who conducts a search look? I don't have to tell you. In the
bureau, among the linens. When I told her that, she stuffed everything into a hole in the wall behind the wallpaper. Low down, under
the settee. Fremde, you know that settee very well. There's a jar-
diniere in the corner," Attorney Szwarc explained to everyone. "It's
a mess—flowers, vases, rubbish. But once, when I was looking for a
glove, I peeked under the sofa, moved a vase, and saw that it had all
fallen out from behind the wallpaper onto the floor! One word led
to another, she got offended and shoved everything into my hand. I
should do it? Where will I hide it? I wrapped it up in paper and put it
in the desk, locked the desk with a key, put the key in my pocket,
and that was the end of that. Better than in a bank. Who would think

of searching a desk in an apartment? A stupid gendarme? Bloody Hands? And even if he should find the desk, where will he get the key? And even if he should get the key, how will he know where everything is? Especially if it's wrapped in paper! But can you keep calm when a woman is hovering over you? She was looking for her nail polish!"

Attorney Szwarc pondered this. "Nail polish! She opened the desk and let out a shriek. In a word, our entire property, packed in paper, was lying exposed in the drawer. She took it and hid it herself. Where? In a mattress. And a couple of days later she comes in with the news: Bloody Hands, Count Grandi, and the Mad Dog are going from house to house. They were at old Lewin's; the search lasted ten minutes. They gutted the mattress with a bayonet and they had everything Lewin owned on a platter. And what was going on in my house? Judgment Day would be an understatement. A revolution plus Judgment Day would be an exaggeration. But a pogrom in a little Jewish town on the day that Jews are celebrating Yom Kippur fits perfectly. All the furniture is moved around, the beds are a mess, and the air is filled with dust. When the bureau was where the sofa had been, and the sofa was where the bureau had stood, my wife decided that the best hiding place would be the chimney. There's a small baffle near the stove: when the stove smokes, the cook opens the baffle, stuffs in a piece of newspaper, puts a match to it, and then it stops smoking. She hid the whole bundle in there—the jewelry and the money. As fate would have it, one day the cook took the morning paper, placed it in the baffle, and in walked my wife, just in time to avert blind fate! I don't have to tell you what went on there! The paper was already burning, there was soot flying around in the air, and the stove was still smoking! She snatched everything out of there and hid it again. Where, I ask you? In the bureau, under the linens! And our misfortune began all over again. People, I have a poisoned life. No peace, day or night. What do you say to that?"

Attorney Szwarc stopped talking and looked at Father brushing blades of eelgrass off his sleeves. He moved his chair over and cleared his throat. "Fremde, you have a boy and I have misfortune in my house. You have a boy who goes over to the other side, and I have to rid my house of this misfortune . . . I have spoken with someone over there, on the telephone. For the time being he can hide everything for me in a safe place. I have already sent my wife away. She's my first concern. And before I join her I have to send him, that man, an installment. I'll stake my head on him. But who will carry the money and letter for me? Time is pressing, my wife is calling. I haven't laid eyes on her for a month and I'm losing my mind."

"And have you also sent your children away?"

"No, no. They're with me."

Father painstakingly brushed the blades of eelgrass off his sleeve, and Attorney Szwarc waited. He held out his hand, but the hand hung in the air.

"Let's make a deal, Fremde."

Mother turned away and covered her face. Uncle Yehuda wheezed and Grandfather raised his head at the sound. His old, faded eyes lingered on Szwarc's face.

"Fremde, there's no need to talk, I understand everything. It depends on the conditions. I'll pay; how much?"

Father shrugged and stiffly spread his arms. He pulled in his neck and it looked as if his arms were growing out of his ears. "I don't want to make such a deal."

His eyelids drooped and his eyebrows rose up his forehead. His temples wrinkled as he grimaced. And when he opened his eyes, Attorney Szwarc was still sitting in front of him on the chair with his hand extended in friendship.

"I assure you, I'll accept any price."

"No price at all is acceptable for me."

"Why? Do I want to cheat someone? To rob? Haven't I said that I'll pay? Who has to be a loser? Everyone knows that Szwarc doesn't say just anything at all. Szwarc speaks the truth and only the truth. My clients have an opinion about that. If you need them, I can give you iron guarantees. Please, I'll pay ahead of time!"

"I don't need any guarantees, not even ones that are posted up there," and Father raised his finger, pointing at the ceiling.

"It's a deal. Tomorrow morning send the kid to me. We're still in our home. I'll give him the address and show him the yellow policeman who'll let him pass."

"Don't bother. He won't go."

"He won't go? To me? Then I'll come here. I'll bring whatever is necessary and the matter will be settled. We're in agreement, Fremde, don't worry."

"For this deal," Father said slowly, "you'll have to find someone else."

"Don't you want to make money?" Attorney Szwarc stood up. "Is that your last word, Fremde?"

Father shrugged his shoulders. Attorney Szwarc stopped at the door. "But why on earth?"

"You're a baptized Jew, so you can't understand why, but even if you weren't a convert you still wouldn't want to understand . . . To make a deal over one's own son? How is such a thing possible? No, no, Abraham would not have sacrificed Isaac for money!"

Attorney Szwarc stood there with his back to them. "It's always the same thing," he muttered, disgruntled, and left.

Grandfather trembled and repeated, "It's always the same thing, amen, amen."

"That's all we needed," said Father. "What do he and I have in common? The child?"

And Grandfather stretched out his thin neck toward Father and asked, "Who is that convert, eh?"

"Czerniatyński, from Sienna Street, the lawyer."

Grandfather was offended; he made faces and groaned. "Oy, I'm not asking about his name *now*. I'm asking what his family name *used* to be."

"Szwarc."

"Szwarc? From Sienna Street, you said? Szwarc, Szwarc . . . I don't remember."

He sat there with his elbows propped on the table and his plucked chin drooping and he crumbled dried bread into a glass of boiled water that Mother had placed in front of him. His pale yellow fingers crushed the crisp rusks with difficulty.

Now Father spoke, looking Mother straight in the eye. "Why did I refuse him even though I could have helped? The boy is going across the wall tomorrow anyway."

"I don't want to hear any more about this, Yakov. It's enough, enough," Mother interrupted him.

"I was blinded by anger and I wronged him."

"Just anger wrongs others blindly, but unjust anger wrongs them deliberately. You won't become a saint," Grandfather assured him. "I have watched you since you were young and I can tell you that there was never much chance of that. Yakov, my eye didn't pick you

out. My heart didn't feel tenderness for you. Of course, an upholsterer—I knew that you'd turn out passably, but no more than that.
So don't reproach yourself. The devil take him, that convert."

"I could have helped him. But he had to reach for his pocketbook
right away."

"A fool thinks that for his money the gates of heaven will be
opened for him, that he can buy everything and everyone, on this
side and on the other side," said Grandfather.

"'Why?' That's what he asked me. When a man asks 'Why?' it
means you have wronged him." Father's voice was trembling.

Mother interrupted. "Sometimes you say one thing, sometimes
the opposite, and you yourself don't know what you want. Be
happy, you've gotten a load off your mind. Do you want to be a
saint in times like these? There's no one that good."

"Oy, no one," said Grandfather.

"There is no one and there won't be anyone," Uncle Yehuda
repeated.

"And since when do you know everything?" Father asked cut-
tingly. Uncle Yehuda fell silent.

"Everyone is pained by the same thing," said Professor Baum.
"There are no better people or worse people anymore. Equality in
misfortune, and that's that. The stick falls equally on every back and
doesn't choose."

After a moment's silence, Father said, "That's only talk. A family
came here from the provinces. A father, two sons, and a daughter.
They rescued a Torah and hid it in the transport. How? Everyone
asks how and no one can believe it happened. Now they walk down
Walicόw with the Torah and beg. They took it to a rabbi, once."

Grandfather asked, "Which one?"

"Reb Itche laughed till he cried. What are they bringing him?
Doesn't he have enough sacred scrolls in his own city? And they
have to bring him one more from the country? He looked at the
sons, he looked at the daughter, and he said to the father, 'Was it
you, Father, who placed their lives in danger in order to smuggle out
a Torah?' And he answered the rebbe, 'Every day, every hour, Jews
risk their sons' lives for lesser things.'

"Have you seen him, the sort of man he is? Reb Itche asked the
youngsters, 'What are these lesser things?' And they answered,
'Every day, every hour Jews risk their sons' lives for bread.' Reb

Itche fell silent, and the old man from the small boarded-up town asked the rabbi, 'Is such a sacrifice pleasing to God?' Reb Itche nodded his head and said, 'What can be pleasing to God in these times? If one man dies of hunger, should another also die of hunger?' And they, who walk up and down Walicòw and can't beg even a groschen for a piece of bread, replied, 'If one man dies of hunger, another can also die of hunger.'

"Reb Itche spread his hands and put the following question to the first brother, 'And what if a man can't look on calmly at the death of another man?' And he answered, 'Then his life is worth a hundred times more.' Reb Itche put the following question to the second brother, 'And if a man looks on calmly at the death of another man and doesn't even lift his finger?' And he answered, 'Then his life has the identical value.'

"Then Reb Itche said, 'Then can I, Reb Itzhok Kohen, forbid a man to risk his neck for another man? In the Bible it is written: "An ear that hears and an eye that sees, the Lord made them both . . ." Take your Torah, don't remind me of the words of the prayer, because I know them.'

"He called the daughter over and gave her his bread ration card for the entire month. And they went away without seeing their error. And where was the error? It cost them dearly, so Reb Itche only laughed, he didn't upbraid them. And had Reb Itche not heard about their journey? But there is no payment for faith. They did what they could, even more than they could. That is why Reb Itche laughed. Because he already knows that there is no room for holiness in these times. Nor for scales, measures, or false weights. But who knows as much as he does? Whoever desires to know as much as he does would first have to give away his last bread ration cards."

Grandfather interrupted, "What? I didn't hear. What's their name? Maybe I know them?"

"Szafran."

"Szafran? I don't remember."

"Rescuing a Torah from the flames. Well, well," said Uncle Yehuda. "But really, why? You'll only burn your fingers."

"Why? I don't ask why one would pull a Torah out of a fire," Father said sternly. "I ask what is going to happen? Does everything have to come to naught? Yes?"

No one answered. It was quiet in the room, and Grandfather

slurped the moist rusk gruel in his glass. They could hear the greedy sucking of his toothless jaws.

"Well," said Professor Baum, "that's not how I would have put it."

Uncle Yehuda interrupted him with a chilly laugh. "Baum has an answer. He knows there are things more durable than man."

Father shook his head. He said, turning to Baum, "What? When a man is dying, it's easier for him to close his eyes if he knows that something will remain after him. Not a herd of cattle, not a cucumber patch, not a bank account. He would gladly take his property with him. Couldn't that be so, Baum? But he wants to be sure that something, something or other will remain after him and endure. But no one will give five groschen. What? I ask you, what? I ask you!"

Uncle Yehuda pressed his thin lips together. "But if a Jew is dying? How can his memory remain after him? A Jew doesn't die, he drops dead. Such a death isn't becoming for others."

"This is how it has always been and this is the way it will always be," sighed Grandfather.

Uncle Yehuda hissed at Father, "You just have to open your eyes and ears to know about this."

"God, when will all this end," Mother lamented, holding the comb. She pointed to a place on the box beside her, as she did every evening. "Sit, David."

Uri and Naum walked in, stamping their feet to shake the snow off but bringing more in on their caps. Uri's face was red and his nails blue. Naum unwound a thick, sweat-stiffened rag from his left hand and stuffed it into his pocket like a glove. Ice-covered strands of his curly hair hung over his temples and David noticed his skinny yellow neck where he had neglected to cover it. Uri looked into everyone's face.

"You should see what's going on out there! I almost lost my clogs on Ceglana Street. I'll wait a bit, maybe it will pass by."

Uncle Yehuda set his mouth in a smile and said, "I see that Uri has fresh news today from the front lines."

"Leave him alone," said Father. "Let him catch his breath. Thaw out."

Uri was offended and wouldn't speak.

Professor Baum said, as he wrapped himself in the blanket that had slipped off his shoulders and was dragging on the floor, "It's not only life that they're taking away from us, but also faith in life itself. What can one say? There is suffering everywhere, under every roof. And if the wall were opened, the world would have to bite down on its fingers to stop itself from crying out in horror."

Uncle Yehuda lifted his arm and pointed to the darkened window. "That's why the whole world is silent, silent and waiting for when they will finally drive us into the open pit along with our hunger, our typhus, and our lice!"

David shuddered and squirmed on the box near the fire, and he felt his mother's fingers in his hair, saw her eyes right above him. With the comb in her hand she said sternly, "You were scratching yourself at the table today. Again."

The blanket was back in place and Professor Baum, tightly wrapped up, held one of its edges with one hand while warming the other hand inside it.

"Each of us, each of us has had his doubts, not knowing what use the future will make of this. Europe, mired in chaos—when will it emerge from this? I know, I know: what was is past; what is will pass. There will come a day when a new dawn breaks without shame on its face, when the butchers of today will have to settle their accounts. But before whom? Before their victims? Who will emerge from the pit?"

Uncle Yehuda became agitated and said in a hoarse voice, "Whoever emerges from the pit will be stoned to death on the road."

Professor Baum nodded gloomily. "What restitution can there be after such a crime? Hollow laughter and scattered bones. We won't be here and it won't touch us. Yes, I know what I'm saying. This world that is coming will rub its eyes with hands drenched in blood. A law that is not law will once again want to become law. What visions these are; do you feel them? A terrible, terrible world. Perhaps I wouldn't have said all this on some other occasion. I have become incredibly weak and my fever . . . Am I still alive? What is it I'm looking at? Where am I? And am I that thing? The most awful thoughts assail me at night . . . Ice in a pot, frozen faucets, and not a drop of water. One's mouth is dry. It's the same thing all down the hall. Corpses behind every door. More dead than living people, and how many of those will die before morning? That's when they attack a man! Terrible, cold thoughts. Maybe this is necessity? Then does it always arrive with a knife in hand and use that knife to clear a path for itself?"

Uncle Yehuda pressed his fingers against the table edge, jerked his head convulsively, and his face was enveloped in darkness.

"Do we have to believe in nonsense that even they don't believe? Before they shove the Jews into a pit they order them to shout '*Es lebe der Tod!*' They are afraid of the living; the dead are on their side."

Mother grabbed David's ear. "Sit down. Do you think I get pleasure out of combing such an old horse's head every evening and checking to see if he's covered by lice? Aren't you ashamed? Aren't you disgusted with yourself?"

He already knew that he wasn't disgusted by lice; he was only ashamed that she was absorbed in this louse hunting while Naum was watching him.

Professor Baum wrapped himself more tightly in the blanket and kept on talking.

"To live without believing in life. To gather and glue together shards of pottery. Every day one's strength ebbs away, one's indifference grows greater, and one no longer knows how to defend oneself. Sometimes it seems to me that this nightmare is directed by a cunning, omniscient devil. He calculates the number of lice for typhus, the number of calories for hunger, the terror that leads to apathy. The devil counts, he counts up the mad murderers on his abacus. And over there, the apathetic people go to the pit without a word of rebellion, and when they are suffocating beneath the bodies of the dead, they cry out, '*Noch eine Kugel!*' 'Another bullet!' They are conscious and they yearn for the end. To live? To live with such thoughts? And if I am going to live, will I forget that? Such a life is a disgrace, when your people are dying. To cheat fate and profit from chance. Cheated fate is no fate at all, I know that now. They have made a mass grave out of this land and have placed us all on its edge. So what remains in the final analysis? If man is incapable of being afraid all the time and terror has its limits? Calm, to preserve one's calm. The final use that I can make of my freedom. Yes, but even that has been figured into their conniving calculation! Who is served by the dignity of one little condemned person, a child who goes peacefully to his death, having first neatly folded his clothing? They are, because it hastens his execution and makes it simpler. Up till now everything has worked out just right; the meat grinder keeps on grinding without a hitch. But how does it happen?"

"How?" Uncle Yehuda repeated, and laughed sadly. "A criminal begins by picking out his victims. They are outside the law. Everything that affects him, naturally, is beyond the law. That German babble about an *Untermensch* and an *Übermensch* came from their bandits' goal."

David was curled up on the box near the stove where it was a little bit warmer and where the delousing was taking place. He heard whispering above him: "Sit still. If they crawl all over you it'll be quite a party."

Naum winked at him, crinkling his face in a comforting way and lifting his spirits with his winking. The cold comb scratched his ear; he jerked his head.

Professor Baum was breathing heavily and his voice was breaking.

"No, no, that also sounds like an excuse. It's not only criminals who are working to achieve *Judenrein* but ordinary Germans, too, and then they become criminals. The most average people. Their law is a crime. I'm not asking if there can be such a law. It exists! They have a couple of such laws, so simple that the world is stunned by them. And the noise they make about labor and the new order? '*Arbeit macht frei.*' On their posters a scoundrel postures with a rifle in his hands. So killing can be labor? It's become an art! I didn't understand this before. Evidently, they would have lost their identity by renouncing murder. Now I know what 'identity' means in their language! He who stands over a pit with a rifle in his hand tramples on the evil that gives up the ghost in that pit. Naked evil perishes in the mud; armed good triumphs for eternity. Can there be anything more attractive for the average German? Virtue doesn't have to await its reward in heaven; it will receive its pay on earth, which you can see clearly in the rifle's sight at the intersection between the scope and the German eye. That's a straight line for you! A model. That's the old corporal's ideal borrowed from the rules and regulations of the drill field. The German eye sees this world best of all, the German eye of providence that encompasses a great goal and a small life with a single glance. Oof, I'm not finished yet—I'm not finished, but I've had enough."

The shots on Ceglana Street were coming closer; they could hear the footsteps of people who were running away, the gendarmes' shouts. The clattering of a hastily lowered metal shop-window grate drowned out the noise from the street. The helpless pounding of fists against metal, and a howling that was unlike a human voice—"People, open up!"—which didn't subside until a round of bullets silenced it and the clattering of hobnailed boots grew faint and disappeared inside the gate of the building across the street. A short-lived silence descended, then suddenly there was the sound of someone crying out, followed by an eerie giggle.

"Janitor! Janitor!" Somewhere close by they could hear the thin sound of windowpanes being smashed. The shouts of a patrol marching by.

"Can you hear it?"

"It's Bloody Hands, drunk and with his cronies," Uncle Yehuda responded. "He's been prowling around town since morning, collecting for *Winterhilfe*."

Mother nimbly brought the comb closer to him and said, holding David firmly by the ear, "Oh!"

He sat motionless, stiff; he longed to jump up, run away, hide from his mother, from her agile fingers, from the comb that brushed against his ear.

Grandfather stirred and began to speak in his weak voice.

"Hasn't it been just like this in every place and at all times? My children, my grandchildren. Why should we mourn and rend our garments? Mourn with words that have been used too often? Rend garments that are ragged? Brute force has always clothed itself in eagle feathers and held aloft the scale of justice. Ancient history, modern history. The madness abates when it grows weary of its own shouting. There's an intermission for law, an intermission for peace, and an intermission for civilization. And then, after the intermission? Should I complain? I am weary. About whom and in what words? Should I hate? My days are numbered. The man who is sated hates, the hungry man bows his head and doesn't look anyone in the eyes. I have lived as a Jew. I shall die as a Jew. Together with other Jews. Rebellion leads nowhere, and crying for justice ends in blasphemy. Why? I don't know, but that's how it is. To others, fate has granted defeats and retribution. And to us? Let us smite our breasts before we ask. There is no law of retaliation. Our Lord refused it to Jonah, and then refused it to us. What was it He demanded of Jonah? That he should walk among the inhabitants of Nineveh and proclaim his faith, forgiveness, and a warning. He didn't want to reform Nineveh. And who would have wanted to do that? Jonah was not an inspired prophet and he knew that it is impossible to reform the world with a human hand. But our Lord has His own plans. What plans? That I'll tell you later."

Now she was rubbing the back of his neck and behind his ears with a kerosene-soaked rag. "Oh!" Her two thumbs, with their fingernails touching on the comb, emitted a faint but clear crunching sound and the search for lice continued.

"By now Jonah had boarded the ship in order to flee from the presence of the Lord, from the future, to escape his own path in life. Where was the ship sailing to? To Tarshis. And is it possible to flee from the presence of the Lord in a port, if one cannot hide even on the open sea? This, Jonah did not know. And the Lord found the ship and Jonah, and up blew a tempest at sea. Is it possible to hide from the future if one cannot hide in a mighty tempest? So the sailors cast lots. They yearned to calm the waters, and the lot fell upon him. And the sailors asked Jonah, 'What shall we do unto thee?' And he said, 'Cast me forth into the sea.' The sacrifice was made, the sea was calmed, because that was what the Lord wanted. What was the reason for the tempest, for Jonah's sacrifice, why did the lot fall on him? Did the Lord have His own plans in all this? What plans? That I'll tell you later.

"For three days and three nights Jonah prayed in the belly of the great fish with his head wrapped in weeds, grateful for his miraculous salvation. But the worst was always ahead of him. He already knew why there had been a tempest. In order to destroy him. He also knew what the great fish was for. To save him. But why had the Lord saved him? Jonah prayed and called upon the Lord from the depths of the waters that he might learn His plans. The Lord spake the word, and the great fish vomited out Jonah safe upon the shore. And Jonah went unto Nineveh according to the word of the Lord, because He does not retreat from his plans. That was the reason for the tempest, the fish, and his salvation. Now Jonah did not deviate from his path nor ask about the future. He walked the streets of Nineveh and urged enemies to make peace, and he cried out that for its sins the city would be destroyed in forty days. Is it possible to perish in a tempest? Is it possible to perish in the deep? Is it possible to perish in the belly of a great fish with one's head wrapped in weeds? Is it possible to perish from the stones thrown by the inhabitants of Nineveh? Rather than keep on jousting with the Lord, Jonah went to certain death. But he did not know all His plans. My children, my grandchildren. Do you hear me? The Lord wanted this, and the inhabitants of Nineveh together with their king put on sackcloth and sat in the ashes to repent! There was a miracle. Can one call fear of punishment a miracle? No. Is it a miracle that man fears death and repents? No. Was it perhaps a miracle that Nineveh yielded to our Lord? No. He can do everything. The miracle was that Nineveh believed Jonah, a wanderer among them. That he could not have foreseen, because he was a humble Jew who defended himself as best he could from the Lord's demand that He speak through his unworthy lips. But that is what the Lord wanted. What can one say about this? Why did He want this and what plans did he have? What plans? That I'll tell you later.

"Nineveh repented and Jonah asked the Lord, 'Why didst Thou do this and why didst Thou save Nineveh? I fled before Thee for I know Thy mercy. I hid because I well know Thy kindness. My human heart resisted. My heart resisted the salvation of Nineveh before Thou didst command me to go there, before I boarded the ship, before the tempest blew up, before the sailors wrapped my head in weeds and cast me into the sea. There, in the deep, where I was drowning without salvation for a minute that was longer than eternity and no thoughts of Nineveh troubled me because I saw nothing but the abyss, because I saw only death, there, precisely there, in that abyss, defenseless and weak, without feeling or thoughts, without courage, Thou interceded and delivered me, Thou prepared the great fish that swallowed me and neither returned me to life nor gave me over to death, while I prayed for three days and three nights in its belly, not knowing yet that I am a plaything in Thy hand. Why do I live? Without knowing why. And now I ask Thee, have I lived, fled, perished, drowned, wandered amidst evil and amongst my enemies and been put to tests that Thou sparest even them, in order that Nineveh might be saved? Rejoicing in Thy mercy, it heaps revilement upon the just! But is all of Nineveh, in its greatness and wickedness, worth that one moment of terror when I was drowning in the abyss? After I had sacrificed my own life, had ordered the sailors to cast me and my affliction into the deep. My faith, my death, is the truth; Nineveh's repentance is a lie; and when I ask Thee, is Nineveh worth my life, Thou dost not respond. It is better for me to die than to live.'

"Jonah went out of the city and sat in the desert. The Lord prepared a gourd, the gourd put forth a leaf, the leaf protected Jonah from the sun. Does a man who is disheartened need very much? A leaf is enough, a leaf. The Lord knew this and therefore at night he prepared a worm, the worm chewed on the gourd, the gourd withered and Jonah's torment no longer had this final protection. Now the man lay in the desert, sentenced to misfortune and without hope of rescue. And when the sun had risen, the Lord also struck him with an east wind, and then Jonah said for the second time, 'It is better for me to die than to live.' What do you say to that? That's what was needed! A leaf. Then, in the very depths of his affliction, when the ear hears, the eye sees, and the heart feels, the Lord's plans were revealed to him. Jonah felt pity for the leaf and should not the Lord have felt pity for Nineveh, a great city? More than one hundred twenty thousand people, and not a one of them able to discern what is good and what is evil? And they have a lot of cattle. The Lord saved Nineveh because it was worth it. He had his plan. What plan? That I'll tell you later.

"When a man begs for justice, he must be shown the law. When he demands law, he must be reminded of fear. So there is no law of retaliation? No, there is none. I say this today with a heavy heart. Man may not call down the Lord's vengeance upon another man. And the Lord may not be a tool in man's hand. Rather man, man . . . But is it easy to make one's peace with this? Jonah was among his enemies, alone, weak, disheartened, he knew fear, and was it necessary that his last comfort be taken from him? The leaf? Nineveh was grand, wealthy, it was living in sin and doing evil things, and could the Lord not destroy it when Jonah asked him to?"

Grandfather stopped suddenly; he was wheezing. One of his eyes was closed, covered by his drooping eyelid, and the other was turned upwards. David noticed Aunt Chava's red sweater sticking out from under his collar; Grandfather must have put it on under his shirt, on his bare skin.

Uncle Yehuda said, "Jonah is all of us; let the Germans be Nineveh; and our Lord is One. Always the same, the very same, praise be to Him!"

He got up, walked over to the window, and with one jerk ripped off the throw that served as a blackout curtain. Father hurriedly blew out the lamp.

"Do you want them to break my last windowpanes? Yehuda, what are you doing?"

"Nothing. I'm looking."

"Do you want to bring an evil bullet down on all of us? What are you doing?"

"I'm looking. Maybe the king of Nineveh has covered his head with sackcloth in fear of our Lord and is already sitting in the ashes?"

Uncle Yehuda looked out into the street. They could hear shots now from several directions, somewhat farther off, but constant. Flares pierced the darkness outside the window. Hadn't Father said that Bloody Hands was organizing a carnival? For himself and for us.

After a while Uncle Yehuda hung up the throw, darkened the window, turned around, and said in a dry, angry voice, "Ach, that Jewish faith, that Jewish law. To sit and weep."

Father stuck a scrap of paper into the stove and used it to light the lamp. Flakes of black soot flew up to his forehead. Uncle Yehuda bowed his head and David could see only his sunken cheeks concealed in shadow.

Uri called out across the table to Grandfather, "And don't we have the right to retaliate? Don't we? I understand nothing! Us! And if not us, then who does?"

"No one, my noble young man."

"Then what do we have left?"

"No one has ever given anyone such a right."

"People, back me up." Uri turned his head, looking each person in the eye. "Cauterize the black plague with fire, with iron!" When he spoke, his big wet teeth protruded. "Once and for all!"

Grandfather, his face pale as if from an enormous effort, said quietly and emphatically, "There is no 'once and for all.'"

Uri leaned across the table, looking Grandfather straight in the eye, unable to utter a single word. Naum pushed him away good-naturedly.

"Wait a bit," he said and turned to Grandfather. "And I, I? Do I not die once and for all?"

"Jonah——"

"I am asking where I should seek justice since I do not see any here?" He gestured toward the window. "Just a little? A little more? Always just a little?"

"Jonah——"

"I am asking, does a man have one life?"

"Jonah asked the same thing. Yes, one life, in happiness and in stupidity. In sin and in goodness, in success and in destitution—only one life."

"Then do not I, a man, have the right to insist on justice, here, on this earth?"

"And do you, with your burning heart, believe in human justice, here, on this earth?"

"I do!"

"And you want to redeem your wrong with someone else's wrong?"

Father turned up the carbide lamp. Uncle Yehuda clamped his thin lips into a bitter grimace of distaste. Professor Baum tried to wrap himself tighter in his blanket, clutching at its edges. David caught their glances as they crossed in the air.

"Wait," said Uri and pushed Naum away. "What keeps me alive is the hope that I will have revenge. An eye for an eye, a tooth for a tooth. That's what I deserve."

"Young man, there is no such thing in this world as that one person is deserving and another is not."

"I don't want to hear about that now." Uri was raising his voice now, and Grandfather's words were barely audible.

"Wait, wait," said Naum, infuriated, and pushed him aside. "I don't have to be deserving. A man has a right to a life without being deserving. Let them deny me all my rights, let them think up not one Hitler but a hundred mad Hitlers, each one of them with a pig's curl and a lousy little moustache, let them start not just one war but a hundred wars, let the whole world deny me and the Germans the right to exist, and I still won't make my peace with that! No, I'm not concerned with being deserving. And not in relation to the Germans. What do I have in common with them? The law? Do we share one law with them? That's impossible."

He held out one arm. "One day of my life behind walls," and he held out the other arm, "and all the trouble of the Third Reich!" His arms drooped like scales. "Whose conscience will equate them? What scale will weigh them? I spit on the Germans. What is happening now surpasses every measure and I will not sit here humbly like Jonah outside of Nineveh, protected by the leaf of a gourd, waiting until the Lord decides to prepare a worm for my edification that I might come to know all the abasement of my fate."

When he raised his eyelids they could see that his eyes were burning with a strong, even light and that they did not flinch before the others' glances. "Retaliation, that human law must be granted to me."

Father attempted to restrain him, gently waving his hands.

"Retaliation, instant retaliation. Come to your senses, Israel!"

But Naum wouldn't let himself be interrupted.

"*Untermensch?* Fine, I'll show them all how an *Untermensch* fights with the world. Yes, I'm an *Untermensch!* I accept that. In these times that sounds very good indeed . . . A subhuman! I don't demand equal rights. I don't demand any rights. I am a Jew and whichever way you look at it I have to fight. And if they should win this war, who will I be? Who will the others be?"

"Retaliation, a man cannot relinquish that right," Uri chimed in.

Father waved his hands in the air more and more slowly, until he said, "Retaliation? Come to your senses, Israel! Who is talking right away about retaliation? For the time being there is nothing to defend ourselves with. With what? Our bare hands? Life is running away like a hare and it doesn't even have ears to grab and hold it by."

Uncle Yehuda said with a cold laugh, "Bathed in hot water. It won't hurt. Why? It's even good, that we have such ardent youth."

Uri was fidgeting as if he were sitting on hot coals. Suddenly he raised his clenched fist. "I shall resist until the last moment of my life even without a gun, without a gun, when I stand in the pit, I shall also cry out my 'No!' Death to the fascists!"

"Oh yes, that I understand," said Uncle Yehuda, while Uri grew red in the face as everyone stared at him. "That's the way to talk."

For a moment Grandfather's gaze rested on Uri. He had one eye closed, and the other looked upwards. A sigh emerged from between his slightly parted lips. He shook his head disbelievingly. "A Jew is incapable of vengeance. He is unable to enflame the anger within him. He flares up and dies out. Little fire, much smoke. Look at the Germans, they do everything with cold hatred and without haste. And you have burning hearts for your defense? Children, children . . . My children, my grandchildren, do you hear me? This is how it has always been, this is how it will always be. Everyone jumps on one man. The weak man has his faith as his defense and the fear in his heart, and he has to guard that. As for order, law, that's for the strong to enforce. The weak man shouldn't attempt to defend himself, to insist on justice, because justice can also be eroded by that. And since everything is arranged differently in the world than in the heart, the heart aches. And what do we know about the world? We are guests, guests on this earth for a few score years. Where do we come from, where are we going? Do I know? From where and to where? Everyone asks. Behind us is night, ahead of us night. And we are in the middle, we look around, we seek the light, we rush toward the light like moths. We want to scatter the clouds with our shouting, to rein in the rivers with our hands. One small, miserable life seems like eternity to us, and immediately, as soon as we open our eyes, we want to improve what is not fixed in front of us. Vanity, all is vanity . . . I have lived as a Jew. I shall die as a Jew. I have fear in my heart, and I guard it. Fear for my life? I am already far away. And that is not what occupies my old man's thoughts."

Uri listened, leaning across the table, and his large wet teeth protruded through his curled-back lips. Naum held his hands gently on Uri's arms. Grandfather was silent; his face was contorted; he was chewing over his bitter words. He closed his eyes and placed his long, thin, blue fingers together as if to pray.

He continued in a whisper, "My noble young man, they will not win this war. Not because you yearn for their end, and not because we all yearn and pray for it every day. No one has ever won such a war and no one will. It will end with their destruction. But tell me, you who have such a burning heart, what next? How long will their repentance last? And how long will the world be sick and suffering from the effects of this war? You will survive, you will win. Don't be afraid. I have seen three wars with my own eyes. After each one came the yearned-for peace and the victory of the just. And now, young man with the burning heart, tell me, what does that mean? I wouldn't ask you questions like this that shouldn't be asked of the young if it weren't for the bile within me, only the bile remains. Can I wish you ill? Or myself? *Judenrein, Judenrein . . . Judenrein* is such a small beginning, but afterward, afterward . . . My Lord, don't command me to finish my words, my thoughts! Let my soul fly away from my weak body in the middle of my prayer. Amen."

He turned pale, slid deep into his chair, and froze there with his head bowed low.

They gathered around him, alarmed. Uncle Yehuda stood behind his chair and gestured helplessly. Father bent over him anxiously, and a spot of light from the feeble lamp rested on his yellow bald spot. Mother dropped onto her knees before Grandfather, took his hands in hers, blew on them, rubbed them patiently for a long time. Naum and Uri tried to raise the old man higher in his chair, pulling him by his armpits. Professor Baum, with his face averted, took his pulse while staring at the stove, then placed Grandfather's hand on his knees and waved the edge of his blanket under the old man's nose. He asked if there were some drops available. Drops? There weren't any drops in the house. Mother drove them all away, slapped his cheeks to wake him from his faint, blew on his eyes. She wiped his temples with vinegar. His head swayed on his breast, slowly lifted, and they could see the melted frost streaming from his eyebrows. A weak sigh came from him.

"My thoughts are old, weak. I find no guidance in them. But I tell you, though I am no longer able even to strike myself on the breast . . . It is harder to die a blasphemer than humbly, with a prayer on one's lips. Yehuda, can they hear me?"

He beckoned with his crooked finger; now he was summoning David. He ordered him to stand near him, even closer, and he said in a whisper, "Run away."

David saw the emaciated, yellowed face, the eyebrows covered with melted frost, the cloudy, inward-looking eyes, the old, weary eyes of his grandfather. He heard his whisper and he could not understand it.

"What, Grandfather? What are you saying, Grandfather?"

The old man leaned toward him. "Run away, David. Run as far away from here as you can."

He still didn't understand, but he observed attentively how the furrows around the mouth moved, how the soft words came out from between the worn-down teeth with the spaces between them.

"There are people everywhere, everywhere . . . You're a smart boy, you'll manage."

Mother held out her hands to Uncle Yehuda. He was silent. She implored Father, stretching out her hands toward him, and the comb fell to the floor. "Where can he run away to? They're mad," she screamed. "They are all running away! Szwarc is running away. Mrs. Szwarc has already run away. Now they're telling my child to run away. From me! Where will he run to? If everyone starts running away there'll be no room on the earth! If everyone starts running away, whom will they kill? Whom? Better to sit at home together and wait. What God ordains will happen. And it's always livelier when we're together."

"Livelier to live or livelier to die?" Uncle Yehuda interrupted Mother's screaming, and for a moment she choked up.

"Ech, what does it all mean," she said in a different voice now. "Enough! I won't hand over my child to a miserable life, to I-don't-know-what."

"Shh, don't panic," said Father.

But Grandfather insisted. "It's time, it's time," he whispered. "No one will be left alive here. David, forget that you are a Jew. In order to live you have to forget. Do you hear me, David? Live . . . Live like a mad dog and run through the fields as far away from people as possible, but live. Don't be afraid of anyone, of anything. He who is afraid will be lost. He who is afraid will lose his head. Run away and live."

He was terrified; Grandfather's words and his voice echoed like a curse upon his head. Now the curse had descended and he had to take it upon himself.

"You will be alone. Your father is weak, soft. He thinks twice before he takes a single step. But you can't live that way today. David, do you hear me? Don't think, live. Live in order to run away. To run away, to live and run away. When people say nasty things about the Jews, be silent. When they make fun of the Jews, be silent.

Close your eyes and ears to everything. Forget who you are, who your father and mother are. Forget who your forebears were. Don't let your eyelid twitch when you see your own people driven to the pit. Turn away from that place and walk on. David, do you hear me? You have to have a stone instead of a heart. Do you hear me? Drive us all out of your memory. And live, amen."

He fell silent, turned pale. For a moment his hand still hung menacingly in the air, and then he collapsed heavily onto the floor. His head was thrown back and his plucked beard stuck straight up, revealing his pale, thin, wrinkled neck.

They stood there motionless, and Uncle Yehuda said calmly, "It's nothing. It's only hunger."

He could still hear those words long afterward, when Grandfather was no longer alive, and he sat on his low box motionless, imbibing sorrow, depression, pierced through with a helpless fear, with a surge of disgusting cold. "Turn away from that place and walk on. . . . Drive us all out of your memory." He would never free himself of the curse the old man had laid upon him. He thought about himself with a dry indifference, as if he were someone else. A little pain, a lot of amazement—there was a premonition of longing in the thought. "To live in order to run away." He recalled Grandfather's old lessons, full of the noble confusion of the verses from Genesis about the joyous creation of the world. The elements, unused to displaying obedience, bowed down reluctantly, they froze for all eternity, trembling before the Word, yielding their place to the proud legend, so that harmony might arise out of chaos. A bright light shone in the darkness of light. He recalled raised eyebrows, trembling from the effort to contain laughter, the gentle, snoring sounds of the ancient language. The world that arose from indulgence. In the beginning God created the heavens and the earth. And then? "Live like a mad dog and run through the fields as far away from people as possible . . ." Dust swirled into the air, the blades of eelgrass fluttered. Naum and Uri went away. Grandfather and Uncle Yehuda had already left.

Father was plucking the moldy tufts of dense fibers that he had ripped out of the old mattress. "Don't squirm," he said. "Sit still and thank God that you have a mother who gets rid of the lice under your collar. Otherwise you would have long since come down with typhus and turned up your toes."

Then Father tied the brass springs inside the gutted mattress with the twine, and Professor Baum, who was standing near the door, wrapping himself up tightly in his blanket before leaving, said, "In your own way, you have a first-class profession, Fremde."

"An upholsterer? Come off it. Not even a crust of bread. What about you, Baum, can't you find any work?"

"Today? What can I teach people that they don't already know themselves? How to die? Everyone can manage that, and without a schoolteacher. Such are the times."

"Such are the times."

"Fremde, could I borrow a cigarette for the night? Better yet, two. Until tomorrow."

Professor Baum inclined his head with dignity; his feet clicked together as he bowed, but his torn shoe gaped pitifully and his foot wrapper showed through the hole. He wrapped himself tight in his blanket one last time. His face, with its wild growth of beard, and his rags disappeared into the darkness before he had crossed the threshold.

Drowsiness enveloped David in a tender embrace. His feet were burning; his eyelids were sticking shut. Delousing always made him sleepy. His mother's fingers rested on his neck; he felt the cold touch of the comb. She ordered him to pull off his shirt, and when David had taken the wooden clogs off his feet she carefully inspected the seams, creases, and folds of the cloth, bringing the shirt close to her eyes. Father hammered at the frame of the old mattress: one light blow on a nail held between his fingers and then, when his left hand was lifted and the nail was seated, he could hear a couple of measured, stronger blows. The brass springs clanged and jangled. He saw how his father moved the lamp closer and cranked the burner. With his knees under his chin, he sat for a moment, digging his finger into his ear, and then, fearfully, as if he were plunging into cold water, he pulled the blanket up to his head with a single motion and kicked his feet straight out in front of him onto the cold, damp, sweat-soaked sheet.

"That lazybones, your scoundrel of a son, might help me a little with my work and not tuck himself under a featherbed at eight in the evening when his Father is working as hard as he can so his rascal will have something to put in his mouth again tomorrow."

"Under a blanket," he said.

The hammering stopped at once. "What's that you said, big mouth?"

"I said, under a blanket, not under a featherbed."

The hammering began again, drowning out Father's curses and Mother's hasty words.

"Yakov, calm down, let him get a little sleep. Didn't he cross the wall today? He was gone by six; he came home before five. From six to five is . . . eleven hours. Isn't that enough? And then his lesson with Baum."

The hammering became faster and louder.

"Stop it, Yakov."

And suddenly she screamed, "Isn't it enough that he exposes his head to bullets for your sake?"

He heard his father's heavy breathing. Father had a mouthful of nails and everything was shaking from his furious hammering. He could feel a faint trembling, a definite movement of the floor, as if someone on the floor below, his patience exhausted, was hammering on the ceiling with a mop handle. Father spat out the nails into his hand.

"Oh, go on. Lessons, lessons. I've been saying for a long time that he doesn't need them; only Baum does, for the bowl of soup. It will all turn to ashes anyway, it will all turn to ashes."

All you have to do is squeeze your eyes tight before falling asleep and the black sky opens wide. There, in the space enclosed by your skull, just as in the interior of the darkened globe, streaks of bright lights keep flaring up, fading and vanishing, sucked in by the darkness under your eyelids as new swarms of light take their place. The sound of your blood is magnified and the dark, blind screen fills with a swarm of chaotically moving lights. Are they stars? Can you see stars with your eyes closed? Can you see at all with your eyes closed? Can you see what does not exist? Meanwhile, the spots of light float freely on their way. Oh, they're approaching! The tighter you squeeze your eyelids, the faster they move. The noise in your ears intensifies and it feels as if you are flying into a bottomless pit; your fear looms larger and larger and the space that remains to be conquered expands before your eyes. It seems you could interrupt their flight with your thoughts, stop them and force them to move in the opposite direction. Does everyone have such a small, black sky under his eyelids? Does Eliahu? And what about Naum? Shame on him; he's such a big kid and he still likes to play such silly tricks.

A slight numbness envelops him; that's sleep approaching from far away. It gently covers his eyes, his memory. When the cloud comes near, the stars go out and the sky becomes dark. At such moments, he imagines that he is revolving around the sun together with the earth, and he extracts from his memory the number that always arouses his astonishment and terror: 298,080 kilometers per second. "You, there, hold on to the clouds!" Now the tenement house in the alley on Krochmalna Street begins to move, and also Żelazna Brama Square, covered with snow. A crowd of beggars in ice-coated rags scatters in all directions. They pray, curse, fling out their arms. Now Walicòw is in motion. The wooden bridge over Chłodna Street is moving. Its planks creak in the frost, sag under the weight of the snowdrifts; there's a stiffened, frozen pedestrian draped over the railing. Mordechai's horse-drawn omnibus is moving along. Louse-infested passengers jounce on its hard benches; they look out at the streets as they pass, cleaning the frosty panes with their breath; bitten by lice, they wriggle their shoulder blades. Everyone is rushing along at the same moment, in the same direction, tracing an enormous arc in the sky.

He forced his way up from sleep; he heard Father noisily dropping his shoe on the floor and yawning. He wanted to turn onto his other side but he felt a terrible pain in the small of his back and beneath his shoulder blades, so he lay motionless. It hurt when he took a breath. He'd rather not breathe at all. Now Father had turned out the lamp and he could open his eyes.

The extinguished burner kept on hissing furiously in the darkness, and he heard Mother's voice saying, "Take the carbide out into the entrance. Take it out, I can't listen to it anymore!"

Father walked over to the door, carefully shuffling his bare feet. Far from his face, in his outstretched hand, the gas was spurting into the air. As he did every evening, he drained a small amount of water from the tin reservoir and set the emptied lamp on the stairs so that the remaining damp carbide might air out until morning. The door slammed; a gust of wind snatched at it, scattering a cluster of fading sparks from under the stove and revealing for an instant an enormous, shapeless spot on the wall, which collapsed into the darkness.

"Yakov?"

Silence.

He heard a sudden, rapid, despairing cry. "Yakov, Yakov! Where are you?"

Father was moving slowly, cautiously, feeling his way. He was coming back, yawning.

"Now what?"

"Are you there?"

"I'm here! I'm dropping dead, therefore I am."

She was sitting on the bed, relieved. She checked to see that the matches and candle were lying in their usual place. She walked over to the corner where the army cot was set up. She covered him carefully, checking the length of the bed. She threw an old coat over his legs and tucked the edge of the blanket under his heels.

"David, are you awake?"

For a moment as brief as a broken sigh, he felt terribly sorry for himself. If only he could tell her! But how could he tell her? He lay quietly under the blanket, silent, waiting. Maybe she would figure it out herself.

"Sleep. Good night," she said tenderly.

Zyga had shown him, "That way," and they set off in two different directions. It was halfway between the outlet from Ceglana Street and Prosta, in the neighborhood where the merchants from both sides of the wall met to engage in their illegal trade. That passage had a bad reputation. It was small and narrow, suffocating its victims as they passed. Just a chink that the masons had cut out above the pavement as a sewage drain, where a gutter used to be; the boys from Baruch Oks's gang had chiseled it out at night so that an appropriately emaciated skeleton could squeeze through it; he had observed that passageway for a long time from inside one of the gates and he would have given a lot to be able to shrink to fit it. He looked at the passage distrustfully before running across the street and yearned to crush the wall with a despairing glance. He remembered that it was on this spot that Henio the Herring had fallen with his foodstuffs when his sack got stuck in the opening and he couldn't hide from the patrol in time; and Mordka the Ram, dragged out of there by the Mad Dog and terrified, had flung a kilo of fatback in the mud and escaped in the nick of time. David did things somewhat dif-

ferently: he threw the backpack with the bread and the sack of potatoes (there weren't many of those) over the wall without thinking,
and he himself dropped onto his back, pulled up his knees, and,
pushing himself backwards by digging his heels into the pavement,
squeezed his shoulders into the crack. After that, nothing, emptiness, a gap in his memory. He must have struggled inside the tight
opening with his eyes squeezed shut, but how long did that last? The
first thing he noticed was the bit of crushed wall in his hands. Now
he was wedged in between the bricks; he could feel the weight on his
ribs when someone grabbed him powerfully by the trousers and a
police whistle sounded right above his ear. He flailed his legs as they
beat him.

"Crawl out of there, kid!"

"I can't!"

He resisted and wouldn't let go of the crack, feeling his heart
pounding hard against the stones. Curious people came running
from all directions and the stick went into action. On one side the
Jews could already see his head, and on the other a policeman was
still holding on to his leg, and he could hear raucous voices, laughter,
an uproar. The snow was melting beneath him and the mud ran
under his shirt; that he felt, but not the pain.

"S-s-sentry, please let him go."

He didn't know whose voice that was. But he did know that on
this side hungry people were stealing his bread right under his nose
and that over there they would go on making such an uproar, yelling
and whistling, that a gendarme would show up and batter him on the
spot like a rat.

"Och."

Father yawns, filling the darkness with a drawn-out, steady
grumbling. He claps his hand to his open mouth. The yawn ends
with a muffled groaning deep in his throat, and a melodic droning
accompanies the sound of his hand striking his mouth.

"It will all turn to ashes anyway, it will all turn to ashes. In the
meantime, I'll get my sleep."

That was the sign on the wall of the building across the way and
suddenly a corpse-gray face blocked out that sign and bent down
over him, and he could see the lice on its eyebrows. Motionless, yellow, gleeful eyes examined him; Long Itzhok picked up the bread

with a careless gesture, threw away the backpack gleefully, and walked off, laughing out loud. "David, you don't need anything anymore. It's over!"

With every blow his head bounced off the stones like a ball. The street was rocking back and forth, the sign across the way was rocking, as was Itzhok, running lopsidedly down the street, while right here, close by, were left feet, right feet, stars on sleeves, to which he stretched out his hands. He started screaming because they had stolen his bread. The crowd ran away in fright, and he was wedged inside the crack, screwing up his eyes from fear of the bullet he was awaiting. His own scream echoed in his ears and he felt a new surge of strength; one more effort, some tugging, and he was on his knees.

The tight overhang was behind him now. He hid behind a buttress on the wall.

After he yawns, Father coughs, hawks up phlegm, whistles, spits. He swallows plenty of dust and eelgrass while he works, and as usual, he is having an asthmatic attack before falling asleep.

Mother says, "That carbide. It will poison us all one fine day."

Father, unable to catch his breath, gasps, "It's not that—it's the eelgrass."

Upholstery has eaten up his lungs. He's been a slave to that parasite for too long. When he was twelve years old, David's age, he left home and was never a burden on his father. He achieved everything in life with his own two hands. He had scarcely grown up when he was running from courtyard to courtyard, looking for work. He traveled from one town to another in a charabanc just to get his hands on something, and he became a "wild" porter before he had a hair in his beard, without a groschen for the fee that the labor unions demanded. He concludes as he always does: "And no one handled us with kid gloves. The police would find the 'wild' porters on the tracks and the unions would keep their mouths shut."

He screamed as he ran and on the corner of Grzybowska Street Long Itzhok spilled the potatoes. David didn't know if he should pick them up or keep on chasing the goner, who had turned the corner with his bread; then Kuba the Gelding stuck his foot out to trip him. He scraped his nose on the sidewalk. He sat down, and Baruch Oks's gang was standing over him. They all looked at him attentively and no one reached for his sack.

Only on the stairs, as he climbed up slowly, exhausted, supporting himself on the banister and dragging the sack at his heels like a
dog, did he finally collapse. He was done for! Sura the vendor was in
the entranceway, her gray lips extended in a crooked smile. Fresh
bread? Would he give her some? Then she came down backwards,
moving her feet fast. He dragged himself over to the open window
on the landing and was ready, in a fit of hopeless despair, to hurl the
smuggled goods at them, at everyone, at their heads, but the window
was high and he was exhausted, and before he could pull the load
onto the windowsill his strength left him. His hands and feet were
trembling. He took out a potato, looked dully at the scar on its skin,
threw it back, took out another, and, waving his arm wildly, hurled
it through the janitor's window. The sound of the glass, the uproar,
Haskiel the janitor's shouts, afforded him a nasty feeling of relief.

They were waiting for him at home. Where is the bread? He
looks awful! He could feel their eyes riveted on him. His bare elbow
stuck out of his torn sleeve. He wiped his face in silence, smearing
the mud. He was ashamed and he didn't know what to say. Professor Baum, leaning on the table. Each finger separate. Crossed legs,
the tip of his shoe hitting the floor, and his foot showing white
between the torn-off heel and his gaiter. He's been waiting for more
than an hour! It was Thursday: algebra, foreign languages, physics.

"Yes sir, they kept their mouths shut."

In the darkness a last yawn can be heard. David hears his father
sliding his fingers over the soles of his feet, rubbing off the dust. And
then he says, "Big mouth, where are the cigarettes?"

David joyfully flings off his blanket and runs into the entrance as
if he had wings; he rummages here and there in the dark until at last
he comes across the sack in the corner, spills out everything onto the
floor, and when he finds two dry, untouched packs of Haudegen
cigarettes on the bottom that he had bought that morning he comes
back in and kneels beside his father, blinding him for a moment with
the flare of a match. His father's face emerges from a cloud of smoke.

"You're still not asleep," Mother calls out in an aggrieved voice.

David begins telling them, in a rush, how his backpack and bread
were stolen from him near the wall. In some complicated way, he
wants to justify his incompetence. He laughs, stops talking. He'll get
that louse in his hands yet!

And Father asks sharply, "Who?"

"Itzhok."

"How much was there?"

"Bread? Three kilos."

Father inhales with a loud whistle.

"Tsk tsk tsk tsk, that walking corpse will wolf it down on the spot. He'll kick the bucket before he can turn around."

"No," David objects. He shakes his head. "Nothing will happen to him. But I'm going to get my hands on that louse."

Dozing off, he still mumbles quietly into his pillow. He knows that night protects thoughts. That's what people say. It's enough to repeat it once in the morning and everything will stick in your memory for ever.

The present tense and the past tense of the verb *to be*.

"I am, you are, he is. She is. We are, you are, they are.

"I was."

X

Returning home from the other side, even from a distance David would start looking for the window that was held together by two criss-crossed strips of paper. In his unheated hovel, Natan Lerch, shivering and numb with cold, threw a coarse, tattered cloth over his shoulders; from the window on the second floor, where his worn-out, feverish face shone white behind the windowpane, he could see along the alley all the way to the intersection of Ciepła, where the women vendors barked at the tops of their voices behind their tables, and the swarm of beggars circled lazily around the *Wache*, past which the smugglers were returning with their goods. The sun was setting behind a dirty cloud and in the grayness a trembling light crept among the dark, hazy figures, the murky shadows that spread in all directions at nightfall. The street was dying in wild motion: chaotic noises and roaring, lamentations, the stamping of wooden clogs on the paving stones, shouts hurled loudly from one side of the wall to the other. An OD man with a club in his hand strode out in front of the communal kitchen, wiped his mouth, and shouted something, but the crowd answered him with an enraged choral howl, rhythmically banging their spoons on their metal pots. The pigeons rose into the air in a panic and, with impunity, circled low above the *Wache*. The crowd turned black in the faint, dark blue light cast by the suddenly illuminated streetlamps, and the city was swallowed up by night.

Inside the bare, frost-covered walls from which the wallpaper, loosened by the penetrating dampness, was peeling away, behind the smashed windows that were sloppily boarded up with plywood and stuffed with rags, on the floor with its missing floorboards, burned as fuel to bring some warmth to this cave, mattresses were strewn every which way, and on these mattresses with the stuffing coming out of them, a dozen or so families rested side by side—"wild" tenants who had found their last shelter here. Natan Lerch came out to the entrance hall and stealthily accepted his purchases from David. Felled by starvation-induced fevers, they lay dying on rags spread out in the corners, amid scattered feathers, following the living with their eyes. Faivel Szafran had swelled up and lay dying here all winter long, without the strength to go out into the city to beg or to get soup from the Judenrat kitchen; he was beaten painfully by passersby for his unsuccessful attempts at stealing, for his pathetic, feeble plundering of food supplies. During the daytime he sat propped against a wall, sprawling, sleepy, with his head hung low and his long hair all tangled and matted. His swollen legs lay lifeless on the floor like logs. When he pressed a fingernail against his taut, shiny, grayish-yellow skin, a clear fluid oozed out, congealed, and dried. Devoured by insects, he scratched until he bled. At night, he would come to life for a while and pray, and then he would uncover his darkened face, his little eyes in their large sockets framed by bloody, inverted eyelids.

All winter long, Natan Lerch's "wild" tenants died silently in their corners and newcomers appeared from somewhere to take their place, wandering along the streets of the Little Ghetto in search of a roof over their heads. The first families of deportees had moved in with him while Natan, confined to his bed with fever, was lying alone in the empty, spacious apartment—three rooms, a kitchen, a maid's room, and a pantry—that he had inherited from his parents when they died that autumn of galloping dysentery. One day he woke up next to Long Itzhok, who was snoring in his face and shedding lice. He fled to the pantry; he dragged his iron bedstead there, his straw mattress, and that's where he slept. During the severe frosts the refugees from the provinces left their hideouts in the ruins en masse, invaded open apartments, and spread out their bundles wherever they could find shelter from the snow. They chopped up furniture for fuel; what they couldn't burn, they sold. They spread out straw and sacks on the floor, laid out their bedding, and slept at night with their heads on a bundle, ready to get up in the morning and stand in line at the communal kitchen, yawning and limping

from the predawn cold, and then, prepared to trade their last belongings or to steal, they went begging along the route taken by the column of workers who left the Ghetto in a guarded convoy every day.
They picketed sullenly (there was one word, "Hunger," on their
placards), carrying their children in their arms. Exhausted by their
own timid, shameful crying for alms, whole families of them lay
down on the sidewalk, and when they no longer had the strength to
get up, they drew up their legs spasmodically and, relieved of their
cares, left their little ones to the mercy of the street, whimpering for
a long time beside the stiff corpses until they, too, were finished off
by the cold, by thirst, and by hunger. Those who had enough
strength dragged themselves back to the hovel after a full day of begging in order to last one more night under a roof. The crowd milled
around, died under the naked sky, wandered from street to street in
search of bread, in the hope of some chance earnings.

There was a period when Natan Lerch would go over to Leszno
Street and play dance tunes all afternoon on his famous violin in the
restaurant Under the Fish. A playbill was posted at the Solna Street
outlet, near the wooden bridge. David read it: "Leading off the pro-
gram, a weight lifter and a juggler . . ." The arena—a circle a couple
of meters in diameter, surrounded by chairs—was illuminated with
the cold light of three hanging carbide lamps, and the guests sat at
little tables like those at the railroad station with their coats unbuttoned, dressed in sweaters and windbreakers, ski boots, furs, all sorts
of clothes. A buffoon in the brightly colored pants of a jester came
out and placed his finger over his lips; then he turned somersaults
and told Hitler jokes. The skinny skeletons of out-of-work circus
performers came on stage in colorful gymnasts' outfits. They tossed
bottles, plates, and balls, and a sinewy strongman with biceps that
tensed like balloons, muscles protruding from his arm and leg bones,
placed a thin little girl on his shoulders and performed acrobatic
tricks, while panting from exhaustion and baring his teeth. She was
dressed in blue tights, a white tutu, and golden shoes. She was shivering from the cold. David, Eliahu, and Zyga clapped in the street.
Evidently, the patrons of Under the Fish demanded variety, and
after the circus act Natan Lerch appeared on the playbill and was
temporarily able to earn a slice of bread.

NATAN LERCH ARTIST FROM SAN FRANCISCO
PASSING THROUGH THE GHETTO
WILL GIVE A CONCERT TOMORROW
FOR OUR RESPECTED PUBLIC
ATTENTION
MELODIES FROM OUR BACKYARD
HANDEL'S LARGO JAZZ AND POPULAR PIECES
WHEN THE WHITE LILACS BLOOM AGAIN
I MISS THE SUMMER SO
RESTAURANT "UNDER THE FISH" AT 17:00
DANCING AND BUFFET ON THE PREMISES

They could see it all through the window: Natan Lerch tuned his violin and David, Eliahu, and Zyga gaped in the street, staring as he rubbed his bow with a block of rosin. Smoke, voices, a noisy din, the clattering of glass, loud chewing. Red-faced waitresses in filthy white aprons brought sausages with horseradish to the guests. The headwaiter, a monstrosity with a face as yellow as a pickle in a jar, with a dishcloth around his waist, stood beside the zinc counter, with a pencil behind his ear and a tiny yarmulke on his bald spot. Behind him was a cardboard sign: "5% rebate for our frequent customers" and "No Beggars Allowed." Deep inside the room, on the podium, the beet-colored plush curtain was raised. After a moment, Natan Lerch began playing a mournful piece, the guests enthusiastically devoured their sausages with horseradish and listened to the violinist with one ear; a few of them made their way to the bar, others stepped out onto the parquet with their girls, and when they came back to their tables, David, Eliahu, and Zyga were still peering inside and blowing on the frost-covered window.

"Sin, debauchery, Nineveh," said a passerby in a black gabardine, shaking his head. It swayed precariously on his neck, as if it might fall off at any moment.

"Swear on the red wig of the old rabbi's wife."

The man flew into a rage and stomped on his foot.

"Whether you eat sausages or you don't eat them, it will all turn out the same. It'll be absolute nothing either way, *Judenrein* either way! It's all the same, but I would eat."

Shaken and weakened by the sight, David gulped down the saliva that filled his mouth. Zyga stared fixedly; his eyelids didn't even quiver. Since his typhus, he'd had dead, glassy eyes. He made an effort to think.

"But people are dying like flies in the streets."

Eliahu stood with his head resting on the display window, and when one of the guests slapped a young waitress on the behind, he stuck two fingers between his teeth and whistled derisively. Making a face and spitting, he said, "People, what kind of people are they? Tell me they're Jews."

Natan Lerch kept sawing away at the same sad, long hit, the sausages grew cold on people's plates, the pasty-faced fellow behind the counter took the pencil from behind his ear and used it to push his yarmulke back onto his sweaty, freckled bald spot, and the wait-resses cried out enthusiastically at the kitchen doors, "One sausages and horseradish!" Nineveh looked tempting, not awful, somewhat dirty, boring, because that day there were no attractions on the pro-gram other than Lerch. His feet were rooted to the ground and, feel-ing the damp cold, David stood motionless, with his head tucked down between his shoulders, lacking the courage to take a step away from that place, to insert himself into the crowd of pedestrians. Zyga and Eliahu had left. The quivering of fingers on strings ceased, the melody broke off, Lerch's violin fell silent. The foggy March after-noon drove the cold under his collar and placed its chilly, wet paw on his neck. Everything became enormous in his eyes when he began to stare. The interior, warmed by people's breath, sprinkled a dull fog over the windowpane, and the figures moved fluidly, hazily, as if they were in water. A rickshaw was approaching, its wheels squeal-ing and its chain clanging. The coolie's coughing carried a long way down the street.

Someone called out in the twilight, "Under the Fish. Let me off here!"

He shuddered, stepped back. Black, oozy slush, churned up by the wheels, splashed against his legs.

Did Jonah light a candle in the belly of the great fish? No, he played the violin in order to make time pass and to disperse the abysmal darkness with his music. You could picture that. In the deep of the stormy sea, the monster fish is swimming, and in the fish's maw sits Jonah, swallowed up, and playing the violin nonstop. The enormous fins are carrying him in an unknown direction. How many days and nights did he spend on his journey? And how could he know? There was eternal darkness and no light penetrated to the watery deep where the sun no longer acts as a clock. Did Jonah pray during his journey? After all, he didn't have candles or a menorah. He didn't see the clouds above him, the sky, the stars, where the east is and where the west. He only had his violin, and if you have a violin you can travel around the whole world. And did the great fish hear Jonah's music? Did it like violin music and did it swallow him in order to have a concert while it traveled? That cannot be known with any certainty, because nature hasn't been thoroughly studied yet. But in general, why did it swallow the poor man? The enormous fins carry Jonah in an unknown direction.

You can picture that and imagine it. The violin and silver candlesticks. The violin and the fish in the watery deep, the stars, the clouds . . . From the first floor, from the hovel filled with dying people, the sound of the violin resounded, and since the violinist sometimes played in the tavern on Leszno Street over which hung the shield "Under the Fish"—for some reason the story of Jonah became linked in David's memory with the fate of Natan Lerch. David had often heard that Lerch was a famous violinist, but he couldn't bring himself to believe that when he saw his neighbor on the stairs, already terribly emaciated. He usually paced up and down near the windows of his apartment, looking for something, waving his bow once or twice; he would drop his hands in despair, stroke the instrument pensively, and the violin would wait, leaning against the windowsill, without emitting a sound, and only the thin fingers clutching the neck touched the strings despite themselves and then a thin, pitiful, yelping twitter would be heard. Bent over, his face thrust forward, Natan Lerch measured the wall with his dead eyes.

Mordka the Ram barked out as he ran through the courtyard, "Natan Lerch is off the playbill!"

One day Eliahu saw the violin player on Grzybów, where he was leaning against the wall of a house and playing in broad daylight for a crowd of smugglers. He had lost his job and was running a fever.

"He's bad off," said Haskiel the janitor.

"It's bad," said Mordechai Sukiennik. "When someone comes from America to see his old father right before the war breaks out, to visit his family, to take a look at the Saxon Gardens and the Zyg-

munt Column, and then is unable to go home for a scheduled concert and is dying here together with the Jews, behind a wall, well, of
course, it's no good at all."

The cabby lamented and the janitor, with broad, angry motions
of his broom, swept the rubbish into the guarded rubbish bin. Feh,
it's a shame to even speak of it.

He no longer left the house; he opened the window wide, placed a
handkerchief on his shoulder, tucked the violin under his chin and
played so that the entire tenement could hear, and the entire tenement heard him, instead of those people in San Francisco. Baruch
Oks's gang stood under the window. Their necks were blue, their
eyes protruded. Something dripped from their noses, mouths, and
eyes as they rowdily cried out, "Start playing!"

Long Itzhok tore off his stinking rags and threw them up in the
air. Yosele Egg Yolk giggled softly and the sound he made was like
laughter and sobbing. Kuba the Gelding squatted, pressing his temples with his elbows, and emitted a thin squeal: "Eeeee!" There was
movement, excitement on every floor. From the third floor Kalman
Drabik looked outside, curious. Mordarski the merchant slammed
his window shut in a fury. Buba the street vendor moved old
Papierny's chair closer. Mordechai stood near his stall unmoved,
cleaning his boots with a piece of yellow felt, and a black spider
crawled up the stairs from the sub-basement, a hunchbacked little
body, wobbly legs, thin arms twisted in a gesture of astonishment
and wonder: Yankiel Zajączek in his tailor's apron. They listened
and chatted quietly. On the other side of the ocean the public is
waiting for Natan Lerch's concert. Over there, there are flowers,
applause, bravos, encores. Over there, fans carry his instrument for
him and when the concert is over a large black Ford drives up to the
theater to fetch him. The crowd carries him enthusiastically on its
shoulders, and he kicks his feet in the air, smiles, protests, gives auto-
graphs. Natan Lerch signs his name in album after album, across the
white shirtfront on his own photographs. He writes slantingly,
expansively, with a short, fluid motion of the hand, *Lerch, Lerch*,
and half the world knows the swirl under his name and remembers
the tone of his famous violin. He plays, he holds the violin's neck
lovingly, caresses the strings with his supple fingers, directs his gaze
far into the distance. When he lifts the light bow, the last sounds fade

and die away. The public sits quietly, deep in thought—black tail-coats, evening gowns, fluttering fans, the aroma of perfume—and detects the slightest movement of his hand, the softest rustle of his instrument. Quiet, silence, then a storm of joyful applause and shouts. *Bravo! Bis!* And from the back row . . . Regina Zajączek drags herself out from her sub-basement into the light of day, lifts her greenish-gray face with its network of black wrinkles toward the second floor, and raises her hands, gathering the tears from her cheeks like water. In Regina's squinting eyes there is incredible sub-missiveness. Timidly, shamefacedly, she steals a glance at Natan Lerch. For whom is he playing? Is he playing for himself? The vio-lin's voice floated down from the second floor and lingered; it seemed to them that it would never cease. They are waiting for Lerch in Chicago, in New York, in San Francisco. And does no one here yearn for him to don his tailcoat and give a concert? Natan Lerch was a dying man who was totally emaciated from hunger, who clumsily and anxiously embraced his violin. He had lost his hearing; other people heard his music, but life was departing from him along with the slops from the Judenrat kitchen, fifty groschen a bowl.

Mordka the Ram shouted, "Natan Lerch is off the playbill!"

When a commotion broke out they shrugged their shoulders. They drove Baruch Oks's gang away. They hushed each other, they whispered.

Everyone was standing in the back of the courtyard, emaciated beyond belief by now, like shadows, and their whispers dispersed, flew about in the air like a spiderweb of short-lived, rapid gestures.

"Ah, how beautifully Natek plays."

Haskiel the janitor, leaning on his broom and deep in thought, swayed to the music, listening with tightly closed eyes, with his head bowed.

Faivel Szafran, his sons, Nahum and Shulim, and his daughter, Estusia, had settled down for the winter in Natan Lerch's apartment. Consumed by typhus fever, Natan was lying on the floor, because one of the "wild ones" had pulled his iron bedstead from under him. Snow and wind blew into the interior through the smashed windows and the deportees spread their bedding around the little stove and its stovepipe. One day, the merchant Lewin showed up, brushed the frost from his caracul cap, and looked into all the corners after making sure his nose was thoroughly stopped up with a handkerchief. When he noticed the weak, desiccated body on the mattress he shook his head sadly and asked who was sitting with the sick man. He took out ten zlotys and thrust his clenched fist into Estusia's hand. He pinched the girl's cheek in gratitude. He was a friend of the deceased elder Lerch. He promised that he would look in. He had a deal for Natan. He left and for two weeks Estusia turned the sick man, gently tended to his bedsores, bathed the inflamed skin, and soaked his feet in hot water with salt and potato peels. Sura the street vendor insisted that potato peels "draw out the inflammation." And Haskiel the janitor helped Estusia fill out the ration cards for Lerch. In the meantime, Natan lay there like a block of wood and was delirious. Women came from all over the tenement house to give advice, to inquire about his health, to carry in boiling water, whatever anyone had at hand. Everyone cared deeply about Natan's surviving the typhus.

He did survive. And when he opened his eyes, the hovel was filled with a crowd of "wild ones." Passing neighbors glanced in freely through the open doors that could not shut tight and in any event had no locks. Breath froze in the air of the unheated apartment, and the metal stove emitted the stifling odor of smoke and fried food and weak puffs of heated air that swirled around the soot-coated pipes. A woman screamed and pulled some smoldering rags from the pipe, and Long Itzhok put rubbish in the flames and laughed. Naked to the waist, Estusia was holding her brassiere in her hands and killing lice. Nahum and Shulim opened one prayer book between them beside the window. Faivel Szafran, wrapped in a ragged *tallis*, prayed softly, swaying in his tight corner between the red-hot stovepipe and the pallet on which an infant, extracted just a moment before from its wet rags, was happily flailing its legs. It had a gray, wrinkled little face and a transparent blue body. A man in a woman's yellow sweater was carefully slicing bread on the windowsill and, with his back turned, blindly kicked at the people who were crowding him. Mordka the Ram and Kuba the Gelding were fighting, leaping across the mattresses and the people sunk in sleep. In the center, jostled by them, a five-year-old girl sat on a chamber pot and picked her nose with a gloomy, stubborn look on her face. Someone woke up suddenly, sat up on his pallet, and cried out,

"Pesia, have you gotten that food ready yet?" In the evening, after an entire day of wandering about, the "wild ones" were busy with chores that they performed with particular passion and attention: killing bugs and putting together a meal from the odds and ends they had accumulated. Something gurgled out of an overturned pot. The man in the yellow sweater shouted at the Ram as he ran past him and punched him in the back of his neck. Mordka the Ram dashed through the open doors into the hallway.

"People, you can't just leave it there. Someone will get up at night, step in it, and, God forbid, break his leg."

They moved about lazily in the tight passageway, preparing for sleep. An old woman grabbed her granddaughter. "Lusia, enough. Get off. You're going to dig a hole in your nose if you sit there any longer." And she carried her away on the enamel chamber pot. A man who was covered by a soldier's overcoat thrashed around in his corner, delirious.

Mordka the Ram shouted, "Jews, listen, a flea bit the rabbi!"

And Faivel Szafran waved the hems of his *tallis* at him. "Tss!"

Baruch Oks's gang whistled through their fingers. Flat-nosed Nahum slammed the door to the hallway and leaned his shoulders against it. A soft, trembling voice could be heard. It rose in a despairing wail, a lamentation, swelled to a shout, and filled the hovel. There was a commotion among the people who were lying helpless along the walls.

Gray specters emerged from the corners, loosely covered with rags. They walked, they crawled.

"Who brought in so much mud? Where did all that snow come from? You could drown here!"

A woman who had come inside with her child in her arms carefully avoided the people lying down as she headed for the wall heated by the stovepipe, which had been bent with the help of elbow connectors and pushed into the bare bricks. Clods of snow melted in her tracks.

"Where's my place? Who took it? Now where am I going to go with this child?"

She tugged at the soldier's overcoat, but to no avail. The man mumbled incoherently in his sleep. He didn't move. Finally she sat down and leaned against him. She took her feet out of her boots and, resting, wriggled her toes for a long time. The child fell asleep instantly, as soon as she was laid down on the floor, wedged against the edge of the soldier's coat.

"Yesterday, a person still had somewhere to sleep," she complained. "Lately, they take away your place and the bit of roof over your head as soon as you turn your back. What people!"

They pushed their heads forward, stretched their necks. Weak smiles spread tenderly over the starving people's faces. They gathered around Szafran wordlessly, watching as he adjusted his phylacteries, winding the strap tightly around his arm, forehead, the back of his head.

The crowded man raised his elbow. He was still snoring and he got up from his bedding only after a long moment, rubbed his eyes and looked in amazement at the skinny, tiny woman who was sitting there, firmly propped up against him.

"Who are you leaning on? Find yourself a corpse."

He waved his hand, pulled his coat over his head, and fell asleep. Long Itzhok entered, carrying a drawer full of papers. He crumpled some sheets and threw them into the stove. Ashes blew out. Flakes of soot flew about in the smoky air. Long Itzhok warmed his hands, smiling quietly, and the fire colored his thin ears red. A woman with a frying pan walked over to the stove. She pushed Itzhok away with her elbow.

"Clear out! You'll only smother the fire with those pieces of paper. Get out of here, ragman."

Long Itzhok squatted on his heels against the hallway wall and listened to the prayer through the open door that Faivel Szafran was trying to pull closed, and the woman placed her frying pan on the stove, having first thrown in a clump of kerosene-soaked rags. It flared up; the smell of crude oil and fried onion filled the air. She wielded a poker to keep others away from the fire. Thick black smoke billowed from the fire box.

Faivel's lips moved quietly as he fingered the folds of the *tallis*. His nostrils were distended. He twisted his beard impatiently, as if something were in his way. The skeletal men anxiously observed his naked, rosy lips inside the curly tangle of his dark beard.

"Lusia, don't go near the pipe, you'll burn your hair."

The little girl tugged at her dress. She rubbed her face with her dirty little hands and let out a shrill yawn.

"Supper will be ready in a minute, Lusia—why are you pushing like that? I'll be done in a minute and you'll have my place."

The man in the yellow woman's sweater had sliced his bread on the windowsill and walked over to the stove with his soot-covered kettle. He stared greedily at the fried food, at the woman's hands, which were greasy with oil and creosote. She raked the coals, stuck her scalded thumb in her mouth, and sucked on it. He drew closer and watched with a sad, insistent gaze as the contents of the frying pan darkened. The wind blew puffs of smoke out of the stove. Shoulder to shoulder, the man and the woman stared fixedly at the dying fire.

"Sha!"

"A flea bit the rabbi!"

"Ha ha ha ha ha!"

Baruch Oks's gang was carrying on in the cold hallway in an effort to keep warm.

His gluey eyelids opened. Faivel's sharp, far-sighted eyes no longer saw the ruined hovel or the figures that surrounded him, the louse-infested, ragged men, the tormented, blackened faces, the eyes that stared at him, awaiting a word. Somewhere in the corners of the hovel a pious sob could be heard. They crawled over from their separate nooks, and those who lacked the strength to drag themselves out of their bedding lifted their heads for a moment and their eyes glittered in the semidarkness with a wild feverishness. David stopped for a moment on the threshold, listening to the fervent lamentation, a lament without end, a stern melody built on just a couple of bars of music. The emaciated men slipped out of the dark corners. Pale, contorted faces approached him. They were whispering. What were they whispering? What kind of a crowd was this? Where did they come from? Arms folded in prayer, raised up toward heaven, shaking with exaltation and rage. A wet, dark day: what kind of a day was it? "Corpses ou-ou-out!" A cart pulled up to the gate of the tenement building and Elijah's young helper, a filthy boy who was all skin and bones, bellowed his orders and then stealthily slipped away, offended by the obstinacy and the turmoil of impudent life. There was a mob inside Natan Lerch's apartment; Estusia was there, pale and silent as a drowned maiden, in the midst of an uproar and piercing cries.

"Sha!"

The "wild ones" quieted down after the prayer. The candle stubs burned down, the stove grew cold. Faivel Szafran shuffled over to the wall, exhausted. Flat-nosed Nahum carefully folded his *tallis* and flakes of soot flew up from the stovepipe. Shulim quickly rolled up the straps of his *tefillin*. The crowd lay down to sleep, side by side. Estusia turned around, straightened the pillow under Natan's head, and adjusted the blanket over his legs. In the dim, cramped space, the floor was teeming with people.

Whenever David went over to the other side to buy food, his ears were filled with the din of voices emanating from the hovel. He would always stop in front of the place, shaken. The "wild ones" would fling themselves at him, screaming, holding out money, imploring him to let them buy a roll. Their needs were beyond his strength. Estusia would come out into the stairway and stealthily slip him a couple of zlotys for bread for the sick man. (He bought bread for Lerch, too, but he never told anyone at home of this, as if he were robbing them of something about which they ought to know nothing.) Food was dearer than life. He had become accustomed to getting past the *Wache* all the time and coming back one way or another; as time passed, he became numb. He found out that fear is the worst evil, and as he walked along the forbidden streets he learned to take off the armband with the star at the right time, to slow his pace without thinking, to pass Germans and policemen indifferently, and not to panic. He was still afraid, but it was a new kind of fear. He noticed that premature flight evokes pursuit and that it was better to maintain one's composure to the end. He thought cold-bloodedly about those who stayed behind the wall and believed that he alone had somehow been spared by fate. He coldly calculated his chances; apparently, they were not bad. He took care of his appearance so as not to attract attention through neglect and dirtiness. He worried about whether he "looked like a Jew"; when he left his house he carefully cleaned his shoes and his clothing. Gloomily, sternly, suspiciously, he checked his reflection in the mirror.

Grayish hair of an indeterminate color, parted on the left side. A bitter grimace in the corners of a wide mouth. Something in his own face struck him. He knew what. The timid glance of his brown eyes flickered skittishly to the side, and when he tried to straighten it out and look resolute, it was even worse. His gaze assumed a fierceness behind which anyone could easily detect his anxiety. He walked with his head down, not looking at the patrols he passed or at other pedestrians, and it was better that way. Sometimes he was unable to restrain a sudden reflex: he would stop unexpectedly in a crowd, lift his head, and, taking a deep breath, look straight ahead, far and high, squinting . . . At those times, as he well knew, his face took on an expression of painful uncertainty, and the hidden smile, the timid grimace, was the result of his momentary reverie. Long ago, in school, when his class underwent medical examinations, he had found out about his myopia. He didn't connect his dangerous squinting with the fact that he was nearsighted. He knew that when he squinted and looked straight ahead, craning his neck, particularly at those times, fearful, panicky, roused from his reverie in a crowd of strangers, he "looked like a Jew." He went over and he came back. When he came back across the wall, once his tension had passed, he cheered up, breathed freely with a sense of relief; he made a face, just like that, for no reason at all, curled his lips in a cynical sneer, and instead of answering inclined his head toward his left shoulder. He gesticulated unrestrainedly, and the terror, the constraint, the reflexive courage dissolved in a jumble of aimless movements, glances, hops. He wasn't afraid to be himself, and he felt better.

People must differ from each other somehow, since they can tell each other's past at a glance. But how? No one spoke about this clearly. He observed other people's behavior, their appearance, dress, gestures, and way of speaking. When he crossed the wall, he began to distinguish a difference in accent; pedestrians from Wolska Street spoke the same language differently from the inhabitants of Krochmalna, although the distance between them was no more than a few hundred paces. There were other, more surprising differences, since people who lived on Płocka and Karolkowa talked differently from people who lived on Hoża and Złota, and they were not separated by the wall; they talked one way in the Ochota neighborhood, another in Śródmieście, and yet another in Stare Miasto. People behind the wall also differed from each other in many ways: the violinist Lerch never pronounced words with Yankiel Zajączek's drawn-out, singsong accent, and Mordechai Sukiennik cursed just like the drunken drivers in the back alleys of Wola. The Szafrans, deportees from the eastern borderlands, spoke differently from the neighbors he had known since he was a little boy.

He weaved in and out, changed direction, passed by neighborhoods where he might be remembered. In order to buy a loaf of bread, a couple of kilos of potatoes, and a bit of fat, before he could build up the confidence to enter a store, he would sometimes walk straight ahead for several kilometers. In nearby Ochota he drank in, transfixed, the unkempt slang, full of truncated and contracted words, that were uttered knowingly, like the trusting wink of a drunken eyelid. From underneath the caps that they wore pulled down low over their eyes, they spat out contemptuously blurred vowels, lisped with a sly smile, peppered him with curses and exhalations of crude tobacco, the breath of taverns and the rotten gusts of wind that blew in from the clay pits on the outskirts of town; they slapped him jovially on the shoulder, and all of this was accompanied by unceasing, dizzying, endlessly drawn out curses that took his breath away. In Śródmieście his ear grew attuned to the smooth, gray language of office clerks and petty salesmen, whose precise elocution was barely veiled by the rhetoric of banal, sour politeness. In Stare Miasto and in Powiśle he heard the same language, but older by several centuries, forceful and ceremonious, full of weighty, archaic dignity, of a melodiousness that reminded him of the language of the countryside, the groaning cries of sand diggers on the river, church songs—a language that a coachman in a navy blue cape might use in the shadows of twisting little streets, or a vendor at the market, an inconspicuous master shoemaker napping for days on end at Fukier's, a yeoman, forgotten by time and people. An elderly gentleman in a gray visored cap brushed drops of rain from his gray moustache as he sat stock still on a black bench that had grown carbonized with age beneath the Kierbedź Bridge, with a flotilla of wrecks and barges moored chaotically near the bank—barges into which garbage was being dumped by the basketful, swept up from the escarpments of Mariensztat. He coughed and his old man's coughs echoed resoundingly in the fog, one after another. Walking through Mokotów, David heard the passersby speaking a noisy German, because that was the district where the *Volksdeutsch* and

Reichsdeutsch lived, with their barracks on the corner of Rakowiec-ka from which the loudspeakers endlessly blared lively marches, the elegant Olympus movie theater on Puławska Street, directly across from the outlet of Narbutt Street, and the office of the German political police close by.

At times he overheard a phrase broken off in mid-sentence, a whispered warning, a loud cry; he caught nasty and contemptuous glances. Thrown back on his own resources, he had to figure out the meaning of everything by himself; he was ashamed to ask his father about it. He saw how the street urchins imitated Jews, and their caricatures taught him a great deal. He tried not to draw out his words, not to hamper his speech with a singsong aspiration, not to gesticulate. He remembered to speak slowly, a little carelessly, and not to ask a lot of unnecessary questions. How many questions are there in this world? Everything can be stated in such a way as to become a question. Because he noticed that that made some people laugh, he stopped doing it. He took care not to distinguish himself in any way. He listened attentively to Professor Baum, but the old man spoke with an exaggerated, old-fashioned correctness, distinctly emphasizing his nasal vowels and soft *l*'s, and that grated on him. Any detail might attract an unexpected observation; observing how Uncle Gedali flapped the hems of his long overcoat, tucking his head with his unkempt hair into his raised collar, he could already visualize him on the other side of the wall, trapped, exhibited before the thoughtful glances of the ever-vigilant police. From then on he never raised his collar, even during the worst frosts. Although in the depths of his soul he was moved by the noisiness, the speech, the sad sense of humor, broad gestures, and openness of those who surrounded him, he himself had to avoid such behavior.

Despite this, he was never sure of himself, of how he looked in others' eyes. He had to keep quiet about all this; at home, too, he could not discuss it with anyone. He became secretive, uncommunicative. He grew instinctively nasty. He saw that the sufferings and wrongs of some people only arouse laughter and mockery in others; so then, it was necessary to lower his head and walk past without hurrying, as if nothing were happening. He judged himself harshly, thinking it was fear that guided him at such moments, and he was ashamed, for himself and for the people who were beaten; with time he came to recognize that one could become accustomed to this and he grew indifferent.

A man's clothing wears out and turns into a rag, his face shrivels from thirst and hunger, long-lasting hunger transforms him into a skeleton of skin and bones; in the end, the rags fall away along with his habits and a man is once again what he always was. It is hard for a hungry person to conceal his hunger. Every glance, every movement of his hand betrays him. Looking terrified at the crowd of "wild ones" who jammed the hovel on the second floor, David thought with desperate clarity that they no longer had anything left to hide. Chance had buffeted him blindly, senselessly. Up until now he had somehow always been able to scramble out of its way. He owed it to chance that he was not now at rest in Okopy. How little it took to become a whimpering, weakened, dying man! And who was he, that he deserved a different end? And how had it happened that passageways opened before him that were closed for other people? He felt guilty before those who did not have the strength to live.

Courage appeared to him in the form of a small, coarse man who is able to bow his head and do everything necessary to endure. He saw himself as such a person. With concealed emotion and pride he cherished in his memory the porter from Solna Street, Aaron, who even as he fell under a hail of bullets still shook his fist at the gendarme; little Chaim, who had run against the gun barrels when he could no longer endure his hunger. The courage of those who wanted to exist bordered on humiliation and demanded a calculated, dull submissiveness. It turned out in the end that bravery is the same as the desire for life. How could it be otherwise? In moments of depression, he disdained everything; on such days, he walked down the middle of a guarded street with contempt, gritting his teeth, drenched in sweat, and approached the gendarme, who, prodding him meaningfully in the back with the barrel of his gun, let him pass freely with the food he was carrying. Then he felt contempt for the Germans and for those who, whining pitifully, waited, undecided, begging the laughing guard for mercy. He felt contempt at those times for the entire world: someone was doing evil deeds, but someone else was acquiescing in that evil. In his childish dreams everything was so simple! If only the Jews would fling themselves against the walls with their pickaxes, the Ghetto would cease to exist. He observed that deliberation turned grown-ups into cowards. They did not resist, and after all, it was the unruly kids who had long ago turned a frivolous idea into action: they ran straight ahead in a mob, and the guard could fire off a couple of shots in haste, kill one or two on the spot, but the rest would clamber across the wall safe and sound, with a howl of triumph. Why? Food was dearer and more worth saving than life. That thought took up a lot of space in the empty heads of the little smugglers.

Sometimes he was given peculiar, incomprehensible orders. Dr. Obuchowski wrote out a prescription in his presence and David took it across the wall. They looked at him attentively in the pharmacy; he didn't know that the prescription had betrayed him, because the distraught old doctor had used a prescription pad with his own name and address. It was handed back to him without a word, and Dr. Obuchowski slapped himself on his forehead and screamed that he was a stupid ass. What good luck the boy has!

David smiled modestly; he had to quietly admit it was the pharmacist who deserved the credit. He carefully transported syringes in his small rucksack and watched how Dr. Obuchowski pricked Natan Lerch's skinny legs and poured a colorless fluid into them, the contents of the glass ampules. Dr. Obuchowski, wearing his white lab coat over his overcoat, held the syringe up to the light, adjusted the needle for the last time, energetically stretched the frail skin that hung loosely on the sick man's body, and slowly injected the medicine. He covered the prick with cotton soaked in sky blue alcohol.

"It's cachexia, dear Nataniel. Your organism is consuming itself. It gives up more than it takes in. First the fat feeds the fire, and then? Self-combustion."

He rubbed the pricked spot and looked at it, then rubbed it carefully again. A crowd of people who had crept out from all the corners formed a close circle around him.

He said, "You are dying of self-combustion. The muscles disappear, you grow frail and the skin becomes loose, the bones soften. Yes, my dears. What used to walk proudly erect on two legs begins to crawl on its stomach. The lord of creation turns into an amoeba."

They snickered.

"It's not at all funny. Oh no! The spleen contracts, the stomach, kidneys, liver. A splendid organ shrinks to the size of a walnut and that is exactly what a cachectic patient's liver looks like. The lungs weaken, the heart stops working properly. The pump stops. Drowsiness caused by hunger sets in. Sleepiness. Apathy. Lethargy. Gradually, the entire organism yields to self-poisoning. A lack of nourishment, oxygen, blood, tissue. That's what cachexia consists of. What do I advise you, my dear cachectics? An injection, powders? Nonsense! You need to gorge, gorge, gorge yourselves, but that I can't supply for anyone, not even for myself. You need sunshine, and that I can't create. You need air, and I am not God. I am only a little, harried physician, who has already worn out more than one pair of shoes on these stairs."

Dr. Obuchowski threw the dirty needle into a nickle-plated can. He fished around in it with a pair of tweezers and pulled out another needle. He affixed the syringe to it.

"Starvation sickness is cruel self-digestion. Mercilessly, day after day, hour after hour, you feed on your own blood, your own marrow, your own flesh, your own bones. Until the end. A feast, isn't it? Lick your fingers! Look what a pantry nature has prepared for you at the end! It's a miracle that you're alive. The grippe ought to knock you off your feet, and you survive typhus. How is it possible, tell me, people? Is the production of white corpuscles still going on? Continuing and not slowing down? But it has to be even greater . . . Life holds on longer than life itself permits. There, that's your sickness in a nutshell. Give me your other leg, Nataniel. We'll stick it."

Dr. Obuchowski gave him the injection and kept on talking.

"Medicine has not yet posed this question, Nataniel. When does a man cease to be a man? That's the question. Old Baum babbles something about freedom and other twaddle, and I can't understand a thing. The belly rules the world of the hungry. 'Eat, eat!' That's the cry of the last living cell and there are none that are deaf to that cry. It's a dependency from which it is impossible to be liberated, and nothing that lives is free from it on this earth. If you must talk about freedom . . . Keep him warm, Estusia."

Estusia covered the sick man's legs with a blanket. Dr. Obuchowski changed the needle. A goner, as transparent as glass, stood in front of him; his loins were dark blue. He swayed weakly and raised his long shirt. Without saying a word, he closed his eyes, and then he fixed his feverish, burning gaze on the doctor.

"And if we must talk about freedom, then let's stop this proud lying. Hmm, what's this? A leg? What have you done with your buttock? You're losing your resemblance to a human being. Stand sideways and raise that nightshirt a little higher. Come closer. That's good. And forget about yourself. A body is something that a doctor can stick a needle in. And if the needle no longer goes in, it means that the body is gone. Finis! What remains is the spirit, freed from all cares. You can tell that to any university nincompoop. And what is a doctor supposed to heal, I ask you? Astral bodies?"

Dr. Obuchowski grimaced and pulled a handful of loose skin away from the dry calf. Compressing his lips, groaning, he forced the needle between the bone and the gray swelling on the goner's pelvis.

"Good. Done. This injection will cure you. Tomorrow you'll get up full of energy to fight for life. You don't believe me? You're laughing? Ha! A patient's faith accounts for half the success of a cure. Drop your shirt. Thanks. Next!"

The man who'd gotten the injection walked away, laughing softly. He looked back, bowed, and his long shirt waved on his skeleton.

Dr. Obuchowski changed the needle. Estusia boiled water on the stove, and he took care of the lacerations, swellings, ulcers, and with rapid movements of his tiny lancet opened festering boils. The goners, laughing, amused by his chatter, approached him from all sides.

He chatted with them in a kindly way. "People, my hands are numb by now. What kind of a hellish dance is this!"

Flat-nosed Nahum snorted, "But this is just the beginning," and he impudently looked the doctor straight in the eyes.

The old woman asked for a prescription for a sweet syrup, lemons, and something for a cough for her granddaughter, Lusia. Dr. Obuchowski prescribed cod-liver oil. The man in the yellow sweater rubbed his hands and insistently demanded to be sent to the hospital where he might recover a little and get some rest, and the old doctor nodded his head understandingly and injected a full syringe of distilled water into him, after which the patient rubbed the painful pricked spot for a very long time.

Others stood by in silence, patiently following Dr. Obuchowski's graceful, energetic motions.

"And what about my payments after the war? What a fate! Nataniel, I am of less significance on this earth than the lowliest grave digger who won't dig even a hole unless he's paid! Do you hear me?"

Natan Lerch, propped up helplessly against a wall, half-seated on his bed, gripped his little bottle of pills spasmodically and would not lift his glassy, staring gaze from it. After a moment's reflection, he shoved the medicine under his pillow; every so often he took it out and examined it anxiously. He looked hesitantly at Estusia.

"It won't disappear here?" he whispered.

She shook her head no.

"Thanks—next!" Dr. Obuchowski called out in a loud voice. The goners crowded around on all sides, with foolish, trusting smiles on their faces.

The man in the yellow sweater pushed his way through to the doctor again, waving his hands; he had rings on his fingers. "I'm going to die!"

Faivel Szafran roused himself, raised his head from his swollen abdomen, and announced in a coarse, hollow voice, "One man dies standing up, another dies lying down. No one dies while eating."

The goners shoved the interloper aside and hissed. Flat-nosed Nahum spat into his face, "Give me a crust of bread and I'll survive for a whole day!"

Furious cries could be heard on all sides, "Give it to him! Give it to him!"

Flat-nosed Nahum stood in the doorway and gazed at length out into the stairwell. Shulim watched over his shoulder. Malka was walking down the stairs, shriveled, stiffly erect, wearing a long skirt over a violet slip which glimmered through the filthy tulle, with the mangy red fox wrapped around her powdered neck. Her eyes were screwed up slyly, and she clawed at the air with her sharp, crooked, hooklike fingernails.

"Ram," she simpered, "call the doctor for me."

"You're three-quarters of the way to death; what do you need a doctor for?"

"Ram, Ram, sweetie, call Mordarski for me immediately."

"Malka, what do you need a merchant for?"

"Ram, call Szwarc over here right away."

"What do you need a lawyer for?"

"Ram, darling little Ram, call Mordechai."

"What do you need a cabbie for?"

"Ram, in that case call Reb Itzhok."

"Malka, what do you need a rabbi for?"

"Ram, you blockhead, bring me Loniek, my beau."

"What do you need a beau for? Anyone else?"

"Wait a minute, let me think."

She grabbed the fox's head and tossed it over her shoulder. She fanned her face with the fox's perfumed tail.

Mordka the Ram turned away, made a low bow to Kuba, grabbed his nose between two knuckles, and gave it a yank. In a clear, joyous voice that filled the entire entranceway, he bellowed, "Thaaaanks, next!"

She moved on.

Flat-nosed Nahum leaned over the stairwell. Resting his chin on Nahum's shoulder, Shulim watched her go. She giggled. The red fox waved its mangy tail in the dark entranceway, fixing its cold, ruby-red glass eye on them; when she reached the exit, Malka turned toward them her dead face, on which she had drawn immobile eyebrows and lips with black and red chalk.

"Malka, anything for you!"

Baruch Oks's gang greeted her with deafening whistles, shouts, and laughter as she walked down the street in the afternoon, wiggling her backside with great effort. From corner to corner.

A long time ago, Eliahu had told them what he had seen in the ruins on Walicόw. Zyga and David listened avidly. How Malka lies down. How she boldly removes her lilac slip. How she caresses her breasts and takes money. How she unfastens one garter and slowly pulls down her silk stocking. It's suffocating, terrifying, there's a buzzing in their ears. These stories always ended the same way and everyone knew how, only Zyga pretended hypocritically that he didn't know. Eliahu told his story expansively, at great length, and then they went into the ruins, raising a ruckus just to give themselves courage. The moon over Hale cast a silver glow over their pale faces, over the spacious, shadow-filled ruins, till the cries of the sentries on Żelazna Brama Square echoed right there, and their hearts beat sharply against their ribs when they made their way stealthily, silently, carefully, across the rubble to the place from which they could clearly make out the forms that were lying in wait.

Hungry prostitutes loitered in the ruins on Walicόw.

At twilight they could hear loud breathing in various alcoves. From men who were turning stiff in the arms of women, and women who were turning stiff from hunger. It was like a single, immense beast that had been brought to its knees and was dying, tossing about and unable to find a place for itself. At twilight on Walicόw the beggars' whimpering faded away, as did the importunate lamentations of the cantors, the prayers. At twilight the whispers of the dying rose above the ruins. Final wild fights erupted. Rags dropped off bodies. Skeletons stiffened in the nighttime cold and their breathing died away. Vacant pupils, upturned toward the sky, went out together with the light of the fading day, and there was no hand to pull down the eyelids.

"Ooooo . . . Och!"

Heavy, broken sighs and the curses of the beggars and whores who were locked in embraces hovered over this spot. A loose gutter, dangling in this wilderness, clanged as it struck a downspout on a bare wall. A crumpled roof that had been torn loose hung with one wing suspended over the precipice. The cackling of the wind, the groaning sound of the sheet metal, the furious voices floated over to them from the dark, grating, deformed ruins.

From the second-story level, Eliahu, David, and Zyga leaned out over the edge of the rubble and looked with wide eyes at the people lying down below. It was windy and cold. Pretending to laugh, David stuffed his fist into his mouth. Zyga pounded on Eliahu's neck with a show of high spirits. He looked as if he were going to burst from laughter. Their hands were frozen.

On Żelazna Brama Square a guard fired a shot. The trolleys emitted sparks and hisses, sending a green light into the ruins and a swarm of formless shadows.

"Aaah . . ."

A white walking stick and a bedraggled felt hat had been flung down on the bricks. Nearby was a girl's hand, groping over the stones. A sudden cry resounded in the darkness and lingered there, slashing the sky like a raised sword.

"Iiii!"

The monotonous whimpering, which was unlike a human voice although it was still the voice of a human being, died away slowly, lingeringly.

"Let's go," said Eliahu. "That's enough."

With fear and curiosity, with a modicum of shame that could not overcome their curiosity, clinging to the crumbling rubble, they stayed there. The trolleys, halted in front of the *Wache*, noisily rang their bells. Sparks crackled time and again, whole clusters of them kept flaring up. In the darkening light, the girl lay still and the shadows of the ruins slipped over her body, swallowed up her wasted thighs, her sunken belly, her dress pulled all the way up to her eyes, and next to her sat a beggar, motionless, in a warm felt hat, covering his face with his hands. When he stood up, they could see that the girl was touching him gently.

"Here, I'll brush off the dust. You can't walk around like that. It's different for me."

He picked up his white stick and walked away. She raised herself awkwardly on her elbows and knees. Kneeling there with her head hanging low, she beat her fist feebly against a stone.

Malka's cries carried along the street and they could hear her somewhere nearby.

"What am I doing? I'm out of my mind, selling myself for free!"

Darkness had fallen; a blue moon, trembling in the murky air, rose lightly over Hale and drifted over to Grzybowski Square, and on the other side of the boundary wall, in the ravine of Krochmalna Street, the wind-swept sky still glowed with the cold fire of sunset. The sun was burning itself out behind the solid mass of the new brewery.

Eliahu whispered through dry lips, "She'll find a new guy right away."

"Oy," Zyga groaned. "And they pay her for that?"

"Yes, for that."

"Only for that?"

"Only for that."

Eliahu placed two fingers together and snapped them without making a sound. He rattled off a bawdy rhyme without taking a breath.

"Aha, I understand," said Zyga. He shook his head, disenchanted. "So that's what it's all about."

In an alcove on the burned-out ground floor they could hear laughter, a drunken voice, and disconnected, drawn-out words.

"Oy, leave me alone. Oy, just don't tickle me. Oy, I'm going to die laughing."

They turned back.

"Let's go," Eliahu repeated. "Enough, that'll do, nothing else is going to happen today."

Near the Szafrans' deserted den they passed a woman who was pinning up her disheveled chignon and shoving a beggar away with her other hand.

"Wait a minute, there's no rush."

"I have money! I'll give you money!"

"Eh, for such money dogs and cats eat meat."

He offered her half a quarter-loaf of bread.

"The whole thing!"

He pulled out a broken-off chunk of bread and she started eating immediately.

"There, take it."

She stood with her legs wide apart on the sloping pile of rubble next to a collapsed low wall. The rubble slipped away beneath them, rustling. She swallowed loudly, and held the hem of her skirt against her ribs with her elbow. The beggar carefully pawed her shriveled leg. They fell down together, their knees drawn up, and tumbled down the short incline, dragging their entwined legs stiffly behind them. She squealed briefly.

"What have I turned into," and she began to tear herself away. She fled along the wall on all fours, a brown shadow against a deep blue sky. The beggar ran after her clumsily, plunging his hands blindly into the last pale stripe of daylight.

The laughter stopped abruptly and yawning and grumbling could be heard from inside the alcove. "But I told you I'm afraid of tickling."

Near the exit from the ruins, on a bed made of straw, paper, and rags strewn on the floor in a corner of the gate, something started moving sluggishly.

"Now who's there? Tfoo, I beg your pardon, but they don't give a man a moment's peace all night long!"

Out on the street, the mangy and by now sweaty fox was hopping about, glaring with its glass eye, and slipping off the powdered neck.

"Tee hee . . ."

"Nu, nu, nu . . ."

"Don't you lay a hand on me, you creep!"

"Hand it over, swindler!"

"Fetniak! Now what? Buy yourself a corpse on Kercelak!"

The sudden, tangled brawl startled Waliców, and Malka cried out in her thin voice, inciting them, sitting down delightedly in the roadway. She tore off her lilac slip and wriggled her feet in a grotesque, furious dance. A fine beginning to the night! A couple of ragamuffins were standing idly by; they stealthily surrounded two goners who were flailing around—Kepele the porter and the deportee, Nahum Szafran. A third goner was lying near them. She moved a little closer to them. A wordless howl was building up in her throat. David saw all her teeth bared, the quick movement of her hand grabbing the knife from under her garter, and the sparks of a hurried glance from under her lowered eyelids. Flat-nosed Nahum and Kepele shuffled their feet aimlessly, hopped toward each other and hopped apart.

She yelled something, and Shulim, bloodied, quietly and cautiously got up from the ground and threw a stone at them; David, Eliahu, and Zyga ran away like hunted dogs. Back home. By a round-about route, by way of the ruins, over the tall mound of rubble from the bombed-out outbuilding, they tumbled into the second courtyard gasping for breath, and from there they reached their own building. A shout chased them: "I'll show you!"

During the last weeks of winter Waliców emptied out. The severe frosts abated, and when the thaw set in, flu carried away those whom typhus had not killed.

The dead lay lined up among the living in the street. Moans, whimpers, feeble sobbing floated down Waliców from Chłodna to Prosta Streets and along Krochmalna from the wall to Żelazna Brama Square. Ulcerated skeletons tore themselves from the ground with their last ounce of strength and ran straight ahead, with madness in their eyes, laughing hideously. Malka staggered around like a phantom, back and forth between Żelazna and Ciepła, all day long. When they caught sight of her, the gendarmes made funny faces; amused, they patted the barrels of their rifles. She would stop at a distance from the *Wache*. The red fox was completely bald; all that remained of it was a shiny, hard skin, but Malka kept creeping along the walls, gripping the ragged bundle that she didn't let go of until the very end. She would try to seduce passersby, pulling up her lilac slip and displaying her crooked thigh, which was blackened and shriveled like a rotting branch. Apparently, she was begging for alms in her own way, unable to find the right words; the fever had made her confused and she reached out blindly to passing men.

"How are you, love? Take a look at me!"

A walking stick with a silver ferrule and delicate shoes with beige gaiters that carefully, attentively stepped around obstacles. You can still make a living in our profession, of course. But for how long? Attorney Szwarc was on his way back from seeing a client, looking up at the pale, spring sky.

"Don't you remember me, pussycat? Think about it. Well, well . . ."

She stood before him, adjusting her filthy garter. She displayed her long, yellow, loose teeth in a gloomy smile. Szwarc started running.

"You're running away! But you defended me in court and a whore's groschen didn't burn a hole in your pocket."

A soft, wide, black hat and hair that was blown back as he walked. A pained, embarrassed glance that asked forgiveness for all the prayers he had not been able to say in time. Reb Itzhok emerged from the synagogue on Ciepła Street, emitting an odor of parchment and unburned candles. People in the street bowed to him.

"Stop, Rebbe."

She clutched at his wax-stained gabardine. She implored him, "Rebbe, sweetheart, have a heart; take pity on an unclean girl in need."

"A heart? A girl? And unclean? Isn't there too much of this goodness?"

Reb Itzhok sighed. "Oy, Malka, Malka, everything has been turned upside down, for the glory and joy of the Lord."

He bowed his head and began to unbutton his coat. He hastily searched his pockets for some loose change.

"Mordarski, where'd you get that belly? You, come to me, you!"

Mordarski the merchant was walking past in an unbuttoned fur coat—the upper part made of English cloth lined with civet, with a shawl collar of beaver fur—softly moving his fat, moist lips. If twelve smugglers each carry in three kilos of fat across the wall twice a day, how much does Mordarski earn in a week? You have to honestly deduct the porters' provisions, the middleman's profit, the bribe for the gendarme, the losses of goods and of people killed. Net profit is . . . Quiet, sha! Malka has blocked his path.

"Are you coming, love, are you coming?"

"I have time, I'll wait."

"Mordarski, you may be alive and stuffed with goose cracklings, but you're going to drop dead like everyone else!"

"Tfoo, unbelievable."

Mordarski the merchant spat and walked on, completing his interrupted calculations. That day there was hardly any wind. He breathed and counted.

Loniek Papierny came strolling toward the *Wache*, wearing the yellow armband of an OD man, with a rubber truncheon at his waist, his new officer's boots creaking. Fattened on police bread, he thrust his knees out high and stamped his heels. He polished the stiff brim of his cap with his sleeve. As soon as he caught sight of her in the distance, he started to mock her.

"Count Grandi bows low before you, respected lady. Are you coming, Malka, are you coming?"

"With you, never."

"Life is a barefoot dance of skeletons . . . with figures! Malka, I need you to make a couple."

Dr. Obuchowski was on his way down the street to visit his sick people, out of breath, wearing his white coat over his overcoat. He stopped, carefully set down his doctor's bag on the sidewalk, and attentively examined deformed, bulbous knees on thin, fragile legs, bony hands, dry collarbones that protruded like hooks, and a spectrally emaciated, shriveled little face, the ears stained with rivulets of dried blood, the eyelids dust-covered, a swarm of lice in the hair, and a black hole in the shadow of frail temples; the forehead was slashed by a vertical, bulging, desperately pulsing vein over the bone. Malka waited patiently, blinking her eyes cunningly.

"Doctor, I'm still looking for you."

Dr. Obuchowski took hold of the skull, which was densely covered with dark, brown, pitifully scaly skin, and pulled down a wrinkled eyelid with his thumb. He whispered, "*Atrophia et anaemia organorum. Mors.*"

She bent down swiftly; in a hollow, choking, soundless voice, she ordered, "You go first. I'll follow you."

Mordechai Sukiennik was on his way back to his stall, drunk. His feet and tongue were twisted. He was mumbling something, singing. Gee, Gee! A horse grows old, a wagon grows old, and on the wagon sits a coachman. Walking along the empty street, he broke off his song and started talking to a chestnut horse that was pulling a cart down the middle of the street, reins dangling carelessly, without a whip. But one wheel was caught on the gas lamp in front of the gate? And the other wheel was rolling over the ledge of Kalman Drabik's window? And the shaft had started swaying and pierced a cloud? The cart broke apart into pieces! The horse was already galloping through the heavenly air, effortlessly moving its golden hooves, and its mane and the loosened straps of its harness were flying behind it. Did he want to urge the horse on? To stop it? No one was driving down Krochmalna Street; it was empty. He stumbled and, as in the old days, shouted hoarsely, "Cheee-stnut!"

He was lying down now, blindly groping at the stones. Suddenly, she stood over the cabby and placed her bony, ulcerated hand on his cloak. She bared her loose teeth right near his face. She scratched her head furiously and lice flew out of her hair.

"Are you coming, old man? Are you coming?"

And Mordechai answered, "I've got nothing, whore, nothing."

A relapse of typhus finally knocked her off her feet and for the second time she was admitted to the hospital, sent to Czyste by Dr. Obuchowski. Two weeks later she came back, fed, her head shaved and covered with a square of cloth, and she continued to cruise the streets, always returning to the same spot. Her post-typhus skeleton was covered with swellings from neck to feet. She was alive . . . until the spring. She implored and ran after people in the street, and they fled from her in a panic. They avoided the hungry monster like death. Gripping her ragged bundle, she lisped indistinctly, "How are you, corpse, what time is it on your clock?"

Once, people saw her walking with some bread and then Long Itzhok grabbed the bread from her before she had a chance to run away. He tore the bread and gulped it down in huge pieces. She beat him awkwardly, and when he bent over and began to pick up the crumbs from the ground, she flung herself on him with all the weight of her swollen body, scratching at the goner until he grew still beneath her—stuffed, bloated. She gathered up in her skirt whatever was left and ran off. The next day, a cry could be heard on Waliców again: "Malka, Malka, lift up your skirt."

Long Itzhok leaned out of his lair in the ruins and called out to her. She found him there and began to beat him. She destroyed his shelter, and the rubble and dry rot from the collapsing hut fell behind her collar. For a couple of days he walked around silently, gloomily, near the walls of the houses, but when he passed her in the passageway he raised his insistent cry again. She threw herself at him every time and crushed him against the ground with her swollen body. Winter passed and Long Itzhok lay down with his tin can at the intersection of Żelazna and never got up again. He lay there, growing stiff, for four days and three nights. On the evening of the third day, by the light of the moon, he called out to the woman in a weak voice as she passed by, "Malka, lift up your skirt."

"Oh!"

She lifted it up. In mute rage she pulled her skirt up to her shoulders and bent over him, groaning, heavy, swollen, and the moon colored her shamelessly distended naked buttocks with its living light, like a huge yellow melon.

The next day, Elijah the Grave Digger drove past and smelled the remains of Long Itzhok; wrapping his strap around the stiff feet, he dragged the weight over to his cart. A little farther on, around the corner, lay Malka, her skin cracked and bloodied by the hoar frost. She looked up and down the street with a long, attentive gaze, watching until Long Itzhok's skeleton was resting in the cart, and thick tears ran down her stiffening cheeks, because that evening the frost was biting. The old porter came over to her once more, took a look at her, nodded his head understandingly as she helplessly moved her lips, unable to produce a sound, and he said to her, clearly in farewell, "Tomorrow, early in the morning. You won't have long to wait."

XI

Had a louse bitten him?

The light was cold, white, repulsive. He held his breath. Totally absorbed by the sight, he looked at his bare left arm, on which there were a number of tiny, raised, blood-filled dots. He remembered that he had a scar from a smallpox vaccination in approximately the same place, a bright red stain that always awoke in him the same sense of astonishment. He had to crane his neck, but then he was able to see that the small dark pimples were growing rapidly and that wartlike bumps the color of dried blood were already sticking out of his skin. He tried to count them and then he realized he was waking up. They were growing in a cluster, in a small, isolated circle. He couldn't make himself stop looking at his arm, and with terror and loathing he watched as five growths developed on his own skin, slowly and gracefully unfurling their caps. Now he could see them very clearly. They were vanishing with the roar of a fleeting dream, embedded in a patch of his living skin. They were mushrooms, inedible mushrooms!

That's how his illness began: with fever and delirium. As soon as he opened his eyes he was racked by a fit of coughing. It felt like he had to cough up a sharp iron broom that was scratching and burning him. The spots were spreading over his skin now and soon they covered his entire body. He knew what that meant. Then the spots grew darker, turned a bluish-red, and the rash became the color of blood. How much time had passed? Blinded by fever, he tried to dress himself ever so slowly. Dark rings whirled and blinked in front of his eyes, drowning him completely in multiplying circles of waves. He sat stock-still with his wooden clog in his hand as palpable breezes rocked him, but it was only the fever filling his ears with an audible hissing and with the words of a song that floated up from somewhere: "Stone on stone, stone on stone, and on that stone another stone . . ." He saw, as if through smoke, his father's yellow face and the sallow hollows on his mother's temples. Their elongated forms floated toward him from far away, swaying, rocked by the breeze. Bending over him, they took his hands in their cold hands and examined him. They said something to each other. The sky outside the window pushed its way indoors like green gas. A gray dawn without end permeated the dim apartment; a rotten new day was beginning. He tied his shoes and wept with rage at being so weak. Like a beast, the spot on the wall attacked him. He walked downstairs uncertainly, holding tight to the banister. It seemed to him that he was still dreaming, but he'd been walking around the courtyard for quite a while. Darkness enveloped him completely and a faint light flickered before him far ahead where the gate was. There was an important reason he was walking, he was absolutely certain of that, but he had forgotten what it was. Out in the street, Haskiel the janitor was covering corpses with newspaper. He placed sheets of paper over the stiff corpses that were curled up into balls, their legs drawn up against their chests, and the old newspapers rustled loudly in his hands. It was windy, so he weighted them down with chunks of broken bricks, grabbed at them, held on to the sheets as they slid along the sidewalk. "Who is better off?" A dead man lay there with a piece of bread in his mouth. Haskiel looked at his handiwork and breathed heavily. "Man burns down like a candle; one never knows when." David didn't have the strength to walk any farther; anyway, he had forgotten where he was going. Moving his legs stiffly, he went back upstairs, lay down on his bed in his clothes, thought about how he wanted to cover himself, and fell fast asleep before he'd had a chance to pull up the covers. With his last glance he took a close look at the dirty hand that rested on his forehead. The world became as small as sleep.

It was Seder night. They were seated around the table, eating raisins, drinking wine from tiny goblets, digesting the words of the Haggadah. David, at the end of the table, was quietly and patiently awaiting Elijah the Prophet until he fell asleep, his head on his arms. When he opened his eyes, the tablecloth was pulled askew and there were red stains on it; the candles were melting into warm icicles that dripped from the candlesticks, emitting the stifling odor of soot. The night, the holiday night, was finding its fulfillment in the dreams of those who had eaten and drunk well. The moon grew pale above the silver platter and sprinkled all the signs of the zodiac with its soft light. Sleepily, he traced the outlines of the figures that were carved into the dented, old, well-worn metal platter. A heavy head with a sharp horn—that's Taurus. A six and a nine—Cancer. A high back with the loop of a long tail—Leo. Waves—Aquarius. Three lines and a rounded belly—Virgo, a side view. Huge horns curving downwards—Aries, a frontal view. Scorpio, barely visible, concealed by a layer of verdigris. Libra, worn smooth, dirty, covered with old stains. And Pisces pierced with a fork. He set the lightweight rim spinning. Motion, a blur. All the signs of the zodiac danced around in a circle, whirling against the darkened sky. But the goblet beside the platter was empty. He looked at it in disbelief, his surge of hope frightened away by the mighty snoring that interrupted the night-time silence. Who drank the prophet's wine? Had it spilled out on its own? Most likely . . . The next day Mother was tugging Father's arm, because it was noon and he was still asleep, snoring and whistling. And it was time to go to synagogue. "You drunken sot, what on earth are you thinking of?"

The great ark rose above the *bima*. Two golden lions, leaping. They climbed straight up on either side, standing guard, their shaggy paws resting on the tablets of the commandments. A grapevine unfurled its branches and wrapped its tireless arms around the lions, the tablets, and the commandments. Only birds could settle so high on the arms of the grapevine, their open beaks above the dangling grapes, their wings fluttering in their brief flight, their talons seeking a place to rest on a branch amid the sweet fruit. The birds circled on high, the lions rested on the tablets, and down below the oil lamps gleamed, swaying gently, swaying wildly, among the exhalations of the living. The lofty ark towered above the crowd, above the golden lions, above the grapevine that spread across the curtains, above the tiny flames of the oil lamps lining the altar. The walls were elegantly decorated with moldering tapestries, blackened collection boxes, heavy candlesticks, metal plates that gleamed like old dimmed mirrors. The endless folds of the Torah scrolls swam in the white glow of candlelight that flooded them from all directions. The doors of the ark were closed now, the chanting welled up, and the praying

Jews were bathed in bright light. Their holiday *talesim* shone brightly on their swaying shoulders, and the jangling of a chain could be heard from the rear of the room. That was a penitent, with shackles around his arms and neck, praying alone in the anteroom. On this holy day a beggar was obliged to rattle his chains, shackled to the stocks. Was this to demonstrate remorse for his sins, or to pay with his humiliation for the alms he received? Who knows? In any event, the light of the candles did not reach that corner, nor did the lions stand guard over the commandments there. The branches of the grapevine that spread so wide over the praying crowd did not extend that far. Suddenly, a deathly pale face appeared in the high little window and then disappeared, and a moment later a psalm burst forth in a chorus of high-pitched voices.

"*Alle Juden raus!*"

What is it? Are *they* here again? They can hear the crashing noise of hobnailed boots: smash-bang-bang, an arm, a leg, smash-bang-bang. A patrol goose-steps past as if on parade. A cry: "*Ruhe!*" They walk on. But a bucket of sand stands ready on the street. Quietly and obediently, the condemned walk over to the wall. Next. Next. Hands behinds the neck. Back to the wall. Meanwhile, the patrol looks at them with curiosity, at the people who have become their target. They lift their rifles. They will be preparing to fire and then lowering their weapons throughout eternity. Someone gives someone orders; someone else is ordered to translate. The translator's eyes are crossed in terror. He has long, dirty fingernails, he speaks loudly and slowly as if he is not there, and looks in the opposite direction. The people standing against the wall understand everything even without him. After they have been taken care of, he will be the last victim. One of the policemen loses his nerve, flies into a rage, demands that the scum be quiet. "*Du, komm hier, Junge. Du hast Glück. Du bleibst leben. Weg!*" He waves his arm. If someone moves . . . Good; next group. But hurry up; after all he's not going to spend the night here because of a couple of lousy heads that push themselves in front of the gun barrels. It's a good idea to count them: thirty and not one less.

The corpses pile up under the wall.

"Move those dirty Jews off to the side and sprinkle the street with sand. On the double!"

Somebody drags over the bucket without enthusiasm. Someone

else shouts, "Sentry, it's going to pour any moment now. Why give people a hard time?"

Angered, the policemen whirl around. Who broke the silence with that cry? No one answers. Whoever it was who shouted should run and get another bucket immediately. Barefoot Jasio from Wronia Street stands in front of the *Wache* and issues orders to the Germans, and the Germans laugh. And why not? Red-faced, furious, he waves his long, torn sleeve under the policemen's noses and shrieks, "Get that out of here right now and sprinkle the street with sand!" The policemen turn away indulgently from the madman.

They're gone. They're pushing up the daisies. Barefoot Jasio runs along Wronia Street, disheveled, wearing a cap with its rim torn off. He claps his hands to ward off the cold and giggles in a thin, pitiful voice. He's the one who can recognize any Jew at a glance, by the nose. They can't fool him. "Hitler hasn't done away with you yet? Then I'll get you!" Poor, unfortunate Jasio from Wronia Street. Everyone knows him here, from Kazimierz Square to Kercelak and Bagno. A policeman returning from his beat suddenly spits and crosses to the other side of the street when a black cat runs in front of him. "But they were shooting people all morning! On the corner of Żelazna. It's impossible to get by." That motorman on the front platform of the trolley always had a loaf of bread in plain view behind the windshield, next to the brake handle, and when he drove through the Ghetto he would slow down, ring his bell for the beggars, and throw the bread into the street for them. They pulled him out of the trolley and shot him right next to the *Wache*; it was because of him that those thirty Jews perished.

You have to watch where you put your feet. One, two . . . It's such a long way from the table to the chair. He moved his feet with difficulty. They didn't belong to him yet. He stretched out his arms in front of him. His arms didn't belong to him.

Between them was a huge space which he was seeing for the first time. And in that space was the hard chair that caused him so much pain. Far away, beyond the chair, was a black shoe. It was his mother's shoe, with a little strap and a tiny button. She stepped backwards and screamed. He walked toward her, but she moved farther and farther away from him, and she was no longer his. If he looks down, he'll fall. As soon as the thought crossed his mind he fell down. It didn't hurt at all. She leaned over him and her hair tumbled down in unkempt strands. Her face grew longer and darker in the shadows, her nose became sharper, and her arms wildly stretched out toward him in fright. Her eyes, half-closed, white, rolled inwards, were covered by her eyelids. Then he began to cry. "Hand in hand, hand in hand, let's go to a lovely land!" Nothing hurt. Why should it?

No one will enter and no one will leave. Barefoot Jasio from Wronia Street drew a circle on the ground; inside the circle, a broken cross, a swastika. That much he could do. He looked at everything attentively. The Jews on the posters had rats on their shoulders, lice instead of eyes. "*Juden, Läuse, Typhus.*" Come, come, closer, don't be afraid, here all are equal. The madman drew a swastika on the poster and signed his name. Even Bloody Hands laughed at the sight of this and threw a rusk at the poor man's feet.

"And you want to become an accomplice of international Jewry? Beware, the Jews rule the world!"

That goes without saying, *Herr Zugführer*. The lice crawled down from the poster onto the street in an enormous column, in ranks of four, carrying unfurled banners. A military band was playing a march. If it itches, scratch. The whores went out into the city to greet the victors, straight from the beauty parlor. Dirty blood flowed onto the paving stones; that was the lice trampled underfoot by the marchers. Stone on stone, stone on stone, and on that stone another stone . . . Who's screaming over there? Ernest is playing on a comb and Zyga is screaming bloody murder, showing all his teeth. The moon, like a solitary streetlight that has been saved by chance, shines its cold light on the ruins of Waliców. Rags on living bodies, rags on dead bodies. "Scram, brats!" Malka's yellow and green backside rises above the ruins in the corpselike light. Afterwards, for a long time, people said that Baruch Oks was walking around there in the ruins. No one knows if it's true, but anything is possible. To be certain you'd have to prove it yourself. Who said it first? There's no fooling around with Baruch. For whatever reason, he'd fallen on hard times during the past year, and not many of his gang were still with him. The Crip caught a bullet in the head when he was carrying some goods. Chaim the Orphan walked right into the guns himself. Long Itzhok is gone; he died in the street. All of them, dead and alive, were marching to Madagascar.

When Jacob set up his ladder to the clouds, the porters from

Krochmalna Street climbed onto it. The first rung, the second rung, the third, fourth, fifth rung—on every rung a porter with a sack. What's over there? One beggar said gold. Another beggar said diamonds. A third said it was old man Lewin's treasure that had been hidden until now on the other side. Dreams wrapped up in sacks were handed across the wall. And the porters stood on the ladder while Jacob kept on struggling with the Archangel. But what was in those dreams?

"Seven sacks of pure wheat flour and two sacks of salt. One spilled out onto the road."

It's Mordarski's headache. He'll take it out on the porters, but there's no allowance for overweight, if you know what I mean. Jacob struggled with the Archangel, and in the meantime the porters passed their bundles from hand to hand. The porters called the sentry, who was a Gestapo stoolie, "the Archangel." It was the sentry who ratted on them. A ladder's a ladder. Flour is flour. Porters are porters the whole wide world around. But who was that Jacob, who placed the ladder against the wall?

In fact, the Archangel did not have the sentry's face. Wings fluttered at his shoulders when he hung above Jacob. When was that? In their frenzied life-and-death struggle the man had pushed him away, and his angel's feathers, ripped from his splendid wings, floated down to earth, like feathers plucked from a hen. But where is the hen, where is the soup?

The vault was so high and he was afraid to raise his eyes to the spot from which the light of the burning candles poured down. An enormous spider-chandelier hung over him, waiting to fall onto his head. He could hear the rustle of *talesim* hurled against chests, flung violently aside. Sturdy necks were bowed and from the swaying prayer shawls an odor of naphtha and soap arose, of piety, of meticulous poverty. The cantor's voice flew into the air on a high note and the soft twanging of the chandelier's crystal pendants rang out. Then it blended with the spasmodic sighs and exhalations and, carried away on a wave of sobbing, ebbed into silence. Finally, a drawn-out word resounded as the note faded away. A pure voice, pained yearning, a sweet note. They listened obediently, expectantly . . . Warmth flooded their faces. And they were all together. Such quiet, small, gentle people, so raptly attentive. What were they waiting for? What more could happen? It was the Passover holiday and the cantor sang. *L'shono habo-o bi'Yerusholayim!* David saw his father, saw his worn *tallis* with the large hole in it over his shoulder blade. Uncle Gedali closed his eyes, his eyebrows raised, and there was a smile of disbelief, of gentle sorrow on his face. He saw his Uncle Yehuda's face, with his painfully compressed lips, straining forward. He stood stiffly erect, not bowing beneath his *tallis*, one end of which was slipping off his shoulders onto the floor. He stepped over the *tallis* and David suddenly imagined that Uncle Yehuda would move, stumble, and topple over. The air shimmered from the flickering candles and his eyes closed of their own accord, blinded by the glare. Were they here, huddled together in a crowd, or over there, dispersed along the roads of flight and exile, to which the cantor's voice was leading them? And was that voice resounding here or did it come to them from far away, like a lament from the depths of memory? Somewhere a child began to cry in a high voice, then fell silent when people hushed it.

The cantor stopped singing. The melting wax crackled. A chubby rabbi gathered the folds of his ample *tallis*, keeping his elbows close to his sides, while the holy men, lined up along the walls, pointed their fingers at him, their hands pressed together in a mute display of obedience and duty. There were the sounds of noses being blown, coughing, the murmur that precedes prayer, the shuffling of shoes, footsteps on the platform, the rustling of the parchment scroll as it was being unwound. The boards of the *bima* creaked beneath the cantor's feet. The stifling odor of the candles, of soot and wax, mixed with the smell of root vegetables and human sweat. The synagogue was filled to overflowing. Again, a child began to sob in a corner, impatient hushing sounds could be heard, quiet whispers demanding silence. There was a commotion at the entrance, someone was escorting out into the fresh air a child who was blue in the face from crying, while heads turned slowly, cautiously in that direction. Not much time remained before the prayers would begin. "The rain will fall in a moment and wash the stones clean."

There is no way to walk past there. *Eintritt verboten!* But all you have to do is board the trolley on Chłodna Street and you can ride through the center of the Ghetto all the way to Theater Square. The people who were shot had to be hanged as well. Despite the sentence, they were swaying provisionally—their heads flung back, armbands on their sleeves, with clenched fists. They were dangled on high in order to terrify the others. They were supposed to hang like that for all eternity, but the sanitary codes wouldn't permit it, so they were soon taken down. People from the other side pressed their white faces against the windows of the trolley, exhausted by their own impotence and terror, and stealthily bade them farewell. The motorman who was shot was survived by his cry, "Long live Poland!" And for a couple of days the trolleys passed slowly, like one funeral procession after another. The bells of St. Karol's rang for no reason, all day long, openly and out of tune. In the evening, a car drove up, two fellows in black rubber raincoats got out, and they went in and got the priest. The church was plainly visible from the windows of the Jewish quarter, along with the car and those two men in the black raincoats. People said the Gestapo wore such coats. But what would those guys want with a priest?

It is common knowledge that everything has to be prepared for that day. A pattern, an easy equation of the first degree, a structure along three axes. When Professor Baum points out the fourth dimension, time, they will transfer their motion onto the second plane of coordinates and, ups-a-daisy, tripping over the ruts of Lorentz's equations, they will skip into another dimension. He is waiting so expectantly for that day to come. All he will need is a pencil and a piece of paper, and heaven and earth, the entire universe, everything will be solved so easily. In his notebook he sketched a linear system of three coordinates while Professor Baum stood over him and mocked him. Is that supposed to be a straight line? It's a crooked crescent bun. And where is the zero point of the axis, where is x, where is y, where is z? You can't see a thing. And is there going to be room for a fourth coordinate in such a mess? Where can time be fitted in? That straight line is disappearing crookedly somewhere; not very nice of it. Is it possible to understand the nature of multidimensional space and the relativity of motion on such a sloppy graph? No, it is not possible. Professor Baum scowled at him, and he bent his head lower and lower over the notebook in order to conceal his feelings of shame. But what's going on here? The pencil is slipping, it's riding off along one straight line all by itself. And there, on a second line, Professor Baum is disappearing into the distance, becoming smaller and smaller, and one of his bare, dirty feet is protruding rakishly from his well-worn shoe. Freezing, wrapped in a lousy blanket, he's making a last effort to come closer and now, from afar, from out in space, his hectoring voice can be heard. "The fourth dimension is missing and the world is collapsing!" The voice circles and trumpets like an echo. He looks behind himself in despair and feels the abyss beneath his feet. "You forgot about time! About time!" The stars shine straight into his eyes. He shudders. In his precarious position, he is afraid to look down and the speed takes his breath away. Probably millions of light-years have passed. When? Where? He hears a satanic giggle in front of him and a howling noise surrounds him on all sides, as if a hundred factories had suddenly switched on their power and filled the night with the revolutions of their flywheels. A star passes him in its flight, roaring and puffing like a foundry.

Eternity is empty; it gives birth only to fire. With a cry, he rushes forward into space, stretching his hands out to the distance from which no voice reaches him. The world may yet exist; perhaps there once was life; now there is nothing. He waits and waits. But can this be called waiting? And what is he waiting for? For the arrival of the living, whom he strains to see in this endless darkness. For people who do not exist. "Where are you, people of the future?" His cry comes back to him. In the black, endless, emptiness he is all alone. Alas, it is lost, lost forever; he had forgotten about the fourth dimension. After all, Professor Baum said very clearly that without it the measurement of events must be incomplete, and an event itself will dissolve into eternity, it will be unstoppable, it will escape like noise and light. Poor little Euclidean world, condemned to destruction! That is self-explanatory, *Herr Zugführer*. "The Jews rule the world, beware, beware, beware." The scum are supposed to be quiet. Ultimately, he will have to deal with them. Is this beautiful world supposed to be trampled underfoot by some sly Jew? Up against the wall, everyone up against the wall. *Nimm doch den Dreck und schmeiss an die Seite!* Quick, roll up your sleeves and get to work: squash those lice.

"*Juden, Läuse, Fleckfieber.*" Is that Mother's dry, gray face looking at him from on high? From the poster on the wall? Soon, soon, little one, it won't last long; lullaby, lullaby, my little one, lullaby;

when the fever passes, you'll grow weak, and it will all be over. It won't be so bad. Who said that? Who leaned over him? And how long did it all last? Until he heard a voice, without knowing to whom it belonged, "That child's in bad shape; he won't last long . . ." His mother couldn't have said that. But who knows? He stole a rotten apple, so he's meeting his just fate. Oh, there goes Mordechai Sukiennik, he's running, he's holding a feverish Leibuś in his arms, pressing him against his side like an empty briefcase, lullaby, my little one, lullaby, head thrown back, dangling, lips parted, corroded by blisters, faintly moving. It was he, David, who stole the rotten apple from the stall. Ha! What a shameful thing! The little face disappears. Lullaby, my little one, lullaby. Leibuś's tiny face grows black and disappears in the darkness of the hall as Mordechai carries him up to the fourth floor, while down below, Yankiel Zajączek dashes out through the basement window, coughing, in a cloud of sparks and smoke.

"Mordechai, where did you find such a little white colt?"

And a little colt with thin white legs slips out of the stable in the ruins, stepping softly, and licks the sparks from the air, swallows the fire and the smoke, smothers the fire in the tailor's burning beard with its pink tongue, smothers the fire in the tailor's burning suit with its wet, pink tongue, smothers the stall, the entire tenement building, and when the fire has already died out inside the colt's mouth, Yankiel Zajączek is sitting there in the ashes, on a pile of embers. His beard is singed, there are coals in his hair, his elbow, protruding from his smoldering sleeve, is smoking, and in his hand he holds an enormous letter, like a kite. "Regina, pour in some more water!" The green light burns with a hissing noise, the gas burns with a hiss. In a moment he will order him to read the letter by this light, but he'll run away, run away from this disheveled and singed beard, he'll run away from this letter in the gray envelope, he'll run away from himself, clambering on hands and knees over the ruins of the destroyed outbuilding, from stone to stone, from floor to floor, from chimney to chimney, but there, on the ledge, Long Itzhok is waiting, barefoot, black, skinny. "Gotcha!" He holds out his horrible corpselike hand, shoves him violently into the rubbish bin, and slams down the heavy lid. It's dark, the candle gutters and then flares up, vermin are crawling around the flame, and Father grabs David and covers him with his *tallis*, because the prayer has just begun. They are in the synagogue, the cantor has interrupted the psalm, and two old men are slowly unrolling the endless, yellow scroll of an enormous Torah. And the holy man begins telling the story of the flight of the Jews from the house of captivity to the Promised Land. "*Sh'ma Yisroel* . . . Over your camp stands a column of fire by night, and a column of smoke by day . . ."

The alleys of the Little Ghetto pushed onward to Madagascar. The trolleys, houses, trees, streets, and squares. The ruins of burned-out tenements, a forest of jagged stumps, naked chimneys and walls, roofs hurled into the air by the blasts of the September bombs. Arks that preserved old scrolls inside them swept past, altars, and silver-armed menorahs that glittered with the unextinguished light of candles. Stones, cemetery stones that had cast off the fragments of buried generations, swept past. All the Fridays, all the Saturdays decked in garments deserving words of faith and thanksgiving went bounding by, and in their wake came ancient tomes from whose yellowed pages psalms, soaring prayers, curses, and the sighs of simple hearts were scattered on the wind. Billy goats, nanny goats, and kids swept past. Sheep, rams, and lambs swept past, bleating in alarm, stiffly digging their slipping hooves into the clouds. A shepherd counted the scattered animals as they wandered lost among the stars. Shepherds and holy men tugged at a rope, scattering raisins and nuts onto the earth from their loose, wide sleeves—miracles created before the eyes of the holy *tsaddikim*. A poor schoolteacher from a small town where he had instructed dimwits all his life chased the lost letters that the malicious cattle were scattering on the wind. *Alef, beys, giml, daled, hey, vov, zayin*—all fled before his old eyes, arranging themselves somewhere far away in space into verses he had never seen or heard of. Sins swept past, hungers not completely revealed by the poor, their dreams full of fish, pancakes, fruits, the abundant dreams of the poor. Seraphim spread their wings to shield their naked, blackened bodies in flight. Streams, pure streams swept past, the flow of their waters reversed. Wedding canopies, baldachins, swept by, and in the shade they cast came sleepy girls, dreaming, violently dragged along to heaven by matchmakers. Everyone but everyone was traveling en masse to Madagascar. Lovers in the blind delirium of love flew above the clouds in jasmine

groves and the sun drank the dew from their bare bodies, their
sweat, and tears of yearning. At sunset the day parted from the earth,
spurting red in its flight. Shoemakers, still weighing golden slippers
in their hands, scudded along on high. Beneath gossamer wings, corners of squat huts swept past, glued together by the sweat of generations, by soundless labor, by the quiet breath of spiders. Birds, fish,
and flowers swept past in one harmonious and unimpeded stream. A
wall swept by, Jericho, Jericho, and the sounds of the trumpets vanished without crushing the stones. Silent instruments swept past,
seeking living hands to touch their strings. And finally a procession
of patriarchs with stern faces swept past, their stony profiles eroded
by time, accompanied by the fruit of their loins, rank upon rank of
their sons sunburned the color of bronze, and the sons of their sons,
generation after generation, Kenan, Mahalaleel, Jared, Enoch,
Methusaleh, Lamech, Noah. And the sons of Noah: Shem, Ham, and
Japheth. And the sons of Shem, Ham, and Japheth. "Can this be
real?" Yankiel Zajączek shook his weak, thin chin, sneezing and
scattering ashes, and smoke rose from his charred sleeve. All the
signs of the zodiac swept past in the darkened sky: Aries, Taurus,
Gemini, Cancer, Leo, Virgo, Libra, Scorpio, Sagittarius, Capricorn,
Aquarius, Pisces. "To Madagascar? Can this be real?" A voice still
resounded in the empty cellar.

Lethargic skeletons rose up from the streets where they were
lying, and supporting themselves on each other, they groped their
way forward, gray, emaciated, covered with husks of scaly skin. The
bones of their shriveled legs lifted their fragile ribcages through
which the beating of their hearts, their weak fluttering, could be seen.
Those were birds, birds flying out of those bony cages and beating
against a sky filled with clouds and smoke! *"Alles Scheisse . . . Nimm
den Dreck weg und schmeiss an die Seite!"*

They had wounds instead of eyes. They looked at the world with
amazement through the wounds of their eyes. Anxiously, they gathered up the rags that kept slipping off them. Anxiously, they
wrapped up their scattered belongings. Anxiously, they tied up their
bundles with string, slowly and awkwardly preparing their packages
for the road. Those who were swelling up had a hard time walking.
The heavy ones shuffled behind the others, barely able to drag their
deformed limbs. Their brown, brittle skin cracked under the pres-

sure of their swollen, softened muscles. They moved sluggishly, torpidly, and the clogs dropped from their enormous feet. Their distorted faces, swollen, featureless, like huge and monstrous death masks, floated above the crowd. All of them were on their way to Madagascar in the gigantic procession that followed behind Elijah's wagon. Ghostly figures crept out from dark alleys, from the hallways of tenements, from basements and attics, into the light of day: children abandoning their fathers' corpses, women abandoning the frozen skeletons of their infants in the ruins. They squinted in the blinding daylight and staggered under the gusts of the spring wind, unshaven, with disheveled hair falling wildly into their eyes; they joined together in a parade of skeletons. Emerging from their lairs, they covered their nakedness with rags. In their blackened hands they clutched pieces of pottery, cans, tin spoons, knives, bowls, what was left of the provisions they had kept in reserve for this day. Who were they? Where were they heading in such a crowd? All of them, all, were headed for Madagascar. Covered with dirt, dust, ashes, with gangrene that ate through their skin till it bled, tormented by itching, bitten by insects, they came together in that huge procession to nowhere.

They walked and walked, blindly moving onwards. *"L'shono habo-o bi'Yerusholayim!"* Skinny specters, bearing no resemblance to living human beings, they crawled out of the gates, out of the ruins of the dead tenements, like moths, with their last failing strength. What day is it today? What month, what year? They must stumble onward like this, in the full light of day, in the glare of the enemy sun. One more step, a stone in the road, an effort. Forward, soon they'll be together, forward. Who was it who said that soon they'd all be together? A beggar—a beggar, who was once a saintly holy man, dying of hunger with the others and raising a cry in this enormous crowd, crowing in his whistling, thin voice. *"Hallelujah! L'shono habo-o bi'Yerusholayim!"* Next year in Jerusalem. An old pastor, a pauper, a mortal, a shadow destroyed by hunger. His blood flowed out; hunger drove his cowardly heart. Who paid attention to him? Who still noticed him? A soldier's cry overtakes the beggar on this final march: *"Alle, alle Menschen weg nach Madagaskar!"*

A specter emerges silently from its den in the ruins, its legs wrapped in rags, a tiny corpse in its arms. Lullaby, my darling, lullaby. She rocks the dead burden as she walks across the city, her head raised, indifferent, her black eyes, deep as a well, fixed straight ahead. What did she see high above? Where had she come from and where was she going? To Madagascar. She glides by silently, her bare feet wrapped in rags. Lullaby, my darling, lullaby. People hurry to get out of her way, move aside out of fear, out of the superstitious fear of the mad. She laughs. But what is there to be afraid of? Whom in particular should they fear? She laughs. She rocks the dead little body in her arms, presses the dead burden to her breast. No one will tear her treasure away from her; no bitch allows someone to touch her dead pup. Lullaby. She will wander like that until she stumbles across a merciful guard who will lay that crazed, shattered head on the paving stones with a single bullet. Once upon a time there was a merciful policeman; that merciful policeman had a merciful rifle; and from it he fired a merciful bullet. Lullaby, my darling, lullaby. The cold corpse of a Jewish woman rests beside the wall with the tiny cold corpse of a Jewish infant.

The sun beats down on the slivers of smashed mirror in the ruins of the destroyed outbuilding and scatters brilliant gleams of light. The cabby chases Long Itzhok's corpse-gray skeleton away from the stable. Long Itzhok whispers a lament and his words are barely audible: "Ai, is the Feast of Tabernacles supposed to last all year long for me alone?" It's summer, before the Sukkoth holiday. And Riva is carrying a table, a bucket of water, and a rag into the court-yard. The horse snorts in its stall. Yankiel yawns on the staircase, warming his face in the sunshine at the entrance to the cellar. Long Itzhok, struck by the wet rag, straightens up, looks around dully at the janitor's wife, and hobbles away, holding his arm. David, sitting next to the window, presses his cheek to his warm book and looks around with sleepy, half-closed eyes. A vague feeling of numbness comes over him, just like a catnap; it's as if he felt a weak push and he sees himself in the window at the same time he is standing in the courtyard. His memory still holds that sudden motion from one place to another. But where was he? Here or there? He remembered himself sitting by the window and he remembered himself watching himself sitting by the window. Riva, the janitor's wife, was nearby, scrubbing the table before the holiday. He came to and watched her from above. The shattered mirror in the ruins emitted tiny flashes of light all around. "What are you smuggling, Jew-boy?" Bloody Hands was standing in front of him with his riding crop and pistol, and he didn't dare lift his head any higher. He turned his sack inside out and shook out its pitiful contents. "Life!" His ears were burning. But he was lucky that time. Bloody Hands wheezed and went on to the next person, who was kneeling beside him, his eyes shut tight, hunched over, with his head tucked between his shoulders. He waited for the shot.

But there was no shot this time. "Eat, eat, a sack of carrots, a drop of blood." Mother had said this to him a long, long time ago . . . He was walking through the woods, gritting his teeth against the cold and his fear. Rooks and jackdaws were cawing high above. His heart contracted at this mournful, pitiful sound. The woods, the black woods.

But in April the woods smelled of moss, of decaying leaves, of bracket fungi and early violets. Through the trees he caught sight of a pale girl with a quiet smile on her face; as if deep in thought, she held between her fingers a closed shell from which the gray body of a snail was emerging, enticed by the warmth of her palm. It slid out and crept across her skin. She chanted, "Snail, snail, show your horns!" Revived, the snail crawled sluggishly, cautiously, across the girl's palm, extruding its mucus, and the girl slowly rotated her hand, holding it outstretched in the pale ray of sunlight. He jumped up and down with joy and amazement at this sight and ran out of the woods. The black birds cawed and cawed behind his back. That was a memory. But the girl came to the Hrybkos' later on with a basket of vegetables or something. She walked barefoot, then she ran, because it was raining, there was a sudden summer downpour, but she only shook the kerchief off her blonde hair and, grasping it by a corner, held it high over her head with a light, graceful, deliberate motion, so it would catch the wind. What was the name of that village? Where was the village located?

Near the woods, near the woods. There was a valley there. But an SS man in a black rubber raincoat is waiting for them with his automatic rifle. Sand scatters, the shovel remains standing in a clump of dirt. You can hear every breath in the silence; the convoy's dogs are barking on all sides. "Have a stone instead of a heart. When you see your own people driven to the pit, turn away from that place and walk on." Grandfather's plucked beard stuck out stiffly from his dry neck when they lifted him up from the ground.

It was Seder night and all the living were sitting together at the table. So quiet, so pale. They snapped the thin white matzohs between their fingers. In their prayers, the Jews fled far away through the desert of the night. On the clean tablecloth was the old silver platter, and on the platter was a large goblet of wine. The quiet song sounded so pure, and his heart beat with such joy and strength. It will never be like this again. Repeat after me! *"L'shono habo-o bi'Yerusholayim."* His whole long life was still ahead of him. Is that a sin? He inadvertently touched the goblet on the silver platter. Feh, what is he doing? They all burst out laughing. The wine is for Elijah the Prophet, who will come during the night. If the goblet is empty in the morning it's a sign that the prophet drank the wine. When Elijah finally comes, he will gather all the living, the living and the dead. "Hand in hand, hand in hand, we're going to a beautiful land!" Mother used to whisper this in his ear long ago. A sweet voice can be heard only once in a lifetime; years pass, the voice grows hoarse and coarse. It's time, it's time. Oh, he can see! Elijah has come for them with his cart. Grandfather settles himself comfortably, his eyes fixed on the heavens, lifting the hem of his long overcoat, and behind him walks Aunt Chava, carrying her leather-bound prayer book, and Uncle Gedali, with a sad smile of disbelief, and Uncle Yehuda, with his lips sternly pressed together, and . . . Beloved, where to? Only one little person is still left. He's running, wait up! They drive off. He stands with his head tilted back, watching their escape. But over there, everyone is moving in a disorderly crowd. Is it the end of the world already, and where are they rushing to in such a huge crowd? "Hey, you there, hold on to the clouds! Hold on to the wind!" Then Walic\u00f3w begins to sway and soars into the air like a gigantic kite; the beggars are running around in terror, and the earth is slipping away from under their feet, they are begging for sunshine, lifting up their arms, and caught up by this gesture they fly off into the distance. Torahs with frozen scrolls, sealed with a seal of ice, carried from door to door by old Szafran and his sons, fly out of their hands and flutter above the cupolas of Hale. In front of them is Elijah the

Prophet in his fiery chariot, in a cloak of clouds and smoke. "Another transport. What times these are!" Mother's heavy sighs and the swirling of the stars.

A beggar grabs at the prophet's coat and tugs him, pulls him toward himself.

But even that wasn't the crisis. He came to, rested his feet with pleasure on the hot bricks that Mother kept placing under his sweat-drenched blanket, closed his eyes, and then, stretched out, his neck stiff, aware of the shudders that convulsed his body, he fell into a deep sleep. Voices reached him from far, far away.

Dr. Obuchowski was arguing with Mother about that brick that lay in his bed. David tossed and turned, threw his covers onto the floor. He opened his eyes and, suddenly surfacing, caught sight of the slanting, tumbling world. And that passed, too. The crisis came: he ran into an enormous black dungeon and fell down in there, sweating like a mouse. And when he got up, because he did get up, he immediately felt himself to be terribly weak. His hair fell out in clumps and even a month later he didn't have the strength to drag across the wall even a small sack that could hold just five kilos of potatoes. His diseased blood, sucked out by lice, had already entered other veins, poisoned other people, but he had reached a stage of protracted emaciation, of apathy, that kept him from any exertions. He lay there, staring absently at the large mildew stain that grew on the wall near the door and he could not recognize what it was. A sack full of rusks, dug out of hiding, pressed against his side. For two years Mother had thrown crusts and ends of bread into it, and now she urged him, stealthily, to take a dried rusk as if she wanted to conceal her deed from herself. From somewhere she extracted a bottle of cod-liver oil that she claimed was purchased in a pharmacy sometime in the past at its former, reasonable price. The cod-liver oil was greenish, clear, it shone like gold in the light. David greedily inhaled the fish smell that used to nauseate him and moistened the dry bits of bread in the oil. His shriveled stomach worked like a siphon.

"Here, eat, I saved it for a rainy day."

She placed her hand on his head, from which his hair was falling out.

He ate and slept. He awoke overcome by a ravenous hunger, and when he finished eating he fell asleep instantly. A smile deformed Father's gray face and his nose grew longer, casting a shadow on his sunken, bloodless lips.

Of all the hungers he remembered, this one was the worst. It didn't come gradually and slowly, signaling its arrival with a sickening sucking action, with exhaustion, irritation, and headache, like the hunger of those who were chronically on their last legs, a hunger he had come to know in the first year of the Ghetto. This hunger overwhelmed him suddenly, made his heart race, and blinded him. He dreamed of a piece of onion, but Mother warned him it would twist his intestines; anyway, there was nothing like that in their home. Uncle Gedali brought an onion and he looked at it, his jaws clenched painfully. He'll steal it. Dr. Obuchowski came one day and said that nature takes care of itself. He allowed him to eat the onion but he told them to throw the brick out of the bed. It lay there all the time. He tapped his thin back, wheezed, exhaled his cold breath against the back of David's neck, and promised them a place in the hospital. After the doctor left Mother went into a rage and hurled the rest of the coal into the stove. Not on her life! They'll take a healthy child into the hospital and send him back dead. She warmed the brick in the stove, wrapped it in a rag, and held it against her cheek to be sure it wouldn't burn him.

The street fled sideways to the wall, and the houses stood crookedly when he went into town for the first time. He walked carefully along the slope, passing the crowd; everyone overtook him and he was amazed at how rapidly they moved their legs while he, unnoticed, was pushed and buffeted sideways against the wall. He stopped, having caught sight of a rickshaw at the stand on Ceglana Street. Father sat on the seat, his legs dangling, breathing heavily. His mouth was half-open and his teeth were sticking out. Uncle Gedali was telling him something; a sack protruded from his pocket and he held his hand on the handlebar and wouldn't let go.

"You'll lose a day of driving? Too bad! It can't wait any longer. We have to salvage it. Is David coming with us?"

Father steered the rickshaw, driving alongside them right next to the sidewalk; he wore a metal strap on his trouser leg and the cloth was rusted through at that point. The other trouser leg was rolled up to the middle of his calf.

In the tenement house on Stawki a small handwritten poster was pasted on the bare wall beside the gate; later, they noticed others like it at the entrances to outbuildings, warning tramps and passersby that entry into these quarantined areas was officially forbidden. They went up to the fifth floor, just under the attic itself. The air was saturated with the oppressive odors of Lysol and excrement. It took them a long time to adjust to the dimness as they went stumbling over the lime-covered floor from which the boards had been ripped out. At last, streaks of corpse-colored light, which had laboriously penetrated into this den through tiny windows concealed behind thick curtains of dirt and cobwebs, floated toward their eyes and they caught sight of a fat gray rat right in front of them. When it saw them, it froze where it was, on top of a table, beside an empty, gnawed coffee can, its tail caught in the folds of the torn tablecloth, and it made a heavy, clumsy motion as if intending to leap at them, and then it slid onto the floor, dragging the tablecloth behind it, and scurried away, squealing, along the wall. Only then did they hear scrabbling and squeals in the semidarkness, distinct movements, leaps, the rustling of rubbish, rags, and various items the rats bumped into as they moved around.

A vague form loomed in the corner, a head rose from its pallet, an arm shot up and dropped back weakly. Nearby, a pale spot of light glowed faintly on the wall. A weak voice could be heard, "*Eyli, eyli shebashomayim!*" The head fell back onto its pallet in a fit of coughing.

"How many of you are there?"

Immediately, in this death-filled hovel, sighs, agitated breathing, and voices responded.

"Abram, is that you? Abram, chase the rats away!"

Suddenly, a man burst into horrifying sobs, and a child disengaged itself ever so quietly from a woman's corpse that was lying on the floor and crawled over to the living.

"Abram?" It was the same voice.

And then another, "Who stole my aluminum monogrammed bowl? You can't hide anything. Shame on you, thieves!"

Someone lifted the mattress on which he was lying, raising a cloud of dust and complaining. Someone else hurled a bowl; it banged into the wall and smashed into pieces on the floor. Aunt Chava rushed over to them, crying, "You're alive? You're still alive? God, how good it is . . . that I should see you. Yakov, David, it's me!"

Rapidly, disconnectedly, she told them about some kind of search, about the police, a family shot in the gate, about hostages being taken to Gęsia, a sick man thrown out of his window from the second floor, about neighbors barricaded in their rooms day and night. She was unrecognizable; her wig, pulled crookedly down over her ear, covered her sweaty forehead. She touched them in her desperate fear that in a moment they would melt away in the darkness and disappear. She looked into their eyes, smiling faintly, tiny, standing on tiptoe. She hurriedly pulled up the thick stocking that had slipped down into her warm carpet slipper, revealing her chapped, ulcerated leg.

"What must I look like? With all this I don't even resemble a human being anymore, do I?"

Sidestepping the pallets that were spread all over the place, they found Grandfather at the rear of the hovel, in a tiny little room that was buried under a pile of prayer books and whose window was covered with a dusty *tallis*. Phylacteries that had been hurled to the ground lay unwound on the floor and the leather coils caught at their feet. The desiccated corpse with a yarmulke on its head sat stiffly at the table over an open Bible. Bile had flowed from his mouth onto his beard and eaten through the pages of the open tome. Beside him on the table, to his right, lay an axe.

Uncle Gedali untied the sack and Aunt Chava hurled herself at it with outstretched hands; they couldn't calm her down until Grandfather was lying in it. Father forced a lump of sugar into her mouth and, groaning, she began to suck on it, but the tears continued to flow from her eyes along the dirt-filled furrows and wrinkles. When Uncle Gedali had flung the sack over his shoulder, she pulled a grayish linen rag out of a chest.

"What about his shroud?"

Uncle Gedali waved her off and walked out, humpbacked beneath his burden.

They waited for Aunt Chava to pack her things. She rummaged about, rustling furiously in the corners for a long while, and finally she extracted a small cardboard suitcase without a top from beneath a pile of rubbish, placed a sheet of carefully folded paper inside it, wrapped it all up with paper, and tied it with a string. The little parcel looked exceedingly neat, but there was nothing in it. For a moment she thought about it, shamefacedly and fearfully unwrapped it, checked it, looked at the bottom of the suitcase, then wrapped it up once again. She brought over yet another sheet of paper and a skein of twine that was wound around a pencil. Then she placed a perfectly nice lightweight coat on a chair. She shuffled out into the hallway and returned with a dust-covered shawl, which she beat against her knee for a long time while the people lying in the corners watched her sternly and attentively. She stood there in her thin coat with the little parcel in her hand, looking out the window with peculiar tension and anxiety, shielding the parcel with her arm as if at a loss as to how to conceal something from them. Without batting an eyelid, Father took her skinny elbow and escorted Aunt Chava outside, practically carrying her down the stairs, and the trip through the city began.

In the evening, Uncle Gedali returned from Okopy minus the sack. Mother stood in front of the low stool and said, "Chava, Chavele, take a drop of soup!"

And she answered, "Under no circumstances. I cannot. You are taking it out of your own mouth, my dear."

She ate quickly. She drank the thin soup straight from the bowl and then, looking around to see if anyone was watching, stealthily wiped the empty dishes and sucked on her wet finger, her eyes closed. She sat curled up on that stool next to the stove with an uncertain smile on her face.

She was calm for a couple of days; she wandered sleepily around the apartment, stood at the window sunk in thought, quiet, indifferent. And then she began to run away. Father brought her back twice from her distant neighborhood. When she began to prepare for flight the first time, they didn't understand what it meant and didn't protest. She spent a long time packing her little parcel, wrapping and unwrapping the lidless suitcase. In the evening, Father found her on Stawki. The second time she ran away no one was at home and two days passed before they found her. Uncle Gedali spotted her on Miła Street, emaciated, gray, exhausted, asleep inside the alcove of an entrance gate. She shook her head to show that she didn't want to go back, but she didn't resist. Uncle Gedali and Father put her in the rickshaw, carried her to Krochmalna Street, and placed her on a straw mattress under a blanket, and Mother brewed some camomile tea and gave it to her to drink, looking sorrowfully into her dim, dark blue eyes. When she got her strength back, she ran away again, apparently in great haste, because she didn't take her parcel.

Two weeks later, Uri recognized the little coat on Solna Street. He said her reddish wig was lying nearby. But when they went to Solna they didn't find anyone. The street was empty, and Elijah, stopped beside his wagon, swore that he hadn't laid eyes that week on either a black coat or a reddish-brown wig.

XII

Reddish-brown calves and cattle stiff with terror flew over the wall. Lambs flew over the wall, bleating meekly. Hogs sailed over the wall. Cows scudded along in the dark blue twilight of the summer sky, helplessly moving their hooves among the clouds, flailing with their tails at the lemon-yellow moon that floated near their udders. The animals bellowed, the crane creaked under their weight, a man on the other side shouted enthusiastically, "Swing it, Fela!" A bribed gendarme observed the procedure discreetly; he stood guard and laughed, magnanimously turning his back. In an exuberant mood, he summoned a blue policeman. The policeman was running now. He raced back and forth energetically, supporting his dangling pistol holster with one hand and holding on to his cap with the other.

"People, you've got to do it quick as a flash!"

He was directing the smugglers when a red calf became suspended high above the street, bleating loudly and dropping dung at his feet in its terror.

"That's right, Mr. Policeman, that's right, oh you! Swing it, Fela."

They heard a voice from behind the wall and then a curse. A crowd gathered, and for no obvious reason people said the crane was ruined for good.

It was dusk and they were in Okopy, where the dead were buried with sounds of lamentation during the day, but where at night, at dawn, and in the evening hours the smugglers carried out their trade in meat. They were watching the animals dangling among the clouds in the sky above the rooftops, transported by some miraculous power from the other side of the wall to the Jews inside, where butchers dragged them off to a hasty, forbidden slaughter. They saw how the cattle, restrained in rope nets, were hoisted skyward by a tall crane and then swung through the air across the cemetery wall. Ernest stood there, his mouth agape, tilting his head way back and rocking back and forth in shock, as if he had caught sight of a flock of doves flying across the sky above him.

"Look," he said. And he held tight to David's arm. "Look, look."

The air above the cemetery was clear and bright on that mild summer evening. The wall, the tenement houses behind it, and the graves all looked blue. The six-pointed stars on their armbands also seemed blue, as did the slabs of the tombstones covered with ancient script. The fading sun brushed the bodies of the butchers' cattle with a golden light as they rose high in the air; it was as if the sun was in silent accord with the people who had created this miracle and the people who believed in it. For a moment a lamb hung motionless against the sky. Just for a split second.

"Hurry!"

They passed the cry along from mouth to mouth, people vanished from the street, the smuggling hour was coming to an end. The power that crushes stones and moves walls went into hiding.

"There's nothing for us," said Eliahu. That evening they had to return home with empty hands.

Ernest asked, "How many cutlets can be carved out of one small calf?"

"Enough."

"Who for?" said David. "It depends on who it's for."

Darkness was falling.

"There's nothing for us," Eliahu said again. "We should go home."

"Just a little longer," Ernest begged. And David cried out, "A golden deal! To hell with it! Tell me, Eliahu, why did you drag me here to this bone yard?"

It had started in the autumn of the year before this one, when Eliahu took them to get rutabagas from a fellow he knew who raised vegetables. The turnaround for the number 22 trolley was on a circular wooden platform on Father Janusz Street; that's where they transferred to the number 22B suburban line. They had passed the military airfield and gotten off before the end of the line in front of a wooden church in Boernerów; then they cut across to the forest. Eliahu lay down and scratched his back against the moss, suffocating his lice. He rolled around wildly, slapping the tree trunks in his joy.

He gathered handfuls of pine needles and gobbled up the mushrooms he uncovered. *Ah-ooo!* He shouted and listened open-mouthed as his voice echoed back at him. Laughing, he removed one of his wooden shoes, unwound his foot rags, and soaked his filthy foot in a muddy ditch. He closed his eyes tight, stretched out his neck to the sunshine, plucked a blade of grass, and gnawed at the sweet stem. David and Ernest looked around timidly; with a sigh of relief, they raced through the woods to the quiet, empty clearing carpeted with dry, hot straw. Leaves fell onto the moss, rustling soundlessly, and Eliahu sprawled under a tree, smoking a cigarette and telling unbelievable stories; he was talking them into this deal. They went on a few more outings in this direction, but they changed their route; they purchased potatoes at the Kaputy estate, and once they went as far as the outskirts of Ołtarzew to the farm owned by the Palatine Fathers. October passed, November, the first snow fell. They had to stuff thick rags into their clogs. The snow melted and their foot cloths were soaked in mud, then there was frost again and their wet foot cloths froze and stayed stiff until February, until the great thaw, and Ernest couldn't wait for the day when he and Eli would go to Okopy. He wanted to know everything, what and how. Eliahu had taken a mouthful of water and held it in for half a year. He didn't want to say too much until the very end. He said that he couldn't tell. He said that the time hadn't come yet, and he wouldn't say when that would be.

"When?" Ernest insisted. "And what? Tell us."

"In due time . . . any moment now," he said, until one day he came running up to them, out of breath, stuck his head under a faucet, noisily gulped down some water, and wiped his wet face.

"Where's Albino? We're going," he said, when David had already managed to forget about it. "What do you mean, you don't remember? He came back. And he was at my place."

"Who was at your place, Eli?"

"I'm telling you. That guy."

"What guy, Eli?"

That's the sort of conversation they'd had.

"The one from Nowolipki," said Eliahu, and ran off to find Ernest. They went that same day and came back with nothing. The next day, Ernest came running over just before dawn.

"Tra-tata-ta! Let's go! Are you coming?"

David didn't feel like dragging himself over to the other end of the city with them, to Okopy, and getting involved in who-knows-what. Who-knows-what, who-knows-what. It was supposed to be a golden deal.

"Bite your tongue," Ernest cried. "Don't you remember? We're talking about a fat *mues*."

"*Mues, shmues*," said David. "I don't want to do business with you." And he looked at Eliahu. "Well?"

Eliahu didn't say anything. He hesitated, dug into his pockets, searching for a cigarette.

"Say something, Eli." And he had to repeat it three times, "Speak, Eli."

"Boy," Ernest cried, "pull yourself together. Let's go."

"It's all smoke and mirrors and a photomontage. You won't talk me into it. I'm not going."

"No?"

"No!"

"No is no," said Eliahu. "We'll go by ourselves."

They left immediately. From the courtyard he could still hear Ernest's voice and now he was ready to go along with them to Okopy.

"David!" Ernest was yelling. "David, David!"

And when he went over to the window he could hear the rest of what he said: "You'll see; you'll be sorry."

David slid down the banister and, no longer hesitating, rushed after them, and Ernest grabbed his arm in a sudden fit of joy.

"Let go of me, Albino."

The three of them walked out through the gate, taking enormous strides in their haste.

The huge square was sprinkled with slaked lime; the paths between the old, trampled graves were strewn with lime; the pits next to the mounds of freshly dug clay were steeped in whitewash, the trunks of the felled cemetery trees were covered with white paint, the wall and the stalls near the gate on Okopowa Street, along which—from Pawia Sreet and Kacza and Smocza and Gęsia, Żytnia and Pokorna and Miła and Niska, from Gliniana, and Dzielna, and Żelazna, from Nalewki and Nowolipie, and Długa and Biała and Orła and Solna, and from Żelazna Brama Square, from Zimna Street, from Mylna and Sienna and Ciepła, from Bonifraterska and

Świętojerska, and from Stawki, from Walicόw, and Karmelicka, and
Kupiecka and Zegarmistrzowska and Elektoralna, and from Leszno
and Przejazd and Krochmalna and Szczęszliwa, from the Little
Ghetto and from the Big Ghetto, in horse-drawn wagons and on
handcarts, in boxes with bicycle pedals attached to them, on
upturned mattresses, in jute sacks and in sheets—the living transported and carried the dead from their houses, from the streets
where their bodies lay helplessly, from the ruins where they knelt
down in their hour of anguish, in the blackest hour of their lives,
never to rise again; they carried the blackened, leathery corpses of
those who had died of typhus, their naked skulls covered with fuzzy
growth: these had priority here; they carried the dead who had collapsed onto a sidewalk, tormented by dysentery, green skeletons
from which the disease had sucked the last traces of blood and
lymph; they carried those who had dropped suddenly and in a most
ordinary way from hunger, their corpses stiffened in violent contortions, the way they were found, with the knees drawn up to the
belly, dark blue like the flesh of animals killed by lightning, shrunk-
en and lightweight, wrapped in the bunched-up lousy rags that were
their last garments and their burial shrouds. In the great square, the
melancholy, condensed silence of a cemetery no longer reigns; the
cemetery trees are gone from the great square. The maples, chestnuts, and birches have all been cut down, the gravestones piled in a
heap. Tomorrow they will pave the streets and roads with these
stones and trample on the ancient names under which a Jew was laid
to rest once upon a time. No one says prayers now for the dead. It's
a slaughterhouse. Here people have to dig them in, dig them in, dig
them in fast! As the authorities have ordered. Those who are dug in
will not get out alive, will not spread diseases through the city, will
not cry for bread.

Eliahu pulled out a wrench from his pocket and Ernest turned
gray.

"Don't you want to do this work, Albino?"

Eliahu held out a pair of steel pliers, comfortable and lightweight,
with rubberized handles. Ernest looked him in the eyes like a dog.

"Take them."

"Let me out of this," Ernest said quickly and softly. "I won't say
anything. To anyone. I'll be as silent as the grave."

"I'll smash your skull in with these," Eliahu threatened and shoved the pliers under his nose. "Take them, take them, and don't jabber so much."

But little Ernest started again in his singsong way, begging, pleading, "Let me out of here, Eli. I want to go home."

Then Eliahu bellowed, "Sha, Albino, I'll bash your mug in." And then he said in a quieter voice, with his jaws firmly clenched, "You'll stay right here. Who rushed headlong into this? Who yelled the loudest? And now? *Mues! Mues!* Here's your *mues.* Well, take it," and he threw the pliers to the ground. "Get going, both of you, and don't make me repeat it."

Ernest suddenly fell silent and didn't have to be told twice; he did everything that he was supposed to do.

Eliahu got down on his knees and was the first to begin. They both watched how he did it, and it was easy. Crouching attentively, he moved just as fast as he could, until he was out of breath, then he stopped, got up off his knees, wiped his brow, and looked around at little Ernest, who was following behind him.

"Is this how?" he asked.

"Right," said Eliahu. "Right." But suddenly he shouted, "No! Not those. Don't touch those." He leaped up and shouted again, "Don't touch the ones with typhus, God forbid!" And from then on Ernest stayed close to him, like a shadow.

Eliahu's shout reached him through the soft words of a prayer, a monotonous, interminable whisper.

"Daa . . . David, come here, yes, you!"

"Coming."

He heard the words of the prayer, the soft voice of an old man who was standing, head bowed, at the edge of a pit, his hands resting on a walking stick and his beard, its long, greasy strands waving in the wind, pointing up to heaven. There was no one nearby; he was the only one taking leave of the dead. The shadow of his long black coat stretched across the mound of newly dug wet clay opposite him and fell across the bodies that lay there like hunting trophies, barely covered with paper, rags, sacks, or sheets of newspaper; it fell deep into the open pit, into which sand was disappearing with a soft sifting sound. The old Jew's eyes were white, upturned, and wide open, as if yearning to ingest the sky. The old Jew was crying out at sunrise at the edge of the pit. David could hear what he was saying.

"Lord, Thou alone dost look down from the heights upon this pit, amen. We are burying our dead amidst trampled roads. O Promised Land! A handful of your dust is sacred to us, it is our last relic that we pay for with blood and gold, with our whole life. O Promised Land, we are burying our dead . . ."

They bury their dead and place a stone beneath their head, press a stone into their hand, drop a stone onto their breast far from you, O Promised Land. Where there is wormwood and thorns, weeds and thistles, and they must bury their dead in a burial shirt taken from their own backs. And this is how they do it. On their knees, on their knees, on their knees they fall, and with feeble hand scoop out a shallow hole in which to lay a dried-out body to the words of a difficult prayer.

He heard his name muffled by distance. Eliahu was calling him.

"Daaaa . . . David!"

"I'm looking."

David picked up a lump of dirt, crumbled it in his hand, and let the pieces sift slowly through his fingers. He looked around, walked on.

The old Jew was crying out at sunrise at the edge of the pit filled with dead, naked bodies.

They bury their dead here, where the enemy burns their bones and scatters their ashes to the four corners of the earth, and not a word of welcome greets them from any direction, only a shout: "Out! Scram!" With a finger on their lips, so that not even a murmur should alert the watchman, and with rags muffling their steps, their foot cloths erasing the trail to the dishonored grave. Stealthily, like a thief entrusting his last and only treasure to the earth. They bury their dead without hope, they lay them to rest in an alien land, in this empty, dark, cold earth, without any hope that they will find eternal sleep. Here, where there isn't a single peaceful day, a safe night, a season of life for the sons of Israel, where only the dogs mourn for them and the wolves rip at the face of the earth with their claws in order to bury their snouts in the hearts of the dead.

David walked on, picked up a small coil of copper wire from the ground, bent it between his fingers and slipped it into his pocket. He turned back, discovered a piece of a water pipe that ended in an elbow, held it, weighed it in his hands, wiped off the clay that clung to it, swung it a couple of times, banged it against a stone, threw the pipe into the air, caught it in flight, tucked it inside his belt. He took the soft coil of wire out of his pocket, placed its two ends together, wrapped them around each other twice, twisted their ends into a hook, and slipped it inside his belt.

"Daaaa . . ."

"I'm coming."

The old Jew was crying out at sunrise and praying for the dead, kneeling at the edge of the pit.

We bury our dead in alien earth amidst trampled roads, our graves among the ruts and in the beds of rivers into which flows blood, the water of the wanderer's life, and the accursed bones of the sons of Israel. We bury our dead in alien earth, and it casts out the bodies onto the surface, into the sunlight, grudging them its bosom. We bury our dead, who weigh us down like a burden and become as a curse, and they inscribe traces behind us by which our enemy tracks us down. We bury our dead in an hour that is also the hour of our own death, because there is no good cheer in the hearts of the sons of Israel. Accursed, accursed! We bury our dead as if we were laying ourselves in the grave. We bury our dead, counting aloud all the generations that have passed since our ancestor Abraham, and weeping for the generations still to come. We bury our dead, rejoicing with them and encouraging those who have departed this life, and wish ourselves, the living speaking to the living, a speedy end. The living to the living. The dead to the dead. We bury our dead and grieve that we have remained without them, instead of them, in life. We bury our dead as if we were burying ourselves.

The old Jew knelt at the edge of the open pit.

David walked quietly away from there, lit a cigarette, took two deep drags on it, carefully stubbed out the rest, and put the long butt into his pocket. He walked over to Eliahu, stood over him, took out what was left of the cigarette, lit it, took one drag, and placed it between Eliahu's lips.

"David, are you falling apart?"

"I'm looking."

"Start working."

Eliahu smoked without removing the butt from his mouth. He coughed drily and the butt fluttered to the ground. Ernest jumped up.

"Couldn't you bring something from home, David?"

"Shut your trap," said Eli. "Shut up, because no one's asking you." He covered the butt with his wooden clog and crushed it. "Don't move, and do what you're supposed to do, Albino."

And Ernest did what he was supposed to, and David did what he was supposed to do. They were down on their knees, following Eli, who showed them the way.

"Oh, there!"

"Quiet, Albino. Pay more attention."

Ernest fell silent, but not for long.

"Look what I found!"

They knelt there, indifferent. He bellowed, "Oh God, what I found!"

They came closer and saw that he was holding in his hand a metal ring with a red glass inset.

"What great loot, isn't it?"

"Albino," said Eliahu, "don't be a fool and don't play around like a child, okay?"

He hurled the metal ring far away, aiming at the mound of clay.

"You could have let me keep it. What does it matter to you?" Ernest complained loudly.

"Albino," Eliahu warned. "Watch where you're putting your feet. And don't holler like that."

He had barely gotten the words out when an ancient Jew rose up before them. The specter emerged silently from among the graves and began to scream in a human voice, tearing at his beard and spitting with revulsion, threatening heaven with his stick.

"Rats!"

He looked as if he had long been at rest in the shade of the Okopy cemetery trees, caressed by the soughing of the wind through the old maples, poplars, and birches that were even older than he, beneath the words of prayer chiseled into stone, the name that had been bequeathed to him by his fathers and grandfathers who lay even deeper in the earth.

"What am I seeing? What do my old eyes behold? Rats have invaded the living body of Israel!"

"Quiet, Rebbe, be quiet, sha," Eliahu begged him.

"May this sacred earth swallow you."

The old Jew clutched at his head with his hands and swayed from side to side in a daze. He trembled feebly. His dark, dirty beard stuck to his gabardine like a wet rag. He whispered, "A Jewish child."

"And what of it!" Ernest raised his head. "Maybe you don't like it?"

Eliahu shook the wrench. Ernest brandished the pliers. David got behind the old Jew.

"That's it," Ernest shouted, "take a good look, old man," and thrust the steel pliers under his nose. Eliahu signaled to David. David picked up a small stone and threw it lightly between the old man's shoulder blades.

"Bandits! Murderers!" the old Jew screamed over and over again. "Bandits!"

And he started to run. Ernest ran after the old man and grabbed him by his gabardine.

"Come back."

Ernest kicked the old man and he collapsed to the ground with a loud shriek.

"Ernest, come back!"

He was struggling with the old man, circling, buzzing courageously like a wasp; they could hear no words at that distance. They saw how the bearded specter blindly waved his stick in the sunlight, how Ernest grabbed the stick, and then how the two of them, at either end of the stick, went around and around in circles. The old Jew dropped the stick with a horrifying wail, Ernest fell down, and the Jew ran heavily toward the gate, yelling for the porters to help him.

"Eeer-nest!"

He turned around, and from far away, a small figure on the high mound of clay above the empty pit was explaining something to them with abrupt, rapid gestures. He slid down into the bottom of the pit, emerged after a moment, and ran up to them, panting from exhaustion.

"The deal's off," said Eliahu. "There'll be a stink. Tfoo." He spat and hollered at Ernest, "Let's get out of here!"

"I'm coming," Ernest wheezed. "Wait—" His arms made rowing motions. "I lost—now!"

There wasn't a moment to waste. A swarm of people were running toward them from all directions. Crowbars, spades, and pickaxes surrounded them. They heard vengeful wheezing in the absolute silence, anger expressed without words.

"Take to your heels," Eliahu whispered, and pointed out the direction. "Over there."

But wherever he pointed, between the hollows and from out of the hollows, as if from out of the earth itself, arose drivers, porters, a whole throng of shovel wielders.

"That way," he said, but that way, too, was blocked by now. They zigzagged and circled among the old and new graves, but they were trapped on all sides.

"*Halt! Halt! Halt alle bis auf den letzten.*"

Germans were standing at the cemetery gate. The officers approached the people, and a resolute, controlled menace could be detected in their voices. One brandished a revolver in his raised hand; the other held a Leica at the ready. The silvery braids of their luxuriant adjutants' cords fluttered around their shoulders. And behind them, at a distance, came highly amused civilians, raucously expressing the nonchalant attentiveness and exaggerated freedom of tourists. Gentlemen with their knees covered by wide, loose, pleated knickers, their calves sheathed in plaid woolen socks. Ladies in bright, flowery summer dresses. In the distance, a yellow parasol was swaying; under its shade was a light gray suit, below it a silk stocking, and lower yet, right on the ground, a dainty black shoe. The dainty shoe got stuck in the clay on the mound, the foot in the silk stocking pointed upward, the yellow parasol dipped, swayed, and sailed along in the sky like a light little cloud.

"*Hilfe.*"

Loud laughter erupted among the newcomers. The officer, holding his revolver lightly and easily in his raised hand, turned around at the sound of the woman's cry and, in a clear, pure, resonant voice asked, "*Lotte, was ist los?*"

Sand poured out of the little shoe, the bare foot touched the thigh in a ballerina's movement, and sighs, trembling, and lazily enunciated words could be heard from under the yellow parasol.

"*Bei Gott, das geht über alle Begriffe. Hier darf man nicht gehen.*"

The other officer lifted his Leica to his eye; the porters slowly and reluctantly retreated into the cemetery, among the graves. With an abrupt motion of his arm, around which the braid of his adjutant's cord was fluttering, he stopped the crowd for one moment and then drove them away.

"*Abtreten!*"

And he hurled a question at them from the other side of the ditch, a question that rose above the pit like a lump of earth that has been thrown by a strong hand. He had caught sight of David, who was standing there stiffly. Eliahu and Ernest moved closer to him. The officer raised the Leica to his eye, looked into the sun, made a dismissive gesture.

"*Wie alt bist du? Sprich!*"

He was looking at Eliahu and aiming his Leica at him.

"*Vierzehn, Herr Oberleutnant.*"

The officer pointed at David.

"*Du?*"

"*Zwölf.*"

"*Das genügt!*"

The yellow parasol dipped, swayed, and sailed on. The leg, bent at the knee, was shod in the air with the help of the other officer.

"*Bei Gott, das geht über alle Begriffe! Es ist schmutzig dort. Bei solchem Wetter setzt sich der Staub in die Kleider und das schneidet mir ins Herz.*"

That officer, too, was now standing at the edge of the pit. He inhaled the cemetery air into his nostrils and expansively waved the revolver that he was holding in his hand.

"*Lotte, wonach schmeckt das? Herrlich! Schnauben Sie nach Luft.*"

"*Gott behüte.*"

"*Pfui! Kurt, das ist schwer, ja, unmöglich.*"

"*Ein Gedanke steigt mir auf . . .*"

An expectant silence fell among the newcomers.

"*Ruhe! Was wird er wohl sagen?*"

"*Ich bitte, sagen Sie, Kurt.*"

"*Meine Damen und Herren, da liegt der Hund begraben.*"

The newcomers became very lively.

"*Bravo, Kurt!*"

"*Ja, ja, ein Mann, ein Wort. Aber noch mein Vater pflegte zu* sagen: *da liegt der Hund begraben. Ich sage: da liegt der Jude begraben."*

"Mit der Zeit pflückt man Rosen, Oswald."

Laughter erupted amongst the newcomers; there was general merriment. They slapped each other on the back and thighs.

"Bravo, Oswald! Wunderbar, Kurt! Tränen standen mir in den Augen."

The yellow parasol floated nearer and now was waving daintily beside the great pit. The little black shoes kicked sand onto the bottom; it flowed softly downward with a constant sifting sound.

"Wie gut es sich trifft, Oswald? Oswald, ich habe eine Bitte an Sie."

"Was befehlen Sie, mein Schatz?"

"What do I want? A venerable, horrifying, and elegant skull from a dead man. *Bitte schön."*

"O ja, mein Schatz, aber zur grösseren Sicherheit, haben Sie Geld bei sich?"

"Oswald, Oswald, eine treue Seele . . . Das ist nicht mit Gold aufzuwiegen."

The officer walked around the pit and, without lowering his revolver, approached the boys. The yellow parasol fluttered back and forth. The officer with the Leica at his eye called to the stragglers, who were scattered about the mound.

"Meine Damen und Herren, still!"

"Totenstille!"

"Nicht wahr?"

"Bei Gott, es ist zum Totlachen."

"Damen und Herren, jetzt die Totalansicht!"

"Leute zur Arbeit. Los, los."

"Was ist los? Das Schlimmste ist zu befürchten."

"Ans Werk!"

A noisy excitement ran through the newcomers; there were shrieks of joy, laughter.

"Meine Damen und Herren. Bitte stellen Sie sich jetzt auf. Das Gewitter zieht auf. Schnell! Aber doch sicher treten Sie ans Licht. Ans Licht! Gut, gut. Momentverschluss hundert . . . Molliges Bildchen. Lotte! Lotte, halten Sie sich rechts. Jetzt. Ich schiesse, bums! Danke."

308

"Uf!"

The yellow parasol broke loose from its restraint, floated freely and lightly over the open pits.

"Holla, Kurt! Jodallali-iii . . . 'Mein Liebchen komm zurück . . .'"

"Mit einem Blumenstrauss."

"Mit wendender Post!"

"Halt, eine wunderschöne Bildfläche. Nochmals."

The civilians again stood in a tight formation, the women in front, the men in back, a couple of men kneeling at the feet of the women in the front row.

"Ruhe . . . Bums! Totalansicht."

The group in front of the lens dissolved again.

"Jodallali-iii . . . Jodallala-aaa . . . Kurt, Kurt!"

"Da kommt er."

"Holla, Kurt! Was? Was—pfui, tun Sie es ja nicht. Wie sind Sie darauf gekommen?"

"Jawohl, mein Schatz, es kam mir in den Sinn . . ."

The yellow parasol concealed the officer's uniform at an angle.

"Meiner Treu, er ist kinderlieb."

The officer, without letting the revolver out of his hand, lined up the boys at the edge of the pit. He ordered them to stand closer, closer . . . They stood closer. He ordered them to put their arms around each other. Eliahu, David, and Ernest put their arms around each other. But since their eyes were downcast, he shouted at them to lift up their faces and look straight ahead. So they looked straight ahead. Kurt and Oswald measured the distance, measured the light, carefully photographed the boys, who stood there, helpless, blinking, and stretching their necks toward the sunlight. Eliahu was wearing a tattered cap made out of an old rabbit skin; the Germans evidently liked its dangling earlaps and broken visor, and the fact that it was as dusty as a mattress. The cap and Eliahu were photographed separately. Then Oswald discovered David's clogs; they were Dutch-style clogs that had been chiseled from a single piece of wood, lined with rags and wrapped with wire so that somehow or other they stayed on his feet. Now it was their turn. The clogs and footrags were photographed separately along with David's knees.

They were standing at the edge of the pit and they were free. They stood at the edge of the pit patiently and quietly, and looked straight ahead with slightly parted lips, from between which their warm breath escaped, and their dirty faces were contorted by grimaces of fright, exhaustion, and chronic hunger. They stood at the edge of the pit and looked straight ahead with that doglike look of all the condemned and the damned, and in their eyes, which were both wild and obedient, glowed the dark flame of the fever that consumed their emaciated, anemic, maltreated bodies. They stood at the edge of the pit and, at every movement of the officers, they sensitively turned their bony, misshapen, shaved skulls, covered with stubby bristles and poorly healed ulcers. The Germans took photographs. Heads bowed crookedly on frail, bending necks. The film advanced. Fragile ears jutting out from heads. The film advanced. Heads with smudges of dirt on darkened, gray skin. Faces with dull, sunken eyes in which the light has been extinguished and which conceal a barely hidden accusation. The Germans took photographs, as souvenirs. They stood at the edge of the pit and they were alive; it could go on like that until the film was used up and as long as their shadows survived.

"*Die Krankheit tritt verheerend auf, Oswald.*"

"*Jawohl, je eher, je lieber.*"

They were at the end of their rope, but that was obviously no problem for the men in *feldgrau* uniforms who were walking around them, observing them intently and photographing them from various positions. David avoided looking at the uniforms as if out of a shame-tinged fear that he would see in the eyes of the Germans the sentence meted out to him. He stared fixedly at a point above the wall.

Red calves and cows and lambs and hogs were flying over there among the clouds. Stones covered with ancient script, cemetery gravestones, animals rising lightly into the air, cattle to be slaughtered, stars, six-pointed stars on people's sleeves, all remained, untouched, in his memory. The miracle remained, untouched, in his memory and he who saw it did not have the strength to believe in it or to take in the sight of the world's complete indifference, to lift his eyes to the sun that immutably and majestically warms this spot under the clouds where the blind are born. Nothing worse could happen at that moment.

At that moment the camera advanced the light-sensitive film, the film greedily caught a ray of sun and their motionless faces, frozen in a grimace of terror; the film advanced obediently in its dark interior space, sheltering their faces in perfect blackness, empty and funereal, from which—preserved and frozen in a spasm of pain, of fright lost in the past—other, unknown hands would extract them, other eyes would look at Eliahu, David, and Ernest at that particular moment, on that day when they stood at the edge of the pit in Okopy.

"*Auf die Seite. Los!*"

They were free.

Running away, they still heard the sound of that voice that reverberated rapturously over the pits with a sudden rush of joy and pride. "*Bravo. Meiner Treu, er ist kinderlieb.*"

Behind them was the huge mound, the porters, the crowd of living and dead people, and the Germans, and that yellow parasol, swaying lightly in the sky above the pits in the hastily excavated earth, from under which issued sighs, a slight shiver, lazily unfinished words that died away in languorous enunciation, carelessly drawn out German phrases. Behind them was the good-humored laughter and those words tossed into the cemetery air, "*Tränen standen mir in den Augen!*" And the tourists who came to the other side of the wall to view the Jewish corpses, and the piles of dead bodies wrapped in rags and paper, and the pits left open in anticipation of those bodies, and the bearded old man who threatened heaven with his stick, and the man in the *feldgrau* uniform who hadn't let go of the slim revolver, and that other officer with the camera around his neck, who shouted, "*Ich schiesse. Bums!*" And then advanced the film. They fled from there, cutting across the ruins overgrown with luxuriant weeds, losing their clogs in their haste. Just one more street lay dozing in the full sunlight. The blackened ruins of a burned-out apartment house opened onto the street where their nostrils caught the smell of soot, the sour stench of the rain-soaked crushed bricks, charred in the flames. Then the little square full of rustling paper and trash that entangled their feet . . . And then the film advanced and announced, "*Totalansicht.*" Then they ran down Gliniana Street, which wound around and stretched out like a bad dream; they galloped at full speed into the dead-end ravine on Libelt, retreated to Smocza, ran down Smocza past the cross streets of Gęsia, Pawia, Dzielna, turned into Nowolipki, passed by the church on Nowolipki, crossed Karmelicka without slowing down. And finally they stopped at the corner of Dzika, where Eliahu left them inside the gate. He gave Ernest his wrench and slipped the salvaged metal into David's pocket. He counted it up: eighteen single crowns, five double crowns, and two bridges.

"Wait for me," he said. "And if something should happen, give Albino a push. He should make a run for it with all the goods. He can put the loot in Baruch Oks's hangout. Oks will keep it safe. Remember, apartment 12," and he pointed out the building from the gate. "Well, I'm off. And don't go upstairs until I come down. And if someone comes down for you, tell them to let me come out first. Otherwise, don't go."

"Fine, fine," Ernest encouraged him. "Go."

"Take it easy, Albino."

David asked, "Could it be a rip-off?"

"What, him?" Eliahu thought a moment, waved his hand dismissively. "As long as we have the loot, he won't take off. He won't budge from here. And if something should happen, I'll signal. David," he whispered in his ear, "he's an old dog. It could be a set-up."

And he dashed up the stairs, taking two steps at a time. They could hear the pounding of his feet and the silence when he stopped; one flight. Pounding; another flight. Pounding; then silence. The man lived on the fourth floor. They didn't even know if he was an ordinary scoundrel or a policeman, too. Eli's always that way: in the worst rainstorm, he looks for a gutter. David thought, what's worse? Ernest asked if the guy might cheat Eliahu. David shook his pocket until the metal jangled.

"There, do you hear?"

"I wouldn't go up to that hangout by myself for anything in the world." Ernest moved closer and closer to him, and clasped his hands.

"You! There's a huge difference between you and Eli." He looked at Ernest's dirty hands and at his own.

"We don't even know who he is." Ernest's eyes, with their colorless lashes, were wide open and blinking despairingly.

"The same sort of bandit as us. Now do you know?"

Ernest was taken aback.

"Just like us, only even more cunning! Take it easy, you won't lose a hair on your head, none of us will. As long as he doesn't have anything in his hand, Albino, he won't touch you."

Ernest retreated inside the gate. David extended his skinny fist. "Are you yellow?"

Ernest tripped and sat down on the step.

"You're yellow, aren't you?"

"No," he said softly. "I'm not, just a little."

"I'll show you. When we go up, remember: hang back and keep behind me, always in back of me."

Frightened by this, Ernest looked at him distrustfully.

"Why?"

"Do you hear what I'm saying to you? Stand like this, as if you had—" He fell silent and didn't speak while someone walked past them and went out through the gate. " . . . a pocketful of metal. You can rattle the wrench and the pliers. Got it? That will make a good impression, Albino. Got it?"

"I've got it, I've got it."

"So stand near the wall."

"Albino!" They heard Eliahu calling. "Albino, get upstairs now, quick!"

"Get going."

Without a moment's hesitation, he pushed him onto the stairs. Halfway up to the third floor, Ernest stopped resisting, but on the fourth floor he lashed out in a brief, wild struggle. His clogs clattered noisily on the cement landing. Eliahu was waiting in the doorway on the fourth floor. He winked. The man was alone in the apartment, with a razor, a shaving brush, dressed in long underwear, and yawning. He stood near the window with his back to them, puffing out his cheeks, looking into a mirror that was installed behind a broken windowpane.

He asked, "Is that them?"

Eliahu nodded his head yes, all of them.

He pushed aside the handle of the razor with his little finger, bravely and firmly drawing the open blade against his taut skin. And asked, "Well? How many do you have, rats?"

A little later they were following him submissively. They walked down Dzika, Niska, Pokorna to Muranowski Square and from there they went behind the Brauer factory. He said here, that's where they should wait. There weren't any occupied buildings nearby, only a gate standing in the rubble, and over it a sign in letters as large as cattle: EXCELSIOR CINEMA. Inside, there was a small square and the wall of the old boiler room hanging over their heads like a terrifying precipice that takes your breath away. The wall of the sky, concealed behind the high wall of bricks, lay in ambush for them, waiting to collapse onto them while they stood there patiently, craning their necks and visually measuring the distance from the spot on which their tired, swollen feet were planted all the way up to the very top, as far as their eyes could see. But it didn't collapse; nothing shook the air except for the muffled clatter of pistons in the distance, the sobbing of pounded iron, the crippled bellowing of machinery: *pah, pah, pah, pah, pah*. How could this be? David looked at his feet. How had he dragged himself here? He heard the clattering of the machines, he heard the lazy noise of the blood in his own body, he heard the voice of that guy who had asked them an hour ago, "Well? How many do you have, rats?" A soft, gentle voice that spoke in short bursts.

And Eliahu had answered, "Eighteen single crowns." He'd stopped.

"And?"

Eliahu was silent, hesitating.

"And?"

There was nothing to be done, so he added a little. "And five doubles."

The man was stubborn and probably knew what he was about. Only that "And?" broke the silence. In the absolute silence they could hear the razor sharply sliding along the taut skin with a rustling sound. "And?"

Eliahu lied. "And that's all."

Then he hissed, halted the blade, but he wasn't even wounded. "You, come here, you!" The razor moved and slid loudly across the skin. He didn't turn around until then; he looked in the mirror, quickly and skillfully shaving the stubble off his face. He had soap on his throat and moustache; there were only two motions that he performed with the razor. They watched the light, fluid strokes in silence; he stopped the razor, puffed out his cheek with his tongue, and with the very tip of the blade made the skin in that spot smooth with short, imperceptible movements of his arm. "And?" He stubbornly repeated his one word.

Now Ernest cried out, "And two bridges!"

"So say so!"

The words crossed each other in the air and reached David here, where the muffled clatter of the machines could be heard, *pah, pah, pah* . . . He had a soft, quiet voice and spoke in short bursts of breath. Ernest didn't take his eyes off him, hypnotized by the man's graceful movements, the flash of his razor in the air, the sharp scar that sliced across his bare back from shoulder blade to neck. And then they saw the faint motion of his lips in the mirror behind the shattered windowpane and heard that cautious voice once more, "And nothing else?"

But it was not a question and Ernest repeated after him, "Nothing else."

He dried his hands on a towel, pushed the soap away, bared his teeth at the mirror. "That'll do. It's time to do business." He stroked his face caressingly, looked at one side of it and then the other, rubbed it dry, and when he'd gotten rid of the last traces of soap, he poured a couple of drops of eau de cologne into his palm, its sharp smell permeating the stale air of the hangout, rubbed his fingers on his temples and throat, hissed, huffed, carefully squeezed a bit of vaseline on his skin, rubbed it in, and slapped his neck resoundingly once and then again. He was almost ready now. "Yes, it's time to do business." He was almost ready now, and they were waiting. They were standing like this: Eliahu, David somewhat to the side, little Ernest in the doorway, well hidden by the two of them; they knew that he would run away first with the guy in pursuit, and meanwhile David, with the scrap metal in his pocket, would disappear quietly with Eli. The guy was scratching his leg glumly. "Yeees." And standing there in his long johns, he stretched his sinewy neck and buttoned his shirt. He knotted his tie gracefully with a small, firm knot. "Yeees." His shirt was already buttoned, he stuck a finger under the tight collar, moved his head stiffly. And counted out loud, "Twenty single crowns." The words were barely audible.

Eliahu interrupted, "Eighteen."

The guy hesitated. "All right. Let it be eighteen. Eighteen times two is thirty-six. And four double crowns."

"Five," Eliahu corrected him.

"Five," the guy repeated. "Let it be five. Five times four is twenty. And thirty-six? Altogether fifty-six." Then he hesitated and stopped speaking.

"Two bridges," Ernest interjected smoothly; he'd caught on last.

"And two bridges," the guy repeated after him. "Full ones? Two full ones?" he asked. He glanced for a moment at little Ernest, whose pockets were bulging with the wrench and pliers.

"Yes," Ernest said quickly.

"Okay, two times fourteen is twenty-eight. Twenty-eight and fifty-six? Eighty-four total. Right?" Eliahu held his jacket and the guy stuck out his arms. "I owe you something else for the road. And I give you my word, it's a golden deal. You're making a golden deal at my expense, you rats. Absolutely, absolutely." In the silence the floor creaked under his bare feet as he moved heavily around the room and lazily prepared to leave. He put his socks and shoes on last. "A fine *mues*. I'll round it off to ninety, thirty per head, rats. I'll give you fifteen in hard cash, the rest in paper. You want to do business?" Eliahu was silent and they were silent. Then he turned around quickly and said to Ernest, "Put the gold on the table right now!"

What kind of a place is this? With a soft rustling sound the poster that covered the small, flat clump of rags lying in the corner of the courtyard lifts up, the paper tears away and reveals the dead face of a girl; the sign, weighted down with stones at her feet, begins to flutter. UNITED FUND MONTH OF THE CHILD CHILDREN ARE OUR TREASURE GIVE TO UNITED FUND UNITED FUND. Absolute silence reigned here in the air that was tawny from the dust of the rubble, a silence broken by the muffled, measured noise of the machines. Then, "Take out the gold." He'd whirled around to face Ernest. He was all dressed when he said it and looked at them one after another. Eliahu, David, Ernest. Not a word from any of them. The guy began to walk slowly around the room. But he no longer had any money in his place. He remembered that he didn't keep money at home. If they want to, they can go along with him. Not far, just a couple of houses away. He'll just drop in to see his partner who keeps their cash. The partner will pay on the spot. It will all be taken care of. And if they don't want to, they can wait for him in the hideout, he'll be right back. So if they want to wait, they can wait. And if they want to go, they can go. That's what he said, but he didn't say again that Ernest should put the gold on the table.

He came out to them with his partner a quarter of an hour later. He emerged without a sound from some hole in the ruins where his partner must have been waiting for him, forewarned; and now they approached quickly, walking one behind the other, separated by at least a couple of meters. They walked around the girl who was covered with the sheet of paper. Eliahu went to meet them. Two against three. Not so bad in case something should happen. They walked on, not even glancing at Eliahu. Right up to little Ernest.

"Take out the gold, and be quick!"

"No," Eliahu shouted. "No, no. Nothing doing, nothing doing. Is this a set-up? First the money, then the goods." And to Ernest he said, "Scram!"

"Quiet, rats!"

The guy ran heavily, wheezing. His voice came in short, rapid breaths.

"It's a rip-off," Eliahu said. "You take off first. Remember," he warned David. And aloud to the men, "Leave him alone, Albino doesn't have anything. Albino's empty!"

Little Ernest had already managed to run around the whole square in a panic.

"Which one?" the partner asked. "Which one has the spoils?"

"Grab Albino," the guy hissed at his partner.

He held Ernest down with his knees and started choking him beside the boiler room wall, while his partner nervously searched him, tearing at his clothes. Instead of turning his pockets inside out, Ernest resisted, scratching and biting like a wildcat. Suddenly, he began to scream in a horrifying voice, and once he'd begun screaming he couldn't stop, and since he couldn't stop screaming the guy grabbed a brick that just fell into his hand, and he made Ernest stop with that brick. When Eliahu ran over, the partner jumped him.

"Run away, David, heh-h-h. Run," Eliahu groaned. "I'm done for."

The guy caught up with David only outside the gate, on the street. He dragged him back along the ground like a sack. And he had a heavy fist. David tucked his head between his shoulders, thinking, "Not yet . . . Now!" With his free hand he reached into his pocket and flung a handful of the metal out onto the street with a wild motion of his arm, and once again, as much as he could hold in his hand. The guy pushed him away violently and ran out into the street. Staggering and deafened, David headed for the courtyard. Ernest was lying near the boiler room wall, and the guy's partner was bending cautiously over Eliahu, who was on his knees, shielding his head with his elbows. He was panting, *heh-h-h, heh-h-h,* like someone who's been strangled. The blood flowing from his mouth and nose blocked his breathing.

"Fajner!" They heard a shout outside the wall. "Fajner, here! Leave them. Come, come."

David heard him call the name of the partner, who walked out of the square like a sleepwalker, moving his legs stiffly and pressing his motionless hands against his trousers. They were alone. Eliahu lay on his back and waited patiently for the blood to clot.

"I don't want to worry you, David. But when they come back, that thug and his enforcer, they'll do a worse job on us than on Albino."

They weren't there anymore. The omnibus was driving down Leszno Street. Mordechai Sukiennik, his left arm thrust way out in front of him and the reins wrapped tautly around his fist, was sedately driving a pair of city-owned geldings; from on high, towering above the city, above the crowd of noisy beggars, he doled out shouts, curses, heated invectives to the horse skeletons with their badly damaged skin and mangy coats. They climbed high up on his coachman's seat and huddled close beside him. They didn't have any money to pay for the ride. The chattering, laughter, whimpering of a sleepy child, the conversation inside the omnibus, would not cease. He remembered, "Put on his shoes." David remembered what he'd said when, after some time had passed, they'd dragged themselves back, battered, swollen, and hungry (because they hadn't had a thing to eat since morning) to the square in the ruins next to the wall of the old, destroyed boiler plant. There was no one around. Ernest lay there in the ruins, alone, one loosely curled hand resting against his ear, the other, clenched tight, holding a rock. They couldn't recognize his face; dirt clung to his blood-soaked skin and hair. Eliahu picked up the shoe that was sticking up out of the pile of rubble and placed it closer to him, near his foot. "Put it on him, don't let him lie there barefoot." And Eliahu obediently put the shoe on his left foot. It went on easily, because that left shoe was too big for Ernest. Big blue flies were buzzing around him. "His old man is sick with typhus, he won't find out about it too soon." "Typhus?" "Yes, he never talked about what was going on in his home." "Him? You never could find out anything about him." The crippled horses snorted and Mordechai shouted sadly and kindheartedly. His arm shook, the reins wrapped tightly around it, the wheels of the cart shook as they drove over the cobblestones; the voices of the beggars they passed shook feebly, the passengers' skeletons shook on the hard benches. Flies buzzed around Ernest and there was a rock in his clenched fist. They drove away from there at the unhurried pace of the worn-out draft horses, listening to the cries of Mordechai, who, without excessive anger, compassionately and contemptuously, kept crying out, "Hooligans!" At a bus stop, he halted the team, moved on, and again cried out, "You're hooligans!" And Eliahu stealthily touched the knotted rag under his shirt. There, in the ruins, David had taken out the scrap metal that he still had with him. Eliahu had spread the rag out on the ground, placed the corners of the cloth together, and tied it up. "Is that all?" "That's it; you can search me!" He walked straight toward Eliahu, who retreated before him. "Search me!" Eliahu said he didn't feel like searching him. "Search me, because if you don't . . . I'll smash all your teeth, okay? Damn you, you and your golden deal!" A bus stop, the jam-packed omnibus stopped at the corner of Leszno and Solna, the passengers all got out together, the heads of the weary horses drooped toward the ground, flies gathered on their sweaty scars and bloody coats. The team moved on, snorting. "No. You don't have to." That's what Eliahu said then and, in a different voice, "I'd like something to eat. A piece of bread." He hid the metal under his shirt. "Let's get out of here, David." They walked away.

Mordechai had only to glance at them and he already knew; he spat onto the pavement over the shafts and between the horses' hooves, and when the omnibus, swaying and shaking (the chorus of complaints inside the coach never let up for a minute) turned into Żelazna Street, Mordechai, looking straight ahead, over the stumbling team, into the dark outlet of the street, said between one tug on the reins and another, "You're hooligans," and lashed the left horse's flanks. "Now what, you brats?" He lashed the right horse's flanks, but with feeling. "Now what? And nothing to show for it. Hooligans!"

He tucked the handle of his whip under his knee. He removed his cap, took out a cigarette, and carefully replaced it on his head. His long gray hair stuck out from under the lacquered peak, and the dark blue light of his shaded lantern trembled on it.

"Move over a bit. Can't you see that I'm falling?" Eliahu said, and shoved David.

"Don't bite each other, you rats, as long as you're riding here in the same wagon."

It was dark when they returned home. Where had he been all day? He knew what would happen now. How could he forget it? The house was hidden in darkness and his father's voice reached him from there. He waited for the first blow and counted rapidly, "Eighteen times two is thirty-six, eighteen times two is . . ." What had Fajner's partner said that afternoon? That they'd each get thirty. Thirty what? Frightened, hunched over, he waited for the blow and in the darkness saw a dim streak of light that filtered in from above through the dusty panes and fell on his father's head. *"Aber doch sicher treten Sie ans Licht. Ans Licht!"* He knew that the blow would land suddenly, before he'd have a chance to cry out, to run away. Yellow and red stripes flashed before his eyes. He thought he would go blind from terror. Had he walked in just as his father was praying? "Rats have invaded the living body of Israel! What must my old eyes behold?" Yes, he was praying right now. He threw off his *tallis* with one movement. He straightened up and snatched the *tefillin* off his forehead. He swung his fist blindly and the thick strap of the phylacteries whistled through the air. David heard the hiss of the damp carbide flying from the extinguished lamp, his father's loud, agitated breathing, the wild blows that he didn't feel.

"Tell me where you were."

He beat him in a rage, blow after blow, until he drew blood. With his fist, with the handle of his upholsterer's hammer, with a piece of wood, and when he dropped that, because everything was falling out of his hands, he again grabbed the strap that lay on the floor in long, tangled coils.

"That's not enough yet," his mother said. Pacing restlessly, making wide detours around him, she repeated, "Bandit!" She wrung her hands until her fingers cracked. "A bandit for no reason at all."

Squeezed into the corner between the trunk and the door, David sank onto the floor with every blow. His head knocked painfully against the edge of the trunk. He heard his father's words as he beat him tirelessly, furiously.

"Have you had enough? You've had enough. So I'll add another bit."

He slid along the wall, crouched in front of him. Grabbed by the collar and made to stand on his feet while he was beaten some more, he heard his mother's words, "You monstrous dog."

And then his father, "I'll give you a deal. I'll give you a golden deal."

He staggered, but he did not run away. He gritted his teeth and didn't even cry out. He was weak; a whole day had passed and he hadn't had a bite to eat. He lay still beside the wall in the corner between the trunk and the wall where he'd fallen, shut his eyes, and listened to what they were saying. As if they were talking about someone else. Who was the old Jew in Okopy praying for?

"I don't want this to happen again!"

Weak, emaciated, skinny, like sleepless specters they moved around inside the walls. They bent their yellowed faces over him, shook their fists. They hissed at him with fear, rage, and disgust.

He lay there with his eyes closed, and the coolness of the damp spot on the wall against which his shoulders were resting made him shudder violently and eased his pain; light and empty, he heard his father's words.

"Do you want to bring typhus into this house?"

Who was the old Jew in Okopy praying for when he knelt at dawn at the edge of the open pit? He wants to bring typhus. Light and empty, he felt a burning in his throat, he was ready to burst out laughing. *"Die Krankheit tritt verheerend auf, Oswald."* *"Jawohl, je eher, je lieber."* The loud, exhilarated voices of the Germans drowned out his father's words, the clamor of the running porters who were approaching from all sides and . . . "And?" Fajner's partner repeated insistently, and the razor, rustling, slid sharply over his skin.

That night, agitated, angry voices were raised over him for a very long time.

Butterflies flew away and landed in the darkness of the closed Excelsior Cinema behind Brauer's factory. The gate still stood in the ruins, and in back of it was the wall of the destroyed boiler plant, and beside the wall lay the little corpse of Ernest, whom they had called Albino for ages and ages. For a long time afterward they didn't want to show old Bierka where his body lay; finally Five-Fingers Mundek brought him a torn, bloodied shirt and stealthily threw it inside his door. Mordechai Sukiennik cleaned his boots and went to visit Bierka, who was recovering from typhus. He sat beside the sick man in silence, and said, "Following the tracks you can reach a filled-in well. But no one knows who waters his flock in it and who will show his veiled face. I can say nothing more to you, man. Ech!"

Bierka looked straight ahead with the empty, indifferent gaze of a dying man who has reluctantly outlived his dear ones. The body was buried before he recovered and could make his way to the vacant square. There was a great clamor and commotion on Krochmalna. The holy earth still supports those monstrous dogs. Eliahu and David remained with their childish fate, with the rest of the metal wrapped up in a rag, and some time afterward a merchant was found on the other side of Żelazna Brama, a loyal and eager man, who relieved them of this burden. Eliahu divided the *mues*; he kept six coins for himself and tossed ten notes at Ernest's father. Again there were cries in the apartment house. "Oy vey, a golden deal." And the women who went to work in the Brauer workshops blabbed to one and all, as if they were paid to do so, that Eliahu and David had smashed little Bierka's head with a crowbar and thrown his body into a pit filled with slaked lime so that there would be no trace of him. Who murdered Ernest? Who murdered Albino? Let them ask Fajner, he could tell them. But no one asked Fajner anything. Thus ended the golden deal for which they'd been screwed by everyone.

❖

XIII

D oomsday!"
On the morning of the second day of the action a gendarme in a long overcoat ran into the courtyard, wiping the sweat from his brow and yelling for water. Everyone was terrified. He distractedly ran around the courtyard and peered into windows, but his helmet prevented him from looking up. Stealthily, in absolute silence, they watched him from behind their windows. On the ground floor, Haskiel the janitor pulled back his curtain a little and waited, but the gendarme did not order him outside; instead, he kept looking uncertainly from one outbuilding to the other. Riva grabbed Haskiel by his belt and pulled him back inside their room. In the window over the gate, Mordarski the merchant sleepily and painstakingly straightened his tie. Sura the street vendor leaned her shaggy black head against the wall in the entranceway and looked out, squinting with fright. On the second floor, Nataniel's face was pressed against the dirty windowpane, white and silent; behind him stood Esther, resting her hand on his shoulder. On the fifth floor, under the attic, Papierny the furrier sat in his armchair, holding his cane, washed and dressed in a black suit for the first time in many years. Buba had moved his chair over to the window, and the old man's unkempt beard trembled above the windowsill, protruding cautiously and curiously when the gendarme turned his back.

Suddenly, Eliahu ran in from the street, his wooden clogs clattering, showed himself in the gateway for a minute, and then vanished.

The tense gendarme whirled around but there was no one to be seen. Regina managed to slam the cellar doors shut while Yankiel stood motionless, his hands still gripping his iron; the damp cloth steamed and hissed, something was smoldering, and there was a

323

smell of smoke in the air. The German crouched and aimed his gun in the direction of the destroyed outbuilding. Someone showed a soapy face in an open window, whistled, and drew back, but then the German shouted something or other and began shooting blindly. Window panes started flying, there was a roaring sound, and shards of glass showered down around the gendarme, shattered under his boots, bounced off his helmet.

"Doomsday! Doomsday has begun for me!"

Mother spoke in a hoarse whisper. Her kerchief slipped down and revealed her short hair, close-cropped after her illness, the hollows at her temples, and the blackened skin on her neck. She was holding a lit cigarette that Father had given her. It was a long time since David had seen her holding a cigarette; now she inhaled clumsily, lifting her thin, bony hand to her lips, her fingers stiffly extended. She exhaled the smoke, blowing it out and up. Her eyes began to tear; she coughed and squeezed her eyelids closed. She handed the cigarette back without saying a word. The butt quickly grew smaller and turned to ash, still sticking to Father's lips. For a moment his black, rotten teeth could be seen and his protruding, flattened tongue. His armband was on his sleeve, which meant he hadn't managed to leave the house on time.

The German shot his fill and, backing out, disappeared through the gate as suddenly as he had appeared.

Mother flung herself onto the bed, covered her face, and pressed her hands against her ears, while on the street the police vans were now driving past uninterruptedly. Horns sounded from all directions as the trucks, loaded with people, turned the corner and raced past the *Wache* on Chłodna Street. A yellow policeman opened the barrier at a run, flattened himself against it, his belly tucked in, and let the trucks drive past. They slowed down in a cloud of dust and exhaust fumes.

The Ghetto was sealed off, the *Wachen* were reinforced, patrols of blue police and black SS cruised the length of the wall, while on the other side of the wall Latvians in moldy-green uniforms were posted on the second- and third-floor balconies, in open stairwell windows, and in hallways, their rifles pointed at the street. Vans filled with gendarmes were massed on Żelazna Brama Square and Grabowski Square, ready for the action. By now, the Germans were

running in and out of apartments and dragging out the petr₁
in the first wave of chaos. It had begun on Wednesday, the
second of July, 1942, when the cemetery carts were suddenly
back from Okopy that afternoon and the gravediggers were
away. On that day the gendarmes rounded up the last beggars, pursuing them into the ruins as they fled; they searched the nighttime
shelters for refugees from the provinces and herded the prisoners
from the jail on Gęsia Street to the *Umschlagplatz*. Those people
were in the front lines. The next day, on Thursday the twenty-third,
the news spread that the president of the Judenrat, Czerniaków, had
committed suicide after a visit from the Gestapo, and that his young
daughter then shot herself in the temple with the same pistol. On
that black Thursday panic engulfed the streets like fire, although
people were not dragged from their apartments on that day: only the
sick from the hospital in Czyste were transported by police van to
the railroad loading platform and dumped next to the track in their
hospital gowns. Apparently, the transport was supposed to leave
only on Friday. The prisoners, the beggars, the refugees from the
shelters had not yet departed, and their presence on Parysowska
Square near the loading platform delayed any further action for one
day. On Friday, seven thousand were loaded, and on Saturday, ten
thousand, and they were sent east by train.

Posters promised work and bread there, in the east. They urged
people to preserve order; they cautioned against panic. He who
works will live. The authorities will not permit any lawlessness on
the part of the Jews, and those who participate in rioting or looting
will be tried by a military court. Those who are employed will be
assigned to quarters in their place of work. All others are to proceed
under guard to the *Umschlagplatz*. The Reich guarantees everyone
work, food, a place to sleep, freedom from worry. The police warn
that anyone who conceals a weapon, foreign currency, false documents with an Aryan name, etc., etc., will be brought to justice.
There is no room for thieves, tramps, rabbis, or subversive liberals,
and these harmful elements will be assigned to reeducation and set
on the path to fruitful labor. *Es lebe der Staat, es lebe der Krieg.*

This order takes effect on the day of its announcement. *Heil
Hitler!*

Father read the poster, gathered up his tools in a sack, and, doubled over under their weight, ran off to seek work at "little" Toebbens, the branch on Prosta Street, where Uncle Gedali had been employed for some time now. Mother called to him through the window: he should come back soon because they'll be driving people out to the square at any moment. If he's late, he should look for them in Trawniki! The wardrobe was pushed away from the wall, just in case. Earlier, they had moved the old piece of furniture, the dust rose to the ceiling, and Mother, groaning and coughing, slipped into the shallow niche in the wall in order to check ahead of time if there was enough room; the hiding place, where she could stand for an hour with her face turned sideways and her arms stiffly at her sides, was ready. Couldn't they see her? Her voice sounded hollow and strange from behind the wardrobe. Father pressed his temple to the wall, looked into the crack, and said no, she couldn't be seen. A spiderweb, picked up by his unshaven cheek, dangled from his nose and eyebrows. David didn't go in there; after all, someone would have to shove the wardrobe up against the wall and then push it away again. He had the key to the cellar in his pocket, and that cellar linked up with others that were covered over by the rubble from the ruins of the destroyed outbuilding. And what if the Germans should look inside it? Mordechai Sukiennik had dug an extra tunnel whose outlet in the stall was extremely well hidden; farther on, concealed underground passages linked up with the spacious storerooms of the soap factory in the neighboring building, and it appeared that from there you could go through an old underground passageway all the way to Hale. That's what Haskiel the janitor said, and he had lived on Krochmalna Street for thirty years and knew all the nooks and crannies here like the back of his own hand. That's fate: the Jews will imitate the rats and stealthily disappear among cellars and dens, they will descend under the earth and hide in order to live. Who will permit them to live? Sooner or later they will be exterminated. It's easier for rats, because no one has yet proclaimed *Rattenrein*. Saying that, Haskiel laughed hideously, and tears appeared in his lashless red eyes and ran down his laughing, contorted face. It was terrible to hear that laugh and to look at those eyes. Father said that David should hide in the cellar and sit as quiet as a mouse, but after the sweep he should go upstairs right away and move the wardrobe, because Mother will suffocate or faint there. She had been stubborn and refused to go downstairs, because someone, after all, had to watch the apartment! She thought up that hiding place behind the wardrobe herself.

That day, a whole squad of gendarmes ran into the courtyard once more, in the afternoon. They were accompanied by policemen.

"Come out, Jews! Leave your doors open . . . Get going, Jews!"

A policeman ran upstairs with his cap in hand, carefully wiping its sweaty rim with a handkerchief. David passed him, flew downstairs, and slipped into the cellar. In the courtyard the Germans were barking, *"Auf die Strasse raus! Schnell, Jude, herunter, du Schwein. Aber los! Los!"*

Feeling his way along the damp wall with his fingertips, he slid along in the darkness for so long that their voices grew distant and faint. The enormous silence gripped his throat, and his heart beat like a tocsin in that silence. He stumbled, fell, and desperately started searching for the key, which he had dropped. He imagined that if he didn't find the key he would be lost. The Germans left a quarter of an hour later; they had needed only a few more people to fill up their van.

On the third day of the action the street gangs came out into the open. Rounded up from all the back alleys, ruins, and hideouts, they came out into the city in a noisy, well-disciplined mass, impudently looking for a convoy; the gendarmes stopped in their tracks at the sight of them, then followed the long procession of adolescents. The older boys urged on the younger ones, put their arms around them, squeezed their hands. Bloody Hands led them off the sidewalk with an amused look on his face, shook his rifle at them in a friendly way, gazed at them admiringly, and they walked on toward the *Umschlagplatz* without a convoy, stopped by no one along the route, shouting boisterously and laughing, pushing forward and rebuking each other for their slowness. At their head marched Baruch Oks and his gang: Baruch Oks, without any baggage or bundles, with only a black leather jacket slung casually over his shoulder. Whenever the column stopped or slowed down, he turned around and, walking backward, waved the leather jacket madly over his head. He smiled a nasty smile and narrowed his eyes as he did before a fight. Behind him sauntered Five-Fingers Mundek, swinging his shoulders, his head thrust forward, looking straight ahead and to each side. He whistled at them, his fingers thrust between his teeth, urging them on. Beside him, Kuba the Gelding limped along stiffly, his clogs clattering; he giggled in a high-pitched voice and said something to Mundek, who cleared his throat and mumbled in response. Yosele Egg Yolk marched with long strides, wheezing; he had a bag on his back with protruding corners that were tied up with rope and stuck straight up, and the rope was strapped across his shoulders and around the sack like the straps of a knapsack. From somewhere a tiny, bowed figure jumped out into the street and attentively watched the marching boys with his restless glance. Mordka the Ram was bent over, tying his clogs tighter, and he called out to them, "Where are you off to, my lords?"

"Madagascar!"

"Come along, don't ask questions. Come for a hike with us."

Mordka the Ram tied the strings of his clogs around his ankles, and whistles and laughter resounded through the column. Yosele Egg Yolk walked off to the side and called out, breathless, "*Kesskuh-say?* Could that be the count?"

Baruch Oks waved his leather jacket in front of the amazed Mordka, who was looking at him with his mouth agape.

"To the *Umschlagplatz*! Are you coming?"

"Where?"

He was answered with shrieks and laughter.

"Fall in with us, Ram. Everyone gets a kilo of bread and a half-kilo of marmalade there."

"You'll stuff your gullet forever, Ram."

"Isn't that enough for you, you starveling?"

"I'll give you double marmalade. I won't put sweets in my mouth. Not with these teeth!"

"That's the truth," said Mordka the Ram, and took off at a run after his own people. He raised his head high, stretched, and patted the rucksack slung over his shoulder.

They walked straight ahead, their canteens jangling and clattering, banging their spoons on their plates, beating time on the broken old pots they were taking along on their journey. *Tram-tara-ram-tam, tara-rara-ram-tam.* Laughing, they marched onward to the railroad loading platform on Stawki, shouting and cheering without stop. A woman hurled herself into their midst, repeating the same name over and over again. Pushed out by dozens of bony hands, she stood helplessly beside the ranks of youths who were marching past shouting, tumultuous, in an uproar of talk and catcalls. She raised her arms and ran after them once more, but then she returned resignedly to rejoin the people detained on the sidewalk. A gendarme smiled seductively, inclined his head compassionately, and the teenage rabble marched on. Wildly glittering eyes, smoothly shaved skulls, gray, bony, misshapen, glided along the street; the wooden clogs clattered against the pavement, making an incredible racket, clanging and banging, and it seemed as if they wanted to drag along with them the people who were lined up there, but the people in the guarded convoys waited their turn patiently, and the fading sound of hundreds of small wooden shoes aroused indignation, anger, and hopelessness in their hearts.

Where had so many of them come from? At a signal from a guard, a gate opened some distance before them. They walked onward, alive, strong with that wild intoxication that envelops a crowd. They walked onward, knowing full well where they were going.

Two vans were parked in the street in front of the house, the Germans were running up the stairs, and Haskiel the janitor was beating his hammer against a rail. The rail, to be sounded in case of fire, hung near the rug-beating grate; the hammer was suspended beside it on a long chain. In the past, in the event of an air raid, the sirens in the Haberbusch brewery would sound first and then Haskiel would hammer on the rail and they would go down into the shelter, that is, into the cellar, and they would sit there in the dark until the all-clear sounded; but today, the gendarmes had ordered the janitor to take the hammer and drive everyone out of their apartments with his banging. Haskiel hammered on the rail and in the meantime they managed to fill the two vans. They left the janitor's family in peace; they didn't enter the second courtyard at all, didn't search the ruins. They took bribes from whoever offered them, and those who had no money walked out through the gate with a bundle. The merchant Mordarski's entire family was shot on the spot: his wife, his son-in-law, and his son. They shot Sura the street vendor in her own apartment because she hid in an empty trunk and when they opened the trunk her bare elbow and coal-smeared calf were sticking out. Terrified, she crouched on the bottom, hiding her head in her skirt. A German fired into the trunk and slammed the lid; it hit her in the nose. But she survived. She was still alive a little later, when Buba found her in that trunk, as weak as a child and with her face blackened with coal. Without bandages, wearing her bloodied dress, she hid in the attic for two more days, groaning and crying out for water. It turned out that the only thing wrong with her was a bullet in the thigh. At night people secretly brought her food, but in the meantime the swelling traveled higher, and when her thigh and belly both swelled up Sura hopped downstairs. She wanted to join a transport but she didn't get far; a gendarme killed her around the corner. Eliahu recognized her corpse by the dark blue swollen leg.

The third day of the action passed, and on Saturday Haskiel was still hammering on the rail, standing in the courtyard with his baggage and his family. The police were running along the dark hallways, shooting into the attic, through the doors of the apartments as they passed, wherever they heard the faintest sound. On that day they rounded up men in the street and for a long time made them carry the household goods downstairs and throw the furniture and bundles of linens out the windows, so that the people wouldn't have anything to hide in or anything to sleep on at night when they crept out of their hiding places. The gendarme called Bloody Hands came back from his inspection and walked through the courtyard, avoiding the heaped-up furniture—a damaged wardrobe with doors flung open, bedbug-infested beds, and a pile of mattresses, a pyramid made of chairs, overturned tables with their legs pointing helplessly upwards, a bureau, and individual drawers from which the contents were spilling out: papers and documents, prayer books, trampled rags that kept getting caught underfoot. Pausing as he caught sight of his reflection in a mirror, he stroked his smoothly shaven cheek and carefully adjusted his cap.

On the morning of the fourth day of the action there was an explosive, reverberating noise; it was caused by a gendarme who, on his way down the street, decided to dislodge the locked gate of the building next door with a hand grenade. Soon a patrol of gendarmes showed up, accompanied by the Mad Dog, who served as their translator. The people in their hiding places could hear what the policeman was shouting. The Mad Dog was drunk and he threatened that if the Jews didn't come out on their own, he'd drag them out of their corners by their beards! They should take their brats and come out! The gendarmes fired through the windows to frighten the people, shouted for a while, and left. Everyone who was still in hiding waited to see what would happen next. They stole out of their hiding places in silence and hastily prepared something to eat. Some barely recognizable people ran in from the street; the policemen had taken Nataniel's shoes, coat, and jacket, and red-haired Estusia was wearing a man's shirt. They shouted for someone to throw them down a quilt. The evening passed peacefully; the Lithuanian *szaulisy* who were posted on the balconies on the other side of the wall opened fire from all directions, emptied their ammunition belts, and left for their barracks as soon as they had used up their ammunition. No more "dogcatchers" looked in on the courtyard. A July drizzle sprinkled the bedding that lay strewn over the paving stones, and the sun was setting in the ruins. People who were able to do so returned to their plundered apartments to sleep, lying down fully clothed beside their wide-open doors, taking care not to strike a light and to preserve a deathlike silence.

At midnight a crowd of strangers ran in to the apartment house and swarmed over the stairways, looking for shelter. These refugees said that they had been let go from a column along the road to Stawki; their convoy guards were supposed to watch them throughout the night, but they had given up and marched off. It was raining, the deportation place was horribly overcrowded, and the last transport of the evening had departed. Apparently, they had been delayed by tie-ups along the way. In the meantime, they were unable to reach their homes because the police were patrolling the streets and shooting at pedestrians. Tomorrow they would get back in line, go to Stawki on their own, and leave. One way or another, there was nothing for them to do here; the evacuation would at least save them from death by starvation, and perhaps they would get work. They crowded around the spigots and drank water. They had been dying of thirst throughout their day of wandering. They proudly displayed their baggage: nothing had been taken away from them. You can take along baggage, provided the weight is within the approved limits. Some of them said you could take eleven kilos; others, three. There were people who said the limit was twenty kilos. Some people had nothing at all. Why?

The next day everyone was up and ready at dawn. The refugees disappeared first and the apartment house once again emptied out; morose voices carried across the courtyard through the smashed windows.

"Riva, Riva, what should I dress her in?"

"Her light blue sweater."

That was Haskiel in his janitor's quarters, calling to his wife as he dressed little Roizele for the journey. From all sides the cries of people packing in haste could be heard. Judah Papierny called to his neighbors to carry down his chair. He was hoarse from shouting by the time his daughter came back from town. She had been looking for a cart in all that chaos so she could transport the invalid to the *Umschlagplatz*. Those Germans have no sense if they think a man whose legs were amputated ten years ago can walk to the train by himself! Buba complained and pushed his chair into the hallway, and Mordechai Sukiennik carried the furrier downstairs. Yankiel kept running back and forth to the cellar entrance. He waved his apron in the air, urging Regina to move faster. And how could she go on such a journey? Regina's complaints rose to heaven. She has varicose veins and is short of breath. Why doesn't he go himself, the stubborn goat, along with that crazy coachman, and she'll stay behind. In the end, she followed the tailor; she carried a suitcase and Yankiel Zajączek walked ahead of her, cradling against his breast the little head of his sewing machine, wrapped up in a piece of canvas. Mordechai Sukiennik stood outside the gate with a small lightweight sack, observing the gendarme.

Judah Papierny, seated in his chair, was asking, "Ajzen, tell me what I should do now. Hide? Or leave?"

"Why don't you all leave me alone. What can I advise anyone in such times? Can I conceal you? With what? Hide you? Where? Under the rubbish bin!"

Haskiel Ajzen was dressed for this day in a pinstriped linen shirt and his woolen *shabbos* suit. He was carrying Roizele, who was dressed in her blue sweater, and his shirttails had come out of his trousers. The child's little shoes dangled lifelessly when he ran. Riva urged on Avrum, who was pressing down the bundle with his knee.

"Come on, Avrumek. Come on, my child. You'll get lost."

Avrum picked up the bundle and groaned. Riva flung the bundle over her shoulder and the veins on her neck turned dark blue.

"Leave it, Avrumek. You'll wear yourself out carrying all of that."

A pack of yellow OD men entered the courtyard and Kalman Drabik's family left with them, in a convoy, to join their relatives in the Big Ghetto, but Kalman himself stayed behind with their junk for the time being to protect what was left of their belongings. The yellow police were generously bribed, and during the next week they helped him transport his property to a district that was not being emptied out just yet; everything had been arranged in due time and the butcher intended to stay in the apartment house until the bitter end. Everyone knows money can do anything. Maybe yes, maybe no, but Kalman Drabik wasn't worried about himself. Meanwhile, like a thunderbolt, came the news that the Germans had shot to death an entire ward of patients in Czyste, right in their beds, along with the nurses and doctors. The news was passed on by Count Grandi, who had come to take leave of his father and stood in front of Judah Papierny that day with his cane and with the yellow armband on his sleeve, dressed in a stiff round cap and officers' boots that were polished to a brilliant shine. He had come to say that the old man shouldn't take anything valuable with him because everything would be taken from him in transit. Instead, he should give it to his son for safekeeping, entrust it to his good hands. Papierny rose in his chair and screamed that he wanted bullets to use against the lout. He began to hiccup in his rage and for many minutes his body was wracked by hiccups. Weeping, Buba followed her brother as he left the courtyard and said, "Oy, Loniek, what more do you want? You robbed Father of everything long ago. And today you have to be heartless toward an old man who has both feet in the grave."

"The old goat gambled it away. Every last bit!"

Count Grandi touched his finger to the lacquered peak of his cap and walked away.

He returned that same day, on official business. The vans were waiting in the street, and children, the old, and the feeble were being herded into them, while those who put up no resistance were lined up in columns. They waited patiently for the street to be cleared, filling the entire stretch from the end of Krochmalna to Chłodna Street in a single dense mass. Bloody Hands and the Mad Dog ran into the courtyard accompanied by a couple of yellow OD men in search of escapees; Count Grandi was with them. First they went through every floor, trying to flush people from their hiding places by looking into every corner and firing blindly. Windowpanes rattled and locked doors shattered under the force of their hobnailed boots. Earlier in the day, before noon, Buba, with Mordechai's help, had carried the heavy chair downstairs, and now the chair stood there in the courtyard with Papierny the furrier seated stiffly in it, being passed by the people who were leaving the building. His beard shook from his old man's constant trembling, a gray stubble covered the frail cheeks that were marked by two long furrows. Behind him Buba stood stolidly, and her thick black eyebrows cast a gloomy shadow over her enormous eyes. A tall toque was perched over her forehead; her wide nostrils greedily sucked in air. She held on to the chair with both hands, and two "dogcatchers" had to beat those hands until the blood ran before she would let go. In the gateway she was still tearing at one of the uniforms, shouting something into the face of the gendarme; she was covered with perspiration and her sweater was torn. Judah Papierny watched in silence from his chair. He saw neighbors driven from the apartment house with kicks, others walking obediently on their own and joining the column in family groups. He bade them farewell with a scarcely perceptible nod, with the constant trembling of his head. Somewhere outside the gate, on the street, Buba's scream could be heard and Papierny bowed his head. The courtyard was already empty, the people had passed by. Those who didn't put up any resistance marched in teeming ranks to Stawki; the others held their breath in their hiding places as the police prowled the hallways and smashed the last panes of glass while Bloody Hands emptied his automatic into the furniture, pulled open wardrobes with a crash, and shot the dust out from under the beds, encouraging those in hiding to come out. But somehow no one emerged and the police rummaged without enthusiasm through their scattered belongings. The people in their hiding places heard steps, a rumbling sound, and then the Mad Dog appeared in Mordarski's window and, wheezing, hurled heavy bundles over the windowsill; they landed with a loud thud on the pavement in front of the janitor's windows. Suddenly, a passerby, numb with fear, ran in from the street, inquiring if the Germans had left yet. He reached the entranceway in a couple of leaps and there, at the entrance, he was felled by a bullet fired by Bloody Hands, who, resting on the windowsill and clearly visible from below, held the barrel of his gun out the window and carefully observed the man lying there before he let loose with a brief round of shots. When the policemen assembled in the courtyard they noticed the furrier. His knees were covered with a gray blanket and his crutches lay across the armrests. Count Grandi halfheartedly shielded the chair with his body and looked at the gendarme. Bloody Hands removed his helmet and smoothed his hair. The Mad Dog whispered something into his ear with a broad smile on his face.

"*Ah so.*"

And Bloody Hands handed his gun to the yellow policeman. Count Grandi stood in front of the German, and between them there was only the automatic revolver and the dangling leather holster. Bloody Hands pushed the gun farther away from himself with an encouraging gesture, while Count Grandi hunched his shoulders and seemed to shrink in size. It seemed as if he would fall when the gendarme slapped him on the back and said contemptuously, stretching out the words: "*Du, Lumpenhund. Vater? Das macht nichts. Ein Schuss, ein Mensch . . . es ist aus mit ihm.*"

Count Grandi looked into the German's narrowed eyes, then transferred his glance to the chair in which old Papierny sat stiffly, urging him, with a scarcely perceptible nod, to take the gun. Or maybe his head was shaking from his old man's constant trembling.

"Loniek, do what the dog orders. How long do I have to sit here and wait? My knees are aching already."

Disappointed, Bloody Hands fired a round into the yellow policeman, and Count Grandi, still standing on his own feet, crumpled up and lost his cap. He collapsed in that crumpled position. Judah Papierny bowed his head and, wheezing through his nose, pressed his hands powerfully on the armrests.

"My blood," Papierny said, and Count Grandi lay at his feet, clawing at the ground with his fingers.

Those were his last words. The Mad Dog took the gun and emptied the magazine; they left the furrier in the middle of the courtyard, and his swollen corpse was still seated in the chair a week later.

Eliahu picked up the key that Mordechai had thrown into the rubble earlier that day and a dozen or so people who had fled to the other courtyard during the uproar took shelter with him. A few people returned from the street and Kalman Drabik stood in the doorway, armed with a spade, and didn't let any yellow policemen in.

Their throats were scratchy from the dust and when they searched in all the corners dry blades of hay floated on the air. Rays of sunlight squeezed through chinks in the boards, and the darkness was striped black and gold; the Jews sat huddled together as if they were covered with a single *tallis*. A woman who had fled there from the street stuck a pacifier in her baby's mouth. The baby spat out the pacifier and the mother stuck it back in. They could hear the footsteps of policemen, shouting, shots, and Kalman Drabik peeked out into the courtyard through a chink in the wall; he almost chopped off the janitor's head when he broke into the stall. He raised his spade when the door opened and in tumbled Haskiel in his striped linen shirt and his ripped and soiled *shabbos* suit. He was looking for someone. He repeated that they had to be quiet. If they could hold out until tomorrow they would be saved. Kalman Drabik laughed in the corner behind the door and clutched the handle of his spade. Haskiel looked at him in a daze. They didn't see him again, but in the evening Avrum appeared and asked for the janitor. It turned out that Haskiel had escaped from the street at the last moment, flung his bundles down, crawled over the rubble into the second courtyard, locked his family into a hiding place in the attic, and then came downstairs by himself. Between the time when he left the stall and when Avrum showed up, perhaps two hours had passed. During this time Mordarski came back minus one of his shoes. He'd had a small amount of money in that shoe and so he'd had to take it off on Chłodna Street. He saw that the guards were on the take, he gave a bribe to a blue policeman and ran away, and now he repeated this news to Avrum. Avrum did not believe him. Haskiel knew all the passageways from here to Hale like the back of his own hand.

To Hale? Kalman Drabik wouldn't let Avrum leave until he told everything he knew. Yes, there's a hidden passageway to Hale, an old one, that the janitor knew about from before the war. Avrum sketched the entire route on a scrap of paper and Kalman Drabik disappeared into the courtyard with that paper and a candle. It was already nighttime. He told them to wait until he returned. But Avrum paced up and down, went back to the janitor's quarters, changed his dirty shirt, and, taking something to eat with him, went to see Riva, who was waiting in the attic with little Roizele without even a drop of water. In the morning, when they peered through the chinks between the poorly fitted boards of the stall, the three of them—Riva, Avrum, and Roizele—were walking toward the gate, carrying their last small bundle. In the meantime, Mordarski, still wearing only one shoe, was arguing with Naum. Where? Where had the cabby dug a passageway, that's what he wanted to know. They awakened the people who were sleeping and a fight broke out. Kalman Drabik came back with a kerosene lamp, a metal bowl, and a coarse woolen blanket. Then Eliahu showed them where the passage was: first they had to push away Mordechai Sukiennik's pallet and his pile of harnesses. The inconspicuous passage had been dug from inside the ruins of the destroyed outbuilding down into the cellars. The cellars had not been destroyed and there were holes in the wall there leading to the neighboring building, beyond which were the capacious storerooms of Leder's soap factory. Old Zelda, groaning as she moved about, had placed candle stubs in alcoves in the walls. They could see the traces of interrupted work everywhere: basins without water, mattresses rotting in the dampness, empty kerosene tins, abandoned tools, and ventilation channels only half carved out. Thus they found themselves in a hiding place with a couple of exits; the destroyed outbuilding provided no access to these cellars and the passageways weren't at all badly concealed. Kalman Drabik kept looking at his paper and tapping the wall; no one wanted to go with him through the dark cave and into the underground ruins of the old brewery beneath the cold, wet vaulting. They returned to the stall with a sense of relief, and he pushed on.

Soon there would come a time when Jews were hunted in the ruins, but nobody thought of this that day. Every hour of delay was a guarantee that they would not be deported, or so it seemed. After all, this hell couldn't last forever! Mordarski was looking for shoes. At night Eliahu slipped into the courtyard and removed Count Grandi's soldiers' boots. The boots were in good shape, with uppers reaching to the knees; the only thing was that the cold, sweat-soaked cloth linings had to be taken out. Mordarski objected at first when he pulled them on, but then he walked around the stall and did knee bends in order to break them in. Eliahu looked on, pleased with himself, Mordarski squatted, and the boots creaked around his calves. Uri came running in, began a whispered conversation with Naum in a corner, and in half an hour everyone knew that Ciepła,

Ceglana, and Krochmalna Streets all the way to the wall had all left for Stawki, along with the last groups of people who were camping in Walic*ów*. Whoever had a residence card and a work certificate was exempt from the sweep. Artisans were going to the factories to beg for work, paying huge bribes to the foremen for a registration number; they were running up and down the streets from workshop to workshop with their tools on their backs, going to Brauer on Gęsia Street, to Schilling on Nowolipki, to "big" Toebbens on Leszno and "little" Toebbens on Prosta, to the brush factory on Wałowa Street and to Transavia where someone knew someone. And they were sitting there in the stall listening to the cries from the street. The Germans must have had their hands full since early morning, there was such an uproar outside.

Some people returned. Apparently it was still possible to escape. Pursued, they darted into the ruins, stealthily vanished inside buildings, ran down guarded streets, and beat on tightly locked gates. Mordarski greased a policeman's palm with five gold coins. Attorney Szwarc bought his release for three thousand plus a liter of spirits. He said you could still do business with the "dogcatchers." Then he wandered from hiding place to hiding place with his little boy, his teenage son, and a wicker trunk, until he reached Krochmalna. He had taken nothing with him, he hadn't had the time. Depressed, he told everyone what was in his apartment; he timidly asked Mordarski for help. Mordarski thought it over and agreed to go to Szwarc's apartment and bring him the rest of his valuables under the protection of yellow OD men whom he'd let in on the deal. Szwarc had no regrets; he spoke angrily about Lewin the merchant who had gone to the *Umschlagplatz* out of miserliness because he hadn't wanted to give some groschen to a policeman.

"They came simply to earn some money. And they knew with whom they were dealing. Lewin flew into a rage and told them all to bug off. All of them, blue, yellow, green, and black! He'll go to Stawki just to not have to see their hideous mugs any more. They could get it out of him by force. But why should they? After all, there are so many people rushing to hand over money and kissing the police on their cuffs for good measure."

And Lewin the merchant went uncomplainingly to the loading platform on Parysowski Square, along with his younger daughter,

Anielcia, and Biała Ceśka. But the *szaulisy* robbed him of everything anyway; Uri was there and saw how they searched Lewin at Stawki.

"Oy. If only he'd paid them off in good time, he'd have remained in his apartment and no one would have dared to touch him."

Attorney Szwarc was angry. Mordarski nodded his head politely.

"It's a fact, not everyone knows how to make use of his money in these troubled times. Lewin was always in too much of a hurry."

The people in the hideout talked about him as if he were still among them.

"Lewin has a sense of honor and won't let just any old snot-nose blackmail him!"

People asked about their friends, their relations. Who had been taken, who escaped, who had bought his way out. News about the gendarmes being on the take and the greediness of the police made everyone feel better, lifted their spirits. What it would be like in the future, no one knew.

Mordarski pronounced in his hoarse bass voice, "As long as a 'dogcatcher' has greed in his heart he's still part human. Bribes are mankind's salvation, the tender voice of a debauched conscience. What else is left to us? Pay, pay, pay until the bitter end! An angel has wings and shields a Jew, but a huge paw reaches out from under those wings to grab the money and count it. You have to hand over the bribe quickly and run for it. As long as you can buy life for gold there's something to discuss. And the accounts can balance. But more than one angel is standing in the road, Jews."

Mordarski scratched himself long and hard. Attorney Szwarc voiced his agreement.

"Of all the commandments only one is left, the last one: do not turn a deaf ear to the fate of your neighbor who has what to pay with."

During the day they descended into the cellars and napped under the rubble of the destroyed outbuilding; at night they lay waiting in the stall. Outside, fewer and fewer voices were heard, it was quieting down, but the gendarmes were still searching house after house, entrance after entrance. Climbing the stairs quietly, they would stop with their guns at the ready, and whenever they heard even a rustle behind a wall they started the search anew. Their forms lurking in the semidarkness filled the hearts of those in the hideout with terri-

ble fear; people whispered stories to each other about the black
police, about their greed, their cruelty, their cunning, their dogs.
They were let loose in the attics searching for children hidden in
crannies; pulling the filthy featherbeds off the feeble old folks who
were burrowing into their bedding on the floor, they finished them
off with a bullet. They knocked on walls. Separated by a thin wall,
only a step away, they held their breath in complete silence and with
horrifying clairvoyance circled around their victims, attracted by
their presence. The Germans walked around with a captured Jew on
a leash instead of a dog. Beaten, he called out again and again, "Leon,
come out; I see you! Yakub, don't hide any more, the gendarme will
spare your life!"

It was Nahum Szafran.

They fetched water at night. In the darkness whispers, rustles,
and clattering sounds traveled far. That's when movement and ani-
mation reigned among those in hiding. Some people sought their
kinfolk, others cooked stealthily, went to their empty apartments in
search of food, clothing, and rags.

They had to pass quietly through the courtyard, in which furniture was piled haphazardly, penetrate the labyrinth of wardrobes,
tables, mirrors in which the moon was reflected, suddenly hurling
into their eyes a substitute light that pursued the living—and they,
stunned, saw their own faces, pale as corpses. The stairs creaked like
a poorly fastened coffin that has just been hammered together. The
wind banged the open windows, doors slammed somewhere, and the
house came to life at that time of night from the cellars to the attic.

It was already past midnight when Mother lit a fire in the stove
and hurriedly prepared some "dumplings." The little flame burned
sadly, the water in the pot barely hissed. It turned white and foamed
up under the lid. Mother leaned against the stove expectantly, holding on to the cold tiles with her hands. She closed her eyes and
bowed her head, and the fire from under the stove top illuminated
her neck, temples, and closed eyelids with a rosy glow. They waited
patiently for their meal, which had devoured the last bits of flour
and two chairs. David swallowed some of the hot, sticky broth, and
Mother pushed away her food after a couple of spoonfuls, saying
hoarsely, "I can't swallow this."

She poured it back into the pot. She folded her hands in the silence and, motionless, stared indifferently into the corner of their ramshackle hovel. When they heard cautious, slow steps on the stairs they quietly doused the fire. The steps moved higher, hesitantly stopped on the landing between two floors, and then came closer again. Someone opened the door; he stopped, moved forward and then, from somewhere behind Mordechai's stall, from the ruins of the destroyed outbuilding, a cry rang out in the darkness.

"Nataniee—"

They heard a muffled groan and a crash on the stairs. The steps stopped in the courtyard and then someone blindly stumbling against the heaped-up furniture ran to the gate; the thud of boots on asphalt resounded clearly, leaving a hollow echo behind.

That night they were not allowed back into the hideout, so holding onto their pot of "dumplings" they waited in the cellar until dawn. David dozed off, slid down the damp wall, and awoke from exhaustion and cold. Shouts were heard a few more times, the hammering of fists on the boards of the stall, but he didn't know if he was awake or dreaming, he stood with his back against the wall and his legs grew stiff beneath him, they gave way, they got tangled up in their lightweight bundles. He couldn't pull them out when he ran across the dark courtyard chasing the man without a face. He was just about to see him in the mirror he had passed when the cry "Nataniel!" woke him from his sleep and he quickly rubbed his eyes.

It was totally black in the cellar and a damp cold blew in from all sides. In the silence, punctuated by his mother's breathing—he could feel her warm breath on his ear—he heard a whisper.

"It's nothing, it's nothing, that's Estusia howling. Sleep a little longer."

Rubble slid down from the ruins of the destroyed outbuilding, creaked under someone's footsteps, landed on the asphalt with a thud. They made it to early dawn. The hideout was still locked and they came back. A dead silence reigned in the courtyard by day and none of the watchmen who were running past had yet looked in from the street. The passageway through the cellars was walled off with bricks taken from the ruins and supported on the other side; they called out in vain. Anyway, they didn't raise their voices. David made an effort to link the nighttime commotion with what he saw, with the blocked-off hideout, and something—terror—prevented him from understanding everything completely. They were cut off from the hideout and they knew they would not be let in. And the noise and uproar of the crowd was increasing in the street. When they poked their heads out from the entranceway the courtyard was bathed in bright sunshine and a blue policeman was sitting on an overturned wardrobe and carefully counting his money, moving his lips all the time. He licked his finger, went on counting. In the gateway a yellow policeman was pulling someone's child away; the child was crying and the yellow policeman was crying, and the Jew who was struggling with him spat blood and teeth on the ground. They retreated to the entranceway but it was too late: the "dogcatchers" came running in from the street, bellowing, and another one of them jumped out silently from the stairs. They walked out. It all took just one moment: a "dogcatcher" grabbed Mother's pot from her hands and hurled it to the ground. She lifted her hands to her sunken cheeks and sadly shook her head.

"What are you doing, man? The last bit of flour. And it was wasted, in any case."

The "dogcatcher," dripping sweat, dazedly looked at his spattered trousers, at the dumplings clinging to his boot. Another one ran up and grabbed Mother by the elbow but she, wanting to get free, raised her arm. She screamed with fury, "Keep your hands to yourself! You lout, don't grab me. I'll go by myself."

When they let her go she swayed on her feet, a frail weakling, and walked quickly toward the gate without even looking back. Her captors followed her but no one laid a hand on David. The blue policeman raised his head, stuck his finger in his mouth, and continued counting his money. David stood still for a moment and then ran into the street. There was a crowd that filled the entire width of the lane, from wall to wall. An overfilled truck shuddered beside the curb, belching smoke. The people who were jammed onto the bed of the truck stretched out their hands and cried out. The uproar was horrifying. Pale faces with gaping mouths appeared above the shoulders of those who stood at the front, vanished, came back into view. A gendarme let down the tailgate with a thud, a few more people were squeezed into the truck, and David saw his mother among them as she grasped someone's helping hand.

Every look may be the last.

"Stop, where are you rushing to? Don't bite, you little wolf!"

A hard hand landed on his face. Desperately pushing his way through the crowd, which was so tightly packed together that at times his feet hung helplessly in the air, David began to yell without stopping for breath, carried forward by some blind force, but since he couldn't hear his own voice in the chaos he fell silent and looked straight ahead with wide-open eyes and with pained amazement, sorrow, and shame that he hadn't even the strength to weep at this sight. The gendarme had already raised the tailgate on the run and was the last to climb up on the running board. The truck moved slowly, clearing a path by the howling of its horn, and the people scattered under its wheels, made way with the convulsive movement of a mob, flowing to the sides, thick and black.

Two more trucks had driven away with their loads and the crowd had not grown smaller. The gendarmes tried to impose order by shouting but were helpless. The crowd moved in waves from wall to wall and the Germans' commands sank in the general chaos; first they began to disperse the crowd, to organize smaller groups around them, and to form columns that were immediately surrounded by guards. They pressed the people who were standing along the edges of the crowd against the walls and held them there, but those who were in the roadway pushed forward. The guard opened the barrier wide so that the people formed in ranks could slip through step by step. They put down their baggage in the roadway, picked it up, walked a short way; they were stopped at the intersection of Żelazna Street because another flood of people was pouring in there and they had to merge with them. That continued until Żelazna was emptied. The gendarmes slowly gained in efficiency and self-assurance, and around midday reinforcements arrived and it was possible to determine the various types of troops in that hastily assembled detachment: individuals from the SS, the Feldgendarmerie, Latvians, Ukrainians, Belorussians, and a special division of youth league members who had been trained for this task. The police guarded the gates of the houses, making sure that no one disappeared, and posted guards along the sidewalk, and the Latvians left their upstairs posts and stood against the wall, on this side of Żelazna. They turned back those trucks that hadn't managed to drive away with their cargo and were adding to the chaos by holding up those who were walking.

There was some kind of a jam over there; a small jeep was stopped at the intersection and some subofficer was perched atop it giving signals from afar. In one hand he held a large white handkerchief, which he waved, and in the other he held a pistol. No commands could be heard in that uproar and when he fired his gun into the air the guards turned their heads, driving the crowd on or stopping them as necessary. No one was let into the roadway from the sidewalk and those who came running to see their families marching down the center were pushed back. The police were going crazy. Out of control, they shoved people against the walls, beating and kicking them.

"Get going, get back!"

But the people pressed against the apartment houses were unable to escape their sticks. Finally, the rows began to run and it became less crowded, and when the thinning column passed the intersection David caught sight of a familiar face: Professor Baum was standing in the middle of the street, and he must have seen him, because Professor Baum's mouth opened wide, closed, and his hand, raised almost imperceptibly in the air, traced a tender gesture of farewell. He had a folded blanket over his shoulder, and a metal bowl dangled from his belt. When they were driven forward and the column began to move, he turned back and shook a gray, clothbound book.

"David, remember . . . ," but he couldn't hear what. The column, driven around the corner, moved on. Those at the head were running now under the blows of the convoy guards and Professor Baum walked straight ahead, limping. The Latvians stood along the wall on Żelazna Street with their rifles aimed at the running crowd stretched out along the bend, and then he caught a glimpse of Professor Baum for the last time. His unkempt, long, gray hair surrounded his head like a silver storm cloud. The roadway was empty, littered with lost articles, covered with trash; a gendarme summoned the men who were near the wall and ordered them to clean up the baggage that was blocking the passage. Those who were being held on the sidewalks were not allowed through.

A patrol of SS men, stretched out in single file, cautiously approached the next cross street and circled the head of the marching column as it emerged from Ciepła Street.

❧

XIV

Moving along as a dense, orderly crowd guarded by a beefed-up convoy, the masses of people appeared to have been given wings.

Silence reigned, punctuated by the Germans' abrupt commands. Their weapons were all aimed at the intersection, from which came a din that grew louder and louder. A policeman tried to cut diagonally across the street at the last moment and an SS man who was squatting in the middle of the roadway jammed his rifle butt into his ribs and screamed, "*Weg!*"

They kept walking.

"*Auf die Seite, weg! Rechts halten, rechts halten!*"

"Hey, yellow, you there. Stand here and make sure that no one escapes around the corner."

"Where are you going, Jew! I'll give you 'to the gate' . . . you'll be kicked to a pulp! That's enough, come back here!"

"*Zurück!*"

"Don't look back, there's nothing left to look back at."

"Where's my Leon? People, where's my Leon? Look for my Leon, he must be somewhere around here."

"*Herr Offizier, wie weit ist es nach Treblinka?*"

"Water! Water!"

"Get a move on. If I give you water you'll get blisters on your nose. Or maybe you'd like some headache powder? Keep moving, keep moving."

"Leon Skorko! Skorko! Skorko!"

"Be quiet."

"Stuff your ears if you're so delicate . . . You see him."

"*Wie weit, Jude? Oho, das ist fast unglaublich. Du, Schwein!*"

"*Herr Offizier, bitte.* Oy oy oy! Mr. Officer, excuse me, but please don't beat me like that, sir. *Herr Offizier, bitte.*"

"*Ich habe dir doch alles genau erklärt, Jude!*"

"At first I didn't understand, but you have explained everything to me perfectly. *Danke, unsere Gendarmen sind von allen geachtete Menschen.*"

"I completely forgot my comb. My God, what will happen now?"

"Mama, mama."

"Madman, where are you running without a coat? Tell them that you can't walk around like this without a coat on and they'll let you go back upstairs to get it. Tell that one, that one . . . Mr. Policeman. . ."

"I don't have the strength to hear all of this. Cries, shrieks."

"Mama, is it still a long way and always straight ahead? Is that man in front of us also going straight ahead?"

"Let me through, I'm not going to drag along behind the women and children. A passport! I have a Swiss passport and I have to get to a gendarme. *Herr Gendarm, ich hatte die feste Absicht abzureisen.*"

"Chaya, Chaya, come back!"

"I'm telling you in all sincerity, please believe me, all this cannot possibly last even two weeks, well, let's say a month at the most."

"Did you take a thermos of tea, Karol? What? A thermos of tea. No? Dear God, has he grown deaf? Of T-E-A!"

"You're staying? Here? In the middle of the street? When we're all going to the railroad station?"

"Don't run like that, honey, don't run, or you'll get lost and Mommy won't be able to find you in this terrible crowd."

"There, there, hold on to it, grab it, or it will be too late!"

"Now what have they stolen from you? What on earth do you own, Uncle, that could be stolen from you?"

"A pass!"

"What use will that pass of yours be to anyone? You can drop dead along with everyone else even if you have a pass."

"Drop dead? Who says drop dead? A decent life is finally awaiting us over there, not a vegetable existence like we had here."

"You'll drag it along and then you'll start complaining about your liver again. You'd better give me the suitcase."

"Suitcase? What suitcase are you talking about? I didn't take a suitcase. I'd better go back. Hold this basket and keep moving, I'll catch up with you."

"Where are you going, you cow? Get back in the column, right now!"

"Everyone's shouting at the same time, you can't hear a thing, it's like the Judgment Day, and the journey hasn't even begun yet, so what will it be like later?"

"*Zurück! Halt!*"

"I'm not going any farther. I don't care if I give up the ghost right here. This rabble is trampling my legs anyway."

"Cheer up, everything will be all right."

"Moishe, where are you, Moishe? Wait up."

"Yes, yes, my dears, the fourth move this year. How a person can stand all this, I don't know."

"Sura, did you take a spoon? A spoon!"

"*Los, los, verfluchte Bettel!*"

"We have to stay together, my darlings. Eleonora, Mieczysław, look after the children. Benius, Reginka, come closer, hold hands. Let's go."

"Get going!"

A window kicked in by a boot flew open and the panes fell crashing onto the pavement. An officer with the rank of Sturmbannführer stood directly across from them. Flanking him were two SS men who swiftly brushed the glass off the windowsill. Swept off from the second floor, it flew onto the heads of the people who were walking past. The news that this was the commander of the action, SS-Sturmbannführer Höfle, spread through the crowd. He waited. He took off his hat, which was shaped like a horse's saddle, pressed his handkerchief to his brow, and his bald head was revealed to the crowd. He put his hat back on. He stood there before them in his unbuttoned greatcoat, holding a leather leash in his gloved hands.

"Jump, Rolf!"

The German shepherd leaped up, placing his front paws on the windowsill and sticking his head out toward the street. Höfle shouted, "Jews! Merchants!"

The speech had begun. The Sturmbannführer's hands rose stiffly upwards and out. All his fingers were visible, except for the index finger of his right hand, which was contorted and out of sight. First Höfle directed loud declamatory questions at the crowd and then he answered them himself. Questions and shouts. Shouts and questions. How long? How long will the world have to bear on its shoulders the yoke of international Jewry? A Jew's corpse lies buried and rotting within the foundation of civilization, and civilization itself is rotting along with it. Now the time has come when the last act of historical justice is about to take place. The Germans are evening the score. *Jawohl*, in the interests of the whole. Both the Führer and the soldier who is devoted body and soul to the Führer have taken it upon themselves to execute a deed that will live in memory: *Judenfreimachung!* The glory of this deed and the actions of German genius will remain in the memory of generations forever. So that the races and peoples of this earth may see with their astonished eyes just what this genius relies on, the Führer has clenched his fist. *Und die ganze Welt . . .* And the whole world held its breath.

"*Rolf, Ruhe!*"

The dog was barking. SS-Sturmbannführer Höfle lashed the dog's back with the leash. The tall, skinny soldier behind him stroked the beast soothingly. It quieted down. Höfle kept on talking.

"The papers were on the chest of drawers. People, the papers were on the chest of drawers! On top of it!"

"Please let us go. My husband is an invalid."

"Mordcheles! Mordcheles!"

"They can stand on their heads, but I'm not going to budge without my baggage. They can either turn me into a corpse on the spot or let me go back and fetch my bundles for just a minute."

"*Marschieren, marschieren.*"

"Is that supposed to be a fully packed knapsack? We're not going to get far like that."

"Wait a bit, do we have to be first? All your life you had to be first. Now you can let others in ahead of you."

"I have always been punctual."

"Being punctual is what ruined you. Mark my words."

Due to the uproar, Sturmbannführer Höfle's words were drowned out, and unfortunately no one could hear them for minutes at a time. A command was given and a patrol of black police linked arms and plowed into the middle of the crowd, creating order and silence by beating people. The Sturmbannführer's voice could be heard more easily for a while and then once again it was drowned in the din.

"*Ein Volk, ein Reich, ein Führer!*"

One Nation, one State, one Leader. That is the real secret of German genius. It was Hitler's eagle thought that soared above the entire German tribe. A healthy race must rule and fight and destroy everything that is sick. To begin with it must eliminate Judaization. Countries—bah! entire continents—are incredibly Judaized. *Jawohl*, the goal that the Führer has shown us is universal *Judenfreimachung*. Hail to the Führer and his eagle thought. The ordinary soldier has picked it up and with his own breast shields and defends the great idea. Oh! It's them, the Jews, to whom the leader has devoted sleepless nights of thinking. Oh! It's for them our valiant German lads are preparing, with dedication and sacrifice, the inevitable fate of the Jews. In truth, this is a memorable deed that the Reich has taken upon its own shoulders. The salvation of the race, the future of humankind, freedom, democracy—*und so weiter*—are dependent on the success of this deed. No. The Jews mustn't think so. The Führer doesn't waste words. The race, the tribe is capable of doing everything. *Alles, alles, alles!* What is said is done and the German soldier marches on.

"Leon, Leon, there was an alarm clock on the stool in the kitchen. Did you take the alarm clock? No? Then how will I wake up?"

"Mr. Sentry, dear, can I go back for my pass? Please, sir, I beg you. It's a matter of life and death. Just a hop and a jump and I'll be back. A second."

"*Schnell, Leute!*"

"We have to hurry to get seats in the carriage before the others do."

"*Geige? Ach so, interessieren Sie sich für Musik?*"

"*Ja, Herr Leutnant, ich interessiere mich dafür.* We have pretty good musicians in our circle. I, for instance, am interested in new music."

"Do what you like, but I don't intend to go on such a journey without warm underwear!"

"*Hast du davon gehört? Worüber hat der Jude gesprochen?*"

"*Ganz und gar nichts. Kleinigkeit. Über Max Regers Stücke für die Orgel.*"

"*Wer? Wer ist Max Reger? Auch Jüde? Schweinerei! Das Judentum ist überall, auf dieser ganzen Erde kreuz und quer.*"

"*Ha ha ha auf Ehre!*"

"Die Wahrheit muss siegen."

Sturmbannführer Höfle braced his hands on the windowsill, his elbows outside, and leaned out the window so that the crowd could see him. And hear him.

All together and everyone for himself. That's the new law, enacted for all times by the Führer. Ever since the blood-drenched flag fluttered above the tribe, Europe has honored this law. Today. And tomorrow? The whole world will recognize it. And accept it as its own. For the German soldier and the German idea know no borders. All other nations that have not been awakened by the spirit of history recognize this with sorrow and respect. A new era is beginning in gigantic endeavors, an era of the national deed, and beyond it on the horizon the future of a proud race is appearing that will bring to life the slogan of the days to come: one language, one culture, and one order for everyone. *Das ist alles!* All together and everyone for himself. The Führer's naked thought will triumph because it is crystal clear. Hail to him! And the bacillus of cosmopolitanism with which Jewry has infected humanity will be defeated and the *National-Partei* has already discovered an effective medicine. Hail to it!

The spirit of history speaks through the barrels of German guns. Whoever has the effrontery to deny this should first look straight at them without trembling.

"Don't give me a headache, man. This is a pass for a one-time passage beyond the *Wache* on a sunny day, issued to a woman with a nursing infant, and long out of date to boot!"

"Mr. Sentry, what about my pass, this one—is it valid?"

"What are you handing him? Money? Paper bills? Those worthless *młynarki*? Yesterday paper dollars were still in circulation, but today since early morning they're only accepting coins."

"Who has gold pieces? Who? Go over there, to the left-hand sidewalk, quick. One-two-three!"

"Hey you, where are you going? They'll take your money over there and give you a kick in the behind, and then send you along with everyone else to the *Umschlagplatz*. You'd be better off keeping your gold for a cup of water."

"Please don't butt in, please don't butt in! Everyone forges his own happiness!"

"You there, Flimoń!"

"Mordcheles, do you hear me? I'm looking for Jureczek Mordcheles, my childhood friend. Pass it on! Does anyone know where
Mordcheles is? The one from Twarda Street?"

"The louse! He says I'll have to be locked up by myself."

"They treat people like cattle. They transport them in a crush,
and make them wait for a transport for hours. Those scoundrels
have no respect for people's nerves or health. It's a circus, a circus,
nothing but a circus. I've never seen anything like it in my entire life.
Mr. Policeman, could you kindly tell me in what direction our train
will be setting out and at exactly what time? This is the first time in
my life that I've gone on a trip without knowing where I'm going."

"Blithering fool! Shut your trap, you stupid idiot, this isn't the
place for nice conversations."

"He's fainted, my God, he's fainted . . . Water! He's so sensitive."

"I don't have the faintest idea what time. What a thing to ask. Do
you see this watch? It hasn't run even one minute fast for the last
twenty years."

"Do you have any idea what you're saying, man?"

Eine Rasse, eine Zukunft, eine Ordnung. One Race, one Future,
one Order. Höfle reveals what is coming. The edifice of the thou-
sand-year Reich bedazzles the eyes of astonished, enchanted humanity. But to build it the labor, dedication, and self-sacrifice of individuals will be necessary. For the farsighted, for those who peer into the
future, a vision of proud dreams looms, wreathed in smoke and illuminated by fire. Man will pass through the fire purified, the tribe
will be saved, the species redeemed. History will not forget this and
already today its most glorious pages are written in blood. History
will not forget this nor will humankind, forever and ever. *In alle
Ewigkeit.*

"Mr. Policeman, dear, would you go back with me? Over there.
It will only take a second. I forgot to lock the doors and now I'm
terribly worried. What? The kitchen and front doors."

"You dropped your handkerchief, ma'am. Here it is."

"Eh, you can't tell me anything that I don't know myself!"

"Do you see that woman in the dark blue sweater? Tap her on the
shoulder; she's calling for me and can't hear that I've been calling her
all this time. It's my wife."

"Not on your life!"

"He was always so frail, I don't know how he'll survive this trip."

"Trucks! They're coming, they're coming for us—trucks!"

"At last!"

"Oof!"

"Aaron, Aaron!"

"That's a fine kettle of fish, Heniuś. And where is your other shoe? Now what do you think you look like?"

"Aaron?"

"I'm innocent, Mr. Sentry, assimilated, the third generation of half-Aryans! Why me?"

"Did you take an umbrella, Aaron? And what if it should rain? You'll get a sore throat again and I'll have to take care of you and if you get sick then of course it'll be all my fault."

Blood! History is thirsty for blood. There is happiness in self-sacrifice, victory in battle. And only they, they were able to clearly understand, without scruples and inhibitions from ideas. The first duty of the German tribe is to fight. The second duty is to fight on. *Und so weiter.* Now Sturmbannführer Höfle turns to them, to the Jews, with the following question: Does the German hero's arm have a right to weaken, to falter for even a moment? No, it does not. He must shoulder the task and carry it to the end. After the Jews it will be the Slavs' turn. *Und so weiter.* Everything is clear and there can be no hesitation. *Eine Erde, eine Gedanke, ein Gott.* There is one earth, one thought on it, and only one God looks down from on high upon the Führer's deeds.

"*Schnell, du Hund!*"

"Mama, Mama . . ."

"Make them go faster. Can't you see that the Huns are getting upset and soon there's going to be a brawl?"

"Jews, who's shooting?"

"Where? Where? Where are you shoving with that bicycle? You tore my suit, you idiot!"

"Tell the driver to come closer. Here! Here! They're milling and shoving something awful around the corner."

"My feet hurt. I can't go any farther and you left Papa sick at home. Now he's lying in bed all by himself and who will give him his tea? Let's go home; it's more peaceful there."

"Sweetheart, come. Come on, pet, we have to."

"Help, they're trampling me!"

"Don't go over to the gates. Keep walking. Stay in the middle."

"Could you please stop stepping on my heels, sir? Because . . . when I get through smearing your face your own mother won't recognize you."

"Guard, where's a guard? An old woman has fainted here, she's lying in the intersection and blocking the road."

"Make sure that people don't run over to the gate before the corner because the gendarmes are running a slaughterhouse there. Stand here. You'll see from here."

"You, have some self-respect and don't make a face like you're walking behind your father's coffin with mourners and an orchestra."

"My luggage, my luggage! People, I can't leave anything, it's all I have."

"Let go of your belongings, lady, and you'll save your life."

"God, what's going on here?"

"Don't stop, don't create an artificial jam. Get going!"

"Take this suitcase. The child can't get past because of you."

The Jew isn't supposed to think. Enough scheming, trading, playing at being smart. The Jew has to pick up a shovel and redeem his sins in the sweat of his brow. Then useless thoughts will fly out of his head. Höfle has said enough. No more of that stuff, swine. That's enough, swine. Clear off, Joo-ooo-ooz; it's none of your business. Is everything clear? It's clear and there can be no doubt about it. They have to remember: *Arbeit macht frei*. To dejudaize humanity. That's the task the Führer set for the steeled ranks of the *National-Partei*. And they won't retreat, not even one step. Let the world say what it likes. In the end they'll admit they're right. They, the fighters for a great idea. Too long has the Jew trampled the earth that was ordained for another race. Guard the future, the pure and bright future of healthy nations like the apple of your eye!

"Mama, I have to pee."

"What's the rush? Have they gone mad? I can wait for tomorrow's transport."

"Wait just a little longer, darling."

"Please close your umbrella; you're poking my eye out! I didn't have anything left to take on the journey. A pretty pickle!"

"Be careful. Pass it back: there's a hole in the pavement. Be careful."

"Now button your fly."

"Lay off my umbrella and give me some peace. Can't you see that it's drizzling and it's going to rain again soon?"

"Mr. Sentry, I can't understand how they can drive an elderly person out into the street when he has such a high fever? Natan, put the thermometer in your armpit and take your temperature, because he has to see it with his own eyes."

"Is this the way to bring up a child? Your little boy wet my whole basket. Tfoo, it's disgusting; I simply can't understand it."

"I can't think about such things now. Why don't you ask mama where she put the knife."

"Listen, what's that to me? Use your head. Why should I care about your temperature?"

"I can't walk any farther; I have a broken leg."

"*You* find a way to relieve a child's bladder in such a mob without sprinkling anybody!"

"Elias, come closer, I'm going to lose sight of you."

"It's not important."

"Help, I'm being trampled!"

"Close his mouth. You there, stand closer."

"Oy, my leg, oy oy!"

"What? Damn, he's screaming his head off. Call a gendarme, a gendarme, he can shoot him."

"Ruben, even before you put on a yellow armband, for some reason or other I had the impression that a louse was walking the earth in your skin. And now you're calling for a gendarme yourself, you SOB!"

"The pierogi were left behind in the oven; I've told you a thousand times already. I completely lost my head from all this commotion."

"Watch out, Jews. There's a man with a broken leg over here."

"He came a long way."

"It's burning! Mania's soap works is burning! Who would set fire to the soap works on such a day? There's naphtha in there . . . God forbid the whole quarter should go up in flames."

"Just can the stupid wisecracks, young man. At such a time."

"A horse would laugh."

"What did he say?"

Höfle was lamenting the state of the world. Culture is sick when Jews worm their way into it by deception. Society is crippled when Jews bustle around in it. And confuse people. The state is unfortunate, unfortunate and weak when it is undermined by Jewish treachery and cunning. Trade, science, labor, culture—*und so weiter*—are being undermined by Jewry. Like weeds, wild weeds, *Judentum* grows at the expense of the healthy grain. Like weeds, useless weeds, it sucks the juices from the fruitful earth. It's time to weed the fields. It's high time to burn the weeds down to their roots. The hour for fertilizing the grainfields of the fruitful earth has struck. *Es lebe der Tod!*

"For what?"

"Idiot, saying such things in front of children."

"Calm down, scum. No discussions, no shouting."

"My good woman, I assure you, this is a public place, and you should know, my good woman, that in a public place one is free to say whatever one feels like saying. So there!"

"Don't confuse me! At such a time."

"Oh, it's you, the *grande dame* from Pociejowa, I'll knock your block off."

"Did you hear, Karol?"

"Mr. Sentry, please remove that . . . that gang. I don't intend to travel in such company. I am a retired civil servant, my papers are in order, and if anything should happen I will be able to find witnesses."

"Please fill out a written complaint. A statement, date of birth and so on, a detailed resumé, and affix three-fifty in tax stamps."

"It's a scandal that a government policeman should speak like that to a citizen while on duty."

"What did you say, scum?"

"Guard the line; people at the back are getting away."

The Jew must remember where his place is. But . . . Höfle paused meaningfully. The necessary order will begin only when the Jew's place is underneath the earth. Each one! When the Jew stretches out his filthy paw to the east and to the west, crumbling a clod of earth in his fist, in this historic moment it is necessary to cut off, radically and once and for all, to cut off the criminal hand together with the knife that it clasps. Overwhelming force will sweep over them. Sacrifice will open people's eyes. All trace of the Jews will be burned out with fire.

There is no room for parasites at the great table at which feasting mankind will be seated. There is none now and there will not be any. *Ein Tisch, ein Brot, ein Herr.*

"I have no idea what one does in such a situation. I am powerless, my child."

"This way, this way. Keep pace, don't push ahead!"

"You must be losing your mind. How could you have forgotten warm sweaters?"

"Push, push to the head of the line! One-two-three!"

"Leave me in peace, I've already told you that they'll get us there in time."

"Hello, hello. Caleb and his wife are behind you!"

"What? We'll wait for you at the corner!"

"Did you forget my headache powders, too?"

"Hold on to me. Hold on to me, or you'll get lost and won't find the right place."

"Everyone worries about himself."

"People, don't stop in the intersection; the gendarmes are shooting up half the street."

"Let them try. Let them just try."

"Inform that blasted moron that there's going to be one hell of a brawl here in just a minute. I mean, you can see that the Huns are making in their pants and are ready to spray everything with their machine guns."

"Jews, put up resistance. Don't let yourselves be shoved into a boxcar like cattle. Jews, Jews . . ."

"Into the gate with him and under the heel, right away!"

"Jews, they're driving you to . . . Aaa—bandits, bandits!"

"My God, I left my perfectly new stockings on the dresser. Now what will happen?"

"You fat cow, don't block the way with your backside!"

"Aaron, Aaron, shut that umbrella already."

"Mr. Sentry, dear, just one moment. I have a legally purchased certificate for emigration to Palestine, so why should I have to go with you?"

"Don't bother him, scum. Bug off, leave the gendarme alone if you want to save your head for five minutes, and as for your certificate, you can wipe your you-know-what with it!"

These are the Führer's words. It is antihistorical to assert the right to reverse history. The Bible, as is well known, is an ancient Jewish lie. It has led culture astray. Henceforth the National Socialist Party shall be the highest tribunal, the judge of all humanity. It is they, only they, who can rejuvenate the world. Let man be a God for man! These are the Führer's words. Hail to him!

"*Rolf, Ruhe!*"

The huge tan shepherd was barking at the crowd and drowning out the Sturmbannführer's words. Höfle kept going. And then mankind will rest, liberated and joyous at long last.

Two lanky soldiers in SS uniforms could be seen behind his back whenever he leaned out over the windowsill and, leaning out like that, addressed the people who were walking past. The Sturmbann-führer's dog rested its paws on the window and, with its ears stiffly cocked, took deep breaths, its blue tongue hanging out of its mouth.

"Who's crying there, is it you, Rosie? You shouldn't, you don't have to."

"Now what? Whatever for! Get back in line immediately! Not even if you had a nobleman's genealogy going back three genera-tions including a princely coronet and five bars in your coat of arms and a great-grandmother with pure Aryan blood!"

"Samek, take the child from me for a while. My arms are com-pletely numb."

"Where are you pushing, can't you see? I'll send you to Abra-ham's bosom for flatcakes and oaten beer. Stop, stop. They're out of their minds from terror. Guard the corner and watch the gate. Quick!"

"*Auf die Seite, weg, weg! Rechts halten, rechts halten.*"

"Don't make me confused, today is Saturday, and on Saturday I never take any bribes. That's my rule. It's out of the question, and that's that! I already have such a butterfly collection that two suit-cases are bursting and a third won't close."

"Shmulek, get the thermos out of the knapsack. The little one's fussing and has to have some tea."

"*Schnell, Leute. Fest, fest.* Is long road. No have time."

"What, you're still here? How many times have I told you that you're supposed to drive over to that sidewalk, you scoundrel. Come on, come on, don't stop to think it over."

"Mr. Sentry, over there. On the fourth floor, there, over there. A child is sitting in an open window all by himself. His legs are dangling over the windowsill and he's going to fall any moment now. Please do something, my dear man."

"What can I do? I can't do a thing!"

"Get him down."

"Are you out of your mind, Jew? I don't have the time. I was told to stand on this corner and keep watch. You're supposed to walk in the middle, not dawdle, not run away to the gates, and get to the loading place. Understand? That's it! I beg you once and for all to remember, my name is Alojzy Mycka, just an ordinary government policeman. I weep for you and for myself and I have nothing at all to do with this."

"Aaron!"

"Don't let anyone through. We'll cross Chłodna first. At least there's somewhere to hide over there."

"Who says I'm letting them? I only take their money! Hans leads them into an entranceway and finishes them off."

"Soldier, help! They're ordering me in my old age to go God-knows-where. And I'm eighty years old, not one year younger."

"Faster, people. The road is long and we don't have time."

Sturmbannführer Höfle finished his speech, got into an automobile and drove off, and the crowd poured into the ravine of the street and walked. It walked without end from nine in the morning to late at night. In the afternoon the eerie laughter of policemen rang out among the walls of the depopulated buildings.

"A riot, gentlemen! Bloody Hands is escorting the black coats from Ciepła Street. There's going to be a solemn religious service any moment now."

"Who nabbed them?"

"The Mad Dog! The black coats had a hideout in Itzhok's synagogue. They prayed until they dropped for two days and two nights."

"Oho, stand here behind me. Let me see it just once in my life."

They were herded along the wall, down Żelazna to the *Wache*. Policemen gathered in small groups on the trolley tracks, craning their necks; one gendarme stood on a balcony, smoking, and observed the procession from there. Reb Itzhok walked in front, his head tilted slightly forward, as if he were having trouble hearing something; dressed entirely in black, he walked along without lifting his feet from the ground. He was wearing his *shabbos* gabardine and soft ankle-high shoes. He shuffled along in those cloth shoes, dragging his feet behind him. His lips moved slightly and he constantly whispered something. There was laughter. A German came out from a gate, disgustedly holding a large *tallis* at arm's length between two fingers. He shouted and flung the *tallis* in the old man's face. Reb Itzhok caught the shawl and kept walking, and the shawl dragged along behind him on the ground. Then someone else hurled a prayer book that struck him in the back and fell to the ground.

"*Halt!*"

They halted and Bloody Hands walked among them to the place where Reb Itzhok was standing. He ordered him to pick up the prayer book and, with a nod, indicated that he should start praying. Bloody Hands' face was dripping sweat and there was a broad grin on it. A command was given and Reb Itzhok started walking. With his right hand, he pressed the Holy Scriptures to his heart; with his left, he gathered the ample folds of the *tallis*.

The old men followed close behind him. Their glances passed over the shouting, laughing guards. Boys with their *peyes* flapping rushed past, hurrying to catch up with the old men. Three adolescents walked past, supporting each other, their heads with their little black yarmulkes pressed close together. The fraternity of artisans from the back alleys of Wronia, Pańska, Łucka, and Śliska Streets walked on and on. These Jews who gathered every Saturday in Reb Itzhok's synagogue—tanners, furriers, boot makers, second-hand clothes sellers, junk dealers, tinkers, metalworkers, porters, wagoners—had spent their last days praying behind the wall of the sealed-off hideout in the golden glow of candles. Driven out of there en masse into the street, they squinted in the July sunshine, huddled together like an anxious flock, deafened by the shouts and the raucous laughter of the gendarmes and the policemen massed along the wall. Torn away from their prayers, weakened by fasting, they tottered on their feet. The sentries in the distance near the *Wache* were already waving their rifles, but the old men walked on in absolute silence. They walked like specters. The little crowd on Krochmalna, surrounded by a convoy, stretched all the way to the intersection, but Żelazna Street, narrow and divided in half by the wall, was swept clean with bullets that afternoon. Bloody Hands and his gendarmes led them there.

The command: "Begin praying!"

Reb Itzhok was silent. A rustle, whispers could be heard in the column. They glanced at each other, at their rabbi. But he kept on walking, without slowing his pace, the prayer book held stiffly before him. He straightened the *tallis* on his shoulders, pulled it up, leaned forward, hunched over, and it seemed that he was praying while marching.

Over there, at the end of the street, a guard descended from his sentry post and waited for him. The crowd at the end of the street watched the old man as he moved onward.

The group was stopped once more and Bloody Hands came running, his helmet dangling from his elbow, cursing, *"Du Schwein!"*

Reb Itzhok raised his hand to his throat in silence.

Caps and hats fluttered from heads. Young men in uniforms loaded their guns and a flock of black yarmulkes rose up into the air. A Jew fell on the ground along with his cap; apparently he had pulled it down too tightly onto his ears. The Germans loaded their guns once more; it was absolutely silent, and the Jews stood there with bared heads, huddled together, pale.

Reb Itzhok began, *"Sh'ma Yisroel . . ."*

With his right hand he pressed the Holy Scriptures to his heart; with his left, he gathered the folds of his long shawl. In a loud, trembling voice, he cried out, *"Sh'ma Yisroel adoynoy eloheynu!"*

The old men repeated after him, *"Sh'ma . . ."*

Their hoarse, breaking voices beat helplessly against the wall. The anxiously enunciated words of the prayer died away amidst the sounds of their labored breathing.

Beaming, Bloody Hands stood at the edge of the sidewalk and listened. Suddenly, someone pushed his way out of the ranks and began walking toward him, wearing only one cloth shoe and stepping carefully over the paving stones in his dirty white stocking.

In front of the gendarme stood a Jew with a round skullcap atop his bald spot. A faded *tallis* hung like a rag from his shoulders.

"Mr. Gendarme, I'm entirely innocent." He stretched out his arms and bowed his head. "I sew the vests, my wife stitches the buttonholes, and the children sew on the buttons, and that's my whole family. My whole business."

Bloody Hands shoved his fist under his nose and the Jew stood there quietly, blinking.

"*Weg, Alter!*"

He returned to the column, bent low, retreating backwards.

Mad Dog ran up and struck him across the face with his club, and then the first shot was heard. No one knows who fired the first shot. People said it was a guard in the *Wache*. Reb Itzhok lay near the wall, his *tallis* beside him, and a blood stain spread over the cloth. Bloody Hands looked around and howled, "The whole show has come to nothing!"

The German in the *Wache* shouted at him cheerfully, "Hey, you there! Stop fooling around and start working!"

And that was the signal for everyone to fire. The gendarmes, nervously loading their rifles, drove the fleeing men toward the *Wache*, emitting throaty, wild, stifled screams.

On this small stretch of road, between the end of Krochmalna and the end of Chłodna, several score people were slaughtered that afternoon.

When the firing had died down, an old gentleman with wire spectacles on his nose dug himself out from under the people lying there and tottered back toward Krochmalna Street. No one stopped him. The crowd gave way before him and he bent over even lower, threw the hem of his gabardine over his head, and covered his face. A gendarme pursed his lips, slowly leveled his rifle, pressed the barrel against the old man's gabardine, and fired. Once, and then again. A groan could be heard from under the gabardine and the doubled-over old man collapsed.

"Clean it up!"

The policemen passed on the Germans' orders.

"Clean Żelazna all the way to the *Wache*. Move the corpses into the courtyard."

An exploding grenade shattered the air; the last barred gate had been opened.

XV

Bloody Hands' patrol returned to its business as usual. The long line of black police, sauntering along behind their leader, repeatedly came to a halt and observed with curiosity as the Jews, shoved up against the walls, fearfully clutched their documents to their breasts. The Jews were lined up in ranks once again but confusion erupted because a dozen or so young men, who had been carefully selected by the convoy guards from among many eager volunteers and assigned to clean up the bodies, were suddenly let go by a passing officer. Just like that, for no reason at all. They vanished into the ruins of the building across the street that linked Krochmalna with the hovels on Walicόw.

Bloody Hands walked down the middle of the street, calling out in a loud voice that he needed twenty porters to pack furniture and antiques. But they'd have to be careful not to break anything.

He asked, "Who wants to volunteer? Step out. I'll spare your life."

The black policemen laughed.

Their caps were adorned with skulls and crossbones that were polished to a shine with chalk; they wore them pushed back at a jaunty angle. They used the caps to wipe their perspiring faces and necks, because it was a humid, steamy day.

And the Jews ran around like lunatics from one place to another; they searched for their relatives, called to each other from a distance. No one knew which group was better, and everyone was looking for the best. In the tumult David heard someone repeating his name incessantly; when a gendarme shoved the people aside, clearing a path with his rifle butt and his shouts so that a porter with an enormous clock on his back could get through, David saw Uncle Gedali in the distance. He was walking toward him along the vacant edge of the street, holding aloft the omnipotent green pass from Toebbens.

"Such an ordinary piece of cardboard with a stamp on it?" David didn't take his eyes off him; coolly, attentively, he observed his uncle's movements, his emaciated face, his deliberate self-assurance, the raised collar of his summer-weight top coat. David was afraid to breathe. And suddenly he began yelling in a dreadful voice that he was over here! Somewhere up ahead, his father, bent under the weight of his tools, gazed indifferently at the sentry posts as he passed through them. He shouted something at a German who had blocked his path and vaguely pointed out which way he was going with a hammer he pulled out of his pocket. He had a folded piece of paper clenched between his teeth; slowly, he started to unfold it. He shook it under the German's nose at length.

Uncle Gedali was standing in front of him now and shielding him with the green pass; he hissed a single word at the Jewish policeman who came running over; that yellow policeman grabbed David by the nape of the neck with his strong hand and dragged him toward the gate, grimly yelling something that made no sense. Panting, the three of them stopped only when they reached the entranceway. Father was waiting there. He carefully folded the piece of paper. The tools and the sack he threw down on the ground.

The yellow policeman nodded politely.

"Oy, why go to all this trouble? If not today, then tomorrow. The same fate awaits everyone."

Father kissed David on the lips.

"Good, good."

And Uncle Gedali took the folded paper out of his hand.

"What's that you have there? Where did you get it?"

Father answered, "I don't know. It was lying in the street and I picked it up at the last moment."

Uncle Gedali scratched behind his ear.

"A smallpox vaccination certificate? What do you know, a real live *Ausweis*. Keep it for the next time."

"Smallpox? I didn't have time to read it, Gedali. But I have a feeling it's a one-time-only pass."

"Yes indeed, the Germans love papers and—order!"

The yellow policeman shrugged, sighed dejectedly, and took one step away from them. Then he turned around. "You got off cheap. Smoke," he announced. Noticing that Uncle Gedali was pushing a roll of banknotes at him, he said, "Dough? I don't need your dough, you fool! I'm up to my ears in that garbage."

Father took a pack of cheap cigarettes out of his shirt pocket. The yellow policeman took a cigarette but didn't go away.

"My colleague smokes, too," he said. He got a second cigarette and then at last he disappeared.

They climbed the stairs, passing the corpses and bundles that lay scattered all around. Bright light poured in from all sides. Fluffy little clouds floated past, behind Uncle Yehuda. He was cooking something and he shook his head when they entered.

"You're here—in the nick of time. The kasha is burnt, the water tastes rusty, and I can't find any salt in this mess!"

A weak early-evening breeze set his hair flapping as if it were going to lift him up and carry him off into space.

The apartment was a pitiful sight and David screwed up his eyes, blinded by the light. There were no windowpanes or windows, the door was lying in the entranceway, and the light rain that had been falling all afternoon had washed the sky so clean that it shone white. The demolished burrow in which they lived was wide open, littered with household items and old clothes that had been thrown into the middle of the room; the floor was strewn with slivers of glass that glittered in the sunshine. The gendarmes and police must have spent a long time here, because in a couple of spots the boards had been ripped out of the floor and there was a discarded broken bayonet next to one of the boards. Holes had been punched in the wall at random with a crowbar and a pile of soot had landed on the floor from the punctured flue pipes. What could they have been looking for in here? David felt a chill on the back of his neck and shuddered. The ruin was bathed in a blinding glare. An exploding grenade had laid bare the iron beams in the ceiling, from which plaster was sifting down, covering everything with a layer of powder. Cables and pipes had been pried out of the walls; loops of electrical wires swayed in the breeze. The July day was drawing to a close and the setting sun was sinking somewhere in the distance, above the rooftops of Wola.

Father wandered like a blind man from one filthy corner to another. He bent over to pick up a piece of Mother's clothing that had been crumpled and tossed onto the floor. He shook out an old rag and a cloud of dust rose from it.

"Look, she didn't even have a chance to throw a scarf over her head." He was holding her black woolen kerchief in his hands.

"You there, you fat cow, don't you go crawling out into the middle of the street, blocking the way with your fat behind!"

The policeman's barked command traveled through the exposed ruins to the end of the street. The convoy guards were rounding up escapees in the back alleys and forming the remaining groups of people into columns for the march to Stawki, but Father kept talking softly to himself, as if nobody were in the room with him.

"It could be cold during the journey—Gedali, will they be cold on the journey?"

Blindly, he stepped on her clothing, picked it up lovingly, and then listlessly dropped it on the floor.

"Others will come here. Others will dig through my poverty. Could my poverty be of any use to them?"

Uncle Yehuda stirred the kasha. "This basin is useless. It leaks and I had to carry the water from the ground floor."

Father walked over to the open cardboard suitcase, leaned over its contents, and listlessly started rummaging in it.

"Look, shoes, a suit, a shirt, a tie . . . She even packed a suitcase for me to take on the trip. We planned to go. But all of us together. And what happened? Who knows. That's what she was afraid of, that they'd separate us. How did she put it? 'A topsy-turvy jumble.' And now what? I'm here and she's there."

Uncle Gedali glanced stealthily through the window opening at what was happening at the intersection. From somewhere around the corner a plaintive cry could be heard, "My cards, where are my cards? I left my ration cards upstairs."

"Come back!"

"I left my ration cards, sir, my bread ration cards!"

"Stop!"

They heard a single shot.

Uncle Gedali backed away, turned around, and leaned against the wall, greedily drawing on his cigarette.

"A man lives. He has a rough life. A couple of years pass and all that remains after him are filthy corners."

Outside the window they could see the demolished Chłodna Street bridge and a dry, charred tree on the square in front of St.

Karol's Church. The Germans had ordered the demolition of the span's wooden skeleton in the first days of the action, but the beams were charred and showed signs of a fire. The last furniture wagon had not yet pulled away and the bodies of the porters who had been shot were still lying there.

Father pressed his fists into his eyes. "Why am I alive?"

Uncle Yehuda picked up the pot of kasha. He lifted the lid and wrinkled up his nose. "No salt."

Father repeated, "Why am I still alive?"

And Uncle Gedali said in his soft, quiet voice, as the thickening twilight filled the room like a gentle sigh, "In order to endure. There's no alternative."

Patrols of off-duty gendarmes were bivouacked on the little square. Relaxing, they unbuttoned their uniforms with their canteens in their hands. A noncommissioned officer stood on the church steps in an officious pose, scanning the windows of the dead apartment houses through his field glasses. There was a huge pile of briefcases and leather notebooks nearby and discarded documents were strewn all over the lawn. The empty trolleys that had been stopped at that point were backing up from the closed-off *Wache* and ringing their bells, yielding to the columns of people marching toward Stawki. A disheveled gendarme walked up the stone stairs, stopped in front of the officer, and handed him a canteen.

"Hershele, I can't see a thing! Don't get lost in this mob! Don't leave me alone!"

David and Uncle Yehuda sat in the corner on his disemboweled mattress, listening to the cries from the street—his blankets, a torn quilt, and crushed pillows lay on the floor, covered with debris—and ate the scorched kasha straight from the pot, a thin gruel made with rusty water. The setting sun heated the red wall of the destroyed house with its warm glow, but crooked shadows crept out from hidden corners of the ruins. The twilight crept upward along the walls.

Father stumbled about blindly. "Gedali, how many transports leave each day?"

"Hmm, I don't know . . . One. Two at the most."

"And will they manage to load them all before nightfall?"

It was growing dark; the jaws of Hale Mirowskie had swallowed the bloody day.

"Maybe they'll keep them there till tomorrow?"

"The tracks are covered with troops," Uncle Gedali said, distractedly stroking David's head. "The transports wait around for a couple of days on the sidings. But the loading platform at Stawki is jammed. After each load moves off, another that is just as large returns to the square. And waits, and waits . . . They're murdering people in that bedlam. Murdering people and losing their own heads."

Father kicked the suitcase. A ragged piece of clothing slipped out of his hands onto the pile of trash and an evening breeze blew through the ruins, stirring up the dusty gray air.

"I'm going."

Uncle Yehuda ran over to him. "Come to your senses, man! Wherever you turn, it's the same thing. There's no help from any quarter. Everything is collapsing! The streets, the whole city is on its way to certain death. And you want to go to Stawki and rescue her from a transport? What for?"

A cold wind blew through their den; it was growing dark outside. "What for?"

"I am going to rescue her even if I have to follow her straight to the *Umschlagplatz* without any belongings."

After a moment Uncle Yehuda said in a deep, angry whisper, "If they don't suffocate you with lime in the railroad car then they'll bury you behind barbed wire. But here . . ."

There was a distant, faint explosion and the first rocket hung over the ruins. Father stood erect and stiff among the thickening shadows.

"But here, Yehuda?"

"No one can promise anyone anything. Our fate is sealed. But I can still defend myself. And you can, too!"

Uncle Gedali said softly, "There is no law that says a man must defend himself to the end against everything and everyone."

David got up from the mattress, "Sha, someone's coming."

The rustling sound was repeated, opened doors slammed somewhere down below. It was Naum and Uri; they had slipped out of their hideout at dusk and crawled through the ruins of the destroyed outbuilding to the other courtyard. Suddenly blinded by a sniper's flare set off somewhere close by, they completely lost their heads. Naum was combing the dirt out of his curly hair with his black fingernails. One of his arms was supported by a dirty, bloody rag, and a several-weeks-old beard concealed his protruding Adam's apple. Uri sat down on the cardboard suitcase, flattening it with his weight, and rubbed his hands together; their hideout beneath the ruins was damp and his face was emaciated, frail and gray as a potato sprout. He flexed his arms and the joints cracked drily. A cluster of rockets flared above the roofs, accompanied by chaotic gunfire. Naum sated his hunger with the kasha; Uri picked up a tie from the floor and tied it around his bare skin. His skinny neck protruded from the neckline of his warm sweater.

"Imagine living on this earth for twenty-two years and being unable to knot a tie correctly."

He undid the knot and tied it again just as clumsily.

"Enough. It's too late, Uri."

"Eh." His large wet teeth protruded from his thick lips as he began eating, smiling broadly.

Exhausted by all the events of that day, David fumbled around in the darkness and brushed the debris off the mattress, the chaotically jumbled books and tools. He lay down and felt a hard object digging into his back. He reached for it; it was a file. He pressed the rough steel rod against his cheek and then slipped it into his pocket.

Father stood in the middle of their hovel and asked, "Yehuda, how much does one little pistol cost on the black market?"

"Ten thousand," Yehuda answered reluctantly. "No matter how you figure it, that's what it costs. But the comrades will get weapons. From the other side of the wall."

They could hear a rocket hissing as it slowly burned itself out.

"Anticipating the worst, a Jew is incapable of imagining the worst . . . Gedali, how much does it cost to get a job? One job, at Toebbens? How much. Tell me. In front of him."

"Well, it depends on the day. The price keeps going up. Three, four, five thousand."

Father stopped in front of Uncle Yehuda.

"Passes, passes. Where can one get them, I ask you? Are they lying on the street? You have to pay through the nose just to exist and then you still have to slip the 'dogcatchers' a bribe before every transport. And then? Papers, numbers. Buying life, selling life. A trade such as the world has never seen. Up till now my pass for life was my trade . . . I don't believe in this whole business. In order to survive for one day in a hideout you have to have a pretty diamond in your hand. And the day after tomorrow? It's the same thing all over again! For an extortionist a Jew is a diamond mine. I don't believe in this whole business . . . What else remains? Work, fourteen hours a day for a bowl of slops. But work for a bowl of slops costs money. Who pays the price? The worker! He works and pays for his own work, for the right to work and for the right to exist. Every day, every hour. In the best of situations he gives illegal bribes, the illegal bribes are accepted from him by equally illegal persons, and those illegal persons swear a solemn oath that they will protect his illegal life. Yehuda, this world is totally illegal. And all of a sudden, without rhyme or reason, I am supposed to make my way in this illegal world? To cross the street, to go from one building to another, you have to have dollars. To hold a gun in your hand you have to have heaps of dollars—and my pocket is empty. No money for a pass, for bribes, for a gun."

A single rocket shot into the sky. It drifted down onto the ruins and in its deathly light his face was white as bone, with black holes instead of eyes.

"It's all very well to fight! But with what? With bare hands? A gun is a luxury."

"Yakov," Uncle Yehuda repeated mildly, "your place is here. With us."

"Fighting is a luxury."

Uri flung the tie to the floor. He broke in, "We'll make our way to the forest. Stay here."

"To the forest? They're waiting for you there with open arms. Go, go . . . To the forest."

Naum encouraged him. "Yakov, we need you. You've earned two stripes; you've been at the front. That counts."

Uncle Yehuda encouraged him. "For us . . . for us you are a man worth his weight in gold."

Father guffawed. "And the others?"

They were silent. In the fading light from the rocket they raised their clenched fists.

"Are the others also worth their weight in gold to you? Them, over there? All of them . . . Tell me, Yehuda."

Uncle Yehuda was silent.

"To me, she is worth her weight in gold, and I will not leave her alone even if I have to go empty-handed with her to Treblinka itself."

"You're mad!"

It was late and the last columns that had been formed before nightfall were waiting under guard for the command to start marching. One after another, rockets rose above the rooftops, illuminating the route to Stawki from on high. The crowds of people coming in from the narrow side streets filled the length of Żelazna all the way to Leszno Street; the sea of heads swayed and an even, muffled noise welled up on all sides in the darkness.

"Gedali, what did that hothead say?"

Uncle Yehuda stood there with his hand outstretched toward Father. "I said it and I won't take it back. Life is cheap. It's worth about as much as a shell after the bullet's been fired. We have to fight for something greater. Not just for . . . life itself."

Father grabbed the axe and started hacking at a stool in his fury; when he'd destroyed that, he went after the box that stood in the corner near the door; then he hurled the pieces of wood into the kitchen until there was quite a sizable pile of firewood. All this time, he was on his knees.

"No, Yehuda!"

It took him a long time to catch his breath; then he stood up and said, "I'm going, Gedali. I can't listen to this."

David crept over to him, cautiously, feeling his way in the dark, and stuffed the metal file into his pocket.

"For iron," he said quietly.

Father grasped the file, clasped David's head, and they stood like that for a moment.

"David, you'll be all alone."

And Father was gone.

"Yakov, stop, wait!" Uncle Yehuda shouted.

His words still reached them distinctly from the courtyard: "The scoundrels, they want me to wash my hands of such a woman!"

And then only the sound of his rapid footsteps reached them as he stumbled toward the gate, walking, running blindly, straight ahead, and repeating over and over again, "They've got another thing coming . . . Imagine, that she should go by herself . . ."

They heard the spectral thudding of the suitcase he had dropped in his flight and which only now was tumbling helplessly from step to step.

"Look what you've done. If it weren't for your jabbering, he might have stayed here. Words, words, you've driven him out to the transport with your beautiful words."

"And what about you? Gedali, do you, too, understand nothing?"

"Of the two of us, I'd prefer being the blind one. The one who understands nothing."

"What more do you want? Wake up! Look at what's happening."

The crowd flowed along the middle of the street.

It went on until late at night. The sentries protected the gates from escapees, shouting out the house numbers in the darkness like slogans, and the police, gendarmes, and *szaulisy* circulated through the crowds. They kept on walking. It seemed as if they were emerging from underneath the earth. The streetlights, covered with blackout material, cast a blue light on their faces. They walked on and on, but the crowd grew no smaller during the long hours of that night. On the next day, the action increased in force. That was the day they used dogs.

The German shepherds barked, the Germans giggled, and the fleeing people protected their buttocks. Whole families were flushed out of the hideouts and shelters of the Little Ghetto; calling to each other, they ran straight ahead in a panic, catching up with the columns and hiding in the crowd from the blows delivered by the fervent guards. With sacks in which they'd packed their pitiful belongings slung over their shoulders; humbly dragging bundles, suitcases, luggage; bent under their burdens, they pushed on submissively so as not to enrage their escorts, who seemed anxious about the crowd and prepared for complaints and resistance. They peered around from under their helmets with quick, suspicious glances, and their hands rested on their automatic rifles with their fingers crooked, poised as close as possible to the trigger. The dogs ran along with their tongues hanging out, barking nervously. Some of the gendarmes, fearful of causing a panic in the ranks, behaved cautiously and from time to time extended a helping hand to the old folks caught in the storm who were feebly dragging themselves along behind the marching line, losing their belongings, and complaining.

"Do they know where they're going? So docile," said Uri. "Like a flock of sheep. This is the end."

Uncle Yehuda tore at his shirt. "It's not the end yet," he said. "May I be struck dead, it's not the end yet!"

All that day they lay in the attic, their skin baked by the sun-heated metal roof. Every movement required an enormous effort; they spent the time until evening dozing in complete silence, not moving out of there from fear of the patrols. There were tiny chinklike windows in the loft that let in a bit of cool air. David removed his sweater and his shirt and wiped the sweat with his fingers. He read these words that had been scratched into the wall with a nail: "Esther and Nat 26 July 1942." So they'd been here just three days ago? Sheets and linens hung on lines, dry now and dusty. In a corner he found a sack that belonged to Haskiel Ajzen; there was a little bit of food among the clothing. The worst problem was water; Uncle Gedali crawled on his belly for a while until he spied light coming through the roof and a piece of torn gutter placed next to it. There was a thin, warm, murky trickle there that looked like a white cloud in the sky; they took turns gulping it down until the gutter was completely emptied and dry. Then they wandered around through the crawl spaces and openings in the walls that linked the lofts throughout the building, but they found no more water. They would have to wait until dusk to slip downstairs and force their way into the hideout. But someone prevented them from doing so.

At night they heard a man who had escaped from the cauldron on Żelazna running along their narrow street. He was running in circles and hanging back. He stopped, ran back to the gate; he ran at full tilt onto the heap of rubbish in the center. He stood up, looked in through the empty windows, and breathed heavily.

Then he walked up and down all the stairwells, and the Jews who were trembling in their hideouts inside the abandoned apartment house heard his terrifying cry distinctly, word for word.

"Jews, listen to me, Jews! I'm from Lachwia, 12 Klonowa Street. Don't let yourselves be fooled by the Germans, they're preparing your death. Don't go obediently to your execution! Everything they tell you is a lie. The truth is otherwise and the truth is terrible. Jews,

I am telling you the whole truth. I escaped from Lachwia in order to tell you the truth! Out there, in the provinces, it has already begun. And now they're getting ready for you. Where is Kobryń? Where is Stołpce? Where is Szerokie? Where is Kleck? They're gone—there's not a soul left alive; everyone was led to the slaughter!"

He tore the hoarse, breathless words from his throat and they spurted out like blood.

"Jews, my brothers, all the towns are empty where Jewish hearts once beat. There is no hope, there is no salvation. The last hour has struck. Take up weapons—weapons! It's time, it's high time. Better to die with a knife in one's hand, with an axe, than over there . . ."

He walked on like a specter, a bellowing specter, through every floor and entrance hall until a guard came running.

"Brothers! They drive people naked into ditches and shoot them in the back. They fill in the pits and the blood flows onto the fields. Like a watery swamp. The blood surfaces above the graves. The earth moves over those graves. The wounded suffocate like cattle in those graves. Jewish women and children are buried alive . . . They have some kind of smoke. They have some kind of fire. They suffocate and they burn. They build huge ovens. They burn Jews in those ovens. The smoke rises to the sky; the smoke can be seen everywhere . . . *Loy yamish amud he'onon yomam ve'amud ho'yesh layla lifney ha'om.* Jews, remember!"

A patrol of gendarmes and a crowd of blue police came running, and the lights from their flashlights swayed and crept over the walls, windows, and pavement. They cursed. Three stories above them, Uncle Gedali repeated the ancient words in a whisper and shut his eyes tight.

"*Loy yamish amud he'onon yomam . . .*"

He stood there, caught in the beams of light, and yelled. He didn't hide, he didn't run away. They caught him at last, dragged him into a corner of the courtyard, and smothered him beside the garbage bin, to the sound of their curses but without a single shot. A flat little clump of blood-stiffened rags lay there on the cement long afterward.

The Germans placed a *szaulis* there with a large supply of ammunition. You couldn't blink an eye; he'd shoot at the windows, shattering the last panes of glass. He didn't go inside; he turned around at every rustle, shouted something inaudible into the darkness to give himself courage, and sprayed brilliant bullets from his automatic weapon. What was he afraid of? The guard remained at the gate until morning. And they had to stay where they were for another night and day, living on the bread from Ajzen's sack—Ajzen, who was no longer among them.

There, down below, the inhabitants of the Little Ghetto were leaving their houses. In broad daylight, squinting at the light, the reluctant refugees crawled out of their dark hideouts and made their way in small groups across the city. Stopped for a search, they timidly raised their hands over their heads and turned their faces sideways. They joined the columns in perfect order. On the other side of the wall, along the boundary of the Ghetto, on open balconies and in entranceways, the Latvians had been standing guard since dawn, watching the tracks, the outlets of the streets, and the crowd from up above. They nodded sleepily over their rifles, shooting without warning at the people who were walking to the *Umschlagplatz*. There were two lines of sentries: one stretched out around the gates the people had to pass, preventing anyone from escaping to the side; the other surrounded the column as a mobile escort. Patrols circulated among the ranks of the column, subjecting women and men to hasty searches. Between the chain of the convoy and the sentries, on the empty, off-limits sidewalks, yellow and blue policemen milled about, and couriers ran with orders from junior officers along the entire route of the march. SS men, with dogs on leashes, stood at a distance. The faces of the people being driven through the city were calm and dull, and when they moved into Stawki like herded cattle not a single complaint arose from the crowd.

Around noon, the sentries were removed and the march stopped. The last gendarmes came to a halt on the littered street; one of them removed his helmet, wiped the sweat from his brow, and looked around distractedly in the quiet, empty alley. The voices of those who had been driven out of there could be heard faintly floating in from somewhere along Leszno. After the people had passed by, the narrow street was covered with abandoned luggage. The gendarme looked around furtively. He was fingering a towel he had picked up off the ground.

"It's funny, isn't it? What people think about when they're going to their death. And it went off without a single shot."

"Yes, yes, in two more hours the whole ragtag mob," another

gendarme laughed, "will be leaving . . . for Madagascar!"

"And the shouting will be over."

He patted the barrel of his gun and looked around. They could be seen for many afternoons, until a group of porters were brought in under escort. In silence, their wooden clogs banging, they wheeled in carts to load up the bedding.

Under the roof, they were tormented by thirst. They went downstairs. Stealthily, one by one, they slipped into the hideout. First Uri, then Yehuda and Gedali; Naum and David came last.

He waited his turn, squatting beside the pile of detritus next to an overturned chest of drawers; sun-baked and tormented by heat and thirst, he had to force his eyes to stay open. A gray, swollen mass sat motionless in a large, upholstered armchair; a week had passed and no one had touched it. A formally posed photograph on thick paper of Papierny the furrier, taken when he still had legs, had been trampled into the ground. Someone tugged at his arm; he opened his eyes and Kalman Drabik was standing in front of him and the door to the shed was cracked open.

In the evening, in the hideout, they had the following conversation:

Uncle Gedali: "Just staying alive is a lot."

Uri: "I spit on such a life!"

Uncle Gedali: "It's sufficient to survive in order to bear witness."

Uri: "Witness? Who cares about that? And who is going to care?"

Naum: "A flock led to slaughter remains alive only until the cleaver drops. The Jews are being led to the slaughter but they insist, out of fear, that they should go to the slaughter obediently in order to stay alive."

Uri: "We should fight in order to preserve life."

Uncle Yehuda: "To fight means to perish."

Naum said that he agreed with him. Yes, there are two roads. Coming out and resisting guarantees certain death. Flight, going into hiding, only delays it. What's to discuss?

"We'll delay until the proper moment."

Uri: "There's the forest."

Naum: "I should wander around in the forest? And starve? And let myself be hunted down like a hare?"

Uri: "Yes, sure . . . Here, they've been hunting me for two years. There, in the forest, I can get hold of a gun. And harass the Germans, and not just defend my own lousy life, sharpening my claws like a rat in its hole."

Uncle Gedali: "Always the same thing—fight, fight!"

They shouted him down in unison.

Then he said, "It's not a disgrace to flee before superior force."

They yelled, "Disgrace!"

Before he left the hideout Uncle Gedali woke each of them in turn and said, "Naum, you stay here as long as possible and maintain contact with me. Kepele and a group of our porters are at Toebbens on Prosta Street. Uri . . . Uri, try to contact Felek Piorun. Or someone from his gang. He ought to show up today or tomorrow. And if he doesn't, it will mean that you should go across the wall yourself and talk with him. Yehuda, return to the Big Ghetto in the meantime. I'm going back to Prosta. I'll see what can be done."

And he left.

Mordarski sowed doubt. Uri quarreled with him in order to keep up everyone else's spirits. He said that they wouldn't let themselves be taken alive. They had to believe in that fervently. Their comrades wouldn't desert them. And if they manage to lay the dynamite at the right time, there will be one, three, five holes in the wall! The crowd will make a run for it and the Huns will lose their heads.

Oh, sure. They're strong, strong. When they herd women and children under guard. But it will take only one unexpected explosion and a hole and everything will turn out entirely differently. How many individuals can they drag into the city? No matter, it will be too few. Every apartment house, courtyard, gate can be converted into an entrenchment. The uprising will catch fire, catch fire. A holy war against fascism will break out. Fritz will turn tail and run away with his pants down. The day is near. Uri can see the day. Their comrades will not desert them.

O people of little faith. Hang on just a little longer. How long will it take the transports to reach their goal? There is the powerful Home Army. The Communists. They are waiting for the signal; they are all prepared to fight. And then? Every trestle bridge will collapse, every rail line will be mined, and the locomotives will fly up into the air. From all over the country, from all over Europe, people are riding to their execution. One day they will tumble out of the opened freight cars to freedom. Into the forest, the forest, to defeat the fascists. Hold on and freedom will be given to you. It's a matter of the fatherland's honor, and the fatherland will not look with indifference at the smoking chimneys of the crematoria!

The comrades will not desert them. And the world . . . In the dark, damp cellars, where the faces of the people in hiding turned green and their teeth chattered from the cold, his words raised their spirits.

Attorney Szwarc had certain objections. People like Uri see a gendarme, a cannon, a rifle, perhaps a machine gun. Fine; but what stands behind them? When panic is spreading here and people are losing their lives, over there papers are wandering from desk to desk. Calmly, with no sense of urgency. There's a plan. How many should be deported? Who and where? Numbers, numbers! An entire city inside one pair of parentheses.

To inventory, isolate, deport, liquidate . . . Szwarc bent down one finger after the other. Here's the plan. How can they fight against that? Against a plan that wasn't drawn up today, on the spur of the moment? That satanic plan has a name: *Sonderbehandlung.*

Attorney Szwarc was putting his little boy to sleep in a wicker basket. He had a pink blanket draped over his shoulder. Uri bent over the basket and repeated tenderly, drumming his fingers, "Coochie coochie coo."

The little boy in the basket asked him sternly, "Has the war really ended already, mister?"

Taken aback, Uri glanced at Naum. "Not yet."

"Then don't act like a fool and stand there pretending to be naive. I know a thing or two about this."

They all stared at him. Attorney Szwarc complained, "He's become dreadfully wise for his age. What times these are."

Shaking out the pink blanket, he said to the basket, "I'm going to test you in a minute. Repeat what you're supposed to say."

"My prayer?"

"Yes, your prayer. You can confess your sins, too. Everything, but with feeling. Kneel down."

After a while they heard a cough coming from the corner and the little boy in the basket began to whine, "I don't want to."

Then they heard Attorney Szwarc's furious hissing as he spat out through clenched teeth, "And forgive us our trespasses as we forgive those who trespass against us. Now you can say amen."

And the boy in the basket repeated, "Amen."

Old Zelda was furious as she listened to the child's prayer, and her eyes glittered in the darkness. Her darkened face was hidden in shadow. She clenched her swollen, enormous hands beneath her chin.

"Now lie down and go to sleep."

"Again in that disgusting basket, Daddy?"

Attorney Szwarc turned around, shook out the pink blanket for the last time, and whispered to Mordarski, "He's become dreadfully wise. And he knows the whole catechism by heart. It's a snap for him to pass as an Evangelical."

Mordarski laughed genially. He said to David and Zyga, "Study, brats! You, too, will have to begin a new road in life some day."

Szwarc and his sons had an entire corner to themselves in the cellar. The teenage boy sat motionless day after day, painstakingly removing bits of dust from his navy blue school uniform; every so often he would take his false identity papers out of his pocket and conscientiously study their contents, getting used to his new name, Stanisław. The little boy showed everyone the tin medal that he wore under his shirt on a string around his neck together with a little bag of jewelry. At night Szwarc would empty the wicker trunk and put the boy into it; the child began and ended every day with a prayer that he repeated with great relish, without stumbling over any of the words. He had developed a cough in the cellar.

Attorney Szwarc finished his conversation with Uri.

"Put out the candles. Enough of this holiday for today," Kalman Drabik interrupted them, and was the first to get ready for sleep.

Nights and days passed, and each of them was like all the others, like one long night.

Zyga found the first smuggled message. Old Zelda, shuffling along in her carpet slippers, emerged from some dark recess in the cellar to look at and kiss the scrap of newspaper that was covered with someone's handwriting. She burst into tears at the sight. There is still a God in heaven. She kept on whimpering and sniffling for quite a while. *Eyli, eyli shebashomayim!* Mordarski ordered her to be quiet.

They learned from that message that Yakov was alive. They should hold out for another couple of days, a week. Kepele will get to them somehow. They are not alone. Does Yehuda know what to do? No signature.

They thought it must have been Gedali. But it wasn't his handwriting. Maybe he sent the news but someone else wrote it down and dropped it while walking past. They didn't know what it meant. In any event, Yakov is alive. Father is alive? He smiled vaguely when Naum showed him the message. He avoided Naum's look. Back in the hiding place in the attic, when he had watched the marching crowd for hours, he had said that his father wouldn't come back from there and Uncle Yehuda had heard him. All you had to do was utter anxious words out loud and it was as if the worst had already happened. Something tightened up inside him and turned to stone. Father is alive? It was hard for him to believe that and he was ashamed that he didn't have the strength to believe. He had buried a living person in his heart. But before that happened, he had had to bury the entire world in his heart.

They congratulated him. David, he's a lucky one!

Kalman Drabik, wrapped in someone else's *tallis*, prayed for a longer time than usual, swaying and whispering, pressing the *tefillin* to his lips over and over again.

Mordarski, covered with a fur on the wet stone floor, said hoarsely, "Everyone pulls in his own direction and saves his own skin without thinking about the others. The Jews are conducting a war . . . It would make a horse laugh! I know beforehand how it will end."

It was night. Zelda lit the candle stubs that were placed in recesses in the cellar walls.

The merchants will extract money until the bitter end. They'll pile stuff into the bunkers. Everything they have. The rabbis will pray. And shake their *talesim* above the fire. And cry out that the Lord is One, his flock is one, and Israel is the chosen people. The flock will listen to that one more time. They'll grumble, but they'll listen. The workers will labor until they use up all their sweat. That's all they know how to do. They know that no one will fill their bowls free of charge. The students? Just a little more time, just a little, and the fighting youth will fall apart into factions and circles. Some will pull in the direction of the rabbis. Others in the direction of the workers. And others still in the direction of the merchants. The few of them who will insist on their rights will extort a couple of groschen from the rich to wipe away their tears and for grenades that they themselves will explode in the air out of ignorance! That's how it will end. He who does not believe in money will have to believe in money.

Uri stood over him and said, looking at the muddied, bedraggled fur coat, "Tell me, Mordarski. How do you know that we won't extort as much money as we need from you? You'll vomit money for us. Vomit it. You yourself will come to plead, 'Take it. I can't hold out any longer!' Just you wait."

"Oy, you child, will it suffice for long? What can I say . . . Pistols and grenades are expensive toys."

When Mordarski had had his say, Kalman Drabik walked over to him and said, "They don't have anything. Why must you take away from them what even you don't have? Keep your truth sewed up inside your shoes and don't tear it out unless it's needed. Leave them their little bit of faith. Don't take away from a man what you aren't able to give him. Mordarski, I'm not going to respect your gray head! Mordarski, I'm going to settle accounts with you. And it's a lengthy bill."

His voice had risen to a shout. He stopped abruptly and rose to his full height. His body swayed slightly as if he were about to jump. His left arm, bare, and with the leather strap wrapped around it, was raised above his head.

Mordarski straightened the fur coat, his blanket, covered himself, and huddled in the corner.

"Enough of this Sabbath for today."

Zelda, gliding along the walls, blew out the candle stubs one after the other.

The hand that had thrown down the first message made itself known once again. Now they knew it was a person who could walk around here freely.

Once a day, Nahum Szafran appeared in the courtyards accompanied by a guard. He ran along all the side streets and called out to the people in hiding. He came back with the Germans, and when they had finished their rounds one of them would shove him into the guard house on Prosta Street in front of the workshops and the patrol would go to the canteen; then they would take him along again for the night. Nahum was fed in the Toebbens kitchen, where he could talk with Uncle Gedali. It's possible that the Germans ordered him to drop those messages; in that case, Gedali was under detention and they still hadn't gotten out of him why he was wandering around in that neighborhood or how he had crept out of his hideout. The Germans were sniffing around and might discover them at any moment. Time was passing and Nahum hadn't led them to anyone. Uri said that he could be relied on; Kalman said that no one could be relied on any longer. Every day, in the afternoon, Nahum's cry echoed in the street, and then a gendarme dragged him into the courtyard, the entranceway, everywhere. Dragged him along like a stubborn dog.

"Whoever comes out will save his head!"

Or: "Jews, come out! No one will be left alive here!"

Kalman brought a fresh piece of news. Father has been seen in the Transavia workshop. He goes over to the other side of the wall, to the square, with a group of men. At first, people said that he had left with a transport during the first days of August, then they even said that someone had seen him shot near the *Wache* on Leszno, and then those two crumpled messages came, and now Kalman had brought this news. They didn't know whom to believe. What was Kalman still looking for here? Had he hidden something that he hadn't had time to carry away? Naum, Uri, and Uncle Yehuda talked it over for an entire day, and when night came they took David with them and went upstairs to cook.

Kalman disappeared. But the next day he was with them again and they kept an eye on him all day long.

Mordarski became furious and broke the silence.

They are fools if they believe that the Germans are unable to find them. The Germans don't want to find them just yet! Bloody Hands and a patrol of black police could clean out the entire district in just a couple of hours and flush the escapees from their hiding places. From everywhere, including this miserable den. Once the district is thoroughly shaken out, the "dogcatchers" will have to report to the high command for the city. That's just it. The SS, the Feldgendarmerie, and the blue police aren't interested. Before they turn over the district they can plunder it for their own pockets; the high command knows this but shuts its eyes. To prolong this state of affairs the Germans are tiptoeing around the last hideouts. *They need the Jews who are in hiding.* No one knows for how long. At any rate, tomorrow and the day after, and even for a week, not a hair will be touched on the head of anyone in the hideout. Later, yes. When the "dogcatchers" have lined their pockets and are stuffed to the gills with Jewish gold. Bloody Hands will don his butcher's apron so as not to soil the uniform of a *Zugführer*, he'll set to work enthusiastically and show what he's capable of. Oho, and is he capable! In the meantime, he doesn't give a shit if a handful of Jews are hiding in the ruins, trembling with fear. Business first, then pleasure. It's hunting season for the "dogcatchers," and they have to make the most of it. No German is as gullible as a Jew. Would he just take it on faith that they have to hasten *Judenrein* when it's necessary to delay *Judenrein*? He would have had to fall off the stove and land on his head to have done that.

A stupid Jew is worse than a convert! Mordarski was wheezing with rage. His voice was hoarse, he was chilled to the bone, and he wouldn't let even the attorney comfort him.

It was an amazing thing: Mordarski's words had a bracing effect on them, even more so than what Uri had to say.

They reasoned thus. The Germans go sniffing around in their own way. And Nahum drops the scraps of paper behind their backs. Gedali made it to the workshops without any difficulty and they took him back. Nothing threatens them from that quarter. One way or another, they won't be stuck in this den forever. Uri must get through to the other side and make contact with Felek Piorun and Yehuda will cross the wall with him. From there he'll have the opportunity to return to the Big Ghetto with the Transavia convoy. The streets in the Big Ghetto won't be made *Judenrein* so quickly; before that happens, a couple of months might pass, it will be winter, and in the meantime Yehuda will manage to prepare the ground for them. Because sooner or later the work in the Prosta Street workshops will come to an end and Gedali, if he should get caught in a selection, also has to know that he has where to run away to from the transport to Stawki.

Naum? He'll stay until his arm heals and wait for a sign from Żeleźniak. He's got plenty of grub, he'll get better. Naum is certain Żeleźniak and his fellow looters will show up legally within a few days. The looters' wagons are already driving around and Żeleźniak and Felek Piorun must be aware of that. Kepele must certainly have let them know and Kepele knows the way to the hideout. Mordarski? Don't worry about him! If the "dogcatchers" rip the fur coat off his back he'll be left with a shirt lined with banknotes. Szwarc? He's fed up. He's going to Stawki. But he's worried that they'll turn him into a corpse at the first intersection. How can one go to the *Umschlagplatz* illegally? There's a question for you. Eliahu? He won't run away. He'll stay with Naum as long as he can. Zyga? He can cross to the other side right now. But what about the old lady? Zelda hardly sees anything anymore. She's going blind.

Kalman wanted to tell him where he should look for a crossing point. They all laughed at him, Mordarski loudest of all; Zyga had been bringing him goods for two years. Who was he going to instruct? A puppy knows more roads than all of them together. And if Kalman wants to go with them, with Yehuda and Uri, it will be a good thing. Kalman didn't want to, and then he changed his mind. He'll go with them. But when it was time to leave that evening, Kalman again began to shake. He and Mordarski whispered together; he hesitated. They didn't know what that meant. Later, some skins came to light and it became clear that Kalman had been guarding his treasure. He was waiting for the wagons. He had a deal with Żeleźniak, but Żeleźniak was showing no signs of life. He either couldn't or wouldn't risk his head for those skins. But when Yehuda and Uri were planning to cross the wall they didn't know anything about this. It was too risky to trust Kalman. They had to go, and they preferred to have Kalman with them. The next day passed and Zelda was doing poorly by evening and they thought she was dying. She hallucinated, she lost consciousness, but she didn't die that easily. She kept on swelling, from the feet up. And she was still alive when they were no longer there. The looters with their wagons and the prisoners from Prosta who walked to work in the city under guard saw her for a long time afterwards, wandering around in the ruins. Apathetic, dressed in rags, she went out in search of water in the daylight. She left a trampled trail behind her in the rubble which the Germans could see. It seemed that Bloody Hands was taking his time, he didn't want to shoot her, and finally, just before winter set in, he ordered them to fill in the underground passages with Zelda inside.

At the last minute Kalman said he was going. He asked them to wait a while, because he expected Żeleźniak any day now with his horses; and then he told them about those skins. Mordarski grumbled. A coward like Kalman Drabik is a burden and a misfortune for others. You have to have something to hold on to. They could quietly wring his neck and they would be justified. Him? Kalman shed sincere tears. Did they think he's an informer? Him? He wept, he found his *tallis* and prayed for a long time that night. And since Żeleźniak hadn't turned up to get the skins, he decided to leave the hideout some two days later. He trembled all over, moaned and groaned, kissed everyone good-bye. He planned to come back himself or give the looter a detailed map of where to find his treasure. Yehuda was supposed to leave first with Kalman; Uri would follow an hour later.

Kalman said, "You'll turn the corner . . ."

He'll count the streetlights, stop at the fifth one. He'll cross two squares of pavement and from there crawl straight to the wall. A long time ago, Haskiel pried loose a piece of brick. It's in its place. If Uri removes that wedge he'll have a foothold for his right foot. Stretch his left arm all the way. He'll find a handhold there; the cement is missing between two bricks. (It was Aaron Jajeczny who gouged out the cement.) Be careful; it's only big enough for three fingers. After he's got his right foot in the wall and his left hand in the opening, he'll have to pull out a hook. The hook will be right over his head, at the very top; it's not too loose. He should feel for it carefully, take his time looking for it. The head of the hook is painted over with whitewash and can't be seen. (Kepele installed that hook.) One, Uri will pull himself up on the hook! Two, he'll throw his right leg across! And once he's lying on top of the wall he'll have to slip the hook back all the way. As for the piece of brick—it can lie there. The wall is pocked with bullet holes now and no one will notice it. Up till now, the wedge was replaced after crossing. Do you remember? Repeat once again.

Uri repeated the instructions.

They left, and then it occurred to David that Kalman would take Uncle Yehuda across by a different crossing. It followed from what he said.

Uri didn't want to hear a word about anything; he wrapped himself up in his blanket and said they should wake him up in an hour at the very latest. After an hour the moon had risen high above the ruins and, avoiding places that were illuminated, they stealthily began to make their way through the courtyards, from building to building, searching for crawl spaces that had been hacked through the walls, wandering cautiously down rubbish-strewn staircases, using their feet to push aside the corpses that were lying in the darkness, feeling their way blindly into cellars, then climbing upstairs and down again. They could see the streets. At midnight a wind blew up; windows and doors creaked in the emptiness and the silence, setting up a mournful howling. The Germans didn't show themselves in such places at night, but they felt sick at the thought of meeting even someone who was in hiding. One attic they had to force open; they spent a long time looking around from there. Somewhere beyond the wall, on the other side of the street, a light shone behind a yellow curtain in a window that wasn't blacked out. They held their breath and it went out after a while. It was an unbelievable sight, like life itself. It was growing gray and the motionless outlines of the buildings grew larger in the predawn light. A gendarme coughed beside the wall. They waited for dawn in absolute silence, growing stiff from the cold. Rustles, sighs, footsteps could be heard on all sides, but it was only a rainstorm and the wind sweeping the rubbish through the open gutters. When it grew a little lighter they went down one floor. From there they could see clearly. On the top of the wall lay a cloak that someone had tossed up onto it; at the foot of the wall was Kalman, with the hook in his clenched fist. He lay there just as he'd fallen from the wall.

As they walked back the rain turned to drizzle and then the beefed-up morning patrols cut them off. They had to put off their return for twenty-four hours; during that time they spent the night being bitten by starving bedbugs in an attic that someone had converted into a hideout, while the voices of the drivers who drove their trucks into the courtyard in order to load the furniture resounded outside.

"Throw it down, throw it down . . . Throw it here!"

Patrols of gendarmes came after them. Bundles, linens, garbage, and dust flew threw the windows until evening.

They went back. There was a commotion in the hideout under the ruins and some time passed before they could get inside. No one expected them to return. Attorney Szwarc fed them and gave them something to drink; he asked them somberly if Yehuda had managed to get across first, before Kalman Drabik? They thought he had been taken alive. A couple of days later Naum brought in a scrap of leather from a mezuzah and showed it to all of them without saying a word.

On one side were the verses of the prayer, and on the other, a couple of words written in pencil, and from those couple of words they learned that Yehuda had gotten across. The leather was damp, it had been splashed by the rain where it protruded above a brick at the edge of the ruins they usually passed. A stranger would have just walked past it; but they knew every stone here. After a looter passed by they were able to recognize his fresh tracks, the things his foot had pushed aside, a piece of rubble that had been disturbed. During the long, empty hours their terror kept growing, and every bit of news from the outside seemed like a curse in this confinement.

Yehuda couldn't possibly have written this! Maybe the Germans already have the hideout under surveillance? If so, they wouldn't hesitate, they'd just sweep them out of here one-two-three. Yes, but they were still anxious, because no one could walk around in this district without risking his life. They passed the scrap of a message from hand to hand as if it were an unholy relic, fate's dark pronouncement, that had been handed to them. He had never before touched an unrolled mezuzah; it had always seemed to him that some terrible mystery must be hidden inside mezuzahs. Now David held the scrap of parchment between his fingers and read the ancient words.

Did this prove that Kalman wasn't an informer? It could be that he was and that the Germans just got bored with him. Naum rewrapped the stiff bandages around his hand. And why did Kalman take that crossing when he had clearly stated that he would use another? That in particular was suspicious. Then, wrapping his dirty bandage, Naum suddenly recalled a second crossing on Żelazna. Just a minute, just a minute: and why did Kalman Drabik not take that one? They should check it out.

After the bandage was rewrapped, the candle burned out. Since Zelda had begun hoarding the rest of the candles, they walked around in the darkness of the cellars with their arms extended in front of them. They got lost in conjectures, they dozed off, and their dreams, too, were a nightmare and a curse. One day Eliahu woke up and said that Kalman had come to him in a dream and revealed to him where he had hidden his trove of half a ton of chamois leather skins. Kalman appeared to each of them in their dreams, but differently: according to one person he was sobbing; another said he was praying, his face veiled by his *tallis*. He pointed out the guilty, made accusations! Mordarski spat. In times like these, the righteous are the worst people to deal with. Since all of them were guilty, there could be no guilty one among them. It turned out that a dead informer is just as dangerous as a live informer.

Where is the truth? On Żelazna Street. Naum left at night and returned late the next morning.

He had gone quite far, all the way to the attics at the intersection of Ciepła and Ceglana Streets, where he ran into a number of loners and a couple of families in hiding. It was the same everywhere. Ruins, corpses, and here and there among the ransacked hovels, shadows of living men. They take off in fright, flushed out by the slightest rustle. He didn't have the words to describe what he had seen. In any case, that second passageway through the wall had been discovered—people on Ceglana knew about it because it was located near them—and that's why Kalman Drabik had returned to the place where Uri was supposed to cross over.

Kalman's corpse was quickly removed from the street when the Germans ordered the prisoners from Prosta to walk around the wall; they marked all the old and newly discovered passages with paint so that the patrols could see their targets from a distance. Patrols moved up and down Żelazna without a break, sowing terror among the people who were hiding from them.

Eliahu, Zyga, and David took turns creeping over there to spy on the guards' movements from a hiding place. The removal of property was still going on. On the other side of the wall, the *szaulisy* sprawled out comfortably in armchairs with a thermos of warm coffee and a rifle between their knees; they had quite a good view from their balconies. At night they left their posts, taking their empty thermoses with them, blindly firing a few last rounds into the ruins. The boys returned to the hideout depressed.

"A mouse couldn't squeeze through, let alone a man."

Day after day passed. And each day's delay might cost them their lives.

Mordarski washed his hands of it.

Zyga went by himself, climbed up into the attic, and patiently observed the street from there. He returned when it was already dark.

"Uri will get through!"

They left late at night, before it started to grow light outside—Zyga, David, Eliahu, and Uri. Naum, Mordarski, Attorney Szwarc and his sons, and old Zelda stayed behind, carefully concealed by those who left. Tomorrow or never. Zyga, David, and Eliahu were barefoot; Uri wrapped his shoes in rags but had to throw them away at the last moment. They moved cautiously in the direction of Kalman's crossing and it took them many hours to cover this short distance; every minute they stopped still, glued to the walls, listening. Every rustle seemed suspect after the dead silence of the cellars beneath the ruins. They looked for the old hidden passageways and couldn't find their way. They moved around in circles, came back to familiar places, and saw that the path had been worn down by people wandering about in the rubble and had been trampled over so many times that now it just zigged and zagged and led nowhere. Everywhere they saw traces of the Germans and the horrifying work of the prisoners whom the Germans must have herded along there; everywhere they saw exits buried in rubble, caved-in tunnels, burned food supplies, smoldering sleeping quarters, hideouts that had been emptied with grenades and turned into shelters for eternity, dry buckets, riddled with bullet holes, through which the water had flowed out; everywhere there were massacred bodies from which the blood had flowed, people forcibly removed from their shelters, shot to death on their thresholds, lying amidst scattered cartridge shells, and rats—enormous, bloated, gray rats that leaped into the air when they saw them, aggressive rats that seemed to want to reach the faces of the living.

They made it to Kalman's crossing just before dawn. There was no *Wächter* at the spot next to the wall. They stood motionless, trying to spot the camouflaged German by the scratching of a match and a light puff of smoke fading away in the predawn air. He was concealed inside the gate directly opposite the crossing, below them, slightly to the left. Zyga whispered to Uri, pressing his lips to his ear; since reaching here they hadn't let a single word escape into the air. Eliahu slid down the banister absolutely silently, his bare feet stretched out in front of him. He came back at dawn. The *Wächter* was alone; he had set up quarters for himself in the janitor's apartment whose door opened into the entranceway. It had grown lighter and he had recognized him by the motion with which he adjusted his machine gun and by the wooden pistol holster that he wore hanging low on a long leather belt. It was Bloody Hands. Uri slipped quietly into the adjacent attic, which apparently was part of the building next door. Zyga leaned against the sloping wall, his hands in his pockets, inhaling the cold air that came through the narrow window. The sun had risen and its weak light fell on his shriveled sad face, his vacant eyes, sunken temples, and lips that were stretched into a hesitant smile. The night had sucked the blood from him and Zyga was as gray as ashes. He hesitated for a moment. He wiped his brow with a defenseless movement of his hand. He wanted to say something else; then he gestured dismissively and turned away in the direction from which they had come. Eliahu slowly rubbed his calf with his dirty bare foot. The morning cold made them shudder and their throats were dry and full of dust. By now it was bright outside. They saw the wall, the chipped brick in the wall, and, higher up, the handhold marked by a dark blood stain; at the top, a short stretch of wall, perhaps a meter long, from which the glass had been removed, was clearly outlined; beyond it, jagged chunks of bottles and sharp slivers of glass jutted up from the mortar in which they were set. The *Wächter*'s green helmet appeared and disappeared. Suddenly they heard the noisy clanging of a tin can that had been thrown into the street. The noise came again. Zyga shouted something from a distance, a couple of buildings off to the right, but Bloody Hands stayed at his post and wouldn't let himself be lured from that spot. Eliahu squeezed David's arm and whispered, "When the Latvians emerge, we're done for." But the Latvians still hadn't appeared on their balconies.

Zyga ran out into the middle of the street and shouted, "Bloody Hands, what are you waiting for? Shoot!"

The *Wächter* fired, missed, and ran off in that direction.

Zyga kept on shouting loudly, stopping inside a gate, running through the courtyards, pausing in entranceways, on staircases, "*Blutighändchen, komm, komm . . . Ein Schuss, ein Mensch . . . Komm, ich warte!*"

Zyga's shouts echoed in the dawn among the bare, bullet-pocked walls, among the dead eye sockets of smashed windows and the shutters that clattered in the wind, and the echo carried through the emptiness of the deaf, narrow, dark, and totally uninhabited street that remained cut off from the city by the wall.

"*Komm, ich warte!*"

The German abandoned his post beside the passage and must have run after Zyga with his gun in his hand.

"Blutighändchen, komm, komm!"

A chase began along the upper stories. They could hear doors slammed in haste, shots, from here, from there, fired blindly in long bursts. They caught sight of a shadow on the left that slipped barefoot across the roadway and before the *Wächter* got back to his post Uri had placed his foot in the gap left by the missing brick, grabbed the handhold, and pulled himself upwards on that hand, ripping his knees on the bricks; he threw his right leg over the top of the wall with enormous effort and knelt all hunched up on the top of the wall for just a second while he rested and checked out something on the street, on the other side of the wall, and then he slipped down head first until he disappeared completely from view. In the meantime the sounds of the chase had died down, and after a while they could hear a number of individual muffled pistol shots, following each other at short intervals. When Bloody Hands finally reappeared, he was dragging Zyga, who was wounded, by the shirt. Zyga's feet were scraping the ground. Bloody Hands dropped him near the wall in a clearly visible spot. They could go now. Zyga lay huddled on the stones, motionless, repeating softly, *"Noch eine Kugel!"*

Bloody Hands returned to his post and did not fire the final shot. And they, as they stealthily retreated after the changing of the guard, could hear the fading groans of the wounded boy for what seemed a very long time.

In the hideout they said, "Uri made it over."

"What? To the other side?"

"Yes."

"Without the hook?"

"Yes."

A day passed, then a night.

Mordarski had long known about the passageway that Kalman Drabik was unable to use when he attempted to lead Uncle Yehuda across. Near the intersection of Ceglana and Żelazna Streets, somewhat farther on, not quite at Prosta, loomed the ruins of a gate; half of it was intact but it was overgrown with grass and nettles, with thistles wedged into the cracks of the rubble; even farther along the street there was an empty little square on the site of a bombed-out building and a demolished tannery where the cobblers and tailors used to set up stalls during the summer and where the smugglers from both sides of the wall used to meet. In the shadow of the gate, abandoned among all the fading stalls, stood a cart, an ordinary two-wheeled flatbed cart with a shaft and a chain. In the gray light before dawn the cart would be dragged over to the wall and people would use it to climb to the top; that was the route that smugglers from Felek Piorun's band were still using last winter. Ever since the Germans had dismantled the workshops on Prosta, the little square that remained after the premises were blown up and that linked the Toebbens sites had been heavily guarded; the trading had stopped and the rotting stalls were shoved into a pile near the ruins where they rotted away. Before that happened, the cart would be pushed away from the wall as soon as someone used it to cross over, and it was turned upside down to look even more innocent. When no one is left to wipe out the traces, such a crossing point can be used only once. And since Kalman didn't cross at that point but retreated to the crossing at the end of Grzybowska Street, the people in the hideout assumed that the Germans themselves had spotted the passage and either moved the cart away or destroyed it. But that wasn't the case. Mordarski, who hung around there at night, found out from a guy who was hiding out on Ceglana Street that nobody had moved the cart but that the two men from Krochmalna—whom he recognized as Kalman and Yehuda—were forced to retreat because a patrol of black police had uncovered the crossing point after someone else's unsuccessful escape attempt. Bloody Hands wouldn't allow them to move the cart; a sentry watched over the new ambush day and night.

Mordarski said that the spot was perfect for him, and that with his dough, any gendarme he met would gladly lead him across the wall with a song on his lips. Just so long as he didn't run into any *szaulisy*: he'd been terrified of the *szaulisy* ever since they bayoneted his family to death in his apartment and wouldn't even discuss taking a bribe. Mordarski planned his escape as he gradually lost faith that Żeleźniak would come for him. Kalman and Mordarski were partners and those skins weighed on his soul, too, since no one else could get to where they were hidden. So he hesitated. Until one day he washed his hands of everything and said that he was going to find a gendarme near the old stalls. Mordarski would wait where they were waiting for Mordarski!

That day Nahum screamed his head off. He howled and he

sobbed. He implored the people to come out of hiding. The groans of a man who was being beaten, interrupted by a cry, "Oy, beloved Jews! Oy, help me—help!" penetrated to the depths of the cellars and underground passageways. They could tell in which direction the convoy was leading Nahum Szafran, and several of them stuck their fingers in their ears in terror.

Mordarski said his final word. He set out and never returned to the hideout. And much later the people in the attics on Ceglana told the prisoners from Toebbens what had happened. He stole across Walicόw to Ceglana at dawn. Shielded by the ruins of the stalls so that the guards on Prosta couldn't detect him, he crawled across the little square and came out on Żelazna near the crossing. There he stood still and waited, in a place where he could be seen. He unbuttoned his fur coat. When the black policeman came out of his hiding place inside the destroyed gate, the merchant took off his fur coat and flung it at his feet. He was shot from close up. People said that the policeman was stupefied when, after the second shot, the merchant still stood firmly on his feet and managed to remove a bag of jewelry from under his shirt. The German fired again. Mordarski dropped the jewelry but did not fall. At the last moment he took out a handful of bills and flung them into the black policeman's face. The German stood there among the fluttering money and fired over and over again to make Mordarski stop throwing that money into the wind, but he kept on flinging money at the German.

"The boor wasn't a connoisseur of civet fur."

That's what the people who witnessed Mordarski's end from the attics of Ceglana Street said.

"Eh, Mordarski's fur coat! It was made of English cloth lined with civet fur and an otter shawl collar."

The prisoners from the Prosta Street workshops told the story differently; their version was almost the same, but not quite. And they had had a good view. According to them, Mordarski bribed the black policeman but outsmarted himself. He removed the fur coat and his gold wristwatch. The policeman was still bargaining with him, he wanted more. Mordarski refused; he was probably afraid to reveal that he had concealed dollars. When the black policeman struck a deal with Mordarski, he led him over to the wall in the ruined gateway and fired the first shot, wounding Mordarski in the hand. The wounded man tore his jacket with his teeth in order to extract the money that was sewn inside and then the policeman fired twice. Before Mordarski died he flung a packet of banknotes around him with his stiffening hand; they fluttered across the square as far as the workshops on Prosta; then the SS man propped his rifle against the wall next to the dead man and started chasing the dollars, and it was high time indeed because a couple of guards left their posts beside the barbed wire and pointing in turn to the ruins of the gate, the pile of blackened stalls, the bombed-out premises that marked the end of their beat, and the guardhouse at the entrance to Toebbens, they argued with him about something or other for a long time.

The hideout was emptying out; they took the blankets off Uri's, Kalman's, Yehuda's, and Mordarski's mattresses and wrapped themselves in them for naps, exhausted by the autumn cold and darkness. Water seeped through the walls of the underground passageways and flooded their sleeping places. Naum's watch stopped and Szwarc overwound the spring; they couldn't tell time any longer, and day and night were swallowed up in darkness. Nahum Szafran stopped calling to the men in hiding. The Germans must have finished him off. The voices of the carters who were loading furniture onto the trucks and the footsteps of the prisoners who were cleaning up the streets and courtyards sounded nearer and nearer. They stopped waiting for Felek Piorun and no longer counted on Żeleźniak stumbling across their tracks in the ruins, attracted by the trove of skins. And Uri still hadn't shown any signs of life. It became harder and harder to come up with food; the prisoners from Prosta realized this and placed bread wrapped up in rags at the edge of the ruins. Old Zelda didn't even notice Zyga's absence. She wandered around through the underground passages, shuffling along in her soft house shoes; she moved slowly on her swollen feet, placing small candle stubs in recesses in the walls—candles that she extracted from some storage place that only she was aware of. Zelda's enormous swollen face had become a putrid shade of green. At night Estusia would crawl out of her den somewhere in the rubble. She forced her way into the locked shed. She walked around, searching for something. Once, when they were on their way to the apartment house for water, they heard a long, muffled cry, a sudden outburst, quiet footsteps, muttering. They stopped still; a shadow passed by near Zajączek's basement apartment. And again the rustling of rubbish could be heard in the darkness, the clanging of buckets that someone had tripped over, the clattering of a loose gutter, and a scream, "Nataniee . . . Natanieee!"

The cry moved away, then circled around the place where they had stopped.

"Is it you?"

She turned around, and they fell face down on the ground. She ran lightly toward the shed. She banged on the boards with her fists. One of her feet was wrapped in a rag; she had a sack around her shoulders to protect her from the rain.

Tired out, she sat down on the bricks. She bowed her head, listened, scratched at the door with her fingernails.

"I'm here, I'm waiting. I still have it. But where did I put it. I threw it away. Where?"

A giggle was clearly audible from the ruins.

"One is getting wet in the rain near Żelazna Brama! Go look over there. The other is hidden in a rubbish bin on Pańska. Next to number 7. The third is lying on Dzika, far from here, under a pile of bones. You'll find a tin can there. A pickle tin. There's a letter inside it. Go to Dzika and bring the letter!"

She got up and ran toward them. "It's you, I can see. Don't run away from me, Nataniel!"

They lay there motionless.

"Oh, I thought I wouldn't make it." She circled around near them, sinking into a rubble-filled crater. But luckily she didn't notice them. They could see her hand stretched out from under her rags. She moved on. "Come, come, I have a piece of bread for you." She sucked on a dried crust. She brought it up to her mouth and pulled it away. She hid the rest and they heard her sleepy whisper, "I've hidden it."

She looked around for a long time. "I waited . . . He said he'd come right back, he was just going to the shoemaker's to get some soles nailed on and they picked him up on the street."

Laughter, sobbing.

David felt his heart contract painfully and he shut his eyes tight. The huddled figure rocked back and forth, humming a song. About how peacefully the king is sleeping.

A regiment of soldiers stands and shouts. Sha! Sha! Oy, just so. Oy, as if the king is sleeping on down. Sha . . .

The girl's a disaster. She'll bring a troop of "dogcatchers" down on them.

Naum, Eliahu, and David waited for a patrol to be attracted by the noise and discover all of them here. It poured all night long; not even a dog would go out on a night like that. Finally, toward morning, when she was chilled to the bone, Estusia crawled back into her den and they were able to escape stealthily and return to their place by a roundabout route through the cellars of the old soap works.

"It's her or us," said Attorney Szwarc. He'd had his fill of terror that night.

Soon he gathered his wicker trunk and his children and left the walls of the Ghetto in a horse-drawn cart, concealed by the driver in a double-doored mahogany wardrobe that was still in perfectly good condition although the veneer had been stripped in places. Szwarc paid off the "dogcatchers" generously. Those who cashed in on his escape were a blue policeman and two German guards from the *Wache* on Grzybowski Square, who raised the price at the last moment when they began to knock at the old mahogany with feigned attentiveness. The wardrobe doors creaked and a hand with a signet ring on the ring finger emerged.

"Gentlemen, have mercy! I'm giving what I can afford. A family heirloom!"

The looters, summoned by the gendarmes, were everywhere. The prisoners whom the Germans employed to clean up the corpses rotting in corners and to disinfect the district swept up the garbage, rubble, and glass after the looters finished, working on one building after another. One day Uncle Gedali and another prisoner crept into the hideout and called out at length to the hidden people, hurling Hebrew verses into the darkness like passwords until the people who were scattered in the cellars reluctantly came out to meet them. Who could have anticipated it? They had heavy pliers in their hands, and the rest of them were working under guard in the neighborhood to free Waliców from its coils of barbed wire and to knock down the iron barriers for scrap. The foreman, who was on his way back with his men to the Toebbens and Schultz factories for the night, agreed to smuggle in a couple of heads; someone was looking for Kalman Drabik and the convoy had been paid off ahead of time that day. Naum and Eliahu went with that group to Leszno. David, concealed in a group of prisoners, slogged along with Uncle Gedali to the workshops on Prosta. The sky was high and his ears were ringing. He kept stumbling and falling against the others; he felt as if he weighed nothing at all. They pushed bread into him, held him up.

He didn't want to eat, he couldn't speak. He opened his mouth and inhaled the quiet evening air and felt as if, along with the oxygen that flowed freely into his lungs, he was ingesting once and forever the image of what was before his eyes: the little street full of cobblestones, the disfigured house waving a rag of a blackened curtain, a contorted lamppost that bowed mournfully to the ground like a vine that has fainted beneath its load, a bombed building raising its deformity high against the dark blue emptiness—and with each breath this vision became clearer and sharper, and the motion, the constant motion of his own body, and the swaying, the constant swaying of his shoulders, his arms, of the heads walking in front of him, brought him to a state of lightness that he had never known before and flooded his heart with tender emotion, overwhelming sadness, and rapture.

When they passed through the wires, a man who had been taken down from a post was dying. His outstretched arms lay unbelievably far away from his torso; next to him was a broken brick and blood on a piece of paper. He'd been shoved into the mud and was covered with a torn cement sack; the guard, wiping his hands on his trousers, yelled in the direction of the column that the *Werkmeister* should assign someone immediately to clear him out of there, and in a hurry!

"Little" Toebbens was over there, on Prosta Street, and they worked there for a couple of months longer, awaiting the command to march to Stawki. Everyone wore a number: a patch in front and a patch on the back. He had a star on his back and on his chest, crudely painted with oil paint that seeped through his clothing and stuck to his skin, and for a long time the itching, burning stains bothered him. He thought the paint would never dry; it did, but the patches continued to burn his living flesh. People over there said that the hideout on Krochmalna was still serving as a shelter for others; someone saw the violinist Nataniel on the old rubbish pile, someone else saw Uri, who had come back from the other side of the wall, wandering around in the ruins, old Zelda . . . It appeared that a couple of families had moved into the cavernous cellars from the attics on Ciepła and Ceglana Streets and there was a man in the Toebbens workshop who swore on everything holy that Felek Piorun had managed to empty out the store of skins before the Germans got there and to take some Jews away as well. He was supposed to have moved out the goods over a three-day period in Żeleźniak's wagon under a covering of old furniture and broken clocks, dirty featherbeds, and piles of clothing.

Yes, but the *Wache* must also have gotten a little something out of it.

He saw his house for the last time in autumn. Whenever they herded them in absolute silence through the dead, vacant district they were never certain if they were going to work or straight to the deportation square. On that day the column stopped on Walicόw; they were supposed to move the iron barriers that blocked the outlet of the side street, carry them over to the rubble, and cut the barbed wire that was looped around the rails; the foreman, taking two workers and a guard, crossed to the other side of the wall. The ruins swayed above his head in the sunlight and the dust-filled yellow air. David craned his neck to look at the familiar window and waited. From here, from this spot, in the afternoon, they saw a patrol cautiously making its way through the nearby entrances. The Germans crept up stealthily, with their knees bent and their rifles at the ready. One of them kicked in the door to the shed and another stood by with a rag and a can of kerosene. They could hear the first man sneezing inside the shed as he groped around for quite some time until he finally found the entrance to the cellars concealed beneath Mordechai's bunk and a pile of harness gear; he must have hurled in an entire string of grenades, because the exit from the cellar collapsed and was completely blocked. The ruins smoked and rocked. The pile slipped softly away from under their feet. But the shed remained standing, and then the second gendarme approached and poured kerosene on the rag; he looked around again to see the old building in flames — its dry, rotted boards, and the ragged, worn tarpaper that covered the roof. He flung the can with the rest of the kerosene through the open door, brushed the dust off his uniform, waited a moment and called out, *"Fertig."*

Soon after he left, the guard in the ruins fired a green flare into the air.

"Fire, fire! It's burning," people shouted. Germans came running down the street supporting their hands on their dangling ammunition belts. In the commotion they pressed the prisoners into fighting the fire. They ordered everyone to throw down their tools and find buckets and basins; a little later a second column marched in from the workshops.

The fire was extinguished in an hour. It turned out that a spark from the shed had fallen on the rotted shutters of the janitor's window, and the windowframes and rubbish piles had caught fire from Ajzen's shutters. The water from the buckets splashed through the window and flowed down the stairs to the entranceway. Two apartments on the ground floor, the janitor's flat, and Mordarski's room on the second floor were burned out. The Germans kept on ordering them to bring water, to stamp out smoldering rags, to soak the smoking walls and wallpaper; as a joke, they kicked one Jew into the flames together with his basin. He came running out without the basin, sputtering and coughing, with his hair burnt. Large holes glowed on his knees; they smoked and grew larger in the place where his trousers bulged. The problem was that the Germans were stockpiling fuel in nearby Hale and had set up a temporary garage for military trucks on Żelazna Brama Square. What if the gasoline blew up? The prisoners overheard the gendarmes' conversations.

They knew about Mordechai's shed, but they didn't want to know anything about the other passages, about the underground corridor, the cellars, the emergency exit through the storehouses of the old soap works. They did what they were told to do. The exit that was blown up and buried by the grenades prevented air from getting into the underground passageways, but it also kept the fire out. The burnt shed collapsed and covered the spot with a pile of charred debris from which wafted smoke and the bitter odor of an extinguished fire.

People from the other side said that at dusk they could see Jews in the upper stories who were running away from the hideout. Hunched over forms leaped one by one from the cellars and, hugging the walls, disappeared into the ruins. The prisoner who brought that news back to the workshop had been with the foreman all day and had stuffed his sack with jewelry purchased on the other side of the wall. He had a bluish-gray beard and, like everyone else, a star on his overalls. The unshaven growth of hair on his face that hadn't been touched for a couple of weeks extended all the way to his eyes. David almost didn't recognize him as Kepele.

"Jews," he said. Sitting on his bunk, surrounded by a crowd of prisoners, he poured the water out of his boots. David could feel the sticky paint from his patch clinging to his skin. He unbuttoned his shirt and the prisoner with the bluish-gray beard, looking straight ahead into the darkness beyond the barracks window, out into the rain, repeated without raising his voice, practically in a whisper, "Jews, hide your bread, whoever is going to Walicśw tomorrow."

After midnight the guard made his rounds outside the barracks. He stood quietly underneath the windows, shone his torch inside, and the light leaped from bunk to bunk, from face to face. The windows were barred and the bars were covered with coils of barbed wire. He ran a key along the wires to check that they were uncut, and the key emitted a sudden eerie grating noise in the silence and the darkness. It took a while for David to become accustomed to it, and at the guard's signal he would spring to his feet and, blinded by the flashlight, his heart thumping, he would look around in panic, not knowing where he was and how he'd come to be there. After that it wasn't long until reveille. Before dawn they fed the hogs in the same barracks, behind a special divider. They were being fattened with kitchen slops; the people got as little as possible and the remainder went into the troughs in the pigpen. But the boys—there were about a dozen of them in the workshops with the foreman's permission and the tacit agreement of the Germans—whispered to each other that the hogs were fed on human meat, on the corpses that were excavated from the ruins and the hideouts. In fact, it was German bacon for German soldiers, and they certainly wouldn't eat just anything. Pigs, too, had to be *rasserein*.

They were fed once a day, at night. The squealing and snorting of the herd of pigs could be heard everywhere, and it seemed to him as he was awakened by them that he was hearing the animal-like noise of a huge crowd of people, the sounds of distant lamentation.

David could hear Uncle Gedali muttering in his sleep. He sat up suddenly and said, with his eyes still closed, "Yehuda, come back, Yakov's been found," and then he flopped back onto his bunk, snoring. A new, unfamiliar fear gripped David at the thought of his father. He was alive somewhere, over there. There, in the Big Ghetto, he was walking around freely without an armband. Should he worm his way into the group that was going to Leszno? To cross the wall. They'll meet. In one place, all of them.

Now he knew what he would do. At the first suitable occasion, when they're driving the prisoners out to work on the other side . . . On the other side!

"*Jawohl, mein ist die ganze Welt. Was nun? Es regnet.*"

"Yes, the whole world is his. And what of it? It's raining."

"*Hundeleben. Pfui, Schmutz. Zum Donnerwetter.*"

"He says it's a dog's life. Filth. He swears you can drown behind the guardhouse."

That meant it was after the changing of the guards and the patrols were heading to the canteen. And the voice was probably concerned; the *Werkmeister* was asking politely whom should he send to Walicóv today. Who should be kept in the workshop and who should be sent to the other side?

"*Ich trinke.*" The commander of the guards ordered him to be quiet. Wait. What? He says he's in a hurry? Well, well, the little Jew is brave. "*Prosit! Noch einmal.*"

And once again the furious guard asks what should he do with the Jew who came out of the ruins. He's been waiting in front of the guard house half the night and asking to be taken to the *Umschlagplatz*. Should they send a convoy for one person?

A truck motor turned over in the garage and a loud, abrupt shout could be heard from the canteen, "*Ans Werk!*"

Amidst the gendarmes' convoluted curses, their yawns, their shouts, and the first commands of the morning, the day began, yet one more day. David waited with his eyes open, listening to the beating of his heart, and thought that he had to run away from there. Run away, and do it soon.

It took a long time for the prisoners to be given their assignments, and the drunken orgy in the canteen went on until noon. Doors slammed, the radio was on. They were standing in a crowd when patrols of black police surrounded the apartment house and the Toebbens barracks in silence, and the guards pulled the last Jews out of their hiding places. Rain mixed with snow was falling and there was a strong wind. The two trucks were barely able to hold all the cripples and old men who were found at the last moment hidden away in dark corners of the workshop. They stretched out their wet hands, took leave of their relatives, clutched at the air and the raindrops with their fingers. The healthy men who had been flushed out of hiding were grouped separately. The *Werkmeister*, white as a sheet, stepped forward and addressed them.

"Rejoice, the commandant has forgiven you your sins and you will go with the others to the *Umschlagplatz*."

Along the way David heard people whispering that some prisoners had stayed behind on Prosta Street and that they had managed to find really good hiding places there.

❖

Jewish Lives

ARNOŠT LUSTIG
Children of the Holocaust
The Unloved (From the Diary of Perla S.)

ARMIN SCHMID AND RENATE SCHMID
Lost in a Labyrinth of Red Tape

ARNON TAMIR
A Journey Back: Injustice and Restitution

BOGDAN WOJDOWSKI
Bread for the Departed